Fugitive Anne

Rosa Praed

Fugitive Anne,

A Romance of the Unexplored Bush

by

Rosa Praed

Fugitive Anne

Part I

Chapter I—The Closed Cabin

IT was between nine and ten in the morning on board the Eastern and Australasian passenger boat Leichardt, which was steaming in a southerly direction over a calm, tropical sea between the Great Barrier Reef and the north-eastern shores of Australia. The boat was expected to arrive at Cooktown during the night, having last stopped at the newly-established station on Thursday Island.

This puts time back a little over twenty years.

The passengers' cabins on board the Leichardt opened for the most part off the saloon. Here, several people were assembled, for excitement had been aroused by the fact that the door of Mrs Bedo's cabin was locked, and that she had not been seen since the previous day.

Mrs Bedo was the only first-class lady passenger on the Leichardt.

Three men stood close to her cabin door. These were Captain Cass, the captain of the Leichardt; the ship's doctor, and Mr Elias Bedo, the lady's husband. Just behind these three, leaning on the back of a chair which was fixed to the cabin table, stood another man evidently interested in the matter, but as evidently, having no official claim to such interest. This man was a big Dane, tall, muscular, and determined-looking, with a short fair beard and moustache, high cheek-bones, and extremely clear, brilliant, blue eyes. Eric Hansen was his name, and he was also a first-class passenger. Further, he was a scientist, bound on a mission of exploration in regard to Australian fauna, on which he had been dispatched by a learned society in his own country.

At the other side of the table, opposite the Dane, and apparently interested too, in the affair of Mrs Bedo's locked door, stood an Australian black boy in European dress—that is, in a steward's dress of white linen, with a napkin in his hand; for it had happened that Kombo, Mr and Mrs Bedo's aboriginal servant, had, with the permission of his master and mistress, taken the place of a Chinese boy, temporarily disabled by a malarial fever. These people were at the upper end of the saloon, near which was Mrs Bedo's cabin. At the lower end, the remaining passengers, with the purser and another steward, had congregated. The passengers were few; a Javanese shipping agent, a Catholic priest, a person connected with telegraphs, and two or three bushmen on their way back from Singapore or Europe, as the case might be. These were all waiting, with gaping mouths and open eyes, for the tragedy which they imagined would be disclosed. For it was openly suspected on board, that Mrs Bedo disliked and feared her husband.

Mr Bedo had been knocking violently at the cabin door, but no answer was returned. He was a coarse, powerful person, with an ill-featured face, a sinewy throat, and great, brawny hands. He had started in life as a bullock—driver and was now a rich man, having struck gold in the early days of Charters Towers Diggings—before, indeed, Charters Towers had become officially established.

"Something must have happened," said the doctor. "Hadn't we better—?" and he waited, looking at the Captain.

"There's nothing for it but to break open the door," said Captain Cass.

"Try it, Mr Bedo."

Elias Bedo put his huge shoulders against the wooden panelling, and as the Captain moved aside, the big Dane stepped forward, and laid his shoulders—smaller, but even more powerful than Bedo's—also against the white door. There was a crash; the door fell inward, and Bedo entered, the Captain following.

The Dane had drawn back again, and the doctor, about to follow, paused, seeing that Captain Cass pushed back the door, and drew the curtain within, across the opening.

Every word, however, uttered within the cabin could be heard by those immediately outside.

A coarse oath broke from Mr Bedo's lips.

"—She's gone."

"What do you mean?" said the Captain, in the sharp tone of alarm which heralds calamity.

"Can't you see?" cried the husband, in a voice more infuriated than despair-stricken. "I've always told you that those window-ports are dangerous. It would be nothing for a thin man, let alone a girl, to creep through that one. Damn her! I was a fool to let her have a cabin to herself. She has gone overboard, and swum ashore."

"That's impossible," said the Captain, curtly.

"How is it impossible?" said the husband. "Anne Marley was a northern girl, born and bred on the sea-coast. She knows every sort of water dodge, and can swim like a fish."

"That may be," replied the Captain, "but Mrs Bedo has been three years in England, and must be out of practice in swimming. And why—?" The Captain paused dramatically, and straightly eyed Elias Bedo. "Why, Mr Bedo, should your wife risk her life in swimming ashore? Was it because she wanted to get away from you?"

Elias Bedo scowled for a moment, and did not speak.

"Well," he said presently, "I suppose that most of the chaps on board have noticed that my wife is a bit cracky—a shingle loose, as we say in the Bush." He looked shiftily at the Captain, who made no reply. For he, as well as others on board, had remarked Mrs Bedo's silent, solitary ways, and had thought her a little eccentric, though everyone had attributed what was odd and unsociable in her manner to her obvious unhappiness. Mr Bedo went on, "I don't mean that her being queer, as you may say, is anything to her discredit. Women

3

get like that sometimes, and it passes. I've had doctors' advice, and that's what I was told. It made no difference to me, except that I've known I must look after her. And that's why I say that I was a damned fool to let her have a cabin to herself. It was your doing, Cass; she got round you, and if harm has come to her, you'll have to answer for it." He turned furiously to the Captain, who met his angry gaze with unabashed eyes, making a little jerky movement of his chin.

"Very well," said the Captain, "I'm quite ready to answer for my share in the business, which is simple enough. When I have one lady passenger, and more cabins than are wanted, I naturally give the lady her choice. Mrs Bedo asked for a cabin on the cool side of the ship, and I gave it her. It was the only amends I could make for letting that rascally Chinaman cheat me at Singapore, so that we were put on short commons with the ice. But abusing me, Mr Bedo, won't help you to find your wife. She's on this ship, or she isn't; and if she is, there's no need for you to suppose she isn't."

Silence followed, except for the noise of pulled out drawers, and the metallic sound of curtains being drawn along brass rods, which proclaimed to those outside, that Mr Bedo was searching the cabin lest his wife should lie concealed in berth or locker. After a few moments, the Captain was heard again.

"There's another thing you've got to think of. Suppose that Mrs Bedo does swim like a fish, and is up to every water dodge, as you tell me—I'm not gain-saying it, for I know what a coast-bred girl can do—how is that going to help her against the sharks? And even if she did the distance safely, there are the Blacks. Mrs Bedo is a northern girl, and must have heard something of what the Blacks are, up on this coast."

"Cannibals," put in the doctor, who, unable to restrain himself, had drawn the outer curtain and pushed in the door. He stood on the threshold, and through the rift in the curtain, the Dane's face could be seen with an expression upon it of horror and perplexity; while beyond, showed the black boy, with a look upon his countenance half terror, half satisfaction, which to Eric Hansen, turning suddenly, and thus coming within view of Kombo, was incomprehensible.

"Come," said the Captain, "it's nonsense to take it for granted that Mrs Bedo must have thrown herself overboard, because she isn't in her cabin. I'll talk to the stewardess, and have the ship searched immediately."

He went out into the saloon, followed by the doctor, leaving Elias Bedo within the cabin, and the Dane on its threshold, between the parted folds of the curtain that screened the doorway. The stewardess, who had come up from her own quarters, was standing beside Kombo, the black boy; and to her the Captain addressed himself.

Her answers to his questions were clear enough. Mrs Bedo had gone into her cabin the afternoon before, complaining of a headache, and requesting that she should not be disturbed. The stewardess had nothing to do with taking in her dinner, but she had brought the early morning tea to the cabin door. Finding it locked, she had gone away, expecting to be summoned by—and-by. Mrs Bedo, however, had not rung her bell, and had not taken her bath as usual that morning. The stewardess went on to say that she had again gone to the cabin door, but still finding it locked, supposed that Mrs Bedo had had a bad night and was sleeping late. Mrs Bedo had often had bad nights, and several times had desired that she should not be awakened till she rang.

Kombo was questioned as to when he had last seen his mistress, and hesitated a moment, but answered explicitly.

"Mine been take dinner last night to Missa Anne, but that fellow no want to eat, and I believe Missa Anne cobbon sick like-it cobra."

Kombo made a melodramatic gesture, pressing both hands upon his woolly head. In speaking of his mistress, Kombo, who had known her from a child, never said Mrs Bedo, but always Missa Anne,

"Missa" being, in the Australian blacks' vocabulary, the feminine of Massa as a prefix to the Christian name.

"And where did Mrs Bedo take breakfast?" the Captain went on.

"Mine no see Missa Anne at breakfast," said Kombo. "Mine wait— give Massa breakfast, but Missa Anne no come. Mine tell Massa, Missa Anne plenty sleepy, and no like me to make her jump up."

Captain Cass left the saloon, giving orders that every part of the vessel should be searched, though, as the stewardess remarked, there wasn't much sense in that, for it was not likely that Mrs Bedo would hide herself in the hold. The general opinion inclined to suicide, and there was much excited whispering amongst the passengers, who now followed the Captain on deck, leaving the saloon almost empty. Elias Bedo remained, still examining his wife's cabin, and Eric Hansen, the Dane, watched him from the doorway.

Chapter II—Cannibals or Sharks?

THE cabin was fairly large, considering the size of the steamer. It had two berths—the top one having been occupied by Mrs Bedo for the sake of coolness—and a cushioned bunk with drawers beneath, set under the square porthole. In these smooth seas the heavy dead-lights had been fastened back, leaving an aperture through which might be seen the glassy sea, the Australian shore, and maybe a coral island, with clumps of feathery palms, uprising from the blue. This window was, as Mr Bedo had said, wide enough for a thin man, and certainly a slim woman, to slip through into the sea.

Could it be possible that a girl of scarcely twenty—a bride of four months—had been driven to so desperate a strait as to choose death, or take the chance of life among sharks and cannibals, in order to escape from a loathed bondage? He—Eric Hansen—knew what the Captain and passengers only suspected, that Anne Bedo detested the man she had married. And was it wonderful? The greater marvel seemed that she had married him at all.

Eric Hansen gave a shudder as he watched the exbullock driver turn over certain dainty properties his wife had left in the locker and on the shelves and hooks; pretty garments and feminine odds and ends, and finally a soft leather desk with folding cover, that lay at one end of the bunk. An involuntary exclamation escaped Hansen's lips. Mr Bedo turned and confronted the Dane, but he was too agitated to speak.

"Can I be of any service?" asked Hansen, commanding himself with an effort. Bedo took no notice of the offer. His eye had been caught by a large square sheet of paper written upon and half folded, that lay upon the open blotting-pad of the desk, from which the leather cover had fallen back. It seemed as though the pen had dropped upon the paper, for there was a blot of ink after the last word. The pen, Hansen noticed, stuck up endways between the red cushion of the bunk and the vessel's side. No doubt, in shaking the garments, which hung on a row of pegs above the bunk, Mr Bedo had displaced the writing-case and caused it to close.

He took up the sheet of paper and held it before him, staring in a stupefied manner at the words traced upon it in a decided and legible hand. He stood with his face to the window, and Hansen, moved by some strange impulse, stepped across the doorway, and read Anne Bedo's unfinished letter over her husband's shoulder.

It was dated in the ordinary way from the S.S. Leichardt, near Cooktown, on the previous day, but had evidently been written during the night. The letter began: —

"My own Mother.

"The moon is shining through my cabin window, a full moon nearly, with just a little kink in the round, that makes me think of your dear, thin cheeks. I seem to see your loving eyes looking out of the moon and asking me things; sad things, dearie, that we mustn't think about. But oh! I long to lay my poor head on your breast and to feel your arms round me, and to look up into your sweet eyes which I saved. Ah! thank God for that!

"Mother, I know the sort of things you'd want me to tell you, and what your first question would be. Well, I'll answer it. Yes, I'm happy, dear, and I'm not sorry about anything. It's 'altogether bujeri' with me, as the Blacks used to say when they had got their flour and tobacco, and were quite contented with things. I've got my flour and tobacco, having earned it by a job that's just a little more complicated than grubbing out stumps on a clearing; and I'm quite content, so you needn't fret about little Missa Anne any more. I'd do the same job over again if I was put to it, for the same end. So never let that thought trouble you, dearie. Besides, you won't miss me so dreadfully now that Etta is grown up, for she is so much more sensible and practical than ever I could be. I couldn't do anything but sing, and not well enough to make any money by it. But never mind, I was able to buy you back your eyes, and for that to the last day of my life, I shall praise God, and thank Him with all my heart.

"Yes, I'm happy, dearest. Don't worry about your little Anne.

"Oh! It's good to be back in the old country; and the whiff of the gum—trees makes a woman of me once more. No, not all the musical academies of London and Paris could change me from what I am, a Bush girl to the bones of me. No, not even if that wonderful fairy story were to come true, and I were really Anne, Baroness Marley, in the peerage of England, as said that funny old burrower in Church registers. Have you ever seen him again, and has he found the missing link in the pedigree? But, of course, it's all nonsense. Mr Bedo told me he had seen into the matter himself. He said that the man confessed his evidence had broken down, and that he only wanted to get money out of poor you and me, who hadn't any to give him.

"Dear, in a few days now, we shall be off the old bay—do you remember? The shining moon reminds me of those hot nights when we used to get up and bathe—Etta and I—with the waves rolling in over us, silver-tipped. And how angry you used to be in the morning, and how frightened because of the sharks! You always said, you know, that I had a charmed life. The moon seems to be beckoning to me now. It's streaming over a little bay so like our own old bay, and I can fancy that I hear the roll of surf on the sand. No, I'm silly; it's the water against the steamer's side. We're not so far off from land, however. Since rounding Cape Flattery, we've kept close in shore. Now, I've been standing up and looking out of my window. I can hardly bear to stay in the cabin; it's like a prison—so hot, and there seem to come living fumes into it, Chinese and Lascar smells, you know! from all parts of the steamer. They poison what little air there is. Out there, where the moon shines, all looks cool and pure and free, and there's just a ripple on the water; and the moonbeams shake and stretch out arms as if they were calling me. Why shouldn't I take a dip?..."

And here the blot had fallen, and the writing ended.

Mr Bedo, absorbed in the letter, appeared quite unaware of the man standing behind him. He turned the sheet over, staring at the blank side for a moment or two; then going back, he read the writing again. When he had finished, he crushed the paper in his hand, and made a movement as though he were about to throw it out of the window, but Hansen put out his hand and stopped him.

"You mustn't do that," said the Dane, quietly. "This should be given into the Captain's charge, in case"—he hesitated, then said straightly,—"in case there should be need for an inquiry."

Bedo swore again. "What business is it of yours?" he cried.

"None," replied Hansen, "beyond the fact that if an inquiry became necessary, which I hope most earnestly may not be, I should be examined as a witness, and should have to give evidence as to the contents of that letter."

"The letter is a private one, written to her mother," said Bedo. "It had best be destroyed; there is nothing in it to throw any light upon the matter."

"I cannot agree with you," said Hansen, quietly; "nor do I think would Mrs Bedo's mother."

"You prying skunk!" exclaimed Bedo. "Do you dare to own that you have been so ungentlemanly as to read over my shoulder what my wife wrote in confidence to her mother?"

"Certainly, I own it," said Hansen. "I will admit also that it was an ungentlemanly action. Yet I'd maintain that it was justified by circumstances. But for my having committed it, you would have destroyed important evidence."

"Do you understand," said Bedo, trying to speak calmly, but shaking either with anger or fear, "that you are forcing me to make public a family scandal, which it is best for all parties should be concealed? My wife was mad, and her words here prove it. All that nonsense about the moon shows clearly that she must have thrown herself overboard in a fit of insanity. She required careful watching, and I ought not to have allowed her to be alone. That is the truth, though for her sake as well as for my own, I did not want all the world to know it."

"I think I heard you a few minutes ago hinting what you are pleased to call the truth, pretty broadly to the Captain," said Hansen, drily. "If there's any family secret, you yourself have already revealed it. But nothing would make me believe that Mrs Bedo is mad— unhappy, yes, but not mad."

"And who are you to judge whether my wife was unhappy or mad?"

Hansen shook himself impatiently.

"Good Heavens! Mr Bedo, why should we stand arguing here? Do you care so little about your wife's fate, that you don't even want to know whether they are searching the vessel?"

Hansen was leaning over the bunk, his face against the window. Now, giving a glance outward, he was attracted by something he saw, and uttered a violent exclamation. He put out his hand, and drew in from where it had been entangled in a rope used for the fixing of a wind-sail, a lock of brown hair, which it was easy to recognise as Mrs Bedo's. He held it up, carefully examining the ends. Mr Bedo, much agitated, seized it from him, dropping at the same time the paper that he had crunched in his hand. Hansen stooped and picked it up.

"That is my wife's hair," said Bedo. "Something must have caught it when she was jumping over, and dragged it out of her head."

"No," answered Hansen, "I see that it is a strand which has been cut; not dragged out. Mr Bedo, this convinces me that your wife did not throw herself into the sea upon an hysterical impulse, but that her escape was planned. No doubt she cut off her hair, thinking it would hinder her in swimming."

The Captain had come in while the Dane was speaking.

"The Lord pity her then," he said, solemnly. "There's been smoke of Blacks' fires along the coast, and yesterday, some of the devils were sighted on the rocks, hurling their spears. But it seems impossible that she could have got to shore; and to say truth, I'd far rather that sharks had eaten her than that she should be in the power of those fiends. Mr Bedo, I'm afraid we must make up our minds to the worst. The first officer is still with the men searching, but we've found no trace, and anyhow, it isn't likely we should. I came to tell you that I must fasten up this cabin. Have you found anything which could give us a clue?"

Eric Hansen told him of the letter; and Mr Bedo, who seemed too stupefied for argument, allowed it to be given into the Captain's hands. The hair, too, was again examined. Clearly, it had been cut off, but was not, Captain Cass said, in sufficient quantity to be any proof of intention, as regards the disappearance. Who could say that Mrs Bedo had not cut off one of her abundant locks for some purpose of her own, and then thrown it away. Perhaps she had done so by accident, some days back. For the wind—sail had been taken down at Thursday Island, and not fixed again.

Chapter III—Elias Bedo's Wife

ALL had been done that could be done on board the Leichardt in order to make certain of Anne Bedo's fate. People felt that the search was perfunctory, yet it was faithfully, if unavailingly, carried through; Kombo, the black servant of the lost woman, being foremost in the quest.

Mr Bedo, after his first sullen stupefaction, roused himself to a fury of anxiety, and stormed at Captain Cass and all the ship's officers, because the Captain refused to man and send off a boat for the exploration of the coast behind them. It was useless, the Captain declared, and would be contrary to his duty to his employers and the Government, whose mail contract he was bound to consider before everything else. Mr Bedo swore in vain, and at last was left to solitary indulgence of his grief.

There was less commiseration with him in his loss than might have seemed natural, for the man—drunken, brutal, and always quarrelsome—had been endured rather than liked, and all the sympathy of passengers and crew went out to the unfortunate woman, who, it was believed, had done away with herself rather than submit to her husband's ill-treatment.

The men admired her beauty in spite of her silence and reserve, which they had at first called "stuckupness," not to be expected from little Anne Marley, whose mother had had to give up her station to pay the Bank's loan—little Anne, who had gone to Europe to make a name as a singer, and had woefully failed, and been obliged to marry rough Elias Bedo for the sake of a home. They had none of them believed in her voice, till one Sunday, when the Captain held service, she had poured out her glorious contralto in a hymn. Afterwards, they gave her no peace till every evening she sang to Eric Hansen's accompaniment on the old cracked piano in the saloon. Then, by the magic of her voice, she had carried each man back to scenes on shore—to opera-nights in Sydney and Melbourne, as she had sung airs from Verdi and Rossini and Bellini, and even from Gluck's "Orpheus"; then to nigger-minstrel entertainments, which the sailors loved best of all, when she had given them "'Way down upon the Swannee River," and "Hard Times come again no more," and "John Brown," and the rest of those quaint plantation melodies.

By-and-by, Elias Bedo betook himself to his cabin in company of a bottle of brandy; and when the steamer reached Cooktown that night, he was incapable of even speaking to the Police Magistrate. This official spent some time of the two or three hours during which the Leichardt discharged and took up lading, in consultation over the affair. It was midnight when the Leichardt entered the estuary of the Endeavour River, and passed into the shadow of Grassy Hill, which overlooks Cooktown harbour. The sky had clouded over; a drizzle threatened, and the moon was quite obscured. Only a few kerosene lamps illuminated the darkness of the sheds, and of that part of the wharf where cargo was being unloaded. A few steerage passengers, mainly Orientals, disembarked at this port, and here, Kombo, the black boy, left Mr Bedo's service, having at Thursday Island announced his intention of seeking his tribe in order to see what had become of his father and mother, and, as he put it, "all that fellow brudder and sister belonging to me."

Eric Hansen, on deck, saw him staggering along the plank with an enormous swag on his back, and a young Lascar hanging on behind him, but soon lost sight of the two behind the low sheds which lined the quay. Hansen was sorry that the black boy had gone, and wondered that he should care to go back to the Bush; but Kombo, though he was well tamed, having been taken young from his tribe, and though he had had three years' experience of domestic service with his mistress in England, gave an example of that savage leaven which somehow or other must assert itself in the Australian native. So Hansen knew that once Kombo had got past the hills behind Cooktown, he would cast off the garments of civilisation and relapse into his original condition of barbarism. The explorer had offered, if he would wait, to give him a place in his own pioneering expedition which was to start from a little further south; but Kombo, with "Mine very sorry, Massa, but mine like to stop one two moon before

I go again long-a white man," had shaken his head and refused the offer. Hansen was disappointed, for he intended to study the northern natives as well as the northern fauna of Australia, and had been getting what information he could out of Kombo, whose tribe was one dwelling inland of Cooktown. It was in his talks with the black boy that he had come into more intimate companionship with Mrs Bedo—curiously intimate, considering a certain half savage, half timid reticence which she showed to almost all on board. She rarely spoke at meals except a word or two to the Captain, beside whom she sat. When the weather was fine and comparatively cool, she would spend much time in her cabin; but in the afternoons, she would usually sit on deck, and there, Kombo would bring her tea, and sometimes stay to have a little conversation with his mistress. Then it would seem to Hansen that she was like some wild, shy creature, brought in from her native forests, and permitted to hold occasional converse with a domesticated inhabitant of her own land. For it was only, he felt, as her face lighted up in talk with Kombo, that he saw the girl as she really was—as she might have been, freed from the galling yoke of an uncongenial marriage. On one of these occasions, when Kombo lingered after bringing her tea, Hansen, walking past, was struck by the animation with which she spoke to her black servant in his own language. The conversation, after the first minute or two, had not seemed to be of a private nature, and presently Hansen drew near, and begged for a translation of some of the words, over which Mrs Bedo was now laughing with unrestrained pleasure. It appeared that they related to certain adventures among the Blacks, which she and Kombo were recalling, in which the girl had played the part of some native deity.

Hansen then unfolded to her his own projects, and his desire to become more intimately acquainted with the language and customs of the Australian Aborigines.

He now learned that Mrs Bedo had been a Bush girl herself, and had lived a little lower down on this very coast till, when she was seventeen, the Bank had, as she expressed it, "come down upon the station," fore—closing a mortgage, and had turned them out. Her mother, who was in bad health and in danger of losing her sight, had gladly accepted the offer of a free passage from the Rockhampton branch of the Eastern and Australasian Steamship Company, and had, with her two daughters, gone to live in England. In those seventeen years of girlhood, Anne Bedo said she had learned the dialect of two native tribes, and now, she told him, was practising the language to see if she had forgotten it.

Hansen, as his mind went back to the occurrence, remembered with what a start she had answered his first question, and how eagerly she had asked him if he understood what she had been saying. He remembered, too, how sadly and earnestly she had been talking some little time before he had ventured to interrupt her, and he wondered whether she had been confiding her sorrows to this sympathetic black friend.

That episode took place after he had been on the boat about a week—he had joined it at Singapore—so that he had really known her for a very short time. Yet it seemed to him that those two or three weeks might have been years, so great was the interest with which she had inspired him. He felt that he understood her—her girlish innocence, her quenched gaiety, so ready to break out when the burden of her husband's presence was lifted—her misery, and her proud reserve—as he had never understood any other woman; and more than once it had occurred to him that were she free and he less wedded to natural science and a roving life, he would have chosen her beyond all other women he knew for his wife. But she was married, and he, even had she been free, was one not given to romantic dreams. So he had put away the vague fancy—not because of the wrong of it—for, indeed, he sometimes thought that the man who delivered her from so coarse a creature as Elias Bedo, would be doing an action worthy of commendation—but rather because he was the trusted servant of a scientific society, and had planned for himself an interesting two years' work, in which there was no place for sentiment concerning a woman.

He had found out her misery the day after joining the steamer, not through any confidence of hers, but by the accident that his cabin adjoined that one occupied by Mr Bedo and his wife. This was before

Mrs Bedo, a few days after the landing of some other passengers at Singapore, had ventured to petition the Captain for a cabin to herself. Partitions on a steamer are thin, and ventilators admit sound as well as air. Hansen had heard Bedo swear at his wife, and reproach her for what he was pleased to term her imbecile obstinacy, in terms opprobious and embarrassing to the involuntary listener. He had heard also Mrs Bedo's sobs and pathetic remonstrances to the man she had so unwisely married. Hansen had the impulse to rush in and denounce the persecutor, but thought better of it; and after the second occurrence, went to the Captain and frankly stated his reason for desiring a change of quarters. Then he found that Mrs Bedo had been before him; and as the only desirable cabin had been allotted to her, Hansen withdrew his claim and remained where he was, suffering no further disquietude except from Bedo's drunken snores.

He thought of Anne Bedo all through that dreary day, during which the boat steamed down along the coast towards Cooktown. The notes of a song she had sung the last time he had heard her sing, haunted him through the hours—Che faro senza Eurydice—the most heart-thrilling wail of bereavement which ever musician penned or songstress breathed. He, too, felt almost as Orpheus might have felt in seeing his love lifeless, her soul dragged down to the pit. His own Eurydice, it seemed, had been torn from him by the cruel teeth of the monsters of the deep. He sat on deck, trying to read, and so occupy his thoughts, which, in spite of himself, would stray among visions of horror, and all the while, his eyes, unconsciously lifting, gazed out on the blue seas dotted with coral islands, or inland to the treacherous Australian coast. Where was she? He shuddered as he asked himself the question, recalling Captain Cass's words. Oh! that she had died without lengthened agony. Better, in truth, a shark for the slayer, than that she should become a prisoner among the Blacks.

A strange hush had fallen upon the vessel since Tragedy had brushed it with her wings. All that day the sailors went silently about their work; the meals were gravely served; none of the passengers seemed inclined to talk. During the long hours between the event of the morning, and the entrance into the mouth of the

Endeavour River, which is the harbour of Cooktown, and, indeed, during many perplexed hours later, Eric Hansen brooded mournfully over his brief acquaintanceship with Anne Bedo.

Chapter IV—Black Boy and Lascar

A BLACK boy and a young Lascar were trudging along a rough track in the Bush, some distance from the coast,—a track that could hardly be called a road; it had been made by the wool-drays coming in from a far-off Western station. The traffic was at all times small, and now the way seemed lonely and quite deserted, for the shearing season had barely begun, therefore the ruts and bog-holes made by the last bullock team which had trodden it, had already become grass-grown.

Both black-boy and Lascar were dressed according to their kind, the latter more fully than is customary among Indians and Malays in Australia, though his garments were wholly inappropriate to foot travelling in the Bush, and were torn in many places, stained with mud, and draggled and limp from the heavy dews. His small, lithe form was pretty well covered by a voluminous sarong, and only a small portion of brown ankle showed between it and his boots, while the upper part of the body was clothed by a sort of tunic in cotton, beneath the outer muslin drapery, which even hung over his arms. He wore a muslin turban twisted round his head, set far forward, and with loose ends, that, from a side view, almost hid his face. He trudged wearily, with a blue blanket strapped upon his shoulders, which seemed scarcely large enough for its weight. Indeed, he was so small and slender as to look hardly more than a child.

The black-boy, larger and more muscular than the ordinary native, seemed to have been a station hand employed by white men. Round the open collar of his Crimean shirt was a red handkerchief, neatly folded sailor-wise, above which his neck showed brawny and black. His trousers were of good material and cut, though they hung loosely, and were turned up in a big roll overlapping the tops of the boots. They had evidently been made for a gentleman, and indeed, any one acquainted with the wardrobe of Mr Elias Bedo might have recognised the garments as having been once his property. They were held up by a strap, from which hung several pouches, a knife, a tomahawk, and sundry articles of miscellaneous use. Round his Jim

Crow hat a puggaree was twisted, and he bore on his back a very large swag.

The two had just struck the main road, having made their way across country, through scrub and over creeks, to a point whence a small digging township might be reached without difficulty. The direct dray road to this township branched off some distance back, but, from the present point, the diggings lay as at the apex of a triangle, and a miner's rude track led to it through the Bush. Presently, on the crest of a ridge in front of them, the black boy's quick eyes discerned two or three men on foot, also humping their swags. He knew that they were probably diggers, and this was the signal for him to call to his companion, who lagged a little, and to strike sideways into the Bush. They soon got behind another low ridge, and walked on in the direction they wished to go, but out of sight of the track. By-and-by, the black boy stopped, looked up at the sun, and peered around. Then he laid down his pack, while he made certain observations usual with the Australian native when he is not quite sure of his whereabouts. Presently, he gave a click of satisfaction with his tongue and teeth, and re—shouldered his swag, beckoning to the Lascar.

"That all right. Mine soon find—im old sheep-station, I b'lieve. Come along now; we go look for water-hole."

The Lascar, who had sunk down upon a log, and was idly plucking and smelling some gum-leaves from a young shoot which sprouted near, rose, and again followed the native guide.

"That all right," the black repeated. "Mine think-it we sit down along-a shepherd's humpey very soon now."

The Lascar nodded and smiled, and trudged on again with a springier step than before.

They went silently through a stretch of gum-forest, wild and utterly dreary. The great uncouth trees rose above them, stretching overhead a latticework of stems, vertical rather than horizontal, and giving little shade. The limbs of the iron-barks were rough and knotted, with perhaps a stalactite of gum, red as blood, dropping here and there from some wound or abrasion on their surface, and were hung with long withes of green-grey moss that gave them a strange look of hoary antiquity. The arms of the white gums were smooth and ghostly white. They had but little foliage, and flapped shreds of pale papery bark that fell from them like tattered garments. Among the gums, there might be seen an occasional wattle, long past blossom, or a weird-looking grass-tree with its jaggled tuft of grey—green blades, thin and unleaflike, and its dark spear as long as the rest of its body. All was dull green-grey, arid and shadeless, from the thin leaves of the gum-trees to the tussocks of coarse grass and prickly spinnifex. These often hurt the bare ankles of the young Lascar, and he would give a little cry, instantly stifled, and then would tramp bravely on.

The Bush sounds only seemed to intensify the loneliness. It was getting towards mid-day, and most of the birds were silent. Those that were awake, had discordant notes, and were mostly of the parrot kind. They chattered shrilly, their harsh cries rising above the tinny whizz of myriads of new—fledged locusts, whose cast-off husks made odd shining blobs on the trunks of the trees. Now and then, the black boy ahead would call to his mate, and point to where a herd of kangaroos were disappearing in ungainly bounds through the tangled gum vistas. Sometimes an iguana would scuttle through the undergrowth, or the boy would stop and tremble for a moment at the treacherous rustle of a startled snake.

About dinner-time, the appearance of the country changed, and the stony ridges, covered chiefly with mournful brigalow scrub, gave place to a less timbered plain. The sun poured on them as they traversed it, and more than once the Lascar took a pull at his waterbag. But far in the distance their goal could be discerned. This was a dim belt of denser vegetation; and as they came closer, they saw a fringe of almost tropical greenery—great scrub-trees, and river-palms, and luxuriant creepers.

Here was the deserted sheep-station of which the black boy had spoken. It stood on the borders of a plain, close to a water-hole, which could be seen in a clearing that had been made in a patch of scrub. The grass upon the old sheep-yard was bright-green; there were still some straggling pumpkin plants, and a rosella shrub almost choked with weeds. Broken hurdles lay around, and close to the clearing was a dilapidated hut. The travellers made their way through vines and weeds, and entered the hut by an aperture, where the slab door hung back on broken hinges. Inside was a plank table, nailed to two stumps set in the earthen floor. Another plank, also supported by two lower stumps, served as a bench on one side of the table, and a slab bunk was set opposite against the wall. The Lascar sat down on the bunk, heaving a weary sigh of satisfaction at having found rest at last. Then he took off his pack, unrolled the blankets, and spread them on the bunk, making a bed on which he stretched himself. The black boy undid his swag too—it was much larger and heavier—and seated himself on the table, grinning benevolently at his companion.

"Bujeri you, Missa Anne!"—the Blacks' commendatory formula. "Ba'al mine think-it you able to walk that long way. You very fine boy, Missa Anne." And Kombo gave a peal of laughter as he eyed the transformed woman.

Anne laughed too. In their keen sense of humour, she and Kombo were at one. It is the redeeming quality of even the most demoralised township black. She tore off the bespattered turban which had covered her head, and showed a short crop of soft hair—dark, but not dark enough to accord with her pretended nationality. Never did Singalese or Malay possess locks so fine and feathery. There did not now seem much of the Lascar in the little brown face, oval of shape, with its delicate aquiline nose, its small, pointed chin, and pretty, finely-curved lips. The eyes were dark-brown, very velvety, with curly lashes and straight, pencilled brows. Only in the hue of her skin, was the girl a Lascar; and how Anne Bedo had contrived, during the hours of her last night on the steamer, to stain herself the colour of a half-caste, was a mystery only known to herself and to

Kombo, who had got the materials from a black medicine man in Thursday Island.

The girl's white teeth shone, as she laughed, between her red lips. Her weariness seemed to have gone; at this moment she only thought of the liberty bought, it seemed to her, so easily. For Anne Marley, in her Bush girlhood, had loved adventure, had been familiar with the Blacks and their ways, had known Kombo since her tenth year, and now alone with him in the wilds, felt no fear.

She got up from the bunk and looked down at her soiled muslin draperies—so unsuited to the life she had been leading during the last few days—and at the tattered sarong, between the rents of which a woman's longcloth under-petticoat could be seen. She put out her slender feet, cased in laced boots, which had been originally made for them, and therefore had not galled the poor little stockingless extremities. She contemplated ruefully the scratches on her ankles, over which the blood had dried and caked with the dust of the Bush, and gave a very feminine shudder.

"Kombo, I'm dreadfully dirty. I want to bathe. Find me a place in the water-hole where I can have a swim."

Kombo shook his head. "Mine think-it alligator sit down there, Missa Anne."

The girl shuddered again.

"Well, let us have something to eat first. We'll see what the place is like when we go to get water for the billy. Now let us find some sticks and make a fire. Quick—Murra, make haste, Kombo. Poor fellow me plenty hungry. Give me the ration bags. Go cut me a sheet of bark, and I'll make a damper on it."

Kombo unstrapped his swag, which turned out to be two separate bundles, each rolled in a blanket, and both together enclosed in another blanket. From the dirtiest of the two—that which presumably held his own property—he produced some ration bags containing flour, tea, and sugar. These he set on the table, and then unfastened a blackened billy, and two pint pots which hung at his waist.

Anne laid hands on the other bundle, and carrying it to the bunk, undid it, gloating, like the girl she was, over certain feminine appurtenances, to which for several days she had been a stranger. Certainly, she had combed her short hair and washed her face, but that was the only sort of toilet she had made. Their one idea had been to push on, in order that as much ground as possible might lie between them and the possibility of re—capture. So they had slept but for an hour or two at a time, for the first day and night, and had only breathed freely since yesterday. A bundle of pocket-handkerchiefs, a change of linen, a grey riding-skirt and jacket, with a crushable cap, a few toilet requisites, pencils and paper, needles and cottons, and some other necessaries, made up all the baggage which Anne Bedo had brought away from the steamer. It had not been easy to take more, and even now she dreaded lest her husband should discover that the garments were missing, and so guess that she had planned her escape. Round her neck, beneath her tunic, she wore a locket containing the portraits of her mother and sister, and also a little bag in which was all her worldly wealth in the way of money.

Kombo went out to find sticks, and make a fire in the bark lean-to which the shepherd had used for a kitchen. Anne lingered in the hut. She had taken a little note-book out of her pack, in which were a few entries—the date of their departure from England, an address or two, and the list of her boxes on the steamer. The last entry had been a memorandum concerning prices of cattle which her husband had desired her to make on Thursday Island. The sight of it brought home to her the reality of her present situation. She turned the page, and, with the pencil attached to the book, scribbled sentences one after the other, with no regard to composition, as a mere vent for the wild joy that possessed her in the thought that she was safe from Elias Bedo, and free henceforward to live her own life.

"Anne Marley, escaped from bondage, rejoices in her liberty."

"Better death in the wild woods than life in chains."

"Anne Marley hails Nature, the emancipator."

"How sweet is the taste of freedom! How intoxicating the joy of deliverance!"

And so on, till the page was covered. Anne looked at her scribblings with the naughty pleasure of a child which has amused itself out of school hours by scrawling over a clean copy-book. It was a very silly ebullition of feeling, which she had cause to regret later.

Chapter V — The Shepherd's Hut

THE crackling of burning sticks recalled Anne to the fact that she was hungry, and going outside she saw a heap of dry gum-twigs making a blaze, which the sun robbed of its redness. Kombo was fanning the fire with his hat, and there would soon be a bed of ashes ready for the damper. Now, Kombo attacked a young gum-tree with his tomahawk, and in a minute or two had cut a sheet of fresh bark, on which Anne heaped flour from one of the ration bags. Water was needed for the mixing, and, searching the hut, she found a battered zinc pail under the bunk, which she gave Kombo to carry, and taking herself the billy and pint-pots, they proceeded down the clearing to the water-hole. This was not so easy a matter; for though the big trees had been cut, and lay tilted against others in the scrub on either side, lawyer palms had grown round them and hung their prickly canes over the path where ferns and undergrowth spread also, making progress difficult. How strange it seemed to Anne to be again treading warily for fear of snakes! This little bit of scrub was a delight, for it was more luxuriant than those she knew further south, and had tropical plants unfamiliar to her. She espied a tall tree on which grew a purple fruit like a plum, and Kombo climbed up to gather it, telling her, when he presented it to her, that it was very good. The water-hole they found was one of a series connected by the dry bed of a creek which had not for some time been flooded. It was dark and slimy looking, with muddy banks and rotting vegetation. A dead log lay half in and half out of the pool, and round it, grew a bed of poisonous-looking plants with large fleshy leaves like those of the arum. At the other end, also half in the water, lay a brown object which Anne thought at first was another log, but suddenly it moved, turned over, showing the pale underside of a hideous jaw, and she perceived that it was a crocodile. Kombo pointed to it.

"Mine tell Missa Anne that Yamin sit down like-it water-hole," he said, using the native term for the Saurian. The muddy bank, the slime of weeds, and dread of alligators, made it not pleasant to dip up water from the hole. Kombo poked about among the palms and ferns on the bank, and presently found a wide, shallow trough which had, no doubt, been dug out by the shepherd who had once lived at this sheep-station. From this they filled the bucket and billy, and here, Anne decided, that she would take her bath when the meal was over.

A scanty repast it would have been of new-made damper and tea, had not Kombo, plunging further into the scrub, discovered the mound of a scrub turkey, and brought back from it four of the bird's large eggs, one of which is almost sufficient for a meal. Two were laid on the ashes and baked. One had in it a young chicken that Kombo ate with gusto; the other was fresh, and Anne thought she had never tasted anything so delicious. When they had finished, Kombo put out the fire, covering it with dead leaves lest there should be Blacks near, whose attention might be attracted by the flame. This, however, was hardly likely. The deserted sheep-station was near the little digging township, as Kombo knew, for he had travelled past it with cattle on their way to a station called Kooloola. It was hoped that he might procure at this township a couple of horses, or even one that could be ridden, also provisions to last them through their journey. He knew the way to the diggings, and calculated upon getting there and back before nightfall. Now came a difficulty which had not been solved in Anne's talks with the black boy on the road. Should she accompany Kombo to the township, or would it be best that she should remain hidden in the hut? Anne, who was leader of the expedition, decided without deep pondering that she would remain. She was afraid to trust herself among white men, whose sharp eyes would perhaps pierce her disguise, and who would possibly carry news of her south, that might reach her husband. Strange as it may seem, she was not greatly affrighted at being left alone in the wilderness. She knew that there were no wild beasts in the bush that could possibly harm her, and crocodiles could not crawl up through the scrub to the hut to attack her. The most serious question in her mind was whether she might rely on Kombo. His fidelity she had proved, and could not doubt, but were he persuaded to drink at the grog shanty, there was no knowing when he might return.

Kombo, however, swore that no blandishments should entice him into the bar, or that were he compelled as a matter of business to enter it, no grog should pass his lips. Anne was obliged to be content with his promise. Never yet had she known him break his word when it had been given to her. In relation to other persons, Kombo's sense of honour was by no means binding, but between him and his young mistress there had always been the strangest affinity. It had been a puzzle to Anne herself; it was a puzzle also to the bushmen who knew of it, and who had no experience of so deep an attachment between black boy and white woman.

Anne untied the little bag she wore beneath her tunic, and taking out of it three five-pound notes, bade the boy use them to the best advantage. She had quickly thought the matter out, and now gave Kombo his instructions. He was first to buy food at the chief store in the township, and there to ask where he could best get a couple of horses. He was not to pay more than five pounds apiece for them, and if he could not find two for sale at that price, he was to get one; and also some sort of saddle, if it were possible to pick one up cheap. Supposing, as the chances were, that he could not get the horses that day, he was to come back, and go in again on the morrow, but he was not to say where he had left his mate. His story, if he were questioned, must be that he and his mate—a half-caste boy—were engaged to help muster at Kooloola, Mrs Duncan's station, some hundred miles further north, and that as time pressed, they did not want to do the journey on foot. The notes, he might say, were his wages which had accumulated from his last employer.

Kombo, like all Australian black boys, revelled in playing a part. He proceeded to set forth his views.

"Mine think-it Missa Anne make very good black boy," he said. "I go along and buy shirt and trouser long-a store, same as black boy. My word! Missa Anne bujeri boy!" and Kombo went off in peals of laughter. "But mine think-it no good for ole Missa Duncan to see Missa Anne like-it black boy," he continued, and meditated for a moment. "Never mind, mine make-im all right. We stop close-up lagoon, outside fence at Kooloola, and Missa Anne put on white

Mary's skirt. Then ole Missa Duncan no make-it noise first time. By-'m-by, Missa Anne tell ole Missus what for that fellow make-im black. That no matter. Very soon, Missa Anne come altogether white again."

Anne laughed too. She had forgotten she was brown. Her first idea had been that she would put on her grey riding-suit as soon as the black boy had departed. Second thoughts now showed her the prudence of Kombo's suggestion. She knew the Blacks' language well enough to find no difficulty in passing as a half-caste boy; and should they meet diggers or stock-men by the way, she would certainly be thus less likely to arouse suspicion. Besides, she could more easily ride in man's dress, for it was not likely that Kombo would be able to buy a side-saddle at the diggings. That in itself would cause remark. Often in the bush, she had ridden on men's saddles, and even bare-back, and had therefore no qualms on that account. So they settled that a Crimean shirt and trousers of the smallest size procurable, were, in the first instance, with rations, to be got out of the fifteen pounds. As to horses and saddles, it was doubtful whether the money would run to all these requirements. She had another five-pound note, but this she had resolved to keep in case of emergency; and it was a relief to her when Kombo proudly brought forth two other notes, describing how he had made Mr Bedo pay him at Thursday Island, and how he had there cashed his master's cheque. Kombo said he would buy his own horse out of his own money, and hinted darkly that if horses were not for sale at the diggings, he might be able to steal one.

Soon the black boy had disappeared among the gum-trees along the belt of scrub. He had only to follow the river bed to arrive in due time at the township; and, alone and unburdened, he could go much faster than when the heavy pack had impeded him, and Anne had been dragging more slowly behind.

Anne was alone. This she did not mind in the least; indeed, there was joy in the thought. She had always as a child loved wandering by herself in the bush. Once she had got lost, and had been out all night, finding her way back the next day according to the methods of the Blacks. She knew exactly how to trace down a gully, or follow a river from its heads, and how to steer herself by the lay of the country, and by the sun and stars. Many a time, too, had she chopped a 'possum out of a log, and unearthed a bandicoot from its hole at the foot of a tree. She wished now that she could find a bandicoot, or if she dared use her little revolver, to shoot some bird by the water-hole.

She had kept her possession of a revolver a secret, and had not shown it to Kombo. It was a tiny pistol which she concealed beneath her sarong—a toy that her husband had given her. He knew what a good shot she was, and she had asked for the pretty little weapon lying on the counter in its open case, which she had noticed when Mr Bedo was buying a gun to take out to Australia.

She had had scruples about carrying off this present of his, but some instinct had told her that it would be well for her to possess it; well also, that she should not make Kombo aware of her possession of it. Brave and lighthearted as she was, Anne Bedo knew well enough to what dangers a woman might be exposed in the Bush. So she had hidden the pistol and cartridges belonging to it about her person, before that early dawn, when Kombo had fetched her from her cabin to the locker in the stewards' quarters where he had hidden her, and where the search party had never dreamed of looking. Anne had then thought vaguely, that were they to discover her, she would shoot herself rather than go back to her husband.

Thinking over that eventful night and day, she wondered whether it had been found out that she had left the cabin door locked on the outside, and whether they had missed the revolver case, which she had thrown into the sea. She thought, too, of the letter she had left behind, speculating as to the impression it had made on her husband, and those who had read it. When she had begun to write, her intention was merely to finish it and give it to Kombo for the post. But in writing the last paragraph, she had suddenly reflected that by wording it in a particular way and leaving the letter unfinished, it might lead to the conclusion that she had, in a fit of mental aberration, thrown herself into the sea.

Anne put the revolver and cartridges away again, and went down the clearing to the dug-out pool in which she had thought of bathing. She peered carefully round to make sure that there was no horrible Ymain lying in wait for her. The only crocodiles with which she had as yet been acquainted were the "bimbies," as the Blacks called them, which are a smaller kind, and comparatively harmless; but even those had filled her with terror, though she had eaten their eggs in the Blacks' camp. She seemed safe, however, from spectators, either human or animal, except, maybe, a stray wallabi or a 'possum in a hollow log; and the birds which, now that that mid-day had past, were beginning to find voice. The strange "miawing" note of the cat-bird, the shrill call of the bower-bird, the plaintive coo of the scrub pigeon fell upon her ear, and another note that she had never heard—a very nightingale-roulade—which, under her breath, she tried to give back again. In old days, she had known how to reproduce the note of every Bush bird, and the temptation was too keen to be resisted. After one or two attempts she got the cry right, for the bird answered her back. Her courage rose; the rich voice swelled louder and fuller. The birds who at first had piped in response, held affrighted silence: they fancied that a strange, invisible songster had risen among them.

The girl laughed in almost elfish merriment. It seemed to her that, after long and weary banishment, she had once more found her home in her native forests, and felt herself akin even with the wild things which inhabited them. In truth, as she had herself said, Anne was a Bush girl to the very bones of her, and now was no more afraid in her own wild woods, than might have been Daphne before Apollo pursued her.

A very nymph she appeared as her garments fell, revealing her small form in all the grace of its early womanhood. She had not taken so much pains in staining herself where her clothes covered her, and below her breasts, to her knees, the colour of her skin was merely pale olive. Her face, shoulders, arms, and ankles were much darker, and she was almost afraid to wash them lest the dye should be removed. But Kombo had been right in his assurance of its efficacy.

She might have been just a little fairer when she came out of the pool, but that was all.

As she dressed, the roaring of an alligator frightened her, and she went quickly back to the hut. Now that the excitement and strain of her flight were relaxed, she felt extremely weary, and her eyelids drooped heavily, for she had not slept much for many nights past. She spread her blankets on the slabs of the bunk, and, making a pillow for her head with her grey skirt, fell into a deep sleep which lasted for hours.

Chapter VI—Kombo the Cavalier

ANNE'S scheme of escape had been carefully thought out during the night-watches on board the Leichardt, after she had told Kombo of her determination to leave her husband. She had not come lightly to this determination; and it is but justice to her to say that, much as she feared and hated the man she had married, she would have remained in servitude had she not become aware that every law, human as well as moral, justified her in freeing herself. Therefore she had appealed to the only friend she had, capable of helping her—the black boy. And in truth Kombo was made of heroic stuff, and would not have been undeserving of honour in the ancient days of chivalry. He had heard Elias Bedo swear brutally at his beloved mistress, had seen him strike her in a fit of drunken fury, and there had then come a look upon his face which convinced Anne that here was her Heaven-sent helper. It is usual to say that the Australian native is incapable of devotion, and does not know the meaning of faithfulness. Treacherous as a race they may seem, but there have been devoted Blacks who have served white masters to the death. "Jackey," of the explorer Kennedy's expedition, is one notable example. Kombo in his, as yet, humbler fashion, was another. Certain it is, that from the time when he had been privileged to hold Anne Marley's bridle at a bad crossing, to weigh the meat for her, scrupulous to the fraction of an ounce, when she was giving out rations, to pilot her on her Bush rides and keep the coast for her when she and Etta were bathing, Kombo had always been Anne's devoted slave. The girl's voice had in the first instance captivated him. All Australian blacks, and especially those of the northern tribes, have an extraordinary love of melody. Their own musical scale is limited, and their Corobberee songs mere monotonous repetitions and compositions of half a dozen notes. But their whole temperament is peculiarly susceptible to harmonic influences, and their passions can be soothed or excited to an almost ungovernable degree by a war song, or one of the ugals with which they exorcise evil spirits. In Kombo's imagination—and the Blacks are wildly imaginative—Anne Marley's beautiful contralto stamped her as a being above all other humans, white or black. He had heard the songs of stockmen and diggers by the camp fire and had been moved thereby, but none of these affected him as did the songs which Anne sang. He used to tell her that her voice was as that of Baiamè, the Great Spirit, whose word had made the world, and as the voice of those wonderful white birds that, according to legend, had flown into the sky singing praises to Baiamè, and had been turned into the Pleiades—those stars which the Blacks believe are the keepers of rains. It was Kombo's fixed belief that Anne was one of these, sent back to earth again, in order that, by her singing, she might move the heart of Baiamè when the fountains of heaven were locked. Once there had been a time of great drought when the cattle had died, bogged in dried-up water-holes, and the sheep had made food for carrion dogs, and when the Blacks had come into the head station and stolen from tanks and reservoirs some of the scanty supply of water. Then Kombo came to Anne and besought her to sing within the Blacks' sacred circle. Assuredly, he declared, in answer to such entreaty, Baiamè would send down rain upon his thirsty people. Anne listened, for she loved the wild superstitions of the Blacks, and was but a child, to whom the earth and inhabitants thereof, and the gods above the earth, were all as one grand fairy tale. She had learned to shudder at the Kinikihar—ghosts of the dead who wander on moonlight nights in the Bush, and she feared mightily Yo-wi, the legendary monster who brings fever and ague, and Ya-wi, the mythological snake, and Buba, the giant kangeroo, traditional father of all kangeroos. So she went obediently with Kombo one moonlight night to the sacred circle that the Blacks had made, in which they had kindled bonfires to keep Debil-debil away, and round which the whole tribe had congregated. There were the warriors in the war-paint of great ceremonials and tribal fights, the elders wealed according to their tale of years, and adorned with frontlet, and necklace, and tuft of cockatoo feathers. There, too, the women crouched on the ground round the circle, crooning and beating time with boomerangs and nulla-nullas. So, in the midst of them, Anne lifted her voice and sang the grandest devotional song she knew—an Ave which their store-keeper, a musician and an Irish Catholic, had taught her. And great Baiamè heard and was merciful, for the next day the heavens were darkened, and rain fell upon the thirsty land.

After that, the fame of her went abroad among the Moongar tribe, and further, even to the far north. The Blacks named her Yuro-Kateena, or Cloud-Daughter, and from this time revered her as a Karraji-Wiràwi, which, being interpretated, is Medicine-Woman.

In those days, Kombo had shown his reverential devotion by bringing her cockatoo crests, the plumage of lyre birds and rare parrots' feathers, and such spoil of the Bush. Later, when disaster came, and the Bank manager wanted to keep him on as stock-rider after the station had been taken from Anne Marley's mother, Kombo had refused to be servant to the enemy of his goddess.

There had been a great woolla, a palaver amongst the Blacks, and much lamentation when their Cloud-Daughter, who they now believed brought them luck in hunting and protected them from evil, was departing from amongst them. It was the chief of the Moongar tribe who bade Kombo go with the Karraji-Wiràwi, and bring her back from over the Great Water that she might once more petition Baiamè on their behalf. So Kombo made his request to the mistress, and Anne pleaded till, somewhat against her better judgment, Mrs Marley consented. A free passage was granted to the black boy also, and Kombo accompanied the mother and daughters to England, where, if truth must be told, he had been more worry than profit. Mrs Marley felt thankful when he asked to be allowed to go back to Australia with Anne and her husband.

Kombo was one of the best specimens of the northern tribesmen, so much higher in the scale of creation than their southern brethren. He was a man, every inch of him; his natural gifts were remarkable, and in sagacity and quickness he was the superior of most white men. He could not be taught to read or write, and all attempts to instil into him the principles of orthodox theology had been a failure; but he could read every chapter of Nature's book that related to the story of his own country; he could mimic any man or animal with whom he made acquaintance; he was a keen judge of character, and he could hold his own among the worst sharpers who ever haunted a shearing shed. With the most guileless manner and appearance, he could plan and carry through a complete campaign of deception, and he loved nothing better than having in the way of work "to make fool of white man." He had once gone on the drink, but ever since, had been afraid of a grog shanty, not from any exalted morality, but because he knew that he had been given doctored grog, which, as he phrased it, had made him "close-up go bong," otherwise, very sick.

In his own domestic relations, Kombo's conduct left something to be desired. He was much given to wooing and then incontinently dismissing his gins, "because that fellow no good," and, according to white law, he might have been frequently had up for bigamy. When residing in the stockmen's huts on the Marley's station, he had been quite contented to live "like-it white man" for a certain time, but about every three years the savage fever seized him, and then Kombo went off to the northern haunts of the Moongarrs, where he committed every aboriginal atrocity, short of assaulting white men. He was even suspected of having eaten warriors of a hostile tribe, though kindred in speech, called the Maianbars, who had fallen beneath his spear. It was because of this habit of Kombo's that he had never been allowed the possession of a gun, which would certainly have given him an unfair advantage over his enemies. He was now again due for a burst of barbarism, and it was when he had announced his intention of joining his dusky brethren somewhere in the neighbourhood of Kooloola station, that Anne had conceived the idea of making him her escort thither. Mrs Duncan, who owned Kooloola, was her father's sister. Some five years before, Mr Duncan had pegged out boundaries beyond even the extreme limits of civilisation, at the base of Cape York Peninsula, and though he had been considered fool-hardy, and even blameworthy, for taking his wife and children among dangerous Blacks, he had died a natural death, and had so flourished on his new station that Mrs Duncan had not felt inclined to give up the place. It was under Mrs Duncan's protection that Anne Bedo had desired to place herself, till opportunity occurred for her to start on a new scheme of life under another name than her own. Beyond taking present refuge, however, at Kooloola, Anne had not considered the future. Here, at least, she would be for a time safe.

Three days were passed in the shepherd's hut before Kombo found two horses and a couple of old saddles. Anne had an idea that one of these was stolen property, but asked no questions, and received back gladly what was left of the fifteen pounds. Kombo had bought for himself an ancient rifle and some ammunition, so that they fared sumptuously on game that he shot and which he broiled on the ashes, or baked, black-fashion, on red-hot stones in a hole in the ground. On the fourth day, Anne donned her black boy's costume of Crimean shirt and moleskin trousers, both absurdly large for her, and a felt hat, the whole a little inappropriate perhaps to the Karraji-Wiràwi part she meant to play, and on which her power of dominating Kombo's aboriginal impulses mainly depended. But she had only to sing a few bars of an Ave or a Gloria, and to point to the pale clusters of the Pleiades, indicating the stars as her sisters, for the subservience of Kombo to become abject. So, fearing nothing, and commending herself alike to the Catholic Saints and to the heathen gods of the Bush, Anne mounted her sorry steed, and the two—black boy and white woman—set off on their hundred and fifty miles ride to Kooloola. They put up at no stations on the way, not even accepting the hospitality of shepherd or stockman, but camped each night in the bush, hobbling their horses and cooking their own food, Anne sleeping under a gunya of boughs which Kombo made for her.

It was a strange, wild journey. Kombo had heard rumours of raiding blacks and of tribes at war with each other and with whites. Once, they met a band of native police with Captain Cunningham, the chief officer, at the head, which was on its way to the outside districts to disperse the Blacks, as the leader put it. This meant nothing more serious than the firing of a few shots, the wounding of an old man or two, or maybe a gin, and the breaking up for the moment of the camps. Anne, in her black boy's dress, astride upon what the Captain was pleased to term "an old crock, only fit to draw my grandmother's corpse," trembled, and tried to hide her face, making pretexts for getting off the track, while the Captain parleyed with Kombo. She had known Captain Cunningham well in early days and feared lest he should recognise her. She fancied that he eyed her suspiciously, and did not like his questioning of Kombo, as to where the black boy had picked up his mate. "Ba'al mine think-it that brother belonging to you. What name that fellow?" said the Captain.

Kombo invented a name on the spur of the moment; and then Captain Cunningham, who had also known Kombo in Mrs Marley's time, enquired about his mistress, and whether the rumour was true that Mrs Bedo had thrown herself overboard off Cooktown. Just then Anne pretended to spy a kangeroo, and putting spurs into the "old crock" darted through the gum—trees. "Billy—Billy!" cried Captain Cunningham, calling her by the name of Kombo's impromptu baptism. "Come here. Mine want to talk to you, Billy."

But Anne would not hear; and Kombo, with a whoop and a black's halloa, spurred along his steed in pursuit of her, leaving the Captain to go on his own way with his troopers. They did not see him again, but the incident frightened Anne. Captain Cunningham had known her ever since she was a child. Often had she sat on his knee, and one of his amusements had been to make her "talk black," and mimic her native friends. She was terrified lest he should discover Anne Marley in Billy, the black boy. Then all would be lost. She was sufficiently well acquainted with Captain Cunningham's views on matrimony and things in general, to be quite sure that he would take her in charge and escort her back to her husband. Each day after that, she rode in dread of again coming across the native police—in dread, too, of Blacks, for the presence of the troopers implied danger in that respect. Of the Blacks, however, Anne was far less frightened. They therefore forsook the track, riding in a course some distance away but parallel with it, and thus avoiding the chance of even meeting a wool—carrier with his team, or a party of diggers, or a lonely fossicker.

The journey lasted longer than it would have done had they been riding better horses, or had they kept to the dray-track. They had many adventures and endured much discomfort—at least Anne endured it; to Kombo, loose again in the bush, discomfort was a joy. It was the end of the rainy season, and the heat was steamy. For two days it poured, and the creeks came down in flood. Once the water bailed them up for a couple of nights; and twice obliged them to swim, clinging to their horses' manes, for the beasts were too weak to carry their weight against the force of the current. Kombo's gun was then disabled and his ammunition wetted, while Anne had some trouble in saving her own concealed revolver and cartridges from the wet. She contrived to tie them on the top of her head beneath her hat, and so kept them above the flood. When the rain ceased, they had to wind along the bank of a river through the tropical scrub, which is common up north, for some distance inland from the coast. In this they suffered greatly from mosquitoes and ticks. But they fared sumptuously on scrub turkeys' eggs, and ground game that Kombo trapped, as well as on the white larvae which they found among the roots of trees, and which is a delicacy for both blacks and whites. Leaner days followed while they rode over the barren ridges they next struck. These were low detached spurs of the great range; and here, one of the horses went lame, thus retarding their progress. Camping on a ridge at night, a terrific storm arose, the most awful Anne had ever seen. While the rain came down in torrents, Kombo, with his head buried in the ground, called piteously on Debil-debil to depart; and Anne, wet through, hungry and frightened, wept like a lost child with her hands over her face. The lightning struck and rebounded upon the iron-stone of the ridge, making wonderful and awesome coruscations, and a tree within a yard or two of their camp was shivered to fragments. Their horses bolted during the storm, and this again delayed them, though the nags were found later not far off, stowed away in the bed of a gulley.

Chapter VII—Birds of Prey

IT would take too long to tell of their escapes, which, after all, are common enough with bushmen who have attacked the base of that north Australian peninsula, though they were sufficiently alarming, even to a Bush girl accustomed to out-country life. There are women, however, to whom adventure is as the breath of life, and little Anne Marley, for all her feminine sentiment and romantic notions, was one of such. Often, in after life, she looked back upon the Bush journey with Kombo as one of the happiest times she had known; and, perhaps, compared with later adventures, it seemed tame and safe. By-and-by, they came upon beautiful pastoral country, the land which had enticed Duncan, the pioneer, from civilisation—rolling downs, slightly wooded, swelling below the basalt mountains and volcanic country westward. There, the peaks, strange—shaped and rock-ribbed, rose some three thousand feet out of dark-green jungle, barring part of the horizon. A little further, the mountains became higher, and multiplied in forms still more fantastic, where, in the far distance, the range turned inward towards a country wholly unexplored, and completely guarded against the inroads of squatters by impassable gullies and impenetrable scrub.

Anne had heard of the wonders and terrors of those mountain scrubs from explorers who had climbed part of the eastern side of the range, but had never penetrated its fastnesses, or gone into the mysterious region beyond. The Blacks had legends of some great and awful Debil-debil, more fearsome than any ordinary Debil-debil of the south, which inhabited these tracts of the interior. Anne knew of the great sandy waste in the centre of Australia which had once been sea; where the rivers lost themselves in the sand, and whence scarcely any traveller returned. But between that sandy desert and the river-shed at the base of Cape York Peninsula, rumour spoke of a tract of country, closed in by scrub, where volcanoes had once raged, and where, according to the Blacks, were small lakes, supposed by them to be fathomless. The Maianbar and Moongarr tribes dwelt near its borders, and it was through stray Blacks who had found their way south, or had been brought by the native police from the outskirts of their own more inaccessible haunts, that these reports came. Otherwise, the region was unexplored. If the ill-fated Burke or Kennedy ever reached it, they did not return to tell the tale. There were all kinds of traditions about this unknown country. Anne had heard one prevalent among the Moongarrs, of a leviathan turtle that had lived in a lake which dried up, leaving the turtle without water. The story went that the turtle had turned into stone, and was now a mountain possessed of magic properties. Then there was another legend of a gigantic crocodile, dwelling upon the top of a high hill, out of whose mouth came fire and smoke; a monster which would still spit flame and ashes, and overwhelm any intrusive stranger venturing into its dominions. It was Kombo who had told Anne the story; he had learned it among the Moongarrs. Kombo believed devoutly in the crocodile "Debil-debil Yamin," and the turtle also — Mirrein, he called it. When Anne laughed, he was very much offended, giving her to understand that this was too serious a subject for profane jest. "Ba'al mine gammon," said he; "plenty black fellow afraid of that fellow Debil-debil Yamin."

Anne asked him if he had ever seen that Yamin. Kombo shook his head. "Ba'al brother belonging to me go long-a Deep Tank, close-up Crocodile Mountain," said he. "Maianbar black, sit down there. Long-ago Maianbar black, brother belonging to Moongarr, talk altogether same. Then many moon back, two fellow tribe fight — oh! plenty fight" — and Kombo's eyes and gestures expressed oceans of gore — "Maianbar blacks been eat Moongarrs. Afterwards, not friends any more. Maianbars one side of mountains: Moongarrs stop this side. But I believe two fellow tribe brother again by-'m-by," added Kombo cheerfully, for his own part quite ready to ignore the blood-feud.

Anne gazed out to a portentous-looking bank of clouds on the north-west horizon, and fancied that they were mountains, and that two of them were shaped like the turtle and the crocodile of Kombo's story. She wondered what was the real foundation of the legend, though it was not difficult to guess that it originated in a volcanic eruption. She knew that extinct craters had been found by many explorers, and she remembered, too, the explorer Hann's account of his find of fossil remains in North Australia, the wonderful antediluvian animals scientists had discovered to have existed in this oldest continent of the world—the gigantic iguana, the Australian diprotodons, the monstrous kangaroos, the enormous horned turtle.

Nearing the lower hills which bounded the great downs they had been traversing, Kombo told Anne that now they were "close-up Kooloola," and that if she wanted to put on her "White Mary's" dress they would camp by a lagoon that he knew, not far from the home paddock, where she could undo her swag, and make herself "altogether like-it half-caste woman."

"Ole Missus Duncan think plenty sun make-'im face black belonging to you," remarked Kombo; and consolingly added, "Mine been tell Missa Anne that all right. That come altogether white by-'m-by."

The lagoon lay between two low, full-bosomed hills, a peaceful tarn, on the surface of which floated the beautiful blue and white water-lily of Australia, and a few blossoms of a lovely pink colour, a rarer kind. Anne wanted Kombo to have a swim, and gather some of these for the old Missus while she changed her dress, but Kombo shook his head.

"Mine think-it bunyip sit down there," said he in a more portentous tone than that in which he had warned her against the alligators. "That water—hole go down long way in the ground. Mine think-it water come out other side," he went on. "Ole Massa Duncan, he try once to measure with plenty thread, but that no good. I believe bunyip catch hold of thread. Ole Massa no find-'im bottom."

Thousands of black duck, teal, and other water-fowl, with their young broods, floated on the lagoon, and now, alarmed by the voices of strangers, uttered strange cries, and rose, a mass of fluttering wings hovering over the water. At one end of the lagoon was a thick belt of casuarina and flooded gums, the white scaly stems of these last, uplifted like an army of ghosts. Anne retired with her swag into the shadow of these trees, while Kombo lighted a fire in a hollow log and set the billy to boil. Close to the bank, he warily waded to pluck some roots of water-lilies, which he laid among the ashes, and roasted like yams.

Presently Anne re-appeared—a trim little figure in her grey riding-habit, with the soft cap upon her short hair, and a veil, which she had brought away in her pack, tied round it, hiding the brownness of her face. Kombo gave a "Tschk! Tschk!" the black's expressive note of admiration, as she came up, tripping a little over her now unaccustomed skirt.

"Bujeri, Missa Anne!" said he; "Ba'al ole Missus see that fellow no look like-it White Mary."

But Anne wondered whether her aunt would recognise her. She had not met Mrs Duncan since she was a child.

The girl and the black boy were hungry, and feasted with a light heart. They ate the yellow powdery roots of the water-lilies, which were very palatable, and a change from their ordinary diet of game and damper. The quart-pot tea was drunk, and then they remounted. Anne had some difficulty in sitting side-ways on a man's saddle, but Kombo and she between them strapped a little hump, cut from a gum-branch, above the saddle-flap, and thus contrived a sort of pommel. About three miles further, they came upon a cattle-camp, which showed that they must be near the station. Before long, the paddock fence appeared, and they halted to put down the sliprails. Some way off, they could see the homestead perched on the side of a hill, just above a long narrow lagoon. Banking the head-station, the hill behind sloped gradually towards a thick scrub which spread upwards over the summits of a broken range, and downwards, in a kind of semi-circle, round the upper end of the lagoon.

Anne, with her Bush knowledge re-sharpened, wondered why her uncle Duncan had chosen so dangerous a site for his homestead, in a country infested with Blacks, to whom the scrub would furnish a very effectual cover for attack. She supposed he must have had some good reason connected with the working of the station; for she knew that, though called fool-hardy, there was never a more thorough bushman than her uncle Duncan. She knew also that he had held theories concerning the treatment of the Blacks, opposed to those of most bushmen. He had always paid them liberally for work they did for him, and, appealing to what he considered their better nature, had constituted himself their protector. The thought flashed through Anne's mind just then—for she was a hard-headed little creature, and, in spite of her friendliness to the natives, knew they were like children whom it wasn't wise to spoil—that it wasn't over safe to be a pro-Black in an unsettled district.

A track, broad enough for the water-cart that supplied itself at the lagoon, wound round the gentler ascent of the hill, past the stockyard, with its heavy railed fence and massive corner-posts, to the back of the cluster of bark-roofed buildings constituting the head-station. They could just see these, partly hidden by a knoll that abutted from the plateau on which the homestead was placed.

Kombo put up the sliprails, but just as he was about to re-mount his horse, something attracted his attention, and he walked on a little way, carefully looking at the grass and saplings which bordered the track. Then he stood still for a minute or two, gazing keenly from the homestead in the direction of the scrub behind it.

Anne called to him to take his horse which she was holding. He turned sharply.

"Kolle mal! Kolle mal!" he muttered, giving the aboriginal words of warning, and went on a short distance continuing his observations. Presently he came back to the girl.

"Missa Anne," he said, "you see, smoke long-a scrub? You see, ba'al no smoke long-a white man's chimbley! What for no fire? What for no smoke? Missa Anne, mine think it wild black sit down long-a scrub. Mine no want-im Missa Anne go first time long-a humpey. I b'lieve Kombo mel—mel—Kombo, look out—Missa Anne stop here—then suppose all right, I come back and tell Missa Anne."

Anne quailed at the scent of disaster, for the black boy looked strangely troubled.

"What do you mean, Kombo? Don't you think old Missus Duncan sit down long-a humpey?"

"Mine no think-it, Missa Anne. Suppose ole Missus long-a humpey, that fellow make-it fire-smoke. I very much afraid of wild black. You no been see long-a cattle camp, one bullock have spear hanging down long-a leg? I b'lieve wild black camp close-up, and this morning he been spear bullock. I no believe ole Missus long-a humpey. I b'lieve that fellow plenty frightened and run away."

"No, no, Kombo. Ole Missus never frightened of Blacks."

"I believe so, Missa Anne. One fellow, black-policeman long-a Captain Cunningham, been tell me Maianbar black come down and make corroboree closeup Kooloola, Maianbar black want-im flour, sugar, ration... Ba'al mine think-it, that fellow look out talgoro (human flesh)." Kombo appeared doubtfully sanguine. "He no like old white. Maianbar black like best young black fellow."

Anne turned very pale, and reeled slightly in her saddle. A more horrible possibility dawned upon her than that ole Missus should have run away.

"Oh! Kombo—don't!" she faltered.

"No fear, Missa Anne. He very bad black, Maianbar black;" and Kombo made a devout grimace. "Ole Missus know all about that, and make altogether white man yan (run away). You see—what for no firesmoke? Mine think-it Missa Anne better stop down long-a hut close-up water-hole. I go look out." Kombo pointed to a bark hut on the bank of the lagoon at the end furthest from them. A fringe of trees and swamp oak spread past the gum-trees, along the side of the lagoon inside the fence they had just passed through, and Kombo's quick intelligence had already grasped the advantage of placing themselves under cover. He suggested that they should get off and lead their horses round along the edge of the water-hole, under shelter of the trees, and then see if the hut was empty, or tenanted by the stockman. He might well be there, for it was near sundown, and work should be over on the run. If he was at home, they might assure themselves that all was well at the station. If the place was deserted, Anne might wait in it, with the horses tethered near, while he, Kombo, crept up the side of the hill near the scrub, and reconnoitred at the back of the house. Anne did not quite care for the plan, and would have preferred to ride straight up to the homestead, but Kombo impressed her by the earnestness of his manner, and she had confidence in the boy's instinct. Besides, a feeling of great uneasiness and desolation, such as she had not yet known during their wanderings in the Bush, had crept over her in the last minute or two. Though she had reached her goal, she could not help, after Kombo's suggestion of the Maianbars' weakness for talgoro, feeling terribly anxious.

Just then, a flight of hawks wheeled down from the homestead hill, close over her head, fierce, red-eyed birds of prey, whose very presence filled her with an unreasoning sense of ill-omen. She resisted Kombo no longer, but got off her horse, and, leading it by the bridle, followed the black boy among the belt of trees to the stockman's dwelling. The door of the hut stood open. Inside, the blue blankets lay in disorder on the bunk, as though a sleeper had hastily arisen. Outside, the fire under the bark lean-to had been laid, but had not been kindled. Two or three fresh bits of wood lay upon the half-burned foundation logs, and there seemed something oddly forlorn in the heap of last night's ashes beneath them, and in the empty black pot tilted on the ground close by. Outside the door, on a bit of stump, the stockman's coolaman—the bushman's wooden washing basin—was set, with the hard square of yellow soap within it. Though in the shade, it was quite dry, and had evidently been unused that day. Nobody was in or near the hut, and Anne seated herself on the slab bench beside the rough table, while Kombo hung the horses to a tree, and then, skirting the upper end of the lagoon and the border of scrub beyond it, began to climb the hill so as to get a side view of the homestead.

Anne waited a long time in the hut—it seemed to her hours, though it was scarcely forty minutes. The setting sun shed a glow on the trees and the bare bit of ground outside, and upon the distant peaks of the range which she could see through the hut door. The mosquitoes, coming with the approaching twilight, had begun to swarm, and the hut was close and ill-smelling. Outside, every now and then, she saw a hawk circling low to the ground. One came after the other, and she wondered what carrion feast had caused the foul birds to congregate. No doubt, she thought, it was the speared carcase of a bullock which the Blacks had killed, and, unable to carry away, had left to rot. She had forced herself to dismiss any more appalling conjectures. Anything else seemed impossible.

The evening birds were beginning to call. She could hear the gurgling note of a swamp pheasant, and every now and then the raucous mirth of a laughing jackass pealed from a neighbouring tree. The Bush sounds which she so loved seemed now only to intensify the nervous strain, which was becoming unbearable. She wondered why she should suffer so, for the first time, now that she was within sight of her aunt's house, and almost under her aunt's protection. For, of course, her aunt was there. She had not felt so lonely and frightened in the shepherd's hut by that crocodile-infested water-hole. It struck her; were there any crocodiles in this lagoon? And then she began to feel thirsty, and searched the hut for water. There was none to be found, and she took a pannikin and went restlessly out towards the fringe of ti-trees which hid the little lake from her view. The sun had now sunk, and a red afterglow illuminated the plain, striking the slab fence of the paddock, and causing scales of ti-tree bark to shine like silver.

Anne walked a little way. All around her, were creepy sounds of animal life, but there was no sign of Kombo. Now she thought that she heard the thunder of hoofs—a rush of cattle, perhaps—on the plain. A hawk rose from among the trees ahead of her close by the bank of the lagoon; another flew up, and another. She pushed back the branches, moving uncertainly, for she was vaguely conscious of some wakening horror, She struck through an odorous thicket of river jasmine, lemon gum, and the fragrance of ti-tree blossoms, and now stopped dead short, and uttered a piercing scream.

At her very feet, the head towards her, the legs caught in a tangle of vine, lay the body of a man clad only in a shirt, with the top of the head battered in, the eyes staring, the mouth wide open, a swarm of flies upon the blue lips; while, as she stood, her shoes were almost wetted by a little stream of coagulating blood. Beneath her outstretched arms, a loathsome carrion bird spread its wings, and fluttered out over the lagoon. The girl gave another shriek, and fled back through the thicket. She understood now. God of mercy! That this thing should be! Had the Blacks massacred every white man and woman on Kooloola station?

Chapter VIII—"Altogether Bong"

KOMBO stood at the door of the hut. He had been crouching at the back of it, even as she went forth to the lagoon, not knowing how he should tell his gruesome tale. He leaned against the lintel, his limbs shaking as though he too had not recovered from the shock of some terrible discovery.

His face seemed ghastly under the outer pigment of black, and his lips were bloodless; but in his eyes there lurked an unholy light, and Anne realised, with a fresh shudder, that the savage beast in him, contending with acquired prejudices of civilisation, was for a moment unleashed, and might have to be fought and conquered.

The girl's indomitable spirit gazed out from her own eyes, and quelled the savage. He gibbered helplessly, uttering unintelligible sounds and laughing with the Black's peculiar note in his guttural merriment. Then he quailed before her gaze, making a gesture of pleading and dismay.

"Kombo!" Anne said, aware that now she held the hereditary tendencies in check, and that he was once more her slave. "Kombo, do you know what has happened? Do you know that he's dead—the man out there? Do you know that the Blacks have killed him?"

Kombo laughed again—a hopeless, helpless laugh, in which, nevertheless, there was a faint triumphant cadence, telling of the race hatred between black and white, subdued in him, but not wholly eradicated.

"Yo-ai!" (yes) he said. "Mine think-it all white man bong long-a station. Plenty dead white fellow—ole Missus; two fellow daughter belonging that one. Young Massa—one fellow Chinaman cook—all lie long-a floor where black fellow been, kill altogether white man. I been tell Missa Anne no smoke—no fire; all white fellow bong— altogether bong, altogether dead."

"Kombo, do you mean that they are all dead—all?" The girl spoke in a whisper, her eyes distended, her teeth chattering. "Kombo, you say all white fellow bong long-a station? You no tell lie?"

"Mine no tell lie, Missa Anne. I believe black fellow come last night kill everybody, take-im store, find-im grog, mumkull altogether with spear and nulla-nulla—ole Missus, young fellow white Mary belonging to her; young Massa Jim—Chinaman long-a kitchen—altogether bong. I creep up close—up humpey. I see long-a verandah ole Missus—I believe black fellow kill that one first with waddy. Inside, I see two young Missee—I believe black fellow take-im that fellow—no kill altogether quick like it ole Missus. Then I go outside long-a store. Young Massa he have-im spear like it back, and Chinaman he lie dead little way off. Mine no see young Massa Tom. Mine think-it that fellow run away and look out—find Captain Cunningham and black police."

Kombo's keen wit had worked out the situation in all its chances and probabilities. He knew that of the Duncan boys there should be two at home, and one was missing. He knew, too, that the black troopers under Captain Cunningham, from whom he had heard their destination, should be encamped a short distance eastward.

At this moment, in confirmation of his intuitive reasoning, the distant thud of hoofs which Anne had heard, deepened into nearer thunder, and suddenly ceased. Kombo darted to the fence, Anne following, and both looked along it, to where now they saw a band of troopers halt for a few seconds, to let the rails down, then pass through in single file and gallop up the slope towards the head station. Each one had his rifle ready, and it was evident the little army was bent on no peaceful errand. No other white man was with the band. Clearly, if it were Tom Duncan who had roused the police, he had been too exhausted to return with them. Maybe he was wounded, and had only dragged himself to Cunningham's camp to die.

Anne and Kombo faced each other—black man and white woman, realising to the full, and without need of words, the danger of the position. On one side were the Blacks, glutted with gore and spoil, their fury satiated, and no doubt prepared for flight into the fastnesses where men on horseback might not seek them. On the other, were the Whites, and in their company the certainty of recognition. Were Anne and Kombo to ride up now to the homestead, it would be almost impossible to deceive Captain Cunningham. Publicity must be given to all details of the tragedy, and the report of the native police would surely mean that Elias Bedo would obtain positive information of his wife's existence and whereabouts.

Better to fall into the hands of the Blacks, Anne thought, than into those of Elias Bedo.

But there was a middle course. It might be possible to hide until pursuit of the plunderers was fairly started, and the southern route clear. Then she and Kombo might either return the way they had come, or wait in the Bush and go northward by the coast to Somerset where there would be a chance of catching some vessel bound for Java. That had been the plan in Anne's mind, when she had decided upon seeking temporary refuge with her aunt. The middle course had also occurred to Kombo as the safest. There was no need between them for preliminary discussion. He seemed to read her mind as she read his. Kombo scratched his head, and thought silently for a minute or two. Then he went back to the horses, unfastened their bridles from the gum-bough to which he had strapped them, re-adjusted Anne's saddle and the pack that had slipped down, then delivered himself of his opinion.

"Missa Anne, mine think-it no good to go long-a station until black police go away. By-'m-by that fellow hunt after wild black in the scrub, but mine think-it very soon, white man from other station come long-a Kooloola. You know! That fellow wear-im shirt outside of trouser and, my word! cobbon woolla—plenty talk and say prayer." Thus Kombo graphically sketched the surpliced Bush parson of his experience. "I believe that white man go look-out Massa Bedo... Tshck! Tshck!" with the indescribable ejaculation of the native. "White man tell Massa Bedo. 'You run—murra, make haste—wife belonging to you sit down long-a Kooloola. Massa Bedo—he think Missa Anne dead.' When white man tell him Missa Anne no dead, he very glad. He ride quick, and pialla (appeal to) Captain Cunningham to bring black trooper. Altogether come—catch Missa Anne and by-'m-by put Kombo in goal. Naia-yo! Naia-yo! That very bad for Missa Anne. That very bad for Kombo."

"Yes: that very bad," said poor Anne. "You must help me, Kombo, to keep out of Captain Cunningham's way. What can we do?"

Kombo ruminated for a minute or two. "Mine cobbon stupid fellow, Kombo. Massa Bedo, he plenty saucy. He got-im money; he make black trooper servant belonging to him. Mine think-it no good to go back long-a Cooktown. Best way to hide close-up Kooloola and look out till black trooper go away."

"But where can we hide?" asked Anne. "Captain Cunningham very good bushman, Kombo. No can hide from black trooper."

"Ole Massa Duncan no like black trooper," said Kombo. "I believe ba'al that fellow know bush long-a Kooloola. Missa Anne, you see!" The boy pointed to a knoll, two or three miles distant, which rose sharply above the scrub. "Big fellow cave sit down over there. Brother belonging to me show me place long time ago, when I bring cattle for Massa Duncan. That cobbon big cave; that very dark cave, very good place to hide. By-'m-by black police take pho-pho, and go shoot wild black. Kombo look out; find saddle, catch horse—bujeri horse, Kooloola brand. Missa Anne and Kombo make quick track. White man no see; police no can find."

Kombo's comprehensive plan was the best in the circumstances, but Anne hesitated.

"Suppose wild black sit down long-a cave?" she suggested, weakly.

Kombo shook his head.

"Mine no think-it Maianbar black stop close-up station," said he. "That fellow frightened, and run away long-a mountain. You come long-a me, Missa Anne; lie down inside cave; make fire and cook supper. Niai kandu...Mine plenty hungry."

Kombo was a philosopher. No matter what the tragedy around him, the danger and the difficulty, he never failed, at the close of the day, to make this announcement. Anne did not feel hungry. Nevertheless, she listened compassionately when Kombo said "Niai kandu."

"Mine show you short cut long-a cave. Mine take-im swag. Mine let go yarraman (horses) and mine plantim saddle. By-'m-by, when black trooper and white fellow altogether yan, mine run up yarraman in paddock—much better yarraman. You see? You think-it that bujeri?"

Anne nodded acquiescence. She could not speak; something seemed to have come up suddenly in her throat and choked her. Her eyes stared vacantly into the bush. She saw before her the dead bodies of her aunt and cousins, and the tragedy re-clothed itself with new horrors. Silently she helped Kombo to unsaddle the horses. When free, the beasts started off with a whinny, and went to drink at the lagoon. She took the two swags in her right arm, while with her other hand she held up the skirt of her riding—habit, regretting bitterly that she had not kept on her black boy's costume. Then she staggered after Kombo, who was laden with the saddles and bridles and his own gun, and was making straight for the scrub. The two skulked behind trees and shrubs till they had reached the shelter of the thicket, afraid that the native police might espy them, but soon they were hidden in the dimness of dense vegetation, and pressed inward as fast as their burdens would allow. After walking for a quarter of an hour, Kombo laid the saddles and bridles in a hollow at the foot of a tree where the earth had slipped, leaving the roots bare, and collected mould and twigs, scraping them backward with his foot, after the manner of a scrub turkey building its mound. Then he gathered other twigs, and before long, the saddles and bridles he had planted were covered safe from the chance of a marauder. The boy then made a discreet blaze on the tree with his tomahawk, so that they should neither of them, on returning for their property, miss its hiding-place. While he worked, Anne gathered her habit round her waist, binding it by a strap that she took from the pack, so that with kilted skirt, progress through the jungle might become a little less difficult. It was still sufficiently arduous, though Kombo went first to move, here a spiked log, or to cut away there, the withes of a hanging creeper. He steered straight for the rocky knoll he had pointed out, in which the caves were situated, though it was no longer visible, and even the stars by which he might have guided himself were hidden by the roof of interlacing branches. But a black boy's instinct of locality is a compass which rarely fails him. Moreover, Kombo was near the hunting-ground of his own tribe, the Moongarrs; and though it was years since, as a naked piccaninny, he had wandered through this region, he had returned to it with Duncan the squatter, and remembered the features of the land.

Night fell. It was much darker in the scrub than it would have been in the open, and the eeriness of it all thrilled Anne's nerves, which vibrated like strings stretched to breaking point. She walked close on Kombo's heels, sometimes stepping deep in mire, sometimes stumbling over stones, sometimes slipping down the side of a gully; her ankles bleeding, her hands torn among the prickly shrubs and tangle of vines.

As they got further into the heart of the scrub, the gullies became steeper, and the great boulders that encumbered them more numerous. Hugh volcanic stones were lying pell-mell, monoliths standing on end, and rocking-stones poised, and trembling at a touch. It was as though, in the beginning of things, fire demons had played here at pitch and toss. After a time, through a rift in the trees, they could see the evening star. The vegetation had become scantier, rocks taking the place of trees, and now they found themselves on a space, clear, but for the stones which strewed it, and with a basalt cliff rising close over it. The base of the cliff was curtained by creepers, and low scrub trees grew out of fissures in its face. Here, a part of the sky was visible—cloudless, of an intense blue, gemmed with stars; the Southern Cross apparently touching the summit of the crag. Anne—ragged, scratched, and sore from the stings of insects and of scrub nettles—sank exhausted upon a stone, a most pitiful figure; while Kombo, marking the position of the stars, took his bearings, and gave guttural clicks of satisfaction at finding how little deviation he had made.

"Close-up cave, Missa Anne," he called, encouragingly. "Very quick, plenty supper, plenty sleep. Come on."

Anne rose; and they moved northward round the knoll, pushing through the scrub where it encroached on the rock, and at last halting before a dark blot on the cliff's surface—a half-circle, in the centre of which was a great bare boulder. Creepers hung round the opening, which, to a casual eye, would not easily be discoverable. Kombo peered about on every side, anxiously searching for any signs of Blacks' fires, but he saw none. Now he bade Anne follow him, and stepped warily inside the cave.

"All right," he called out; and the vaulted roof of the cave caught his voice and sent it back in a reverberating echo, so uncanny that Anne started at the sound. She pressed in close upon him, and, after a little groping on Kombo's part, both stood in a deep embrasure near the mouth of the cave, which was here dimly illuminated by the starlight outside. The light was just sufficient for Anne to trace the outline of a long, wriggling thing, which, at the sound of footsteps and voices, stirred from its lair. Kombo darted forward. "Make light quick, Missa Anne," he whispered hoarsely. "Mine think-it that snake"; and as Anne struck a match which she had in readiness, she saw by its feeble flare that Kombo had brought the butt end of his old gun down upon the neck of a great brown serpent, which, pinioned and powerless to use its poison fang, struck out wildly with its tail, its body half coiled round the body of Kombo's gun. She drew back shuddering.

"Give me waddy, Missa Anne," cried Kombo, stretching back his hand, as with the whole weight of him he leaned on the gun. She handed him a stout stick which he had cut for her as they went through the scrub, and a few well-directed blows made the snake's coils droop flaccidly, its back broken, while Kombo battered in its

55

head. Anne struck match after match, exploring the hollow in which she stood lest other reptile or beast should there have made its nest. But all was safe; the floor was smooth and clean, the walls bare stone, and she leaned against a projection, too frightened to move. The cave seemed to stretch into unfathomable blackness, but was now silent as the grave. How thankful she was that Kombo had bought these boxes of lucifers at the township store, and that they had managed to keep them dry when crossing flooded creeks, by tying them up in the bladder of an animal they had shot. She knew that she ought not to be reckless with her matches, but to remain alone in the darkness of the cave was more than her nerves would bear. Kombo had dragged the snake outside, but presently returned, gloating over the supper he would make from it. He brought in a bundle of sticks and dry leaves, and before many minutes a fire was kindled. Then he took a fire-stick and searched the cave, making another fire in a further recess. Here he took Anne's swag and spread her blanket, keeping his own belongings by the fire at the entrance. He called Anne to come up to her camp—so he named the further fire—and the girl gladly obeyed.

Never had distressed damsel more chivalrous servitor, as Anne had found good reason to assure herself during these wanderings. Each night she had softly sung a prayer, and Kombo, reverently listening, had made the Black's obeisance to Baiamè, the masonic sign taught young men when initiated into the Bora mysteries. Anne knew of those rites, which aboriginal tradition held that Baiamè himself had established when, in long past ages, he had descended as a great white man upon earth. When she had sung, Kombo would retire, and Anne would lay herself to sleep—the first night or two of their journey with her revolver clutched in her right hand close by her side, beneath the blanket. But after a little time she realised the magic power of her incantation, and the depth of Kombo's loyalty to his gods, and to the woman who he believed was their representative. She knew most surely that she had nothing to fear from Kombo himself, and also that his outpost camp was a protection against intruders, upon which she might safely rely. It gave her no anxiety to know that both her honour and her life were at Kombo's mercy, for she realised that they could only be assaulted across the boy's dead body. In her trustful gratitude to Kombo, Anne almost cried sometimes when she thought of the treachery which pioneering Whites had dealt to his race. She was certain that those savages they had ill-used would have been faithful, had they been taught by their conquerors the meaning of fidelity. When she thought of the dispossessed tribe dying out down south, killed by the very vices they had learned from Englishmen, her heart burned with indignation. Setting aside superstition, Kombo loved her and was true to her because she had been kind to him, had never scoffed at his traditions, nor had tried to force on him a religion which experience told him had, on the part of its professors, led to outrage upon the women of his race, and cruelty to its men. Kombo once told Anne of a certain squatter in the back blocks, who, when a camp of Blacks pitched their gunyas beside his water-hole, had called up the chief and palavered with him, telling him that the Whites wanted to make a feast for the Blacks, as it was Christmas Day, and that "a pudding like-it white man's Christmas pudding" should be made for them by the white cook, and given to the chief if he would take it down to the camp. The chief came, the pudding was given to him, and the next day nearly all the tribe was dead, for the pudding had been poisoned. Was it any wonder, she thought, that afterwards white men were speared from behind gum-trees, and that there were murders on the lonely stations?

Anne remembered this story now, and found in it a plea for black murderers. Then the realisation of the tragedy so near, came home to her, and she wept bitterly. Her kind old aunt, her young cousins; why had they, who had never wronged either Black or White, been chosen as expiatory victims for the wrongs civilisation had committed? She could scarcely believe, even now, in the truth of that grim story which Kombo had told her. She could not have credited it at all but for the horrible sight she herself had seen by the lagoon. Her brain was dazed, her senses numbed, the future was a blank. All her plans had been destroyed; she could think of nothing now, but that for the moment, her weary body had found a refuge in which she might lay herself down to sleep. Kombo came up presently with a billy full of water he had found in a hole among the rocks, and with the ration bags of tea and sugar. They had a segment of damper, baked the previous night, and this she ate greedily, not waiting for the billy to boil in order to wash it down with quart-pot tea.

Kombo chuckled benevolently at the sight of her hunger, and produced a bleeding lump of the snake's body which he laid on the embers to roast. It seemed to him that he had provided a delicious repast, to the merits of which his mistress had hitherto been insensible, but which now, in her need for food, she would surely recognise. He had never yet been able to persuade Anne to eat the blacks' favourite delicacy, snake; the easiest food procurable in the Bush. But even now Anne shuddered at sight of the dainty morsel, and bade him take it to his own fire.

"Mine got plenty more, Missa Anne," said Kombo. "That very good, altogether bujeri," and he smacked his lips in anticipatory relish, but Anne still refused the delicacy.

"Mine find-im bandicoot to-morrow," said Kombo, grieved that she should fare so ill, and took the bit of snake to his own camp, where he cooked and devoured it, while Anne ate her damper and drank her tea. Then she softly sang her little hymn, and bruised, tired, and sore, she stretched herself as she was, on her blankets, and slept long into the morning.

Chapter IX—The Cave of Refuge

LIFE in the cave, but for mosquitoes and absence of light and air, was not absolutely disagreeable. The rest from physical exertion was a relief to tired Anne, whose limbs ached from riding a rough horse, and on a man's saddle for so many days. They were stiff, too, after the march through the scrub, and bruised from her falls among the stones. Yet after the first twenty-four hours, her nerves began to recover their balance; for the wild life of the woods, the scent of the scrub, the sough of the wind among the trees, the calls of the birds and other native sounds breaking the solitude, were as medicine to her spirit. In spite of grievous thoughts that afflicted her, it was indescribable pleasure to feel herself once more Nature's child in the nursery of her earliest years. With the adaptability of youth, she set herself to make their rock abode as habitable as circumstances permitted. There was no knowing how long she might have to dwell in it, for Kombo and she had decided that they would not venture into the open until the coast was clear both of Blacks and Whites. The native police, they concluded, would have raised the district in quest of the murderers, and might at any time, in company of neighbouring squatters, turn up again at the station; but Anne hoped that her cousin Tom Duncan, if he were still alive, would return to Kooloola, and she determined, on the most convenient opportunity, to throw herself upon his protection.

They had not heard any sound of shots, and no search parties had come near their retreat. Kombo, taking off part of his garments of civilisation with the gladness of a savage restored to barbarism, and clad only in his dark-grey flannel shirt, crept cautiously through the scrub, and reconnoitred as best he could. He dared not go out of shelter; but from a little eminence overlooking the station, he had seen that a small detachment of troopers was quartered at the homestead, though doubtless the strength of the force had gone in pursuit of the Blacks. It was reinforced, Kombo had reason to believe—from the horse-tracks he had descried round the upper end of the water-hole, and on the edge of the scrub where he had ventured forth—by some white men from the stations eastward, who had hastened to Kooloola on receiving news of the murders.

There was no smoke of camp-fires in the scrub, as far as Kombo's eyes could reach; and it seemed clear, as he had told Anne, that the tribesmen must have fled towards the mountains, where the troopers would have much ado to catch them. They would not go, he said, as far as the fire—spitting crocodile. Into the dominions of that monster no Black would dare penetrate, and from them no White would issue alive—so declared Kombo, and Anne wondered anew if there were hidden volcanoes in that closed region, the existence of which was unknown to explorers. Short of that fearsome locality, Kombo informed her there were plenty of scrubs and rocky places on the side of the range, and where the natives would be perfectly secure from molestation. He also assured her, shamefacedly, that it would not be his own tribe, the Moongars, that had committed the evil deed. Their hunting-grounds, he explained, were further south, this being their extreme limit. He again suggested that the marauders belonged to one or other of a more warlike and much dreaded race, either the Maianbars or the Poolongools, both of which spoke the Moongar dialect, and inhabited the ranges further west.

Anne tried to forget her sorrow in making the cave comfortable, Kombo keeping his camp near the mouth of it, while she remained in the interior. There were grass-trees out upon the stony plateau upon which they had emerged from the scrub, and she made the black boy cut some of the green tufts of these, and spread them upon the floor of the cavern. On a heap of the long blades, she laid her blankets, making an odorous couch; the trunk of the tree they burned at the entrance of the cave, and so managed to keep off the mosquitoes, which would not fly through the smoke. Kombo collected, too, a number of dry branches to serve as fuel for several days; and finding a convenient basin in the cave, they fetched water in their billies and pint-pots, making many journeys to and from a spring Kombo had found, and filled the basin, so that they might have a supply at hand in case of siege.

Anne dared not herself go far outside the cave; but Kombo foraged for native berries and roots; for the larvae which, when roasted, make a dish for an epicure; for scrub turkeys' eggs, and for opossum and bandicoot, so that on the whole, they fared sumptuously. Kombo sometimes wished openly that he had a gin to get food for him, and once tentatively suggested that they should join the Blacks, who, he said, would pilot them up the coast to Port Somerset. He assured Anne that she need not dread ill—treatment at the hands of his brethren so long as she was under his protection.

"Ba'al mine like-it altogether Maianbar and Poolongool black," said he; "but all the same, long time ago that brother belonging to Moongar. Suppose mine say, Missa Anne, been bring down rain for black fellow; Missa Anne, Cloud-Daughter belonging to Mormodelik (the Pleiades); Missa Anne plenty good to black fellow? Then Maianbar black very kind—bujeri look out after Missa Anne. Black fellow no make Missa Anne carry spear, waddy, dilly-bag, like-it gin. Mine tell black fellow Missa Anne like-it Karaji (Medicine man). Mine say, Missa Anne pialla (talk to) debil-debil till that fellow go away. Mine say, Missa Anne make it rain, make it thunder, make-im black fellow very sick—you see! Black fellow frightened of Missa Anne; give her gunya, bring her nice fellow tucker—make it altogether bujeri for Missa Anne. I b'lieve Missa Anne be like-it queen long-a black fellow."

But these gracious promises did not tempt Anne. Indeed, they alarmed her, as showing the trend of Kombo's desires. She thought of the horrors at Kooloola, and even began to be a little afraid of Kombo, who, she saw plainly, was longing to rejoin his tribe; and though she trusted him as regarded her own safety, she could not be sure that he would not yield to the impulse of savagery, which, it was evident, had seized him since the casting of civilisation. She could only beg him to wait until the commotion had blown over, pointing out that, in such case, they would both be in danger of being shot by the black troopers; whereas, if they remained in the cave, by-and-by her cousin Tom would be settled at Kooloola and would plenteously reward Kombo, and maybe cease from hostilities with the tribes because of the black boy's care of her.

Three days passed, and Anne was getting accustomed to being a cave dweller. She mended the rents in her grey habit, combed her hair, and took a bath, stealing to the spring for that purpose. She saw in the pool's mirror that she was less brown than when she had bathed in the water-hole near the digging township, and was half glad, half fearful. She was woman enough, however, not to desire that Kombo should get her materials for re—dyeing the skin that had once been fair.

Things were so quiet, that after the first day or two, Kombo reconnoitred more freely and was out longer at a time; while Anne also, chafing against her enforced imprisonment, took courage and went out into the scrub above which the crag rose. She now discovered that this was not an isolated peak, but the half of a cloven hump, and that it was rounded more gently on the other side, and covered with the same dense scrub which stretched westward among the hills at the back of Kooloola head station.

Seeing the configuration of the country, and realising the shelter which so vast a jungle must give to dangerous Blacks, Anne marvelled again at her uncle's want of bushman-like sagacity in selecting this site for his homestead. She did not know that the scrub, lightly wired, formed an easily-made boundary for an extensive home-paddock, which it would have cost a good deal of money to fence, and that Angus Duncan's Scotch thrift had on that account prompted the choice.

The wild berries were now, as the summer waned, dropping off the trees from ripeness. They were very tempting to the little troglodyte, and a search after an especially luscious plum led Anne one day much further than she had intended. She lost her way, and was some time in striking the precipitous face of the hump; then, being quite out of her bearings, she skirted it in the wrong direction, getting further and further from her own temporary dwelling-place. Seeing a dark opening in the face of the cliff, and mistaking it for the entrance to their cave, she ran towards it, to find that it differed somewhat from the opening she knew, for it had not the grey boulder which there guarded the cave's mouth. She was venturesome enough to wish to explore this new cavern, but was held back by the dread of encountering such another snake as the one Kombo had killed on taking possession of their own refuge. Then she fancied that she heard a Black's cry—the sort of cry Kombo gave when they were separated in the Bush, to let her know his whereabouts, and which he had taught her to imitate. She uttered it now, imagining that Kombo had found the cave before her; but immediately afterwards, a confused sound of Blacks' jabbering fell upon her ear, and at the same time she saw a little cloud of blue smoke blown outward from the opening in the cliff, which showed her that there must be a fire within.

Was it Kombo who had made the fire, or were there other Blacks near? A sudden doubt came into Anne's mind and caused her to retreat hastily into the shadow of a boulder of rock, cowering against it till she should become certain who were her neighbours.

If, in truth, there were blacks near, it was not possible that Kombo should be unaware of them. Certain small circumstances, suspicious in themselves, which she had not at the time thought much of, now came back to her. The black boy had been out an unusually long while the day before, and she had noticed on his face, when they were afterwards in the cave together, an expression which had puzzled her, a suggestion of mystery, glee, and yet of awed timidity in his manner of dealing with her. At the same time, there had been in his demeanour something of repressed savagery, and he had talked to her in his own language entirely, not in the pidgin English—aboriginese—customary among Europeans and half—civilised blacks. Anne understood to a great extent the language of his tribe, but had preferred to encourage him in learning English, an effort which, so far as grammar went, had not been wholly successful. She remembered, too, that he had brought with him a bit of half-cooked kangaroo tail, and knowing that they had no kangaroo meat in their camp, she questioned as to where he had got it, and why he had not fetched more of the flesh home to the cave, but received only evasive replies.

While these thoughts were passing uneasily through Anne's mind, she was startled by the whizz of a boomerang which flew by the rock, and returned towards the thrower. At the same moment there was a rustle in the brushwood by the cliff, and two naked Blacks advanced round the boulder upon her.

The girl kept her self-possession, though the Blacks were fully armed, each holding a nulla-nulla pointed, and a spear poised. She reared herself against the rock, and looking straight at the warriors, said fearlessly in their own tongue:

"Minti into yuggari Mai-al?" which means, "What is it that you would do to a stranger?"

The men fell back and jabbered to each other, astonished at the sight of this brown woman who yet was not as themselves, but who addressed them bravely in their own language. Now, out of the cave a crowd of natives swarmed—young and old, men, women, and piccaninies. There must have been nearly a hundred hidden in the recesses of the mountain.

"Wunti Murnian?" they cried. "Wunti Karabi?" (Where are the police? Where are the white men?) And they waved their arms at her threateningly.

The girl felt for her revolver beneath the flap of her jacket where she usually carried it, then recollected with dismay that she had not taken it that day from the hole beside her bed in the cave, where she kept it hidden. Only the belt with cartridges in it was about her waist. Then she reflected that perhaps it was as well that she had not the temptation of using her revolver. These Blacks, if they were those who had raided the station and murdered its inhabitants, would know the use of fire-arms, and would not regard them as something supernatural, wherein she felt lay her chief hope of alarming the Aborigines. Perhaps one of these very nulla-nullas had battered in the skull of her aunt. She shuddered at the thought. What chance had she among such blood-thirsty devils? Oh! where was Kombo, who might have protected her?

And yet her words seemed to have awed them, for the nearest of the warriors made no further demonstration. And now it occurred to her that she possessed possibly a surer means of self-defence than even her revolver. She lifted both her arms, stretching forth her hands in a gesture so commanding, that the attention of the blacks was arrested, and they all gazed wonderingly at her, and ceased from manacing. She stepped back on to a ledge of rock that protruded from the boulder, and, letting her arms fall at her sides, sent out the full strength of her voice in the Ave Maria of Gounod, that devotional chant, which had once before so impressed Kombo's tribe; only, that for the name Maria, she substituted Baiame, the title of the Blacks' Great Creator. The natives shrank for a minute or two in amazement, and made a circle a little distance from her, as they do in a corroboree when the medicine women dance and sing. Suddenly, a warrior stepped forward. He lifted his spear and, springing to this side and that, began to dance the wild semi-religious dance which preludes the native religious rite of the Bora, to which, however, no women are ever admitted. Anne sang on, and one warrior after another followed the example of the first dancer. The sublime strains of the chant echoed among the forest trees and the great boulders, and were thrown back from the face of the basalt cliff. The girl's soulwas in the invocation. She was singing for the glory of God, and the preservation of the life He had given her. "Ave Baiamè!" Was ever stranger prayer or praise raised to the Lord of Hosts in His wilderness?

She ceased. The warriors continued their dance, but presently stopped too; and now the whole congregation gazed at her as she stood on the raised ledge, her head level with the point of the boulder; her grey habit the colour of the rock itself, falling in straight folds round her; her brown face upraised, with its delicate aquiline nose, its little square chin, and its shining eyes all aglow; her lips tremulous with excitement. The Blacks, spell-bound, regarded her with the wonder and admiration they would have given to a divinity. And, in truth, she seemed like some goddess of their own race, suddenly descended incarnate among them. They waited in awe—stricken silence.

"Nulla Yuggari berren," she said simply. (I have now finished.) Shouts arose, and she could distinguish the words, "Pialla naia nanti." (Tell your name.)

She answered in their dialect—that of Kombo's tribe, the Moongarrs—the words coming to her as if by inspiration, "What would you have of me? I, who am sister of the Mormodelik—the Pleiades—have come to give you blessing."

She pointed skywards. They understood, and with one voice the old men, the young warriors, and the women acclaimed her:

"Mormodelik! Mormodelik! The Spirit of the Pleiades!"

At that moment, from the summit of the precipice above them, another voice shouted, and a spear, hurled down with unerring aim, struck the ground a few paces from the outskirts of the mob.

The voice was Kombo's.

Chapter X—The Sister of the Pleiades

"MISSA ANNE! Missa Anne!" the black boy cried. "Ba'al you jerron (don't be afraid). Plenty mine lookout long-a you."

As Kombo spoke, he swung himself down the face of the cliff with marvellous dexterity, clutching at the saplings and shrubs which protruded from the crevices, and balancing himself wherever a projecting rock gave him a chance of foothold. The Blacks watched his descent, greeting him with friendly yells, and making way for him when he flung himself to earth. He rushed through the little throng to the boulder against which Anne stood.

"Wunda Mormodelik!" he too cried, pointing to the grey figure, and making before it a quaint imitation of the white man's deferential bow.

"Wunda Mormodelik! Yuro Kateena! Spirit of the Pleiades! Cloud—Daughter!" And then Kombo harangued the tribe briefly but forcibly; and Anne, following his discourse, made out that the Karràji-Wiràwi (the Medicine Woman)—meaning herself—was known to all the tribes below Mount Coongoon, the mountain near Cooktown; for had they not heard her sing songs which the Great Spirit had taught her, and did they not know that Baiamè the Creator had taken a star from the sky and made it into a woman; and that he had sent the woman to his children, the Blacks, to bring them rain and food, and to make them victorious against their enemies? Then Kombo proceeded to tell how Yuro Kateena had sung to Baiamè in the great thirsty time; and how Baiamè had given rain to the earth, and had made the rivers run again, and the wallabis rejoice and the fish glad; and so had he provided food in plenty for the tribes to eat. He told how, when Yuro Kateen sang for a tribe, so that its warriors might fight and conquer, and grow mighty men of battle on the slain flesh of their enemies, great Baiamè listened to Yuro Kateena's prayer, and the tribe flourished even as she had asked. And so all had gone well with the Blacks while Yuro Kateena remained among them and sang. But there had come a day when the white man drove

Yuro Kateena from among them, and Cloud-Daughter could sing no more. Eeoogh! Eeoogh! Yucca! Yucca! Alas! Alas! Cloud-Daughter had gone across the big water, had left her children, the Blacks; and Baiamè had been angry with the Blacks because they had not kept his beloved. Then Kombo told that after a great Woolla (Council) of the tribe, he had gone from his people and followed Cloud—Daughter over the great sea to the land where only white people dwelt, serving a queen who knew not Baiamè. There Kombo had seen that Yuro Kateena was not happy with the white people, and that she longed to be again among her brothers the Blacks; and he had brought her home by sea and by land, so that now she was here to sing once more to Baiamè, and thus call down blessing upon the people. Kombo paused dramatically, and again bowed before Cloud-Daughter. The Blacks set up a great shout, and the warriors made a line, advancing to tender allegiance to the Medicine Woman, the beloved of Baiamè. But Kombo had more to say. He had not lived among Whites for nothing. He knew how to bargain, and could turn his astuteness to account even among his kindred Blacks.

So he dilated upon the advantage to the tribe of having a great Medicine Woman among them. He pointed out that if Cloud-Daughter were to remain, she must be treated as the divinity of a once-time star demanded. There must be no burden laid upon Yuro Kateena. Were she tired in marching through the scrub, young warriors must cut a great sheet of bark, and carry her thereon upon their shoulders. Her gunya must be made in the best fashion and held sacred, none entering therein without her permission. The King himself must do Cloud-Daughter honour.

Whereupon an old man, much wealed upon the chest and shoulders, which is a sign of age and dignity, stepped forward and spoke. He said that Multuggerah, King of the Maianbars, was verily King, and all others were his servants. Even Buli—he who spake—oldest chief in the Maianbars, had no will but that of Multuggerah. Multuggerah had not followed the wind of the south, in whose footsteps had trodden Buli, but had remained in the great camp beside Maianbar, which Kombo interpreted to Anne as the Deep Tank near to Kubba Ulala, the Mountains of the Dead. For the King Multuggerah, the old man went on, not even his chief Buli might answer. But Buli the Whirlwind—for he it was who made the warriors and their gins to run fast through the scrub, who laid low the brigalow trees, and carved spears therefrom, who with his weapons of war swept like a tempest over the herds of white men, and killed the white men in the camps they had made, therefore was he named the Whirlwind—he, Whirlwind, would swear now before the sister of the Pleiades, Cloud-Daughter, that he and his warriors, old men, and gins, would obey the word of Cloud-Daughter till, after many days marching through the scrubs, they should reach Maianbar the Deep Tank. Then when Yuroka-Gora, the North Wind, brother of Yuro Kateena, should sweep his children the clouds from off the sky, they should behold, higher than the hills, Kubba Ulala the Mountains of the Dead. So then also when they came to the camp of Multuggerah, he—Buli the Whirlwind—would deliver Cloud-Daughter, unharmed, to the King; and Multuggerah should say whether he would hear or no the song of Yuro Kateena, sister of the Mormodelik, the beloved of Baiamè.

Having thus with much dignity delivered himself, the Chief retired, first prostrating himself before the messenger of Baiamè; and Cloud-Daughter, some guardian power compelling her, sang in recitative in the native tongue:

"It is well, oh! Buli, Whirlwind, and chief of the family which bows before Multuggerah the King. Cloud-Daughter will cause the wallabi to fall beneath the Maianbar's spears, and the roots and the fruit to yield themselves abundantly for Buli and his warriors who shall lead Cloud—Daughter to Multuggerah the King."

But Kombo continued, warily making his stipulations for the safety and honour and well-being of his mistress.

The finest opossum robe should be laid at the feet of Cloud-Daughter, and the first portion of game, and first gatherings of roots and vegetables and berries from the high trees. To all, the word of Cloud-Daughter should be as the word of Multuggerah the King, till the King should himself behold and acknowledge the wisdom and power of Cloud-Daughter. And in return for the honour bestowed upon her, to Yuro Kateena, the Maianbars should be as her own people, and each night would she petition Baiamè for them, that the Murnian (troopers) should not find their camp, that the wallabi should fall plentifully beneath the warriors' spears, that the caves and hollow logs should yield bandicoot, and the earth roots in abundance, and the high trees bear many thousand berries. For all these good things would Cloud-Daughter entreat Baiamè. Therefore every night at the mouth of her gunya, so long as the tribe did her honour, would Cloud-Daughter sing her song aloud, so that all the warriors might hear her commune with the Great Father Baiamè. Therefore, likewise would she hold converse with the gods made by Baiamè over whom the Great Spirit had made her queen—with Munuàla, God of the Waters; with Kurru—Kurru, his wife, Dropper of Dew and Gatherer of Mists; with Woong-goo—gin, mother of the earth's produce; and with Billibira, God of Fire, most cruel and most mighty enemy of gods and men. All these, at the will of Baiamè, even the dread Billibira, were subject to the song of Cloud—Daughter.

Buli, the Whirlwind, bowed his head before the words of Kombo, and said affirmatively, "Yoai Pika," in the manner of the Blacks. But he set before Cloud-Daughter that the gatherings of the forest might be few, and the spearing of wallabi difficult, for the Murnian—the black troopers—were pressing upon the tribe for what they had done at Kooloola; and it had been needful to hide in haste in the caves, because their camp-fires had betrayed them, and there had not been time for them to escape afar—"yan wàra wàra."

Then Kombo related how on that very day he had tracked the Murnian and had found mandowie (foot-prints) going eastward. Therefore he knew that the troopers had ridden, as far as they could, into the scrub, and finding nothing, were gone eastward, believing that the Blacks had fled towards the swamp near the coast. He had been returning in haste to tell of what he had seen when he beheld Cloud-Daughter, and heard the voice of the goddess calling upon her Father Baiamè to hold the spears of his children that they were about to hurl against her. Now, he said, must the Blacks hasten where the north-west wind would lead them—the wind Yuro Ballima, brother, too, of the Cloud-Daughter. "Nalla yan!" (Haste, haste!) he cried. "Let them go quick through the scrub into the places where no white man on a horse might enter; then would they be free from the fear of the Murnian, and might travel as they would, to the camp of Multuggerah the King."

So the Blacks decided the matter. The sacred circle was broken. Buli issued his commands. The gins hastened back to the cave to collect their dilly-bags, their piccaninnies, and a supply of food; also to let loose the tame dingoes which had been imprisoned in a corner of the cave, lest their barking should call attention to the camp. The old men followed the gins; and the warriors, at the order of Buli, defiled before Anne, making a double line, through which she passed with Kombo to the mouth of the cave. As she stood waiting for what should come, and realising with dismay that, though a divinity, she was a prisoner, about twelve of the braves closed in round her, and by order of Buli, constituted themselves a guard of honour, appointed, as she understood, to be responsible for her safety till Multuggerah the King should make known his ordinance as to her keeping. As she heard this command, Anne's courage sank for the first time; and forgetting that she was a goddess, she appealed pitifully to Kombo to save her from the Blacks, and to keep her in the cave they had left till she could give herself up to her cousin. "Mine think-it that fellow Tom dead like it ole Missus," was Kombo's reply. "Mine no see Massa Tom long-a police. Mine think-it that fellow no come any more long-a Kooloola."

It was, alas! most likely that Kombo was right. Anne recognised the justice of his argument. If Tom Duncan had been alive, he would certainly be with the troopers, helping them in their work of vengeance. It was no doubt due to the fact that Tom was dead or disabled that their hiding-place had not been discovered. For was it otherwise probable that Tom should be unaware of caves so close to the head-station? That the troopers had not found them was hardly to be wondered at. Of course it would be supposed that the Blacks had fled westward. No one would suspect that they had concealed themselves so near the scene of their misdeeds. Kombo made a feint of not understanding Anne's English, as she went on alternately pleading and commanding. He turned away and spoke to the guard in so low a voice that Anne could not hear what he said. The girl grew desperate, and addressed the tribe in their own dialect, bidding them leave her behind, for that it was not her will, nor the will of the great Baiamè that she should be taken to Multuggerah. She even disclaimed her divinity. She had been made brown, she said, in order that she might escape from her enemies among the white men. In reality, she was the daughter of a white man and a white woman, not Yuro Kateena descended to earth from among the Mormodelik, the Pleiades.

At her words the Blacks scowled and murmured among themselves much disquietude. Several spears were raised threateningly. Then Kombo, moved by a sudden inspiration, cried, "Unda burgin duriga maial Billibira." "Billibira, the God of Fire, has driven the stranger mad in the scrub."

Scrub madness was not unknown among the Blacks, and they feared greatly Billibira, the fire-smiting god. The men of the guard had been standing at ease, each with his shield of wood lowered against the right leg, the left leg bent, the left foot resting in the hollow of the right thigh, and the weight of the body supported by the spear held upright, its point in the ground. Now they were at attention again.

Among the Blacks an insane person is sacred; and at the words of Kombo, threatening gestures changed to those of commiseration. Kombo, pursuing his advantage, spoke eagerly to Anne in broken English. Would she sacrifice both their lives?—for the Blacks would most assuredly kill and eat them both, unless she sustained her position as the beloved of Baiamè, and the sister of the Mormodelik, in which birthright Kombo, indeed, to do him justice, believed implicitly as a certain occult mystery. Had she not proved that the gift and the withholding of rain was in her power? She was Yuro Kateena; and were she not Yuro Kateena sent down from the sky as the child of a white man and a white woman, born in the Blacks' country, and destined to be the Blacks' saviour, then he, Kombo, could regard her no more as a divinity. She would be to him merely an ordinary white woman—one of those who were the enemies of his race. Besides, he argued ingeniously, how could she remain in the cave and not be discovered, supposing that the Maianbar tribe permitted her to do so? And now that Massa Tom was no longer at Kooloola, would not her husband most certainly hear that she was alive and come to claim her?

Kombo's reasoning was not to be gainsaid; and with the terror of Elias Bedo before her eyes, Anne silently submitted. Then Kombo cried "Undara Bunman," to the relief of the Blacks, who understood from the words that the madness of Cloud-Daughter was now cured.

Kombo subtly set forth in broken English that, once established among the Maianbars as the divinity Kombo himself took her to be, Anne might so rule the people that they would do her bidding even to the sending her from them at the will of the Great Baiamè. So might he and she by-and-by strike north in safety and make for the port of Somerset, according to their original intention. He explained also, that though the language of the Maianbars, and the Moongars, his own tribe, was alike, and that though the Maianbars had undoubtedly heard from the Moongars of the physical existence of Cloud-Daughter, which had been bruited among Blacks ever since that memorable bringing down of rain a few years back, there were many points of difference in the tribal customs, and he would not have the same influence with this race as he might have had with his own. He also told her that the Maianbars and the Pooloongools had the reputation of being the most bloodthirsty warriors and the fiercest among the northern tribes; also that they were cannibals to a greater extent than his own tribe, the Moongars. The Maianbars, said Kombo, lived in a place "burrin burrin (many) moons journey," to which none of the coast blacks had ever yet penetrated, through the scrub and over the mountains.

In the midst of Kombo's explanation, a little wailing, but most tender cry, sounded from the cave's mouth, interrupting his eloquence and causing him to turn sharply round, for Kombo was a gentleman never insensible to the claims of womanhood, even though it might be black womanhood, and for three years he had been mateless. The secret of Kombo's mysterious glee was now explained. A girl stepped forward and pathetically stretched forth her arms to the lover who she feared might be leaving her. She was a comely creature, scarcely matured, with long straight hair, a skin like brown velvet, and dark soft eyes. A smile broke over Kombo's face.

"Kunman Kurridu nungundung inta," he cried, which Anne knew meant, "Darling, I love you." He turned to Anne with the dignity of a man who has incurred family responsibilities.

"Mine no want-im stop behind," he said. "Mine want-im go long-a Maianbar camp. Ba'al mine been have-im wife plenty long time. Now mine got-im gin belonging to me. Name Unda. Come," — and he beckoned with loving hand, — "Taiyanàni Unda!"

Unda crept between the legs of the guard at the call of her spouse, and Kombo presented his bride.

"Unda servant belonging to Cloud-Daughter," he said. Anne bowed to fate in the shape of Unda, and from that day became the goddess of the Maianbar tribe.

Chapter XI—The Magic of Cloud-Daughter

TO ANNE MARLEY—for now she refused to think of herself by her married name—suddenly turned into a goddess, life became a piece of play-acting, in which she dared not give way to natural impulses, lest she should forget that she was an incarnation of one of the Pleiades—Wunda Mormodelik. The rôle of divinity she found, as her experience lengthened, had, with certain compensations, serious drawbacks. The worst of these drawbacks was from the beginning very apparent, when she saw that she was to be denied liberty of action and right of solitude.

Her guard marched her into a furthermost recess of the cave, which was now a scene of indescribable confusion as the tribe prepared for departure. The place reeked with the vile effluvia of animals, unclean humanity, and decaying meat, while the noise was so great that hardly one definite sound could be distinguished amid the babel of voices. Piccaninnies squalled, burning themselves with the scattered fire-sticks as they crawled along the floor, camp dogs wailed drearily (the tame dingo never barks), spears and boomerangs clashed while the men collected their weapons—the only part of the packing performed by lords of black creation—and gins squabbled over pieces of half-cooked flesh which they raked out of the ashes, and stuffed into their dilly-bags; while every now and then, when a gin seemed to slack work, her husband hurled a nulla-nulla at her head. From one corner of the cave, close to the recess in which the poor goddess was imprisoned, there came shouts of ribald laughter among a group of black men there engaged in some operations, the nature of which, in the dimness of the cavern, Anne could not at first determine. But now one of the Blacks threw a branch of dead gum-leaves on his fire. It flamed up, and Anne saw by its light that the men were holding up some garments of white women, and with unbecoming gestures were trying on skirts and bodices that had no doubt belonged to those murdered at Kooloola. Anne turned sick and faint, soul and body recoiling with deadly horror from the companionship in which she found herself. How could she endure to live, even for a day, among these brutes who had killed her aunt and cousins? Alas! a terrible foreboding told her that not for a day only, but perhaps for months, she might be doomed to share their food and shelter. A frenzied longing seized her to escape into the scrub and trust herself to the tender mercies of whites. She begged that she might be allowed to go out into the open air. But old Buli the chief had, with a black's cunning, read her face, and was of no mind to let Wunda Mormobelik, who was to deliver them from their enemies, slip through his fingers. He shook his head, and made a sign to the body-guard, which, with spears uplifted, closed round the troubled divinity, while their eyes gleamed through the flickering light of the cave with, it seemed to Anne, a horrible ferocity. She called for Kombo, but Buli told her he had gone to the other cave to fetch the blankets and rations. Anne thought of her revolver, for which she knew Kombo would not search, since he was unaware of its existence. Had that revolver been now in her hands, Buli and the guards would have fallen dead at her feet. It had several chambers, and she could load quickly. But she was helpless. Since force was not at her command, she tried guile instead, and requested that they would let her go herself to collect her possessions. She tried to work on the cupidity of Buli by promises of tea, sugar, and other delicacies, but to no avail. Then she appealed to his superstitious respect for her magic powers—alas, also to no purpose. Buli was obdurate. Though she was a goddess, and though Buli and the braves had sworn to obey her as they would Multuggerah the King, Anne discovered that she was to have no power in mundane matters; and even her supposed jurisdiction over the forces of nature was limited, by reason of Kombo's unlucky announcement that she had gone mad in the scrub. In reply to her angry questioning, Buli told her that because Billibira had stricken her with madness, though now she was recovered, it would not be safe for her to move in that place without a circle of warriors around her to do battle with the fire-god, and that on no account could she be permitted to enter the cave in which the mighty Billibira had robbed her of reason. Anne laughed hysterically. It was useless to declare that Billibira was made subject to her by Baiamè. Buli thought it better to be on the safe side, at all events, till they had got through the Kooloola scrub and out of reach of the troopers. The girl was now too hopeless and too exhausted to plead any more. Buli would not leave her side, and the guards made an impenetrable wall around her. Even Kombo had deserted her, she thought bitterly, and was no doubt enjoying himself with his new wife.

She did not see the black boy again till towards evening, when she was marched back out of the cave, still with her body-guard pressing close round her, to breathe at last again the pure air of heaven. The tribe had gone before, and the procession was now formed, so that all might round the hump and mount in order, piercing the scrub at the back of the precipice. A band of warriors went ahead; Buli with his old men strode just in advance of her; and behind, marched the rest of the men, and the gins who carried on their backs great baskets of plaited cane and dilly-bags filled with spoil and provisions. Here, Anne caught sight of Kombo, with Unda by his side, her own swag and his, which had been brought from the cave, divided between the two; for Kombo was yet too lover-like a husband to load his gin as if she were a beast of burden, in the manner of other husbands of his race.

The company of Blacks mounted very quietly to the summit of the crag, and then descended again in a north-west direction through the dense scrub towards the lower mountains of the dividing range, which were at least four days' march from Kooloola. There were other hills to the eastward clothed with scrub, and also having caves, and it was to scour these hills that the native police had now gone. From the top of the knoll the surrounding country could be seen, and far away in the hollow, the head — station, out of the chimneys of which smoke arose, showing that the place was not deserted. The stars were shining in heaven, and the moon getting to her full, sent down occasional gleams upon the marching band, through rifts in the foliage overhead. There was a blacks' track through the scrub, which the army followed; but after some hours this became lost in the thickets of lawyer palm which often barred progress, and through which those ahead had sometimes to chop a path.

In spite of the dense vegetation, which hindered any free current of air, the night was cooler than usual, and the march less wearying than it would have been by day. The damp soil and rotting leaves of the scrub sent out a heady smell, which mingled with the scent of flowers and the aromatic exhalations of many of the trees. Towards morning, though it was long before dawn, the scrub awoke. After nightfall, in the early part of the march, they had heard the mournful note of the jungle hen, the miawling of the cat-bird, the coo of pigeons, and cries of many other birds unfamiliar to Anne. Sometimes she amused herself by repeating the note, to the surprise of her companions, who could not account for a sound so close to them. But as fatigue crept over her, she lost zest for any such pranks.

By sunrise they were several miles away from Kooloola, and in such a precipitous part of the scrub that it was not likely any white man would disturb them. But there were the black trackers to be dreaded—the men who, with carbines cocked, would creep through the vines and lawyer palms, and surprise a sleeping camp. So the band made but a short halt by a running stream, and then marched again. Only the terror of trackers, and Kombo's exhortations, could have forced the Blacks to exertions so unwonted. Kombo, as one versed in the ways of Whites, was respected among them, and Kombo had his own reasons for desiring that there should be a considerable distance between Captain Cunningham and himself.

His councils had weight, emanating, as he took care to state, from Cloud—Daughter, whose magic had enabled her to see afar the fire-spitting pho—phos of the Whites, which would bring destruction upon the camp. Billibira, he explained, was the enemy of Cloud-Daughter; and were the fire-spitting pho-phos of the Whites to prevail, the Fire-god would carry away Cloud-Daughter, and she would become once more a star inaccessible in high heaven. Then there would be no more an intercessor between Baiamè and his children.

Kombo's reasoning had weight with Buli and his braves; and so all night, and the best part of the following day, the unfortunate goddess was obliged to tramp on between her guards; and, though they made the way fairly easy for her, pushing back the palms and vines with their spears, before morning Cloud-Daughter was almost fainting from exhaustion. By-and-by they got into clearer country, where there was a break in the scrub. Here Buli, who, in the rapidity of the march, had been trying to act up to his name of Whirlwind, stopped, and bade the men cut a big sheet of bark which was to serve as a litter for Yuro Kateena. Kombo had reminded him of his obligations, but in the scrub, such a mode of travelling would have been impossible. There were some lightly timbered ridges to cross, and beyond the nearer spurs of the range, scrub land again. On the other side of these near ranges, they might consider themselves safe from pursuit. So Anne journeyed for the rest of the day in comparative comfort, lying in her litter on the best opossum rug in the camp, which Buli had consecrated to her use, and borne on the shoulders of four braves. These, however, grumbled sorely at the task imposed upon them, and, but for the exhortations of old Buli and Kombo, would have left their divinity to come along as best she could. That night, the Blacks camped just within the further scrub, and the next day took a welcome rest after their toilsome march. A gunya was built of branches and palm-leaves for Cloud-Daughter in the centre of the camp, and here, upon her 'possum rug, Anne slept in comparative peace.

The next day, the gins hunted in the scrub and brought in a small animal called yopolo, which they found among the leaves, insects' larvae, and fruit that, when baked on red-hot stones, somewhat resembled peas, but were red in colour. The gunya which Kombo and Unda occupied was next that of Anne, and Kombo kept her fire alight and cooked her food, claiming a portion for Unda as well as for himself. The surveillance of the guard was now somewhat relaxed, and she was permitted to bathe in a stream which ran down a gully below the camp, Kombo and Unda keeping watch. On the whole, she was better provided than when in the cave, and but for the uncertainty of her future, and the long distance from civilisation which was lengthening with every mile, she might have reconciled herself to her situation. The girl's buoyant spirits rose in these surroundings, which had upon her an effect at once soothing and intensely exhilarating. Here, amid perils and deprivations, she was happier than she had ever been in England, where the endless bricks and mortar had seemed to her a wall reaching to the sky, in which her prisoned soul fluttered with maimed pinions, where her body languished, and her will became inert and morbid. Here, Nature reclaimed her child.

Anne's heart bounded, her spirit uprose on freed wings, and her voice, she fancied, had never been so strong and so pure as when at night and morning she sang her hymn to Baiamè. Sometimes, she thought, that if she ever again went into the haunts of men, she would not sing that song in its orthodox form, but keep it always an invocation to the Blacks' god, an "Ave Baiamè."

When the camp was broken, they mounted the range by walking up the bed of a watercourse, where, though boulders and pitfalls abounded, there were no thorny vines, nor impassable hedges of lawyer palm. On the summit of the hill they camped again for several days, and there fell in with a strange tribe known as the Poolongools, which surprised the camp of the Maianbars and tried to steal some of the youngest gins. In the dead of night, a spear was thrown into the gunya of Cloud-Daughter, just missing her as she lay upon her 'possum rug; but at her call Kombo awoke, and gave the alarm by hitting about with the butt of his old gun, which, though useless for want of ammunition, he preserved as a potent club. There was wild excitement in the camp. The warriors sprang out and met their assailants. Spears flew, boomerangs whizzed, the heavy wooden swords kept for duels to the death, struck out from behind great painted shields. Two young warriors of the enemy were killed, while one of the Maianbars was wounded, and a gin carried away. At one moment, the tide of victory seemed turning in favour of the hostile tribe, and rout and disaster threatened the men of Maianbar. Then old Buli hastened to the gunya of Cloud-Daughter—in the scurry and confusion of battle he had forgotten that their goddess might save them—and called upon the spirit of the Mormodelik to cry out to Great Father Baiame, and bring down water from Mununduala, the Keeper of Rains, which should sweep away and drown their enemies.

It was a critical moment for the perplexed divinity. Anne looked up to the sky, and saw that it was overcast, and that a pale glimmer of lightning shone low among the trees. Perchance, she thought, Nature

and coincidence would come to her aid; and so, at the entreaty of
Buli and of the gins who wailed while the warriors fought, she lifted
her voice and gave out the first song that occurred to her—one
peculiarly appropriate to the occasion, "God save the Queen." At the
sound of these heroic strains, the war-whoops of the Maianbars were
changed to acclamations, and fear seized the hostile tribe. The spears
ceased whirring, the swords fell. There was a shriek of "Debil-debil";
and while

Send her victorious
Happy and glorious

echoed among the rocks and the forest trees, the enemy fled helter—
skelter, never pausing till the gully was crossed and the opposite
scrub gained. Thunder growled now, making a deep toned
accompaniment to Anne's voice; and presently a wind arose and rain
fell—proof never to be denied of Cloud-Daughter's sovereignty over
the minor gods of heaven. Next day there was horrible revelry. The
bodies of the slain had been dragged to a clear space just outside the
circle of the camp, and there a great fire was kindled. Dear to the
native is the flesh of his fallen foe, both for its toothsomeness to the
palate of the aboriginal, who prefers black meat to that of white man
or Chinaman, and also for the prowess in battle which it is believed
to produce in the one who eats. There was a shout of "Talgoro!
Talgoro!"—which is human flesh—and all the gunyas poured out
their occupants. The whole tribe and the dogs collected round the
fire, and there was a great feast. Even Kombo ate of the dainty
morsels to which his stomach had long been a stranger; and some
would have been taken to the gunya of Cloud-Daughter, had not
Kombo cunningly represented that the Sister of the Pleiades was
forbidden to eat flesh of man. All day Anne cowered in her gunya,
sick with horror; but when it grew dusk, she stole out unperceived
by the revellers, and climbed down into the bed of the gully. Here
she sat, among the boulders which strewed it, out of sight, smell, and
hearing of the cannibal orgie. In her misery, she wondered whether
the time would ever come when she should fail in bringing down
rain or in frightening away the tribesmen's enemies; and whether

they would then denounce her as a false goddess, and roast and eat her as they were eating the dead warriors of the Pooloongools.

Chapter XII—Domestic Difficulties

FOR the present, however, Cloud-Daughter seemed in no danger of denunciation as a false goddess. The old men and braves of this wandering band of the Maianbar tribe lauded her greatly for the manner in which she had routed the Pooloongools. They were grateful for the feast of human flesh, which they attributed to her magic, and were quite ready to believe that Yuro Kateena held an exalted place below the great Baiamè in the council of native gods. And, moreover, the rain she had called down from heaven caused edible fungi to spring up in the scrub, swelled the fruit on the trees, and made succulent the roots, which the gins prepared into a paste that was to serve as food in a time of scarcity. Now, meat was abundant; for the rain also brought game from exposed places to take shelter in hollow logs, caves, and rocky nooks—wallabis, the marsupial tiger, and snakes which the Blacks love; so that each night when they camped in the bed of the watercourse, or in some clear spot on the fringe of the scrub, whole animals were roasted in their fur, and the half-cooked flesh, left unconsumed, was gathered up by the gins and carried in their dilly-bags for sustenance during the day's march.

For a day after the cannibal feast the Maianbars gorged and, lethargic after the orgie, rested, wrapped in their 'possum rugs beside the camp-fires. They did not resume the march for still another day, and, during the halt, even Cloud-Daughter's guard of honour relaxed vigilance so much, that it would have been easy for her to escape had she been within reach of civilisation. As it was, she wandered helpless and hopeless in the scrub till night fell, and it became necessary to go back to the camp, for which she now felt the most horrible repugnance. But so buoyant was the girl's nature that the very wandering distracted her thoughts; and a young opossum, which she caught in a dead tree and determined to tame, helped her still further to shut out from her mind the horrors of the previous evening, and to efface her miserable previsions of a similar fate for herself. Had the victims been white men, her imagination could not have been so easily lulled, but she knew that Blacks much prefer the flesh of their own kind to that of white people; and she hoped, too, that if she could retain their faith she might not only be safe herself, but might gradually bring them to believe that Baiamè disapproved of cannibalism, and had sent her, his daughter, to make known his will. Anne's courage and enthusiasm rose at this thought, and every voice in the scrub seemed to speak to her of the mission she now almost believed that she had been sent to fulfil. What of through her, these Blacks could be civilised, taught to cease from their wanderings and their fightings with other tribes, taught to till the ground, and build huts of wood instead of gunyas of leaves; taught to be clean, wholesome, and righteous in their dealings, to look upon the Whites as their regenerators, and not as their enemies? But here Anne paused and sighed, for how could this be till the Whites also were regenerated? And of that she knew there was sore need.

The next day the Maianbars roused themselves and hunted, bringing in a goodly supply of game; and upon the following morning, they started once more upon the ascent of the range. The hills spread eastward in a series of low spurs with ravines between, till the backbone of the range was reached—a series of sharp peaks connected by narrow necks, which, viewed from the coast side, appeared to touch the sky. Anne knew that beyond the Dividing Range, as it was called—the Australian Cordilleras, which form the watershed of the whole continent—the country at this point was mostly unexplored.

They mounted at first by the gulley, down which flowed a broken stream, swelling later on, Kombo had told Anne, into the river which watered Kooloola station. On each side of the little stream was a stony bed clear of vegetation, though much encumbered by great stones. Sometimes the way was barred by waterfalls—especially just now after the rain, which they perceived had been heavier on the higher hills. Then it became necessary to make a détour through the scrub, and this was a labour of pain and difficulty, for here the growth of thorny palm was thicker than in the hills behind Kooloola. It would have been impossible for a horseman to pierce this jungle, and the black trackers were not likely to venture so far on foot. Therefore old Buli, no longer anxious to keep up his reputation as the Whirlwind, moderated the speed of his flying squadron, and the march was now conducted in a more leisurely fashion during the first week of their progress.

In her girlish days Anne had always been fascinated by the loneliness and weirdness of the scrubs, and had been wont to defy rules, and spend long hours in those which surrounded her mother's station. But never had she been in a scrub so vast and wonderful as this one—a wilderness probably till now, untrodden by the feet of civilised humanity. The solitude of it, which might have driven many a white woman in such a situation to madness, stimulated her romantic fancy, and drew her fears away from the dangers which surrounded her, and the uncertainty of her future. She was like a child traversing a fairy forest, and each day brought her new amusements and interests. At first, the silence of the scrub oppressed her in an almost supernatural manner, for except at early morn and evening, scarcely a bird calls or creature stirs. Then as she became more at home in it, and her ear was attuned to its whisperings, even in the silence, she could hear faint noises, stealthy rustlings of reptiles and insects among the dead leaves and decaying wood, soft flutterings of butterflies, so large and brilliant in colour that they might easily be mistaken for flowers, throaty gurglings of animals hidden in the trunks of trees; strange murmurings—she knew not whether of bird or grasshopper—sometimes making loud echoes among the greenery, or the wild alarm cry of the mound builders disturbed in their work. Many a scrub turkey's nest did they find, and the eggs of these birds, roasted in the ashes, were the most palatable food offered by the Blacks to their divinity. Occasionally, they would come upon the footmarks of a cassowary; and once a man of her guard brought Anne a young bird whose eaglet eyes looked at her in such wild pleading, that she let the creature loose as soon as it was possible to do so unseen.

As a general rule, she was rarely left alone. During the march, some or all of her bodyguard of braves surrounded her, and on this account she was somewhat debarred from mixing freely with the tribe. Moreover, the gins were taught to regard her as a superhuman being, and they brought always to her gunyah the best of the fruit they gathered, and of the roots which they dug up with their pointed sticks. They held her in too great awe to attempt any more friendly intercourse. Even Unda, the wife of Kombo, was afraid of her, though she and her spouse always occupied a gunya adjoining that of Cloud-Daughter; and it was she who gave the peculiar cry which summoned the tribe within hearing of their goddess' invocation to Baiamè, sent up night and morning for the prosperity of his children.

Poor Unda was but a child herself, and, as the honeymoon waned, ceased to enchain the facile affections of Kombo, who very shortly began to follow the example of native husbands, and to chastise his wife with a nulla-nulla. When Anne remonstrated with him on behalf of the weeping Unda, Kombo sulkily replied, "Mine plenty tired of Unda. That fellow stupid—no like-it white woman." Anne was silent, for she saw that already savagery was palling upon Kombo, and she felt glad, for therein lay her only hope of escape. But this seemed to be getting more and more impossible, for they went each day further into the wilderness, further from the haunts of white men, and the chance of rescue. The last vestiges of civilisation were disappearing. All the rations stolen from Kooloola were consumed; there was no flour to make damper, nor tea, nor sugar; though, as a substitute for the last, the Blacks cut down sugar-bags— the wild bees' hives—from the trees; and, as they always presented the best of the comb to their goddess, Anne was able to make a pleasant drink of water from the stream mixed with honey. So she partly satisfied the natural craving for saccharine matter; but salt, for which she also craved, was in no way procurable; and gradually she learned to eat and relish the birds and beasts, and even the tree-pythons without it, when they were cooked in native fashion between aromatic leaves upon red-hot stones, in a hole in the ground covered over with earth. There is no better oven than this, and the bandicoots and yopolo baked in their skins in such manner are excellent as sucking boar and fat young chicken.

So Anne did not find life wholly without charm in this desolation of scrub and mountain. Her own gunya she was able to keep clean; her food, cooked by Kombo, and eaten off plates of leaves or fresh bark, was nourishing and appetising. Her position in the tribe brought her respectful treatment, and the duties of priestess to Baiamè were by no means arduous. Winter was drawing in; and, as they mounted to the higher slopes, the clammy heat of the scrub became less trying in the day-time; and the nights were often so cold and chilly that she was glad to keep a large fire burning in front of her gunya, and to wrap herself closely in her opossum cloak. Days and days passed in this slow ascent of the range, short marches alternating with stretches spent in camp, while the men hunted, and the women gathered roots from which they extracted the poison, by steeping them in a running stream and grinding them between stones, then drying them in the sun, till an innocuous powder was produced, which they made into cakes. Anne now began to occupy herself during these days of rest, and in the long winter evenings Unda taught her to sew the skins of opossums together, and to weave a sort of grass-cloth out of the fibre of a certain creeper and the strands of a kind of grass that grew beside the water-courses. From this grass-cloth she made herself a petticoat, for very soon there would be little left of her grey habit, though she mended it sedulously with the needles and cottons she had saved, and which she kept for that purpose. Unda had shown her how to make needles out of the small bones of birds, and thread from the sinews of wallabis and opossums. The feathers of the birds that Kombo snared, she kept, and sewed on to a foundation of grass-netting into the shape of a tippet. She was vain enough to admire herself in this tippet, which, being composed chiefly of brilliant feathers of parrots and the soft grey and white plumage of pigeons, was picturesque and becoming. Anne was a true woman in her small vanities. It amused her to deck herself with necklaces of berries, and head-dresses of parrots and cockatoo's feathers. When she bathed in some quiet pool amid the rocks, she would look at her reflection in the water and feel very glad that the brown dye was wearing off her skin; she felt pleased, too, in beholding the brightness of her eyes and the delicacy of her features. At these times, she was sorry that there was no white person to admire her, and then her thoughts would stray guiltily back to conversations with Eric Hansen on the deck of the Leichardt. She would recall glances at her from his eyes, which her own had intercepted; and she would wonder whereabouts in the Bush he was exploring—whether he ever thought of her and regretted the tragic termination of their friendship; and whether, by any strange vagary of fate, they would ever be brought together again.

Of Elias Bedo she never thought, except with shuddering relief that she was free. In comparison with that hated bondage her present nomadic existence seemed almost happy. There must have been a strain of gipsy blood somewhere in the Marley pedigree. Anne loved the long days in the open, and the nights beside her camp-fire. She loved the good smell of earth and leaves, the wonderful tropical flowers, the strange plants and ferns—all natural beauties that surrounded her. She loved the sounds of the scrub, the weird cry of the brush hen, the shrieks of giant cuckoos, the occasional roar of the cassowary, the tinkle of the bell-birds, and the soft coo of Torres Straits pigeons.

By-and-by they left the water-course, and pierced into the heart of the scrub, dallying for game, and walking slowly for many days, till, on the opposite side of an immense ravine, they found themselves in more open country, on a raised plateau under the shadow of the highest hills. Then with much toil they climbed to a neck between two peaks on the very summit of the range; and here Buli halted, and made a camp by the side of a river that had its rise in these mountains and flowed down the west side of the range to water the country beyond. Anne now discovered that Buli was in no haste to report himself to Multuggerah the King. She suspected that he did not wish to resign the glory of his chieftainship over the band with which he had raided Kooloola. North of the river, naked crags rose precipitously, and the very neck itself which joined them ended in a fall of rock several hundred feet deep. Below this, lower spurs rolled downward, something like those they had already crossed, but less timbered and less steep. At the edge of the cliff was a high wall of rock, making a shelter for the camp. Game here was plentiful, and a sort of trout abounded in the river.

Chapter XIII—Mirrein the Tortoise

ONE day, Anne waded across the little river and climbed up the side of the south crag, whence could be had a magnificent view of the country to south and west. On the west, another range of mountains bounded the horizon, and here, afar off, was the Crocodile Mountain, a long narrow ridge with a great rock rearing itself like the uplifted head of a crocodile. The rock was of peculiar appearance, and had a curious funnel-shaped opening in its side representing the jaws, whence, according to native tradition, fire had spouted. Probably it was the crater of a volcano, apparently now extinct. All the country indeed, seemed volcanic. Beyond the upheaving spurs of the Dividing Range, as they spread down westward, stretched a space of comparatively level country, though at a considerable elevation. Out of it rose cones resembling those around the Puy de Dôme in Auvergne, testifying like them to the presence long back of volcanic fires. At the upper end of the plain, in the shadow of three or four of the cones, lay a small blue lake, probably also of volcanic origin. This was called Maianbar, the "Deep Tank," for it was declared by the Blacks to be bottomless. Through the plain, appearing at intervals among the cones, flowed the river—a narrow stream that emptied itself into the lake. Beyond and below the lake the cones became less numerous, and the land stretching south from here was level and barren. It seemed indeed to be sandy desert. Anne likened this desert tract, in imagination, to a waterless inland sea, bounded on all sides by mountains. South and west it extended, to the base of a further great range higher, Anne fancied, than the one on which she stood, but invisible from the coast belt nearer Kooloola. Anne had always been told that beyond the Dividing Range, the central desert of Australia began and spread south-westward into the immense and uninhabitable wilderness below the Gulf Carpentaria. But here was a small Switzerland; a sea of mountains, some covered with tropical verdure; others, bare granite peaks and humps, barring the horizon as far as eye could reach. At right angles with the famous Crocodile Mountain, equally far inland, was another even more curious in appearance,—an enormous dome of naked rock rising above the scrub, which clothed its lower slope with a short black fissure in its near side, evidently a deep ravine; and at one end of the huge mound of rock, a large slanting crag of smooth granite rounded at the top, the whole giving a suggestion of some gigantic couchant beast or reptile. Anne did not wonder that the Blacks held these two extraordinary mountains in superstitious awe. Each might indeed have been the fossilized shape of some huge primaeval monster. The day was peculiarly clear, and she could see distant outlines with an unusual distinctness. She asked Kombo, who had accompanied her in her climb, what the natives called this domed mountain. The black boy at first pretended to misunderstand her, and tried to change the conversation, but Anne insisted, calling his attention first to the deep chasm at the foot of the rock, dimly visible, notwithstanding the great distance from which they were viewing it. She showed him the rounded rock at the end which overlooked an enormous and impassable ravine, and made her think of the massive turret of some Cyclopean citadel. Then with bated breath, glancing round as though he were uttering something sacrilegious, and there were a lurking devil that might carry the matter, Kombo told her that it was Kubba Mirrein, otherwise, the mountain of the Tortoise, brother, as he put it, to Kelan Yamina, the old man Crocodile. Kubba Mirrein, he said, was even more feared than Kelan Yamina; the Crocodile spat fire, but the Tortoise had a mouth from which a poisonous breath issued, that killed man or beast upon which it fell. The mouth, he explained, was beneath the Tortoise's head in its stomach, and was full of bones, the remains of animals and human beings that had ventured into it. The mouth was at the end of the great chasm they could now see beneath the rocky head, and it was called by the Blacks, Gunida Ulàla, the Place of Death, since none who went towards it ever returned.

Anne asked how, if the breath killed all who approached, it had been seen that the mouth was full of bones. But Kombo gave a puzzled shake of his head.

"Ba'al mine know, Missa Anne. That what Karraji—Medicine Man— tell Maianbar blacks. Medicine Man say that many thousand moon ago, one big Karraji make friends with Mirrein debil-debil. He go look inside Mirrein and come back again. That murrin-murrin moon—long time since Medicine Man go and come back. No more Karraji go long-a Mirrein debil."

Then as Anne questioned fearlessly, assuring the black boy that the magic of Cloud-Daughter, sister of the Mormodelik, was greater than any magic of Yamina and Mirrein, Kombo gained boldness and waxed garrulous, telling Anne all that he had heard about the race which dwelt under the shadow of the Tortoise. It was not a black race, Kombo declared, nor yet a white race. It was a race of men who were red as the setting sun, and of women tall and beautiful, with eyes like stars and flowing red-gold hair. This Kombo set forth, relapsing into his own language, since his command of English was not equal to the tax put upon it. Anne listened, nodding, and interrupting him occasionally with a question. He sometimes used phrases she did not understand, but on the whole she followed the gist of his story. Then it struck her as strange that she did not always understand his speech, for she had been long enough with the Maianbar tribe to speak their language with ease. Later, she realised that he had been quoting the words of one long dead, who had no doubt incorporated with the vocabulary of his tribe, words in the tongue of a strange people.

The men of this race, said Kombo, according to the description handed down by oral tradition from the old Medicine Man to succeeding Medicine Men, were very large, of peculiar customs, and wiser and more powerful in their magic than any of the wizards of the Blacks. Kombo himself had never seen a red man, nor had his father or grandfather, in the days when Moongars and Maianbars were friends, nor any other of the tribe within historic memory. It was that great Karraji among the Maianbars, who, many thousand moons ago, had gone into the land of the Tortoise, and had brought back to his fellows, accounts of the Red Men, and of the Kubba Mirrein. Also of the Tohi Mirrein, which is the spirit of the Tortoise. For, inside the Tortoise Mount, related the Medicine Man, there dwelt another and smaller tortoise, though that too was greater than any known beast, or fish or reptile; and this tortoise was the Tohi— or soul—of the great Tortoise, and it was its breath that proved manai-manai (poison) to all men not of red race. The red men breathed on by the Tortoise, he said, grew strong and brave and beautiful, for the Tortoise never devoured its own, but only the sons of strangers. It was said, too, among the tribe, that long ago the Maianbars had been richer and greater and wiser than now. They had built houses after the manner of the red men, and altars to the great Tortoise, and for a time had been successful in all their wars, and had subdued all the people round. That was why only the Maianbar tribe occupied this district. Not even the Poolongools or his own tribe, the Moongars, nearer the coast, had been mightier than they, Buli had told him. Still might be seen near the great Tank remains of the houses which Maianbars had built under the instruction of the first wizard, while he was friendly with the Red Men. For the old Karraji had brought back knowledge from the land of the Tortoise, and for many moons after his death, the tribe had remembered it, and acted according to the laws he had given them. But after a time, the Karraji had died, and the Maianbars had ill-used some of the red men, and from that day the breath of the Tortoise had gone forth against them, and none that entered the Place of Death, Gunida Ulàla, had come back to their wives and their kindred. So, too, when generations had passed, the wisdom of the Tortoise had been forgotten by the tribe; though even still, the Medicine Men of the Maianbars were held to be wiser than any other Medicine Men, and the King Multuggerah was greater than any other chief among the Blacks. But Multuggerah the King was not powerful as had been kings before him, nor were the Medicine Men who dwelt by the Deep Tank learned in magic, as had been that ancient Karraji, who was taught by the Red Men the wisdom of Mirrein the Tortoise. When Kombo had finished his tale, he bade Anne never speak of what he had told her, for it was accounted a sin in the tribe so much as to mention the name of Mirrein the Tortoise, or to hint at the existence of the Red Men.

These words must not be uttered lest evil befall the tribe of Maianbar from the magic of Kelan Yamina the Crocodile, and of Mirrein the Tortoise.

Chapter XIV — The Signal of Relief

ONE night, many weeks later, when the tribe, after a long loiter in the mountains, had ascended the range and were within a day or two's march from the Deep Tank, Anne was standing at the opening of her gunya, having bidden Unda give the signal for the assembling of the Maianbars to join in the invocation to Baiamè.

Unda's shrill call was caught up ere it died away and smothered by the report of a gun, which, though a good way off, could be distinctly heard. "Pho-pho! Murnian! Murnian!—the gun of the police," shouted Kombo, jumping excitedly from his 'possum skin on which he had been squatted before his camp-fire. A great commotion arose in the camp; the warriors rushed to and fro gathering up their weapons, while cries came from every side, "Wunti? Yumbu-yumbu. Nalla yan. (Where is it? Quick! Quick! Let us go.) Then old Buli came out of his gunya, and went up to Cloud—Daughter, saluting her in blacks' fashion. A weird figure he looked with his apron of opossum yarn, his many strings of berries, and the raised weals upon his naked body, which denoted his age and chieftain-ship, but a figure not without dignity.

"Wurra-wurra!" (Look! Look!), he cried, lifting his arm towards the blue sky overhead, in which a young moon shone brightly, and all the constellations showed with clearness in the deep blue. He was pointing to the pale cluster of the Pleiades.

"Look! Mormodelik!" he cried, and spoke to the excited braves, stilling their alarm. "That was no pho-pho of white man," said he, "for it was impossible that horsemen and black trackers should have followed by the way they had come. It was Tulumi Mirrein, the Thunder of the Tortoise; Manai-manai Mirrein, the poison of the Tortoise, which had been breathed from Gunida Ulala, the Place of Death. But there was no cause to be afraid," he went on, for the gins began to howl and the warriors to gesticulate. "Had they not Cloud-Daughter, the Sister of the Pleiades, among them? Had not Cloud-Daughter delivered them from the Poolongools? Had not the magic of Cloud-Daughter brought rain upon the earth and given game into their hands? For surely, no evil had befallen them since Cloud-Daughter had besought Baiamè, night and morning, that he would protect his children. See, the thunder had already ceased; the poison of the Tortoise put forth power in vain, while Cloud-Daughter lifted her voice to heaven." And now he bade Anne sing the prayer to Baiamè, so that the camp might sleep in peace.

Then Anne lifted up her voice, which seemed to have swelled in strength and volume during her sojourn in the woods; and "Ave Baiamè" rang through the forest, and reached faintly the astonished ears of a white man who was encamped beyond a projecting spur of rock not a mile distant. Buli crept back to his gunya, and ate composedly of the wallabi which was roasting on his camp-fire. The warriors and the gins followed his example, and, except for the excited murmur of their voices, the camp was quiet.

Great was the faith of Buli. After his manner, the old chief was a fatalist, and believed that most surely, while Cloud-Daughter dwelt with the people of Maianbar, no power of earth or heaven should prevail against them.

Anne sang on. She let her voice out at its full compass, and her nerves thrilled with wild excitement. Then a sudden fear struck her, and changed her joy to terror. What if it were Elias Bedo who had fired that gun? She stopped singing, and called in a low tone to Kombo. The black boy was bending over the camp fire in front of his gunya. He had just taken a bandicoot from the hole in the earth in which it had been baking, and was tearing its limbs asunder, reserving the choicest portions for his mistress and himself, while he threw to Unda the least savoury morsels. The honeymoon was long past, and Kombo's chivalry, as far as Unda was concerned, had died a natural death. Now he treated his gin with undisguised contempt. When Anne spoke, he brought a thigh of the bandicoot to the door of her gunya, and laid it on a fresh bit of bark which served her as a plate.

"That bujeri, Missa Anne," he said, "mine think-it Yuro Kateena plenty hungry."

"Kombo," the girl whispered, "you been hear him gun? You believe white man sit down close-up camp?"

"Ba'al mine think-it, Missa Anne. Mine no believe white man come long—a this place. Too much scrub; too much stones. But I believe that noise altogether like-it pho-pho," he added, doubtfully.

"I believe too," said Anne. "And suppose black fellow come long-a this place, what for no white man?"

Kombo could not answer this argument. "That very like-it gun, Missa Anne," he said. "Ba'al mine believe it Mirrein thunder. Cobbon stupid that fellow Buli. He not been hear white man shoot— never all his life. He been tell me that plenty dark long-a Kooloola when black fellow kill altogether white Mary. Black fellow jump up quick—give ole Missus no time to shoot."

Anne shuddered. During these weeks of journeying, she had been forcing herself to forget the Kooloola tragedy. Now the thought of a white rescuer near, and the faint hope of escape, brought back to her the horrors of her first days in the cave, and also the danger and the helplessness of her present position. If only she could be sure that there was indeed a white man's camp beyond that projecting knoll, and that it was not the camp of Elias Bedo!

"Kombo," she said, "I am going round the hill to look if there are any white man's fires. Suppose Buli say to you, 'Where Cloud-Daughter?' you tell Buli Mormodelik call me."

Anne frequently employed this subterfuge to ensure for herself an hour of privacy. She allowed it to be understood that her sisters, the Pleiades, or even Baiamè himself gave her counsel from heaven, to which no black man might listen. Buli, less vigilant now that they were, as he believed, beyond the reach of the native police, made no objection to her solitary withdrawal upon occasions into the bush.

"All right, Missa Anne; suppose Buli look out, I tell him Mormodelik pialla (talk to) Yuro Kateena, all about Tulumi Mirrein."

For a minute or two, Kombo devoured his bandicoot, ruminating the while, and then spoke again.

"Missa Anne, suppose white man sit down close-up camp, mine think-it Kombo no tell black fellow. I believe Missa Anne and this fellow Kombo go long-a white man. Mine plenty tired of black fellow; mine plenty tired of Unda. Mine want-im go back long-a Missa Anne to Cooktown. Then find-im steamer, and take Missa Anne home long-a ole Missus over the big water."

Anne realised with gladness that Kombo's bout of savagery was at an end, as far as his inclinations were concerned. The black boy continued, still tearing the piece of bandicoot with his white teeth while he talked:

"Missa Anne, Buli tell me we close-up now to Deep Tank where King Multuggerah sit down. Mine been think-it—suppose Multuggerah no believe that Missa Anne come down from sky, no want-im Missa Anne sing to Baiamè. Plenty water sit down long-a Deep Tank. Black fellow no ask for rain. Then I believe Multuggerah angry, and that fellow King, he kill Kombo and Cloud-Daughter, and make it one big dinner."

Anne remembered the cannibal orgie, and shuddered again. The same dread had been in her mind also.

"Mine been think-it like that too, Kombo," she said. Then she reflected that even were it Elias Bedo who had fired off the gun— supposing that a white man was near and that it was a gun—if she were to throw herself upon her husband's protection, she need not fear being killed and eaten, and as long as Kombo remained with her, there was always the chance of getting away again.

"Mine wait until black fellow go to sleep," said Kombo, "then mine come long-a Missa Anne, and we go look out white man. Plenty soon I believe black fellow go to sleep."

This agreed upon, Anne forced herself to eat a piece of the bandicoot for the sustaining of her strength in preparation for what might come. She knew that the probabilities were against their finding a white man's camp so far from civilisation, and that the sound they had heard was perhaps not the report of firearms, but had possibly come from an isolated thunder—cloud, or was the noise of some giant gum-tree, dead at the core, and falling from its own top-heaviness. She weighed these chances in her mind, and came to the conclusion that the sound had been too like that of a gun for them to dismiss it as a mere illusion of the forest.

When she had made a small meal, she went back into her gunya and wrapped her 'possum robe close round her, putting on a cap that she had made out of the skin of a grey duck which peaked over her face, and which, being all of a colour with the 'possum fur, made her look like a shadow of the grey gum-trunks as she glided out of the camp. The dogs knew her too well to bark, and many of the Blacks had their backs to her, while the others were too well occupied with their supper to notice her as she passed. Soon she was out of sight, and was skirting the rocky knoll beneath which Buli had fixed his camp. Beyond, rose an undulating ridge covered closely with acacias and gums, and also with a sort of scrubby undergrowth. Here she need not fear being detected; and even if the Blacks came after her, it would be easy to say that she was communing with her sister deities. She sat down on a stone and waited, her eyes fixed on the point of the knoll, waiting till Kombo should come to her. All the time, her ear was strained for any sound that might betoken a friend's presence, and her eyes peered into the dense bush, seeking the glimmer of a camp-fire. But all was darkness, and silence reigned save for the night sounds of the bush.

By-and-by, she saw Kombo stealthily creeping among the undergrowth near her. He gave a low "Kai!" and muttered the Blacks' adjuration to be cautious. "Kolle-Mal," he whispered, as he

97

beckoned her to follow him up the ridge. She trod in his footsteps, carefully making her way over the stones which encumbered the ridge, and through the thick bushes and creepers growing among them. After a time they had climbed to the highest point, and could look down and up the gully and across to the other side.

The gully was not steep, nor was it difficult of passage. They threaded it upward, walking along its comparatively smooth bed, and skirting the little pools of water which lay here and there among the stones. Its course was somewhat tortuous, and as they rounded a curve, Kombo suddenly stopped short, and Anne's heart leaped to her mouth, for there, some distance off, glimmered a camp-fire.

It had been made evidently with a view to safety, in a semi-circular hollow at the gully's head. The spot was banked by cliffs, and was quite invisible except from the hill above, or from the particular bend in the bed of the watercourse to which they had crept. For this reason, both Kombo and Anne guessed that it must be the camp-fire of a white man. Blacks would not have been so careful in choosing a position. Their doubts were presently set at rest by the sharp report of a revolver, fired at a little distance above them.

Kombo crept into the shadow of a big rock, afraid of the pho-pho, but Anne sought no shelter. She stood fearlessly in front of the rock and gazed into the darkness near her, and towards the faint illumination beyond. It was a bright starlight night, and the moon, in its third quarter, was shining above the gully. Anne fancied she saw a dark shape move, and then become stationary between her point of vision and the fire-glow in the distance. She felt sure that the shape was that of a man, and the indistinctness of its outline made her suspect that it was a clothed man. She strove vainly to assure herself that the figure was not her husband's form, but found it impossible to be quite certain whether even it were that of White or Black. Kombo settled the doubt. He had crawled round the boulder to Anne's feet, and whispered excitedly, "Missa Anne! That all right. I believe that fellow white man."

A Black's "I believe," is tantamount to certainty. Anne thrilled to the finger-tips at once with joy and terror. She bent to the black boy.

"Kombo," she said very low, "you no think that fellow white man Mr Bedo?"

"No, Missa Anne," Kombo replied confidently; "I no think-it that Massa Bedo. I certain sure that no Massa Bedo."

Black man and white woman waited for what should happen. The shadowy form remained still, seeming almost like some tall slim rock in the gully bed. Then the man, whoever he might be, made a movement as though about to return to the camp. Kombo whispered in even greater excitement. "Missa Anne, that fellow go away. By-and-by white man go to sleep. Then suppose we wait and creep close-up camp, I believe that fellow white man jump up quick; think-it strange black fellow, and shoot Kombo. Missa Anne, suppose you sing big song—white man hear and no shoot. Black fellow over there, think-it Debil-debil, make a noise, and run away altogether. Suppose Buli hear—no matter. Buli think-it Missa Anne talk to Mormodelik."

Kombo's quick intelligence had grasped all points of the situation. Anne's song would proclaim their whereabouts and arrest the attention of a white man—if there were one—while it would terrify any strange blacks, who would be too frightened to search for the cause of the sound. And, at the same time, were Buli to hear it at the camp they had left, though this was improbable, he would know it was the voice of Cloud-Daughter, and would only suppose that she was pleading with Baiamè on behalf of the tribe. Therefore he would not trouble himself to investigate the matter.

"Sing, Missa Anne," said Kombo. "Make-im noise. Plenty make haste. I believe white man go to sleep now long-a gunya."

Anne hesitated. The shape which stood out against the fire-glow turned. There was a side view of him visible for an instant. The black boy's keen eyes discerned the profile more clearly than did those of

Anne. Kombo started up. "Missa Anne! Missa Anne!" he cried. "I believe that Massa Hansen. You know—Massa Hansen long-a steamer. He been ask me show him road up north. Mine think-it he find other Black, and come plenty quick long-a scrub. Oh, bûjeri, Massa Hansen! All right now. Sing! sing! Missa Anne."

Then Anne, a great weight lifted from her soul, and a new joy filling it, sang softly and clearly, her voice echoing through the loneliness of that northern forest, the last song she had sung on board the Leichardt, a song Eric Hansen had loved—the immortal plaint of Gluck's Orpheus—"Che faro senza Eurydice."

The man in front of the camp turned again. He paused, and then strode rapidly forward, clearing a fall of rock which banked the small plateau on which his camp was made, and shaking the stones in the bed of the gully upon which he stepped, in his eager passage towards the woman he loved—scarce knowing indeed that he loved her, but with heart leaping at the mere suggestion that she was alive. Anne sang on, her eyes lifted skyward, as was her wont in the invocation to Baiamè. She did not hear the footsteps of the Dane; she would not let herself hope even that it was he; she dared not send her heart out to him as she might have done had she been free, had he ever owned in words that he loved her. And yet a woman's instinct told her that it was Eric, and that free or bound his heart was hers.

Suddenly she heard her name,—"Anne,"—uttered in that deep, tenderly masterful voice which she remembered so well. "Anne"! he repeated. He did not call her as he had always done hitherto—"Mrs. Bedo." She ceased singing, and a great sob shook her body. She tried to speak, but could not: she could only sob and laugh hysterically. She could not even ask his name, and assure herself of his identity.

He came close to her, and took her hand in his, "Anne"! he repeated. "Thank God, I have found you."

She laughed still, though trying to control her hysterical shaking. Her wet eyes met his, which, in the pale moonlight, she could see fixed upon her with a look that is never in the eyes of a man unless he gazes into the face of death, or into the face of his love, at a moment as tragic as might be that of death itself.

And now, the pent wave of emotion swept over Anne, and bent her as the wind beats an ear of corn on a stormy day. She sank back against the rock behind which Kombo had cowered at sound of the pho-pho, and fainted dead away.

Chapter XV—"That Massa Hansen!"

WHEN Anne became conscious again she was lying in a gunya on a bed of leaves and grass, over which a waterproof was laid. Her head rested against a tilted saddle with a folded overcoat for a pillow, and her own 'possum rug was drawn up to her knees.

Water trickled from her forehead, and she began to shiver, for in that high region the nights were cold. She wore over her grass fibre petticoat an upper garment, also of plant fibre, upon which she had sewed parrots' feathers, taking pardonable pleasure in arranging the colours to suit her complexion. But this gave insufficient warmth, and she put out her hand to pull up her blanket of skins.

Another hand arrested hers, and drew up the 'possum rug instead. Then the same hand softly wiped the water from her forehead with a silk pocket—handkerchief. In her dazed state she was hardly sensible of the fact that a civilised being was tending her, but was filled with delight at the touch of this fine material to which she had for so long been a stranger. She fingered the corner of the handkerchief caressingly.

"Why, it's silk," she cried.

"Yes, it's silk," said a voice that she recognised and which sent the blood to her face. "Lucky that I've still got one of them fit for you to use." The girl turned upon her elbow and looked up at the man who was kneeling beside her. She saw a face bronzed to copper-colour, and very thin, the naturally high cheek-bones now standing out prominently under the skin. She saw, through an untrimmed fair moustache, a mouth that trembled, and bright blue eyes which gazed at her with tender fierceness. It was Eric Hansen, but unkempt, and changed from the handsome, close-shorn, and trimly clad man she had known on the Leichardt. She turned away from him, and her hand instinctively moved about her neck where the fur tippet had been disarranged, and her skin, now almost fair again, showed through her ragged under garment.

"It's all right," he said, in a matter of fact way. "I hope you're not very wet. I had to douse you, for I thought you were never coming to again." Anne took the silk handkerchief from him, and spread it upon her chest, stroking it softly.

"You can't think how nice it feels," she said, simply. "I have no pocket—handkerchiefs of my own, nor any clothes either. My swag was swept away when we were swimming a river, and I lost everything except the things I had on. They went to shreds very soon, and I was obliged to make myself some clothes of grass and feathers to cover myself with. I'm nothing but a savage now."

"I think your dress is beautiful," he said. "Yes, you're like a savage princess. It's all wonderful. I can't believe it's true that I've found you at last."

"You were looking for me?" she exclaimed, eagerly.

"Yes; I had got on your tracks. I was combining my search for you and for the marsupial tiger."

"Oh!" She was a little abashed. He had given a shaky laugh when bracketing her with the marsupial tiger. "Have you found it?" she asked, laughing shakily too.

"The marsupial tiger? No, but I've found you. I'm beforehand with the others."

"The others!" she repeated in a tone of blank dismay. "Who?"

"Your husband," he answered, shortly. "He is in tow with Captain Cunningham—whereabouts I don't know."

The girl gave a passionate movement, flinging off the 'possum rug and half rising from the couch. Then she realised how weak she had suddenly grown. He put his arm round her, supporting her for an instant, then laid her back against the saddle.

"Let me go," she cried. "I will go back to my tribe, and ask them to hide me from him."

"Your tribe!" he repeated, gently ironic. "So you're counting yourself a black gin already! And have you become a cannibal too? No, no," he added, seeing the tears drop from her eyes on to her cheeks; "I understand. I know why you ran away, and you needn't think I'm going to give you up to Elias Bedo. I couldn't if I wanted to, for I haven't the least idea where he is. Look here," he went on, "I've got a lot to tell you, but I won't do it now. I'm going to make you some hot tea, for you're shaking all over after the ducking and the fright I gave you."

He went to the opening of the gunya, just turning back his head as he told her to keep still, and she saw him take up some ration bags, and occupy himself with the fire that was burning outside, and with the billy that hung over it from a bent stick.

The mists slowly cleared from Anne's dazed brain, which had been roused only to a momentary activity by the mention of her husband, and the dread possibility of his reclaiming her. A sense of relief and rest came to her. She recollected now all that had happened before she fainted, and knew that she must have been carried from the gully to Hansen's camp. It was as though a miracle had been worked for her deliverance, and she could think of nothing but that deliverance, now that Hansen had assured her of his protection against Elias Bedo. It did not seem to matter that she was still in the far Australian bush, that she and Hansen were perhaps the only white people within hundreds of miles. She was safe; he would take care of her; and by-and-by she would tell him everything—all her misery and despair, and why she had felt that there was nothing for her but to run away and pretend to them all that she was dead. But how had they found out that she was alive? Who had betrayed her? She asked the question, but did not trouble now to speculate upon the answer. Hansen would explain it all. In the meantime, she was in a white man's camp. There was no more need to play the part of Cloud-Daughter, Sister of the Pleiades. She need not now be afraid lest Multuggerah the King should roast and eat her. It was as though she had awakened to find herself in heaven. She caressed the silk handkerchief, which was to her, for the moment, a symbol of salvation. Then, as she did so, a new dread assailed her. After all, it was but an hour or two since the report of Hansen's gun had startled the Maianbars. Their camp was hardly a mile distant. They would soon discover her flight, and would track her up the gully. She rose again on her couch of grass, and called anxiously "Mr. Hansen." He had gone to the other side of the fire, and was just then out of her sight. She called again, "Mr. Hansen!"

He stood in the opening of the gunya, a pint-pot in each hand and from one to the other he was pouring a foaming brown liquid.

"It will soon be cool enough for you to drink," he said. "Be patient for a minute or two."

"Oh! it isn't that. But do you know—have you thought? The Maianbars are camped on the other side of the ridge. They are the fiercest of all the northern Blacks—it was they who killed my aunt and cousins at Kooloola. There are nearly a hundred fighting men, and they'll be mad at the loss of me. They think, you know, that I am a sort of goddess who can bring down rain and help them against their enemies." She gave another little shaky laugh.

"Yes, I know. I've heard about Yuro Kateena—Cloud-Daughter— from my Moongarr Blacks. You're afraid they'll attack the camp, but there's no need for alarm. I've sent out a scout, and I and my gun are a match even for Maianbars. Besides that, you can fire a revolver?"

"Yes, of course. I had a revolver, but I lost it in the cave."

"The cave! Oh, yes, I know about that too. Well, you'll tell me all your adventures by-and-by, when you are rested and feel inclined to talk. They must be the makings of a wonderful tale." He had been speaking all through in a matter-of-fact manner, with a certain brusqueness, which was affected, partly, to hide his real feelings. Now he could restrain them no longer. "Merciful heaven!" he exclaimed, and his voice deepened and thrilled. "I give thanks, gnore.

indeed, for your preservation. Oh! if you knew—if you knew! Day and night I have thought of you in the hands of those demons. And that you should be safe! Oh! thank God!"

"I do thank Him," Anne answered, softly.

Neither spoke for a few moments. Hansen stopped pouring the tea from one pannikin to another, and stooping, held one of them to her lips.

"Drink it," he said, huskily, "and don't shake any more, my poor little woman. I've got you now, and I mean to keep you safe till I can put you on board a home-bound boat. You can trust me. That's all I want to say. Only just tell me this—you do trust me?"

"Absolutely," she replied. Then she took the pannikin from his hand, and drank the tea in slow gulps. "Oh! how good it is! How good it is!" she cried.

"Now," he said, "I want you to sleep, for we've got to break up camp and clear out of this by day-break. I shouldn't care much if the Maianbars did attack us. It wouldn't be the first brush I've had with the natives, and I've inspired them with a wholesome respect for my gun. But it's as well that we should put a day's march between us and them, and I've pretty well exhausted the ground hereabouts. I've made one or two splendid finds, and the blacks have been telling me of some queer beasts in the range opposite. Only the worst of it is that they are in such deadly funk of a monster who, they say, lives in the mountains over there, that I can't persuade them to come with me. Now I won't stop and chatter. Try and get some sleep. First let me take my gun. And don't let yourself feel frightened, for I shall be outside wrapped in my blanket, and you've only got to call and I shall be awake in a moment."

Anne asked after Kombo.

"He's out there having a jabber with the other Blacks, who turn out to be of his own tribe—the Moongarrs," said Hansen. "His chief

anxiety seems to be to escape from his wife and from a certain old gentleman called Buli. You may be quite sure that he'll be ready to start in the morning. I've told him to wake us up if I should happen to oversleep myself."

With this, Hansen departed, first ministering as best he could to Anne's wants, and tucking her opossum robe round her, close to her chin, with the kindness of a woman.

But for a long time the girl did not sleep. Not far from her bed stood a lamp made from a sardine tin filled with fat, and having for a wick a strip of moleskin trouser. How the sight of that fat lamp in the old sardine tin reminded her of camping-out nights at the back-blocks cattle station near her girlhood's home! Its flame cast flickering shadows in the small space of the gunya. Hut it might have been called, rather than gunya, though it was constructed of gum-boughs and palm leaves. But four upright saplings made a loftier framework than is usual in the Blacks' hurriedly built gunyas. Across the side of it, above her bed, Anne saw stretched out the skin of an animal which she recognised as the tree kangeroo, and on the opposite side was another skin of some beast she did not know. Beneath it, were a pile of saddle-bags, one of which gaped, showing a heap of small wooden boxes, square and shallow, such as are used by naturalists for the keeping of specimen insects. These, she afterwards found, were filled with butterflies and beetles, which the Dane had already collected. Over all, hung the faint scent of chemicals used to preserve the specimens. Here and there were various masculine properties; and on a stump which served for a table, was a manuscript book in which the explorer had evidently been posting his diary, for it was open, and the pen lay across the page. But in spite of the primitiveness of the dwelling, it was curiously orderly, and Anne found a strange pleasure in noting the small contrivances which the Dane had made for his convenience and comfort.

Chapter XVI—The Manoeuvring of the Moongarrs

THE Maianbar Blacks were famed in that region as men of war, and the Moongarr Blacks who led Hansen's party were even more anxious than the white people and Kombo to get as quickly as possible out of their reach. The guides adopted a cunning ruse to deceive the enemy. While it was yet night, Anne was awakened by the voice of Hansen, who stood over her with a pannikin of tea which he made her drink. He then told her to follow him, explaining that for this move, the cover of darkness was necessary, and that they would return before long to break up camp and breakfast.

They now passed down the gully by twos, or in single file, and, rounding the projecting spur, made a feint of crossing to the flat country beyond. A long narrow water-hole—more swamp than water-hole—lay beneath this part of the range. The Whites stopped at the edge of this swamp, while the black scouts and Kombo marched a little way in the direction of one of the volcanic cones, hiding their tracks in a bog, then returning on their steps, and re-wading the water-hole.

Anne had waited shivering, as this manoeuvre was performed. Far off in the distance, through the trunks of the gum-trees, the embers of the Maianbar's fires could be seen like feeble glow-worms, but it was evident that the camp was still wrapped in sleep. Old Buli, as Anne knew, had grown careless, believing himself safe from any enemy. No watch was kept at night, and the warriors, heavy after the plenty of game in which they had been indulging of late, were never in haste to rise.

The wanderers now re-ascended the gully, obliterating their tracks by boughs which the scouts dragged behind them, and treading as well as they could in the dim light upon their former footsteps. There was only a pale streak in the east when they reached their camp again.

Here a hasty meal was eaten, of damper and cold bandicoot, and Hansen collected his possessions, and took down the skins from the sides of the gunya, packing them carefully and strapping the saddle bags. He called up the Blacks to receive their burdens, distributing a small portion of tobacco among them to secure their goodwill, for he intended to make a long march that day. Some of the Moongarr men had brought their wives, and these took the greater part of the load. There were six men, not including Kombo, and four gins; also three or four dogs—a half-breed of the station bound and the wild dingo. Hansen told Anne that these had been selected with great care, as they were his best assistants in the pursuit of valuable animals. Kombo shouldered Anne's opossum rug—she had no other baggage—and, after demolishing the gunyas and scattering the fires, so as to leave as little trace as possible of the recent occupation of the camp, the convoy started while yet a few stars were faintly shining.

They climbed the cliffs at the head of the camp, taking every care they could to hide their tracks—not so difficult a matter, for the rocks were bare, and, but for the inequalities on the surface and natural niches, the precipice would not have been easy of ascent. It took them nearly an hour to do the climb; but even then the sun had not risen above the hills to their left, as skirting the range they struck a southerly course towards a dim half circle of mountains which bounded the lower part of that curious cone—strewn extent of level land.

The Blacks all went before, and Anne walked beside Hansen in the rear, he carrying his gun, and, besides the knives and pouches at his belt, a big soft leather wallet slung over one shoulder, into which he put his specimens, and where he carried ammonia and other chemicals, also his note-books. A curious picture they presented as they walked side by side where the rocks and trees permitted, or one after the other, where it was impossible to move except in single file—he bronzed, unshorn, a straggling fair beard covering the lower part of his face, his Crimean shirt a little open at the neck, gaiters to the knee over his moleskin breeches, and boots long since worn out, held together by stripes of opossum hide; his gun in one hand and a stout stick in the other, while a soft felt hat, stained and shapeless, covered his head. He had but a change of shirts and socks, and was in almost as sorry a plight as Anne herself, since feminine ingenuity had not come to his aid in the matter of raiment. Anne had no boots either. A pair of opossum-skin moccasins, roughly put together by Kombo and Unda, covered her bare feet, less dark in colour than when she had first dyed them, but still a little browner than Eric Hansen's neck and face. She, too, had contrived a sort of gaiter made from the hide of wallabis, which protected her legs beneath her skirt of woven fibre, and such tattered under-garments as still remained to her from her original wardrobe.

The tippet of fibre and parrots' feathers came below her waist, and from it her brown arms protruded, only slenderly covered with strips of grass netting. Upon her head was the cap she had made of grey duck's skin, and below it her brown hair showed in short roughened curls. She had a dilly—bag slung round her neck, in which she had brought such small properties as she had been able to carry away from her gunya in the Maianbar camp—a pair of scissors, a reel of cotton, and a few needles—her dearest possessions. She wore always round her neck the large locket with her mother's and sister's photographs, which was regarded by the Blacks as a sort of talisman, and into which she had contrived to fold the last of her five-pound notes. She, too, held in one hand a stout stick, which she used to assist her in climbing, and at her belt hung one of Hansen's revolvers. After heading the gulley, they came upon a low round spur cut out by a precipice, which seemed to fall sheer into the plain below. Yet to call this upland tract between the ranges a plain, was almost a figure of speech, for it undulated here-abouts in land billows, to where the desert tract stretched mistily south-westward, tossing up on its surface, as far almost as the eye could reach, those curious volcanic cones. The spur they were traversing was lightly wooded with gum and acacia, and low green trees which Anne did not know—indeed, there was much of the vegetation of this northern country with which she was quite unfamiliar—so that progress was delightfully easy compared with that they had made through the scrub. The thick jungle which clothes the lower slopes of the Australian Cordilleras they had now left behind, and with it, the more tropical appearance of the vegetation, as well as the intense heat. On the higher level at which they were proceeding, the climate was almost temperate, being chilly at night, though still extremely hot in the daytime, and the fruits they gathered were different, and if less luscious, Anne fancied, more sustaining. On the edge of the precipice they found a species of wild raspberry, and further, a low shrub bearing fruit which was red in colour and strongly resembled the strawberry guava, also a gourd-like creeper on which was a kind of melon that was aromatic in flavour, and seemed to Anne a cross between a custard apple and a rock-melon.

Hansen took careful note of the botanical family of these plants, which he told Anne he had not before seen. About breakfast time they found themselves in a garden-like cup sloping down to the precipice, and here they lingered a little while, the gins digging for edible roots with their sharp sticks and filling their baskets, while the black men spied for ground game After leaving this cup, the country they traversed became smoother; and as they walked along the side of the range, a splendid view was to be had of the cone-dotted plain, and of the distant mountains bordering it afar, which, as the sun rose above the hills behind them, turned from purple to rose and gold beneath the orb's kiss. Through a cleft in the far-off range they could see clearly both the Crocodile Mountain and the Tortoise Hump. Hansen gave Anne his powerful field-glasses, which showed plainly a long deep ravine stretching from the Crocodile's upreared jaws to the naked hump that so oddly resembled the shell of a turtle. This hump shone a luminous grey, terminating at one end in the rounded monolith which the Blacks called the Tortoise's head, and below which—a small triangular blot—was the fateful mouth.

Anne told Hansen all that she had heard from Kombo concerning Gunida Ulàla, the Place of Death, and what the black boy had told her of the old Karraji—the Medicine Man of the Maianbars, who was said to have explored the mysteries of the Tortoise, and to have brought back to his tribe the wisdom of the Red Race. Hansen was deeply interested. He, too, had heard legends of the Tortoise Mountain, and of the existence of a mysterious race of red men who were Tortoise worshippers. The stories of the Moongarrs had set him speculating upon the possibility of a prehistoric race dwelling in the unexplored heart of Australia; and the description of the Tortoise brought to his mind certain altars in the shape of a turtle which he had seen in the buried cities of Central America, overgrown by forest trees, and dating back to an immemorial antiquity.

He told Anne the tale of five years which he had spent in the Yucatan forests, exploring the remains of this ancient civilisation, which pre-dated that of the Children of the Sun, conquered by Cortes. He told her of the hieroglyphic monuments he had unearthed, on which the snake and the tortoise figured so conspicuously—told her how he had compared them with certain Egyptian hieroglyphs and had found points of similarity suggesting a connection, improbable though it appeared, between the two countries. He told her of the old tradition of the lost Atlantis; of the legend related in Plato's Critias and Timoeus, of Donelly's book tracing all civilisations to that centre; of his own meeting with Le Plongeon in Mexico at the dead Palenque, to whom he had handed the tracings he had made, and who had himself arrived at the same theories, and had begun the deciphering of the hieroglyphics on a scheme derived from a comparison with the writings of ancient Egypt. He, Hansen, had regretfully left the great scientist engaged on that work which has, since those days, been prosecuted with results so magnificent, and had obeyed the call which took him back to Denmark and started him on his present expedition. What if his Australian exploration should lead to discoveries more astounding than even those of Le Plongeon! What if in the supposed desert interior of this vast continent, which differs from all other continents in the peculiarity of its fauna and vegetation, he were to find traces of a civilisation going back even further than that of which the Aztec empire was a remnant?

He now ardently desired to cross the upland sea of cones and land waves, and penetrate into that mysterious region over which, according to the Blacks' traditions, the Crocodile and the Tortoise kept guard, and where he might perhaps come upon the traces of an extinct race—maybe the same which had built those Cyclopean ruins discovered in Easter Island, the origin of which is shrouded in an unknown past. Moreover, apart from this visionary object, he hoped to enrich science with specimens of mammals not yet classed in natural history, and which might prove a link between the fossilised remains of prehistoric animals and those now living only in this part of the globe. He unfolded these ideas to Anne as they walked on, and again getting a view of the mountain, they stopped to look through the glasses more closely at the curious triangular gap in the rock side, which, as the sun illuminated it, had a shiny blue appearance as though the interior of the chasm were lined with lapis lazuli.

Chapter XVII—The Promised Land

"GUNIDA ULÀLA! The Place of Death!" Hansen repeated, thoughtfully. It is not possible that the Blacks could have given the place such a name unless it were a grave—possibly the scene of a great battle that once took place between the natives and this strange tribe the old Medicine Man discovered. Or, perhaps, he went on, there may be some natural property of the rock, some mephitic exhalation from the interior of the moutain, which accounts for the tradition and for the Blacks' dread of the spot, as fatal to man and beast.

"Kombo spoke of the poisonous breath of the Tortoise," said Anne; and she related how the Maianbar camp had been thrown into consternation by the thunder of the Tortoise—the noise of that breath which killed.

"That explains everything," said Hansen. "Probably there is an opening from which some deadly vapour issues. All this country is volcanic. One sees it from the formation of the land, and the Blacks' story of the fire—spitting crocodile confirms the notion that there are craters not long extinct. I have been wondering whether over there we may come across a volcano that is still active. Then, too, the exhalation would affect the sides of the cavern, and give it that look of being lined with blue marble. Oh, Anne! Oh, Yuro Kateena!" he exclaimed, "can't you bring some of your magic to bear upon my men and assure them that the white goddess will protect them from the breath of the Tortoise? I am simply longing to explore that extraordinary mountain, and discover the red men who inhabit it— or, at any rate, their graves, if they have ceased to exist."

"Well," said Anne, "why not try? I am not afraid of the Red Men, nor of the poisonous breath either, and perhaps the Moongarrs will believe that I have magic enough for them to go without fear of the breath. Oh! I should like to put that wild stretch of country and the Place of Death between me and my—" She had spoken excitedly, but now paused. "Between me and my pursuers," she said, quietly.

Hansen guessed, however, that she had been thinking of her husband; and this reminded him that she was not, or ought not to be to him, Anne, or Yuro Kateena, but Mrs. Bedo, and that she might have resented his familiarity.

"Tell me," he said, abruptly, "what name am I to give you? I can't call you Mrs. Bedo, as I used, and I am sure that you cannot wish that I should do so."

"Thank you," she said. "No, I could not wish you to call me Mrs. Bedo. I cannot think what madness possessed me when I accepted that name. I think you must understand, though we have neither of us said anything about the matter. Now that I have left my husband, I forswear his name for ever."

"So be it. I am glad. Yes, I think I understand sufficient for all practical purposes—for you to feel safe with me. By-and-by, perhaps, you will give me your confidence, when you have proved to yourself that I am worthy of it."

Anne's heart was too full for words. She turned her face to him, and her lips trembled, while her eyes shone with a light no one had ever before seen in them; then she moved a step apart from him, and gazed out towards the mountain.

"I am going to prove myself worthy," he said, and again there was a short silence. Then Hansen said gaily, "Well, is it to be Yuro Kateena? I see that even Kombo—to say nothing of the Maianbars—believes implicitly in your goddess-ship, and I am quite ready to bow down defore your divinity. So, shall it be Yuro Kateena?"

"I'd rather you called me Anne," she said.

"That's good of you. It shall be Anne; and believe me, Anne shall be as sacred to me as ever was Yure Kateena to the Maianbar blacks. You trust me, Anne?"

"I told you last night that I trust you absolutely."

115

He slipped his gun from his right hand to the left, which also held his staff, and taking her right hand bent his lips to it in a most courtly gesture.

"In token of my fealty," he said.

"Mr. Hansen!" cried the girl.

"No," he interrupted. "If you are Anne, I am Eric."

"Eric, then. Oh, Eric, in all this topsy-turvy world, were ever two people in such a strange position as you and I? We have need to trust each other. From to-day, I am going to look upon you as my brother. I had one once, but he died when I was eleven years old. I shall feel as though you were that brother come to life again."

"As you will, Anne. I prefer to look upon you as a goddess, but it comes to the same thing. Now the question is, what am I to do with you? Were you really serious when you said that you'd like to go with me and try to find the country of the red men?"

Anne blushed and hesitated.

"I did not mean—" she began; then said with some dignity, "I trust you to act by me as seems to you best. I think you understand that the one thing in the world which I should most hate, would be to be given back to my husband. If you did that, it would not be to much purpose, for I should escape from him again, and my last state would probably be more desperate than my first. But I did not mean, when I came to your camp last night, to thrust a burden upon you which would upset all your plans, and cause you trouble and inconvenience. If you feel like that, don't worry about me, but let me turn east with Kombo, and we two will wander on, as we did before, until we get to the coast. We should not be worse off, anyhow, than if we were still with the Maianbars—better off, in fact, for now we have got our liberty, and as it was, we ran a considerable risk of being eaten by Multuggerah the King."

"And if I were to do as you say, you would run an even greater risk of being eaten by the Poolongools, the most bloodthirsty cannibals — so my men tell me — of all the northern tribes. No," Hansen said, decidedly; "I have been thinking things out, and it must be one of two courses. Either we all turn back, and I take you to Cooktown and put you in charge of the Police Magistrate there, leaving you to settle matters with your husband as best you can; and really, I don't know why you should be in such terror of him. He can't force you to live with him if you don't choose, and there's your mother in England for you to go back to."

"You don't understand," cried Anne. "For my mother's own sake, I could not go back to her."

"No, I don't understand," he rejoined. "Then what do you mean to do? You didn't suppose that you and Kombo were to spend your lives among the Blacks?"

"I meant to stay with my aunt at Kooloola till I could find employment of some kind, or till I could make for Thursday Island and get taken in a steamer to Singapore or Java. I have my voice, you know. I thought that I should be able to get an engagement to sing in public."

"In Java or Singapore or some part of the Malay Peninsula! You, an unprotected and penniless woman — for I don't suppose you have got much money."

"I have got five pounds," said Anne.

"My dear," said Hansen, gravely, "rather than this, you had better turn beach-comber, and that is about the lowest profession I have ever known."

"Well, as far as my poor aunt is concerned, my plan is ended," said Anne, mournfully. "You know that they were all murdered by the Blacks — my aunt and cousins — all except, perhaps, Tom. I wonder if you can tell me whether Tom is alive or dead?"

"He is dead," said Hansen. "He just managed to get to the camp of the native police, and died an hour afterwards."

"Then I have no one left in the world whom I can ask to help me," said Anne, sadly. She did not weep at the news of this fresh disaster. She had become too accustomed to tragedies for this last one to move her.

"My child! My child!" said Hansen, "I'm not much of a woman's man, and a poor sort of chap at anything but ferreting out unclassified beasts; but such as I am, I'm your servant and your protector till you can find a better one. I'm not much at protesting either," added the Dane, and an odd little spasm went over his features as he looked at her; "but I can tell you—and you've got to believe me, for it's true—I never felt so badly in my life about anything since my poor old mother died, as I did when we knocked in the door of your cabin on the Leichardt, and found it empty. Now I am not going to say a word more than that if I can help it—about what the finding of you last night meant to me—not a word if I can help it, while you and I are wandering through the bush like two savages. You are my goddess, remember, though you don't want me to call you Yuro Kateena, and as soon as we make a camp, I'll build you a temple all to yourself as the Maianbars did. If ever I come across a Maianbar, Anne, I'll give him a bigger present of tobacco than a black fellow ever had, for the sake of the respect his tribe paid you."

Anne laughed and so did Hansen, but the voices of both quavered.

"You haven't asked me about the alternative course I spoke of," he said. "It is for both of us the best after all, I think. You see you're not keen on making straight for civilisation, and a settlement with your husband, and I'm not keen on giving up my trip before I've discovered the red men, and what's more immediately practical, a new marsupial—a sort of land platypus, I've heard of from the Blacks, a creature that isn't amphibious like the ordinary kind, but yet has webbed feet, while it lays eggs, suckles its young, and carries its babies in a pouch. Now, what I want to do is to catch that beast, skin him and christen him—something Hanseniensis—carry him home to the Museum in Copenhagen, and become famous for ever. Well, why shouldn't we go on together round these mountains and get to the range on the other side, have a peep into some of the old craters—avoiding the Maianbar Tank and Multuggerah the King— then, presuming of course that I have got a good specimen of my Platypus-Kangaroo, make for the Tortoise Mountain and have a look, from a careful distance, at Gunida Ulàla, the Place of Death, and explore for the red men? It's a large programme, but I think we'll have a try for it."

"Very well," said Anne, her spirits rising at the prospect, and her eyes dancing with glee. "I wish that I had been a man," she exclaimed. "I think that I should have made as good an explorer as you, Mr. Hansen. I've always longed so for adventure and discovery."

"We are well mated," replied Hansen. "I see that you are as eager about the Red Men and the Tortoise, to say nothing of the Platypus-Kangaroo, as I myself. Oh! Anne, what a plucky woman you are, and what a comrade I have found!"

"But you mustn't expect too much of me," said Anne. "I have been terribly frightened sometimes, and if you knew what I felt outside that cave near Kooloola, when the blacks surrounded me, and held up their spears as I sang 'Ave Baiamè,' you wouldn't call me plucky. But tell me—you said that you knew about the cave?"

"Yes; you were traced there, and your revolver found. Then the trackers followed into the scrub, but had to give it up. The Maianbars were too cunning for them, and started Captain Cunningham on a blind chase."

"But how was it possible that I was traced to Kooloola? I thought that once I had got away undiscovered from the Leichardt you must all certainly believe I had drowned myself."

"So we did; and it was not till some time afterwards that we were shown some incriminating evidence you had left on your travels, and which proved to us that you were alive."

She questioned eagerly; and Hansen pulled out of an inner pocket a piece of soft paper—the page of a note-book, in which was wrapped a lock of her hair. The page of the note-book was blank, but she recognised it as one from the little book she had carried on board the steamer, and taken away with her. Hansen fingered the bit of hair tenderly, as though it had been in reality a relic of the dead.

"People don't usually cut off their hair as a preparation for committing suicide," he said. "The magistrate and the captain, and most other people, supposed that you had thrown yourself into the sea, but this set me thinking on another track. It puzzled your husband also, I fancy, as soon as he became sober. Several things of yours, too, were missing, and it wasn't reasonable to conclude that you'd want a change of clothes in heaven. Well, Mr. Bedo and I landed at Townsville, and I made for the station that was to be my headquarters in the intervals of my trips. But after a little while I came to the conclusion that I'd go back to Cooktown and start exploring from there. So I took the next coast boat north, and to my surprise found Mr. Bedo at the hotel. He was in a state of intense excitement, for news had just come of the Kooloola murders, and he thought you were murdered too."

"But he had no reason to think I was up there," said Anne. "It was impossible that I could have been recognised on my way. I did not even go to the diggings where Kombo bought our horses and things. I camped by myself in a deserted hut by a water-hole full of alligators."

"Yes, I know all about that. They say, you know, murderers always leave some stupid little trace which leads to their committal. Well, you were engaged in a sort of murder, and you did exactly the same thing. You left the note-book from which I tore this sheet, behind you in the hut, and it gave incontestable proof that you were alive. Do you remember writing in it: 'Anne Marley escaped from bondage, rejoices in her liberty,' and some other remarks of the same kind, with a date beneath them?"

"Yes. How I could have been so foolish I cannot imagine. It was a babyish thing to do. Then I must have forgotten all about the book, for I did not find out that I had lost it till we had left the place several days."

"You dropped it in the hut, between the bunk and the wall. A Chinaman found it there; one of the Chinamen who had been on the Leichardt. He was going with a mate from Cooktown to the diggings, and camped in that place. He brought it back to Cooktown and made some money out of it. Now, if you had not betrayed yourself by that womanish piece of carelessness, neither Elias Bedo nor I would have known you were alive. And that's why I cherish this morsel of paper, and why I bless you with all my heart for having shown yourself no wiser than most women."

Anne was overwhelmed with confusion and shame; and whereas she had not wept at the news of her cousin Tom's death, she wept now over the tale of her own stupidity. This also was like a woman, and Hansen told her so. He tried to console her.

"Much cleverer people than you, my child, have been caught by the police through having made just such a blunder," he said, "but the mischief is done and can't now be mended. Mr. Bedo is on your track, and Captain Cunningham is helping him. They both started from Kooloola about the same time as myself They must have taken a different direction, for I have not seen nor heard anything of them since."

Anne paled. "Then they may be near. They may have followed you to this place!"

Hansen shook his head. "I doubt it. I don't fancy that Mr. Bedo and Captain Cunningham would care to force their way on foot through the prickles of a scrub of lawyer palm. The prickles funked even me, and I gave up, and turned south-west till I got into desert country. I crossed that, and got over the range through a sandy gap, till it became a case of scrub again, and leaving the horses. My impression is, that Bedo and Cunningham tried rounding the scrub to the north. Of course, it's possible that they have reached the open country, for your husband's determination to find you seemed equal to any danger."

Anne was silent; she appeared to be weighing the situation. Just then, they came to a bit of difficult walking over boulders and through clumps of scrub. They made their mid-day camp shortly afterwards, and then the Blacks turned sulky, and needed persuasion and more tobacco to continue the march. It was only Kombo's vivid description of the war-strength of the Maianbars which induced them to quicken their paces. By-and-by, the party came upon a track made by beasts going to water, and found a tiny lagoon embosomed among the swelling slopes. After this, the path became easier, rising and falling over lightly wooded spurs of the higher hills, as they marched along the side of the Dividing Range, not daring to ascend into the open till a much greater distance separated them from the land of the Maianbars. They could now see that the Deep Tank, which they had fancied close to the opposite range, was in reality much nearer this one, for the further mountains receded like the shores of a vast bay, showing more clearly a flat extent of country which they believed to be desert.

Anne abruptly resumed the conversation.

"I cannot understand why my husband should go through so much to find me. It cannot be because he cares for me. He told me himself before I left the Leichardt that my moodiness had completely destroyed any affection he had ever had for me. Why then does he want me back again?"

"I believe that I can explain that to you," replied Hansen. "Mr. Bedo himself let out his reason to me, when we were at Cooktown, after he had been drinking rather much champagne. He was greatly excited by some news the mail had just brought him. Do you not guess the explanation of your husband's anxiety on your behalf?"

"No," she answered; "I have no idea of it."

"Yet the letter you left unfinished in your cabin before you disappeared, rather suggested that you understood. You spoke in that of the possibility of your being a peeress in your own right."

"Oh, that!" Anne laughed. "I wrote it as a joke. The whole thing had been proved a mistake. Mr. Bedo told me so. But you shall know the story. While we were in England, an old man who had been busying himself in hunting up pedigrees came to my mother with a long story about our own. It appeared that a barony and a great fortune had lapsed, or was going to lapse, to the Crown for want of a proper heir. This old man said he believed he could prove our descent and heirship if we would give him money for the search after some missing link in the evidence. Of course we had no money to give him, and no documents to prove anything ourselves. In fact, there are several reasons for supposing it all a fairy-tale. Mr. Bedo saw the old man—that was before our marriage—and then again afterwards, just as we were sailing,—and he told me he was sure the whole thing was a fraud."

"Mr. Bedo was deceiving you for his own purposes, judging from what he himself said to me," replied Hansen, gravely. "Possibly he did not wish to raise expectations in your mind before your position was fully established. Anyhow, he gave me to understand in Cooktown that there was no doubt about your being Baroness Marley, and that a large fortune as well as the title—both of which would otherwise go to your sister—depended upon his finding you. That is why I believe he will leave no stone unturned to do so."

Again Anne appeared to be pondering the matter, her face showing pain and perplexity. At last she said:

"If it is true that I am a rich woman, will the money be mine absolutely?"

"I cannot tell you," answered Hansen, "for I am ignorant of the conditions in such a case as yours. Ordinarily speaking, I believe that, according to English law, and unless there is a settlement to the contrary, a wife's money is her husband's."

"Then," said Anne decidedly, "my mind is quite made up. I would much rather be dead, and that the money and everything else should belong to my sister Etta. Then my mother would be independent of Mr. Bedo."

"But you are not dead," objected Hansen.

"It doesn't matter. I should have been eaten by the Maianbars long before now, but for their superstition about Cloud-Daughter. I'd like everybody to believe that I had been killed and eaten."

"I'm not sure if it's practicable," said Hansen, dryly. "Murder will out, you know. But Anne, never mind about that for a moment. Tell me, if I may know, was it for your mother's sake that you married Mr Bedo?"

Anne looked at him with a surprised expression in her brown eyes.

"I thought you would have known that," she said. "Why else should I have married him? Not for my own. I'd rather have died first. It was for mother that I did it, and I'm glad I did; and though I said that I must have been mad, if it had to be done over again, there would be nothing else possible for me. You see it was this way. I had failed in my trial as a singer. We were in debt. Mother was almost blind, and we had no money to pay for the operation that afterwards saved her sight. Do you understand? Mr Bedo asked me to marry him, and I consented on the condition that mother should be provided for, and the operation tried."

"Yes; I guessed as much before. There's one thing I ought to confess to you—which is, that I played the sneak and read the letter you left in your cabin, over Mr Bedo's shoulder, and I'm not at all ashamed of having done so in the circumstances, though eavesdropping and reading other people's letters isn't a habit of mine. It would have been destroyed otherwise, and a valuable clue would have been lost. Do you forgive me?"

"There is nothing to forgive," said Anne. "I thank you for having cared so much about my fate."

"Your marriage was a cruel sacrifice," said Hansen, "a wicked sacrifice, one for which heaven will require atonement."

"I did it of my own free will," replied Anne. "No one coerced me. Having done it, I had to take its consequences. Perhaps I was wrong in having run away from them; and yet, I can't think that any law of God or man obliges a woman to live with a husband she hates, and who has been brutally unkind to her, as well as other worse things. Yet I knew what I was about, and if he hadn't sworn at me and beaten me, perhaps I should have acted differently."

Hansen gave a stifled sound of indignation, but he said nothing. Anne went on.

"You are thinking that I am a wicked, heartless woman, and I often think so myself. I know that if I were to ask a clergyman what my duty is, he would tell me to go back to my husband. Perhaps my own mother would say so. Everybody seems to think that because a poor girl takes a vow at the altar to love, honour, and obey, and to be faithful until death, she must carry it through, no matter that she is suffering a living martyrdom; no matter, too, whether the other one in the contract be true to his oath also. Suppose that you cannot love or honour, must you obey? Is it not enough to be faithful in the one sense? ... And then what about his share of the bargain? Has he loved and cherished me? Has he even been faithful to me? No. Can you wonder, then, that I felt myself absolved from my oath?"

"My poor girl!" said Hansen, hoarsely. "Was it as bad as that? Then you were absolved—you are absolved."

"That is what I felt. And from the day that I found out that, I determined I would leave him at the first opportunity. Mother was all right; the money was secured to her, and she could see again. So I made up my mind that when we got to Australia I would run away and hide myself among the stockmen and the Blacks—I knew that they would be kind to me—and manage somehow till I could make a living for myself. I didn't look forward very far, and even to that I couldn't make up my mind quite till he beat me again, just before we got to Thursday Island. Could you blame me afterwards?"

Again Hansen gave that smothered exclamation. He dared not trust himself to speak.

"Even Kombo—that ignorant black boy—saw how impossible it was that I could ever live with Mr. Bedo. He would have killed my husband, I think, if he had seen him ill-use me again. So you see that even for Mr. Bedo's sake it was better I should go."

"Yes," repeated Hansen, "it was better you should go; but I'm thinking of you, not of Mr. Bedo."

"We made the plan, Kombo and I," Anne continued, "just before the steamer got to Thursday Island, and it was then that I decided to go up to Kooloola to Aunt Duncan. But I needn't tell you anything more about that. You know how everything happened, and how well I should have succeeded if it hadn't been for my abominable stupidity and carelessness in writing as I did in my note-book and leaving it in the shepherd's hut. Yet, even still, if you'll only be true to me and never say how you found me, or rather how I found you, they'll think I was killed and eaten by the blacks, and Etta will get the money and be Baroness Marley in my stead—that is, if there's really anything in the story, for I can't quite believe there is. Mr Hansen— Eric, will you promise not to betray me?"

"I don't know how to answer you," Hansen said after a pause. "I couldn't give an unconditional promise of that sort, for what you would call betrayal might be my duty, and I should have to do that at any cost. Do you think," he went on, his voice deepening as it did when he was moved, "do you think, Anne, that I could give you up to Elias Bedo, if I were not convinced by every human argument that

I ought to do so? And whatever happened, I'd stand by you and advise you, if you'd let me, so that you might free yourself legally and honourably, and still enjoy your own. Only in that case, I suppose I shouldn't be the person to help you. But you have your mother, and surely she would so advise you."

Anne's face fell. "You don't know my mother. Publicity of that sort would kill her. But never mind." There was a pause. "Then you won't help me?" she said, with the dejected air of a child rebuffed.

"Help you?" he cried. "Haven't I just said that nothing but sheer compelling force would make me give you back to your husband? You told me not long ago that you would trust me. Won't you go on trusting me? I'm not a man who jumps at once to a conclusion. I must think this matter out. In the meantime, I'll look after you as though you were my own sister. After all, why should we worry about that just now? If your husband follows and finds you, he finds you, and we'll make our fight. If he doesn't, there's plenty of time to consider the situation before we get back to civilisation. The point is—are we going back or not? You know now who you are, and what you may be losing. If you really are Baroness Marley and a rich woman, it seems to me—knowing nothing of English law—that you've got the whip hand, and that matters might be arranged somehow to your satisfaction. I'm just taking a common-sense view of the position. But if you go on with me, you're risking a great deal, and there's no knowing whether we shall ever return. Of course, I'm supposing that we explore yonder mountains. I'm resolved to find out all that there is to be found out about them and the mysterious Red Race, if not now, then later. But it does seem a pity to turn back when with great danger and difficulty we've got in sight of the place."

"Oh, yes, yes," cried Anne. "You must not turn back."

"It's only a question of time," replied Hansen. "I shall come back by-and—by; and, if you wish it, I'll gladly take you to the coast now. Perhaps, after all, it would be better for my own sake that I should go back, and then make a fresh expedition on different lines to explore the Tortoise Mountain, which appears to be quite unknown to all previous explorers. So Anne, do not let the thought of my disappointment weigh with you, should you decide on the civilisation scheme. I really believe it would be far wiser for me—speaking from the explorer's point of view—to start anew with a better equipment."

"And if I decide on the scheme of barbarism or rather of exploration," she said, "what then?"

"Then," he answered, fervently, "I will even more gladly take you with me into all unknown dangers, and I will guard you with my life against possibility of harm."

He waited for her reply with an anxiousness he could not hide.

"I have decided," she said, presently. "I decided before, when you spoke of the alternatives. I will go with you thankfully, and will be as little hindrance to you as is possible. Perhaps my reputation as a goddess may be of greater service than you imagine," she added, shyly. "I can at least bring it to bear on the Blacks, to prevent them from jibbing at the fire-spitting crocodile, and the poisonous turtle."

And so it was settled.

Chapter XVIII—Comrades in Adventure

AFTER that long day's march, which must have covered twenty miles, the wanderers came to more broken country and progress was necessarily slower. They had again got into the heart of the range, having been obliged to head precipitous gullies, and for many days were out of sight of the cone-strewn upland. Twice, being as they believed beyond reach of their enemies, Hansen made a temporary camp, and rested for a day or two, employing the interval in searching for unknown beasts. He succeeded in finding one hitherto undescribed by naturalists, but the mythical platypus—kangaroo seemed, figuratively speaking, a will o' the wisp, never to be caught, but always luring him on. Then for a week, the party was flood—bound on the banks of a roaring torrent swelled by heavy rains in the mountains, though of the rains they had but a drizzle. The bad weather kept them inside their gunyas, however, for several days, and in that time Anne came to know the Dane even better than while they had been marching. For now they had long spells of talk by the camp-fire, and the tale of adventure being exhausted, Hansen had to draw upon the stores of his own mind for her amusement. These were varied and interesting, and Anne came to the conclusion that to be a savage in company of Eric Hansen was a liberal education.

He was very good to her, thinking no trouble too great which might ensure her some little comfort; and after her experiences with the Maianbars, this sojourn in the white man's camp was to Anne a taste of Paradise. When they got down from the higher spurs east, into view of the western range, the opposite mountains appeared to have receded, and to be many miles distant, while the Deep Tank of the Maianbars was now completely out of sight. From their southerly position they looked towards the edge of the cone-dotted upland, which terminated some way off in a natural wall like a cliff on the sea-shore. Below it, stretching to their feet, was indeed a sea, but of sand, not water. Northward and westward, as far as the dividing cliff and the distant range, there was now nothing to be seen but desert.

They had the intention of skirting the southern mountains and of so rounding the desert, but in this plan they were frustrated by impassable ravines and peaks of naked rock rising sheer from the plain below. Besides, as long as they remained in the hills they were sure of water, but if they were to start crossing the desert plain, they might have to encounter all the horrors of thirst as well as of extreme heat. As long as they kept to the highlands the air was comparatively fresh, while the nights were often cold enough to make a fire agreeable. There was nothing for it, therefore, but to strike upward to the wooded ranges where all was scrub again, though less dense than it had been in the earlier part of Anne's wanderings. Nevertheless, it was sufficiently thick to make walking tiresome and difficult. Yet the scrub had its own interest, for it abounded in botanical wonders, and Hansen collected some curious "leaf-butterflies," specimens of the muskbug, the smoke-ejecting beetle, and other Australian insects. In the days of rest, Anne employed herself in the manufacture of fibre garments, while Hansen provided both with new moccasins of skin.

Now they walked in a south-westerly direction as near as they could to this great basin enclosed on all sides by mountains, and which had no doubt been a small inland sea. But crags and precipices soon made the route impracticable, and they saw that it would be necessary to descend. From the face of a steep crag above the eminence on which they made these observations, a stream sprouted in several places, and, gathering into one volume of water, swept down a gully to the left, and lost itself in the sand of the desert below. Hansen told Anne that this was a very common feature of rivers in the West Australian desert, and that they should doubtless find the stream again, re-emerging among the mountains to which they were bent, or possibly flowing still through some subterranean passage which it had hollowed for itself in the heart of the hills.

To follow this gully appeared the easiest mode of reaching the level, and they climbed down with some difficulty along its bed, crawling part of the way upon a ledge of rock overhanging the stream, and for the rest, picking their steps among water-worn boulders. There was a deep pool dammed by rocks some feet above the plain, and from the bottom of this natural trough the river flowed on unseen beneath the sand.

The travellers now found themselves on the brink of that dried-up sea closed in by naked rock as far as they could see, except where above the dividing cliff northward, they had a faint and very distant view of those volcanic cones among which lay the Deep Tank of the Maianbars. There was no sign of an oasis, nor of any other stream rolling down from the higher hills to hide itself in the sand. All along, fringing the desert, the grey cliff rose unbroken. For several days the party camped in this place, and here, the Blacks mutinied and refused to go further.

For some time, there had been dissatisfaction in the camp. The tobacco had given out and game was scarce in these barren regions, so that for food all were dependent on Hansen's rifle and Anne's revolver. The gins and men grumbled loudly at their burdens, which increased as more specimens were added to the pack. Then a favourite dog had been bitten by a snake and died, while two other dogs had eaten of a poisonous fungus in the scrub, or had got their death in some unexplainable fashion, all of which things aggravated the blacks' discontent, and convinced the Moongarrs, who were extremely superstitious, that Debil-debil was hanging round. Not even the magic of Cloud-Daughter was held to be a safeguard against the evil spirit, and to no effect did Anne raise her voice in the awe-inspiring Ave Baiamè. The confidence of the Blacks had been shaken, for whether or not she could produce rain did not greatly matter, since she had not of late brought them wallabis—except of the shy rock kind which is difficult to spear—or serpents of which they had found abundance in the tree ferns of the scrub, and which had reconciled them greatly to the march. The aboriginal stomach craved morbidly for a feast, and as one of the Moongarrs was known as being especially clever in procuring Talgoro—human flesh—it behoved the two white people to take care that no Black ever walked behind them. Indeed, Kombo had given dark hints of a plot to slay Hansen from the rear with a nulla-nulla, and to carry back Yuro Kateena to the Moongarrs' land.

One night a bird sang weirdly over the pool into which the stream discharged itself before becoming lost in the desert, and the Blacks, crying out that it was the voice of Debil-debil, made a wild stampede, and removed their camp from the haunted spot. Possibly, for geographical reasons, as their natural hunting-grounds were further south, the Moongarr, had not the same definite terror of the thunder of the Tortoise as the Maianbars. Their legends were more misty, and their ideas of the mysterious red race inhabiting the opposite range vaguer than those of the Maianbars. It was rather the usual native awe of Debil-debil that held them back. The Debil-debil superstition seemed, however, potent enough. All the next day the Moongarrs were very sulky, and towards evening declared their intention of re-mounting the bed of the stream in search of fish or game. They took all their belongings with them, and even Kombo accompanied them. To start so late in the day was in itself suspicious; and neither Anne nor Hansen were surprised when the next day passed and none of the escort had returned.

Those two nights, the man and woman camped in a sort of cave beneath the projecting cliff. They could not have made gunyas—had that been necessary—for here were no trees nor ferns with which to roof any extemporised hut. The heat was great, being reflected back from the sandy sea on the grey precipices above them, and, but for the good supply of water, they would have suffered much discomfort. Now it was that Anne proved her fitness as the companion of a brave man. An ordinary woman might have wept at the desertion of her black comrade, which was in fact a sharp blow to the girl; an ordinary woman might well have shrunk from the traversing of that hideous strip of desert which lay before them, and from the unknown experiences which awaited them in the opposite mountains—the strange Crocodile with its yawning jaws of stone, and the still more mysterious Tortoise.

Then, too, an ordinary woman might have been over-come with conventional scruples at finding herself thus committed to the solitary company of a man who she guessed loved her, whom she scarcely dared confess to herself that she was beginning to love, and whom, moreover, while her husband lived, she could not marry.

132

But none of these considerations deeply affected Anne, the last one least of all. Since it had been decided that she was to take part in his expedition, Hansen had sedulously guarded his lips and had striven to establish a merely friendly comradeship between himself and the girl in his charge, so that but for the unacknowledged consciousness at the back of both their minds, they might in truth have been brother and sister. As for the difficulties and dangers of their enterprise and the desertion of Kombo, this was not the hour in which to bewail them.

Anne had heroism sufficient to make the best of the situation, resolving not to add to Hansen's perplexities. She laughed, and made light of their troubles, and would not listen when he again suggested that they could still turn back.

Firing here was not plentiful, and the two diverted their thoughts from unpleasant subjects in gathering up driftwood that had been washed down by the stream, and heaping it in stacks, Anne singing the while, as was her way when Hansen showed depression. The Blacks had taken away most of the provisions, and Hansen went up with his gun and fishing line in the hope of shooting some game, and of catching fish in the pool. Anne did not go with him, but remained beneath the cliff, putting into such order as she could the baggage, which had been piled pell-mell by the Moongarrs against the rocks. It was a problem what they should do with the specimens, chemicals, and ammunition, now that the bearers had left them. She put the question to Hansen when he came back with some fish he had caught, and a rock kangaroo that he had luckily shot on its way to water. He decided that they would bury the specimens, and all else that they could not carry, in the sand. By measuring a certain distance to right and left of the pool, they would, he said, find the spot easily on their return, as the gully would form a landmark. Water was what they would most need; also ammunition, of which they must take as large a supply as possible, as well as such food as they could carry. This he set himself to prepare for transport, slitting the fish they did not eat, and drying them in the sun, as well as portions of the wallabi. He settled that they would camp in this place for a day or two longer, in order to get provisions together and to recruit themselves near the water for their journey across the sand. Thus, too, they would give Kombo a chance of finding them, should he think better of his ill-deed. Of the other Moongarrs, Hansen had little hope, but neither he nor Anne could believe that Kombo could seriously desert them after the perils he had already shared with his mistress.

It was soon proved that they were right. Kombo's better nature had triumphed over his superstition, or some more potent fear had driven him back to the protection of the white man's gun. The third night after his departure, Anne and Hansen were awakened by a stealthy native call, and then a cry of woe, which sounded from the bed of the stream a little higher than the pool into which the water emptied itself and disappeared. Both started up, Hansen with his gun in his hand, and Anne having her revolver ready. At first, they hardly recognised the voice, which was drowned by the rush of the river, but presently knew it as that of Kombo.

"Eeoogh! Eeoogh! Poor fellow me! Missa Anne! Missa Anne! Massa Hansen! Kombo plenty close-up bong (dead). This fellow altogether sick—no got him arm! Poor fellow Kombo! Eeoogh! Eeoogh!"

Hansen mounted in the direction of the call, and in a few minutes Kombo, half led, half carried, presented himself before his mistress. He was a pitiable object. His old flannel shirt—all that remained to him of his wardrobe, which he had discarded during his residence with the Maianbars, resuming it after the example of Hansen's men—was torn to shreds and caked with blood, while one arm hung helpless from a flesh wound near the shoulder. The boy was in an exhausted and almost starving condition, and before he could speak, fed greedily on a piece of cooked wallabi, drinking long draughts of cold tea which had been made from the last pinch left in the ration bag. Afterwards, Hansen examined and bathed his hurt, binding it with the silk handkerchief he had given to Anne—another last remnant of civilisation. He saw that the wound was a small matter, its chief importance being the fact that it had been caused by shot from a gun. The black boy told his tale.

"Ba'al mine want to run away," he pleaded, evidently deeply ashamed of himself. "Mine plenty frightened long-a Debil-debil, and Moongarr black fellow, he say, `Suppose you no come, Kombo, then black fellow kill you.' Mine no want to run away from Missa Anne. I been think-it me go little way long-a Moongarrs, then wait till sun fall down, and by-and-by come back when black fellow not looking. But that no good. All the time, Moongarr black stop close long-side of Kombo. No chance to run away. My word! Black fellow walk quick! I believe Moongarr black very much frightened too of gun belonging to white man. So all night Black make light with fire-stick and climb up mountain, then sleep a little while and climb up again. One black fellow find-im hole where mountain split like-it melon when that fellow plenty ripe. Black fellow altogether creep long-a hole a long way, and get down close-up scrub on other side. Then mine been see horses with hobbles—mine go little way and mine been see black trooper—then mine been see—" Kombo paused dramatically—"Mine been see—Massa Bedo." Kombo's pantomimic gesture was expressive of utmost dismay. Anne gave a little cry.

"Are you sure—are you sure, Kombo, that it was Mr Bedo?"

"Mine plenty sure, Missa Anne," replied the black boy. "Mine see Massa Bedo. I b'lieve that fellow long time long-a bush. He look like-it wild man. I believe certain sure that Mr Bedo. He no been see me. Mine climb up big tree while Moongarr black make camp and look out snake in scrub. Suppose like-it this—" And Kombo made a sort of diagram with his hand, pointing to a boulder near him, and then to a lower ledge half way down it, and to imaginary scrub in the distance. "Here you see, big fellow rock." He went on: "You see, Kombo up on tree close-up top; Massa Bedo down bottom of rock— good way, but that close enough for gun to find Kombo. Mine been frightened,—suppose Massa Bedo see me, and so mine been crawl down tree. Then one big fellow branch break, and Massa Bedo he look up, and I believe he think Kombo one fellow wallabi. He put up pho—pho—Ow!—he fire off gun, and one little baby bullet hit Kombo. My word! that plenty hurt—altogether blood run down, but ba'al mine make a noise. Mine frightened. Mine think, suppose Massa Bedo fire again! Mine stoop down and run along like-it snake, quick up the mountain, over other side. Then mine stop little while, because plenty blood come. But mine no like to stop long time. My word! Kombo plenty make haste—run—run. Then mine find-im hole, and crawl like-it first time long way. Ba'al mine stop for eating, but by-'m-by mine lie down. Eeoogh! this poor fellow altogether sick. Mine believe Debil-debli marra (take) Kombo, make that fellow go bong. Then mine think, suppose Kombo go bong, Massa Bedo climb up, look out blood, and see poor fellow Kombo—then soon Massa Bedo find Missa Anne. He very saucy—Massa Bedo; he no go back. He got-im horse too. But ba'al mine understand how horse come along through scrub. I believe black trooper bring him other way. My word! I been very sorry because no can steal horse belonging to Massa Bedo. When mine think like-it that, mine get up and walk—all night, all day—all the time mine very sick. Poor fellow Kombo! Nothing to eat! By-'m-by, I find-im river. I got-im spear and catch-im fish and eat-im. Afterwards ba'al mine sick. Now can run. I want to tell Missa Anne and Massa Hansen, you look out—Massa Bedo, he close-up. Suppose he give Moongarr blacks ration, they show-im road. Missa Anne, you no want-im catch you. Then, you make haste—up stick and yan. Nalla yan, Massa Hansen, before sun jump up."

Thus Kombo delivered himself, and the manner of his delivery was even more graphic than his words. The tears came into Anne's eyes, as she realised how the brave boy had dragged himself along in his maimed state, conquering the tendencies of his race, for when a Black is wounded he gives himself up for lost, and thinks only of getting among his tribe to die. Kombo had left his tribe to save her, and for her sake he had even ventured back to the regions of Debil-debil. While he spoke, his teeth chattered with intense fear. It had cost Kombo a good deal to descend the haunted stream alone. Mercifully, the wild bird had not again piped its mournful cry, or superstition might have driven him back. The girl put out her hand, and stroked the black boy's dirty paw.

"Oh! Kombo," she said, "you altogether brother belonging to me. Bujeri you, Kombo! Good boy, Kombo!"

Hansen also was moved. "Bujeri you, Kombo!" he repeated. "Mine brother too belonging to you. And you very clever boy, Kombo. We must up stick and yan before the sun rises. I don't think Mr Bedo will catch us just yet. Now see, I will put medicine on this sick place, and Yuro Kateena will pialla (pray to) Mormodelik, so when the stars go away, Kombo will jump up altogether well. But first tell me—how many men were with Mr Bedo?"

"I been see only two black fellow," said Kombo.

"Not Captain Cunningham?" asked Anne, anxiously.

"No," replied Kombo; "I only see one gunya belonging to white man. No sign of Captain Cunningham. I believe Massa Bedo all by himself with two black trooper."

"So far well," said Hansen. "Now Kombo, you go to sleep, and remember, you'll be all right when you wake up."

The black boy rolled himself over, and almost before Hansen moved away, was fast asleep.

"Anne," said the Dane, turning to the girl who was sitting with a very disconsolate air on the rock which had served Kombo as an illustration of Mr Bedo's position, "I'm not going to let you be downhearted, and I don't intend that Elias Bedo shall find you. You've been the pluckiest comrade man ever had, and you must be brave a bit longer. Shall you be ready to start at daybreak?"

"I am ready to start now," she said.

Hansen looked at his watch, which he had kept in working order, and then at the sky. "It wants three or four hours yet, and in the meantime we must fill our water-bags and stow the ammunition about our waists. I don't want to leave a cartridge behind—as well as the food we are going to take. Kombo won't be up to much weight just at first, but I can manage a good load. You've got your belt filled with cartridges for the revolvers?"

She pointed to it—a bandolier she had manufactured herself out of skin and plant fibre that she wore slung over one shoulder.

"All we have, are there," she answered, "and I have packed my dilly-bag with food."

"That's right. Lucky we buried the rest of the stuff this afternoon. My specimens are the only things that trouble me, but I think they are pretty safe in this dry sand. Now I'm going to give you a bit of advice. Just before you start take off that cartridge belt for five minutes, and lie down in your clothes in the shallow part of the stream, letting the water soak into the pores of your skin. You won't catch cold, and you'll find it a preventive against thirst, so that we sha'n't need to tackle our water-bags so soon. I shall do the same."

"How far do you suppose it is to the mountains?" she asked.

"I should fancy about thirty miles—nothing of a walk. But we have to face the heat and the chance of barren rocks at the end. And we must be provided with grub, and against there being no water beyond this stream we are leaving. It really is no great undertaking, the crossing of the strip of desert, and we shall keep under the shadow of the cliff. The heat will be the worst part of it, and I shall be glad when we get to the uplands again. Then think of what we may discover. It's worth while braving the Red Men and the magic of the Crocodile for that."

Chapter XIX—The Tortoise-Altar

THE Crocodile and the Tortoise—as the lowering sun shone upon them—had the appearance of gigantic primaeval monsters. The yellow orb hung over that grey hump which so curiously resembled a turtle's shell, and specially illuminated the slanting monolith in which to the north, it terminated. So natural did this monolithic head appear, protruding, as it were, from beneath the upper crust of the mountain, that it was difficult to believe Nature had not been assisted by man. That, however, in this remote region, could hardly be thought possible. Below the monolith, and carrying out the Blacks' tradition of a mouth in the reptile's stomach, the mysterious blue lips of Gunida Ulala were partially visible. Yet it seemed that the opening into the valley where the wanderers stood, might even more appropriately have been named the Place of Death. Never was scene of wilder desolation. At this point, the range of mountains turned inward, and thus formed the gorge which led up to the Tortoise. Gaunt peaks rose at the south end of the gorge, straight from a grey level of loose stones and ashen soil patched with stunted bushes. At the north side, abutting from the ridge, the Crocodile reared its ungainly shape like some petrified antediluvian monster appointed to guard the valley. It had to the eye of a spectator, standing close to the crag, a less distinct likeness to the form of a gigantic saurian than when viewed from a distance, under softening atmospheric conditions. It was, in fact, a long precipitous ridge forming part of the range, the end of which, rearing abruptly like an uplifted snout, was a tall trough of rock, with a jagged rift in its side, that gave an appearance of gaping jaws. The surface of the rock was black and scaly from the action of internal fires, and there could be no manner of doubt that this natural trough had once been the crater of a volcano—whether or not now extinct who could tell? There was at least no present suggestion of activity. The course of the lava flood which had issued from it was clearly indicated, and in one part, seemed to have been broken as by a rush of raging water which had flung it back against the rock, from which it now curled and hung in mighty petrified shreds, like black foam on a giant wave.

The very earth itself had been riven in the struggle, for there was a deep chasm, partly filled in the course of centuries, by soil and scanty vegetation; while beyond, across the valley's mouth, lay huge boulders most fantastic in shape—fragments of a mountain torn in that cataclysmal convulsion—and heaps of grey-black stones which might have been vomited in prehistoric times from the crater-jaw.

Opposite the Crocodile, to the south, at the foot of a great basalt ridge, which did not seem to have been so severely dealt with by the elemental forces, there lay a belt of verdure, where possibly, a stream had once flowed. Closing in the head of the valley, and partly hidden by the tortuous lines of the projecting hills, the grey stone carapace of the Tortoise Mountain lay against the horizon.

This was the scene which met the wanderers' eyes, as, worn out with a two days' march across the desert, where inhospitable grey cliffs had walled them in like the sides of an immense natural basin, baked by the fierce sun, and parched with thirst, they came within reach of their goal.

Hansen hurried as best he might over the uneven surface of a comparatively level stretch of the valley towards the ribbon of scrub. Alas! he found no shimmer of water within its depths. But the sight of the green was hopeful, and calling to Kombo to come on, he helped Anne to climb the boulders till they dropped from a low fall of rock down upon smooth ground in the shadow of great trees.

The vegetation of this scrub was unlike that of the scrub they had already traversed, for here was no dense undergrowth nor any thickets of the prickly lawyer palm.

There were shrubs unknown to them, bearing flowers of different hues, and large, trunked trees, very lofty but bare to a considerable height, where they spread out in horizontal branches. The stems of these trees were white, while they tapered inward at the bottom, and just below the branches, in something the shape of an enormous bottle. There was no doubt that they were a species of bottle-trees, only very much larger than those further south. With his knife

Hansen at once made four incisions in one of them, and taking out the wedge of soft wood found that a few drops of colourless liquid trickled down the stem. He collected what he could of the liquid, and made Anne moisten her lips with the few spoonfuls in the pannikin. She wanted him to do the same, but he shook his head. "There's sure to be water here," he said; and just then, Kombo, who had been scraping the soil with his sharp club, called out that he had found it. The two men made a deepish hole, and before long, they had a bucketful of clear water. Now they relieved themselves of the baggage they had been carrying. It was reduced to ammunition, for all else had been cast aside. Kombo cut some branches of acacia which grew among the bottle trees, and soon rigged up a shelter for Anne. He spread a blanket on the floor; the opossum rug had been abandoned long ago, both on account of its weight, and because the heat made such a covering, even at night, unnecessary.

The girl threw herself down, with a piece of log for a pillow, and sank almost immediately into a sleep of utter exhaustion. When she awoke, Hansen was beside her, holding in his hand some fruit,—a flat long purple plum and a cluster of large red flowers like lilies, which she could but dimly see in the dusk of the gunya. In spite of his own fatigue, there was a look of repressed excitement upon his face, but he said nothing, bidding her eat the plums and stay her appetite till the junglehen he had shot was cooked.

It was now dark, the twilight having abruptly deepened into night, and only the flames of Kombo's fire lighted up the little smooth space among the bottle-trees where they had made their camp. All were too weary for anything but to eat and sleep; too weary also, to feel fear either on the score of Elias Bedo, who they believed was pursuing them, or on that of the mysterious Red Men. They never thought of blacks. For many days there had been no sign of native fires, and it was certain that the Maianbars' superstitious dread of the Tortoise and Crocodile would keep them from venturing into the neighbourhood of these mountains. Only Kombo was uneasy. He would not now, as was his wont, camp over his own fire a little way apart, but crawled close to Anne's gunya, between it and the place where Hansen slept, his gun beside him; and more than once in the night the girl, was awakened by the black boy's whispering voice.

"Missa Anne, you no think-it that Tulumi Mirrein? (the thunder of the Tortoise). You no think-it Kelan Yamina—the old man Crocodile—spit fire on Kombo?" At which Anne would reason with him, declaring that since the magic of Cloud-Daughter had so far preserved him from harm, he might trust it against the breath of the Tortoise and the fire of the Crocodile. But even she was sometimes startled by strange noises and peculiar night cries, whether of the wind among the tall trees or the voices of bird or reptile, she could not tell. The whole place seemed to her strained senses haunted and uncanny, and she was, later, interested in discovering that the history of that wild valley might well justify ghostly alarms. The heat had been terrible for the time of the year, intensified no doubt by the glare of the desert and the reflection of the sun upon the sides of the great sandy basin they had crossed; but it was very hot and steamy even in this mountain gorge, and they became anxious to ascend into cooler regions. For some time the next day they traversed the scrub in fruitless quest of a pool of water, but they found none, and there was no sign of the buried river emerging from beneath the desert sands. They climbed up the northern ridges—which, though inaccessible crags towered above them, were on the lower slopes, not difficult to mount—in the hope that here, as in those of the range they had formerly skirted, they might find a mountain tarn.

But here again progress was slow, for again they found volcanic boulders and banks of loose grey stones upon which, at every moment, their feet slipped. As they proceeded, the vegetation which had clothed the lower spurs at the opening of the gap became scantier, till it ceased or showed grey and withered, as though burned by the heat of the ground on which they trod. There was a sulphurous stench in an intersecting ravine they had to cross, and here and there, smoke issued from the side of the hill; while once, Kombo, treading incautiously, fell through the crust of an earth bubble, and was with difficulty pulled out. The boy uttered piercing shrieks of "Debil-debil," and when he came out was scorched and in places badly burned. This did not add to his happiness, and he went whimpering to the rear, afraid to retreat, afraid to go on; and repeating to himself, in mangled fashion, the Lord's Prayer, which had been taught him during his civilised years, but which he had given up for the employment of his native exorcisms.

"It's like a place I know in Japan that they call the Great Hell," said Hansen. "Keep close to me, Anne, and tread exactly in my footsteps." Thus they went in safety over that part of the Pass, and climbing again, seemed to leave the sulphurous track behind them.

All this time they had been steadily mounting. Though suffering great inconvenience from the heat, they were not tormented with thirst, for they had filled their water-bags at the little wells they had dug in the scrub below. But after a while it got cooler, and by-and-by they found themselves in pleasant pastures, ascending and descending land billows that were green with long grass and shrubby vegetation, above which rose, here and there, the feathery crest of a clump of palms. At last, in a hollow between two of these undulations, they found a tiny blue water-hole which seemed of an incalculable depth, and round the sides of which grew lilies with pale blue and white cups.

"The lotus!" exclaimed Hansen. "The sacred lotus of India, Japan, and Egypt. This is very interesting. I have never seen it growing in Australia."

There were other surprises in store. They camped that night by the little lagoon, and supped sumptuously on Torres-Straits pigeons that Hansen had shot, and on fresh-water fish caught in the pool. The presence of this particular river fish in so small a lagoon puzzled Hansen, and he concluded that there must be an underground stream making a continuous current in the lagoon.

Next day they mounted higher, with still the Tortoise Mountain before them. But it was partly hidden by the projecting spurs of the range which seemed to meet in front of it, so tortuous were the curves of the valley. The rock head of the Tortoise, which at intervals rose above the curving hills, appeared more natural than ever. They could discern some resemblance to the flabby folds of skin that hang about a real tortoise's neck. It was a marvel of nature, if it were indeed entirely due to nature. That seemed almost incredible, but there was no other explanation of the wonder. From this point of the valley they could not see the blue triangular mouth of Gunida Ulàla, for the lower part of the mountain was wholly obscured by a great rocky spur some distance in front of them. There was a still lower spur intervening between the wanderers and the further hill; and as they approached this nearer rise, they saw that what they had taken for a rocky serrated formation on its summit, was in reality a series of monoliths placed in a definite circle with irregular spaces in the circle where great columns were missing. These ruins had certainly been made by no convulsion of the earth, and as certainly, by the hand of man. Such of the monoliths as remained upright, surrounded an oval space, in the centre of which stood a large round stone supported upon another, and with a slight depression in the centre, suggesting an altar of Cyclopean size.

Till now they had come upon no sign of humanity; and even this circle of stones, giving somewhat the idea of Stonehenge, seemed a relic of some race of Titans rather than of human beings like themselves.

Kombo, when he beheld the monoliths standing out against the sky, cried aloud that "Debil-debil sat down there," and hid himself behind a bank of shrubs where he again assiduously repeated what he could remember of the Lord's Prayer. The air was very still; no wind stirred the tree-tops on the mountain side; neither human being nor animal gave sign of its presence, nor was there any sound presaging supernatural occurrences or giving countenance to the Maianbar's terror of the Tortoise's ominous thunder. Had there been, Kombo would undoubtedly have fled back to the desert and to the Maianbars themselves to avoid the greater evil. As it was, he waited, and by-and-by, taking heart of grace, cautiously followed his mistress. Anne ran up the grassy slope after Hansen, who turned, waving his hand to her to remain till he should have reconnoitred this strange spot. But she was not to be holden. Before many minutes she stood by his side, in front of the desolate altar which reached high above their shoulders.

"They must have been big people who worshipped here," Hansen said, thoughtfully. "This seems to me higher than any of the Tortoise altars I have seen in the buried cities of Mexico."

Hansen's eyes were agleam with the delight of scientific discovery, which is greater even than the joy of finding gold. He knew that he had found here in the unexplored heart of Australia—that continent which was declared to have no previous inhabitants but the degraded aboriginals found there on the first explorers' landing—ruins which proclaimed the fact of a civilisation, linked with, and perhaps as great as, the prehistoric civilisation of Central America, traces of man's occupation in remote ages, which might, indeed, change modern scientific conceptions of the former history of the globe.

"Anne," he said, solemnly, "I am now confirmed in an idea which came over me the night we camped in the valley, though I said nothing to you till I had further proof of my theory. I am convinced that this was once a populous region, which has been destoyed, probably long ages back, by an eruption of the Crocodile Mountain. I believe that we shall find the remains of a race similar to that which built the old cities of Palenque and Copan. I know the shape of that altar—a tortoise altar,—though I have never seen it enclosed by a druidic circle."

"A tortoise altar!" repeated Anne, with a puzzled expression on her face. "Do you mean that there were ever any people who worshipped tortoises?"

Hansen did not answer the question for a minute or two. He was too deeply engaged in tracing the lines of some much-worn hieroglyphics which covered the pedestal of the altar.

"Oh! If I had but the drawings I made in Yucatan, to compare with this!" he exclaimed. "But who could have dreamed of such a discovery? It certainly confirms Brasseur de Bourbourg's theory, that there was once a vast continent with a great civilisation, extending from Chili and Peru to Australia. Remains have been discovered in the islands of Polynesia, but till now none in Australia. Who knows that they may not be buried beneath the sands of the great Central desert, or the lava of extinct volcanoes? Anne, you do not realise what a stupendous find this is."

"No," she answered, "but you will explain it to me."

"Yes, as far as I am able. I worked up the subject as well as I could before going to Mexico; and when I got there, the question of that ancient Mayan civilisation interested me so intensely, that I tried to pierce into the forbidden heart of Yucatan, where white men dare not go. You know the legend of a mysterious city, where, it is supposed, is a remnant of the lost Atlanteans? I learned as much as I could of the old Mayan language from Landa's Grammar, and the dialects of the Quichés—which is a corruption of the Mayan—so as to be able to talk to the natives and collect their traditions."

"Did you find the mysterious city?" she asked.

He laughed. "No; I don't think any white traveller is likely to do that. I meant to have a try at it, however, only I was laid down with fever at the start, and when I got well I was recalled home."

"And you never went back?"

"No. It is only a year ago. I came out here instead."

They were walking round the circle, and there were pauses in the talk, for every now and then, Hansen would stop and spend some minutes in examining the monoliths. There appeared no trace of inscriptions on the great stones, some of which were upright, others fallen. The vegetation on the summit and sides of the mound was scanty, indicating no depth of soil except in a line sloping perpendicularly where there was a band of verdure. He prodded the ground with his staff.

"It is as I suspected," he said. "There is masonry under the grass, and I am very much mistaken if here are not steps like those leading to the great temple platform on a hill I've been to in Hawaii. So there must have been mound builders and pyramid builders in this new world, as they are pleased to call it; though it is my opinion that Australia is about the oldest portion of the known earth."

He was greatly excited. Anne caught the reflection of his enthusiasm.

"Let us stay here and dig for what we may find," she cried.

He held out his staff derisively. "With this, and the butt end of my gun! No; we will push on at once to the Tortoise Mountain. I shall be surprised if something astonishing does not meet us there. Very likely this temple, or whatever it was, guarded the approach to the sacred hill. If this people had anything to do with the ancient Mayans, which seems probable, I can understand why they chose this as the site of a city. No doubt they utilised the shape of the mountain in their rites." They had come back now to the great altar. Hansen raised himself and peered over its sides.

"There's a hollow in the stone," he said. "It may be, Anne, that we are standing by the very spot where human victims were laid for sacrifice."

"To a tortoise!" she exclaimed, shuddering. "You have not told me if it's really true that any people ever worshipped tortoises."

"Why, yes," he answered. "All the old religions had a beast or a reptile as the emblem of a cult. There's the winged serpent of Yucatan, the hooded cobra of India, the elephant, the bull, the cat— ever so many besides. The tortoise was a very sacred symbol among the Chinese. Its upper shell was supposed to be the are of heaven; its under one the bottom of the earth, and its body floated on the waters. Therefore, you see, it typified creation."

"I see," she assented, doubtfully; "but I think the idea is rather silly."

"All symbolism seems silly till you get a clue to its inner meaning. They spoke to the people in parables in those days when men were undeveloped animals and only the priests knew anything. But I'm not going to worry you with ancient symbolism till we have had our lunch. You shall hear as much as I can tell you—which is little enough—by-and-by, when we are not hungry. Now I'm going to desecrate one of these old stones by making a fire against it, and cooking the birds. Where is Kombo?" and he gave a cooee.

The black boy came diffidently from behind the bank of shrubs, and sidled up the hill. He was still very frightened; but as neither the Crocodile nor the Tortoise had so far shown signs of animosity, he began to feel more comfortable, and reflected that the Lord's Prayer had proved efficacious.

"By-'m-by, Missa Anne, you tell me again that fellow `Our Father,'" he said, confidentially, to his mistress. "I plenty forget. Mine think-it that frighten Debil-debil."

Soon, a couple of pigeons were roasted, and some of the roots like yams. Hansen deplored the apparent scarcity of game.

"We shall have to get into the mountains," he said, "or we shall be starved out. Now," he added, when the meal was finished, "now for the mysteries of the Tortoise."

Chapter XX—The Place of Death

THE wanderers were at length camped under the very shadow of the Tortoise. The rock head, protruding northward, was slightly slanting in poise. The small face with its round eyes depressed in the skull, its sunken nostrils and slit of a mouth, so strangely resembling that of a senile old man, was now clearly visible, and certainly gave small confirmation of the theory that this effigy of Nature was Nature's own freak. Nature had supplied the monolith, and perhaps the rude outline of a head, but undoubtedly man's hand had fashioned this into its present similitude of the Chelonian species.

Since the discovery of the ruined temple and prehistoric altar, Hansen had become prepared for signs of a bygone civilisation. No marvel of workmanship, on however titanic a scale, would now have struck him with amazement. The greater wonder was the utter depopulation of this extraordinary region. Not a trace had they as yet found of living human occupation; the spot seemed to be shunned even by beasts and birds; for the further that the explorers proceeded, the more intense was its solitude and silence. It appeared as though the cataclysm which, long ages back, had rent the mountains and doubtless destroyed cities and inhabitants, had also scared away, during many succeeding centuries, the animals that had once browsed on peaceful hillsides and the birds that had nested among rocks and forest trees.

As Hansen and his companions skirted the spur nearest the great mountain, there opened before them a scene of even wilder desolation than that at the valley's mouth. A chasm torn in the range met them with yawning jaws, and forced them to descend along its borders to a point where the gap was partly filled by a tongue of earth and rock, grown with straggling shrubs, or more correctly, dwarfed trees of immemorial antiquity—a landslip arrested in its fall and forming, in course of ages, a natural bridge. Beyond this cleft, the spur rounding northward gave a fairly level shelf beneath the overhanging precipice, making a sufficiently convenient camping-ground. From this spur, with its bectling cliff, the ground fell away southward, taking the shape of buttresses to a semi—circular range of high hills, These curved inward to the north beyond the streaked and jagged rock carapace of the Tortoise Mountain, and joined the base of the great monolith, in semblance of a tortoise's head, which dominated the whole scene. Within the curve of the hills, there seemed to be a huge depression as of a deep round basin—possibly a lake, and probably, dry like the desert they had crossed—enclosed all round by precipitous heights.

It was dusk when the camp had been fixed, and the sunset behind the Tortoise's back had left an afterglow of lurid splendour. Presently, a full moon rose almost before the short twilight had ended, and cast long pale rays and patches of black shadow over the valley and on the mountain side. As Hansen and Anne gazed at the mysterious shape of the Tortoise, they were struck by a curious phenomenon. Directly below the huge head with its cavernous eye-sockets, its protruding underlip, and the long narrow slit forming the reptile's mouth, there was a deep hollow, triangular in shape and pallidly luminous. The light in the hollow was stationary, never changing its area, but increasing in brilliance and then fading like phosphorescent gleams upon a tropical sea. As the moon rose in the heavens, this intermittent effulgence waned, brightening again when the orb was veiled by passing clouds.

Hansen wondered whether the effect could be due to a massing of glow—worms on one spot, but decided that this was not possible; then he asked himself if it could be caused by the moon's reflection upon some rock—bound pool. This too, however, seemed unlikely, as they would certainly, from higher levels, have noticed any such mountain tarn. Kombo, returning from an effectual search for food, put an end to their speculations, as he too espied the glimmering patch of light.

"Gunida Ulàla! Gunida Ulàla!" he shouted in deadly terror, and fled to the refuge of the camp-fire. There presently, they found him shaking in a fresh access of superstitious dread.

"Missa Anne! Massa Hansen!" cried the black boy. "Ba'al you stop long—a this place. Debil-debil sit down here. That altogether like-it what old Medicine Man tell Maianbar black fellow. Mine very much afraid that Debil-debil catch Massa, suppose he go too close-up mouth belonging to Tortoise. I been tell you before, poison come out of that fellow mouth belonging to Tortoise. That make bong— altogether dead—white man, black man, kangaroo, 'possum, snake—altogether everything. You see, ba'al you been find-im bandicoot; ba'al you been shoot-im bird; ba'al you been see-im black fellow. I believe Debil-debil been frighten that fellow. Ole Medicine Man been tell the truth. Ba'al can live close-up Gunida Ulàla. Ah! Yucca—Yucca! Eeoogh! Eeoogh! Plenty this poor fellow Black frightened long-a Debil-debil."

Then Kombo wailed the Blacks' wail, which is a fearsome and unpleasant expression of emotion. Again, not all Cloud-Daughter's assurances of her potency against Debil-debil would quiet his wailing. By-and-by, it subsided by reason of sheer physical inability to make more noise, for Kombo had fasted long and was weary; and, moreover, he was overcome with holy fear and deadly uncertainty as to whether he should petition the Christian deity, or his own native gods. Voice failed him, and he could only whisper entreaties that Hansen would turn back even at risk of being eaten by the Maianbars, in preference to facing annihilation from the fire of the Crocodile and the breath of the Tortoise. But presently he lost power to entreat even in a whisper, and, yielding to a more compelling force than terror, his eyes drooped; he rolled himself in his blankets, and forgot his woes in sleep.

The other two were exhausted also, though they had better staying power than the black boy. It was as Kombo pointed out. For the last twenty-four hours no game had fallen to Hansen's gun, and Kombo had looked in vain for yopolo, grubs, or snakes. They had fared poorly on berries—a scanty supply—roots, and the remains of their last supper of fish. A sorry meal was now set forth of roasted bulbs, and before long, Anne and Hansen, like the black boy, were slumbering peacefully in the shelter of a rock.

Food, and not archaeological remains, was next day the chief object of their explorations. Before starting, however, they tried to locate Gunida Ulàla, and made out to their satisfaction that it was a certain blue-looking cleft beneath the Tortoise's head, which they had marked through the field—glasses from the mountain behind. They could not see how far it extended, for the opening was partially hidden by a projecting ridge of basalt that shelved outward, and seemed almost to roof in the upper end of the gap. It was from this opening, in shape an irregular triangle, that they imagined the phosphorescent light had emanated. Only a small streak of the inner walls of the gap was visible through Hansen's field-glasses, and this had the smooth polished look of lapis lazuli. They had noticed that peculiarity even more clearly from the greater distance of the eastern range, which seemed strange, considering how close they now were. But then they had viewed it from a much greater height, and with no near intervening projections. Hansen again remarked to Anne that this blue appearance was probably caused by the action of volcanic fires. Yet this hardly accounted for the faint effulgence they had seen, and for its waning and increasing as the moon's light swelled and was dimmed, nor for the total disappearance of the phenomenon by day. Hansen promised himself considerable scientific interest in its investigation. This, however, was not the time for scientific investigation. Man's most primitive instinct was clamouring, and for this day they could be nothing but hunters of game. All the morning, they traversed the semi-circle of the range, following its undulations of ridge and gully. But the spurs barring the valley northward; were desolate and barren, except for a few berries and some bushes of the Blacks' narcotic plant called pituri, which Kombo gathered with glee.

They were now almost directly under the great rock, shaped like a tortoise's head, which reared itself at the back of a basalt ridge that they had begun to ascend. The ridge dipped, and beyond, the land rose again in wooded slopes to the base of the grey bulging body of the mountain that gave so curious a suggestion of a tortoise's shell. Suddenly a low "G—r—rr—! Yumbu—Yumbu!" from Kombo called Hansen to attention, and he beheld, poised on a crag some distance above, an animal of the goat species, but with striped markings, larger than a chamois; and, as far as he was aware, unknown to

Australian naturalists. This fact, apart from the desire for a meat dinner, fired him with determination to shoot it. He raised his gun, but as he did so, the beast sped along the summit of the ridge and was lost to sight. The goat had bounded downward towards the rift, which ended to the left in that triangular blue patch where had shone the phosphorescent illumination of the previous evening. Hansen darted swiftly and stealthily through the bushes, mounting with alertness, and keeping the gap to his left. For a second the goat showed, outlined on the edge of a cliff, then bounded forward, and disappeared down the face of the ravine.

The hunter pursued his quarry, swerving to the side of the gully and then disappearing also, as he swung himself by means of saplings and undergrowth to a lower level. Anne, who had become an almost more adroit climber than her companion, followed him closely. Hansen had very little hope of bagging the goat, but thought that he might get another glimpse of it, and at least try a second shot.

The two, striking diagonally upward, found themselves — Anne several yards below Hansen — on the brink of a shelving precipice, comparatively easy of descent to a practised mountaineer. Beneath, lay a narrow gorge wide at the base, ending in a cavern that resembled an open mouth, over which curled shining lips of stone. These lips, of which the outside was basalt, seemed to be lined interiorly with something like lapis lazuli — a polished blue marble, streaked and flecked in dark and light lines and splotches. The floor of this cavern was, at the entrance, almost entirely white. It rose in a sort of crest, graduating and spreading inwards and outwards, like the foamy summit of a wave as it breaks on the sea-shore. All down the gorge, the white accumulation spread out in splashes like a drift of chalk or gypsum. For the moment, neither Anne nor Hansen realised the true nature of the accumulation, for the goat had reappeared on a shelf of rock overhanging the bottom of the gorge at the height of about fifty feet. The animal steadied itself for a moment on the brink, but Hansen's second shot struck wide of the mark. The goat leaped after the concussion, gained a lower footing, made some zig-zag steps along the ledge, then dropped into the very mouth of the cavern and was lost to view. Though it had bounded as if unscathed, Hansen could hardly believe that he had again missed his aim, for craning forward he saw the goat touch the white ridge at the opening of the cavern with forefeet extended, and springing towards the interior of the mouth, quiver; and then, as though overwhelmed by a galvanic shock, fall on the blue floor of the cave. He waited for it to give signs of life, but there were none. There it lay, with, as far as he could tell, no trace of a gun-shot wound to account for its apparent lifelessness.

Hansen threw himself down upon the abutting shelf from which the goat had sprung, aiding his descent by the projecting ledges of rocks, and the shrubs at which he was able to catch. He ran along the shelf for some few paces, following the course of the animal. He would have tried to scale the fifty foot precipice between where he stood and the blue mouth of the cavern on which lay the body of the goat, had he not been arrested by a cry from Anne and a warning screech uttered simultaneously by Kombo. Then, as he gazed more intelligently and closely into the bed of the gorge and the interior of the cavern, a slow horror seized him.

"Stop!" called Anne imperatively; "you must not go any farther. Don't you see that the place is full of bones?"

And Kombo cried the native warning, "Kollè mal! Massa, look out! Kvangin! Kvangin! (Evil Spirit). That place, Gunida Ulàla, where Debil—debil sit down and make altogether bong. You see! Bones belonging to white man, black man, kangaroo, bandicoot; altogether everything that come long-a mouth. Suppose Massa go there, Debil-debil make him bong like-it all the rest. Come back, Massa Hansen. Ba'al mine want-im Massa go bong."

Now Hansen perceived that part of the gorge and the blue mouth were indeed a charnel-house—a valley of dry bones such as that of the prophet's vision, only that here there was no spirit to stir them into life. The white heaps and patches were not gypsum or chalk as he had at first imagined, but bones of animals, birds, reptiles, possibly of humans, all destroyed no doubt by the poisonous breath of the Tortoise, in which particular the tradition of the Maianbar men was justified. The mouth of the Tortoise was indeed Gunida Ulàla, the Place of Death. From that surf-like crest at the cavern's opening, the wind playing amid the putrid remains of rotting carcases, had scattered bones and dust along, till where, as the gorge widened, the white specks gradually ceased. Hansen realised that there must indeed be something deadly—a gaseous exhalation possibly—in the cave itself, which had destroyed the goat as it had destroyed all other life coming within its influence. From the height at which he stood, there was no perceptible effluvium, nor did he even feel giddy nor in any way oppressed. This puzzled him, since vapour ascends, and the death of the goat testified to the cave's noxious qualities. Was it possible that death was caused by contact with the shining blue surface of the marble interior, which, as he looked into the furthest recess of the cleft, seemed to emit a pale glimmer? The outer wall gave out, he fancied, a somewhat dull sheen. Over all, lay a sinister suggestion which he had never before come across in his experience of mountain regions in other parts of the globe. Could it in fact be possible that this strange blue marble was in itself a deathstone?

There were no means at hand of solving the question. The goat lay many feet below, and he had no cord to make a lasso by which he could have drawn it up without incurring risk to himself. How he wished that they had brought across the desert one of those long withes of creepers called by the Blacks kàmin, and which, serving as a rope, enable them to climb the straight stems of palms and other scrub trees. The chamois made no movement, and there seemed little doubt that it was dead. He gazed regretfully at the carcase. The species, as far as he knew, was unclassified in Australian zoology, and he would have given much to secure it. He thought that he might perhaps find a withe of creeping palm in the scrub, at the foot of the Tortoise Rock, by means of which he might draw up the animal. With this thought in his mind, he went reluctantly back again to where Anne was standing, pale but excited. It was as much want of food, as mental perturbation that caused her to tremble. She went forward, and impulsively put her hands in his for a moment, as she exclaimed:

"Oh! I am so thankful you are safe. If you had gone down! Oh! if it had killed you!" She shuddered.

"I'm all right, dear comrade," he answered. "You may trust me not to run any risks—for your sake."

She withdrew her hands, but with his words, comfort had stolen into her heart.

"I was not thinking of myself," she stammered. "But it is true—what should I do—oh! what should I do if anything happened to you? Eric," she went on more steadily, "Kombo is right. There is no doubt that we have stumbled on Gunida Ulàla—the Place of Death. That old Maianbar Medicine Man knew what he was talking about. There's always some foundation for these Blacks' legends. Oh! Eric, let us get away from here as quickly as possible. We can climb this ridge higher up; and Kombo says he has seen a thick bit of scrub close under the Tortoise's Head, where he thinks there's water, and where we may find a scrub turkey's nest, or perhaps a kangaroo rat. Come, let us go."

"I'd like first to have a try at the goat," said Hansen. "If we could fish it up we should get a good dinner at least, and the skin of a new specimen into the bargain."

"Oh! no, no!" she pleaded. "Leave the thing where it lies. How do we know that it is not poisoned by the breath of the Tortoise, as Kombo would say? I couldn't eat it, if you did pull it up out of that horrible cave. Besides, if we climb higher up the hills, we shall most likely come across other goats. It seems fairly easy going as far as the Shell—I can't help calling that rocky hump the Shell, it is so exactly like a turtle's back. Eric, there must be some meaning in it all. Look at the head, how it seems to poke forward—and the queer little eyes, and the nose! Oh! it's uncanny; but I'm sure it must some time or other have been carved by men—civilised men, not savages."

"Yes, I'm sure of that too," he answered. "The whole place fills me with a longing to explore. I believe, Anne, that we have come upon the home of the Red Men, and that we are on the verge of tremendous discoveries. Don't tremble, my child, you must not be afraid."

"I don't feel afraid of the Red Men," she answered, "but I can't stay any longer in the Place of Death Oh! Nalla yan, Nalla yan—which is what Kombo has been imploring for the last ten minutes."

She was still trembling. He had never in their wanderings seen Anne so unnerved. Kombo too was shaking, and his face showed livid under its black skin. The boy was kneeling, and again gabbling faltering repetitions of the Lord's Prayer, in feeble hope of thus exorcising the demon. He had got as far as "Gib us dis day," but broke off, his practical mind seizing a hitherto unconsidered point.

"Mine no understand, Missa Anne. Ba'al mine think-it Big Massa long-a hebben have flour like-it white man. Ba'al mine believe that fellow God make-im damper." At which Anne laughed in spite of herself. But Kombo was in no mood for levity, and gravely went on with his devotions. He stumbled hopelessly over the forgiveness of his trespasses, again appealing to Anne in frantic perplexity.

"Ba'al mine know that fellow treppass, Missa Anne. Mine been lose him altogether. Bujeri you pialla that big Massa long-a hebben. Big Massa listen to Missa Anne—ba'al he listen to Kombo."

So at the boy's petition, Anne knelt on the rock beside Kombo and very reverently made her own and his supplication in the simple and sublime words of the Master who first spoke them in Galilee. And Kombo was soothed, and rose at her bidding to follow her, thankful to escape from the Place of Death. Hansen took Anne's hand in his, and they mounted together like two children, hastening over the rocks and through the stunted herbage, but scarcely speaking till they had gained the patch of scrub below the rock carapace and the towering monolith, which, now that they looked up at it, scarred as it was and worn by time and weather, seemed less defined in outline than it had appeared from a greater distance. The scrub was moist and comparatively cool. There were bottle-trees in it, and native plums and scrub vegetation, also palms; while in places, the ground was carpeted with a low-growing plant, bearing bright red blossoms—the same that Hansen had gathered at the entrance of the valley. They found a little stream trickling between banks of fern; it had its source in a fissure in the basalt wall that rose overhead to the height of about a hundred feet and then rounded backward, forming the Tortoise hump of almost naked rock. The wall was jagged at its upper edge, much as might be in miniature the striated margin of an ancient turtle shell. It was seamed with clefts and burrowed with holes, while here and there at the base, there were projections of the cliff forming natural buttresses. Between these rock buttresses lay cave-like shelters, strewn with boulders that had fallen from the face of the cliff, and with rain-worn niches and ledges. Anne seated herself on a ledge, her back to the mountain, too wearied even to help Hansen in collecting sticks for the fire he now set himself to light. When he had done this, he took a billy to fill it at the stream, while Kombo marched forth, carrying his pointed stick, in search of a mound-builder's nest, or a layer of big ants' eggs beneath the bark of a decayed tree. He had hopes, too, of finding among the orchids and parasitic ferns, that native delicacy, the pouched mouse; and Anne watched him take up here and there a handful of earth or rotting vegetation and smell it, then start off with a reassuring "Y—ck! Y—ck!" having ascertained that there was a chance of his quest being successful. She felt that it would indeed be pleasant to eat a full meal again, for one might have fancied that a upas blight lay upon these mountain fastnesses. Except for the goat, many hours had passed since they had seen a sign of animal life. There was no rustle of birds' wings, nor stealthy sound of reptile, nor any of the soft cries and gurglings common in the scrub.

After blowing up the fire, and setting the billy to boil, Hansen shouldered his gun; and bidding Anne not to be afraid, as he would not go beyond sound of her voice should she call, crept along the side of the precipice in the direction of the Tortoise's head. He hoped that he might sight a rock wallabi, which would furnish them with meat.

He had not gone far when he came upon a tunnel in the mountain which struck him as not entirely natural. It was a hole some six feet high by about a yard broad, that seemed, when he peered into it, to descend into the interior of the hump, and in which, as he explored it from the opening, he seemed to discern the outline of rude steps. Greatly excited, he stepped a few paces within the aperture, having leaned his gun outside against the rock. As he moved on, he found that the hole got higher and that he could stand in it upright, though presently it narrowed so that he could not square his elbows. His fancy had not deceived him; there were certainly rude steps leading downward several feet, and beyond, he felt, rather than saw—for a faint current of air met his face—that a long tunnel stretched into impenetrable blackness. The sides of the passage were, as far as he could grope with his hands, of smooth rock, and he could tell that it went for some distance, by the reverberation of his voice when he raised it in a Coo-ee, though the Coo-ee gave back a broken echo, showing that there were obstructions in the way.

He went a little further along the tunnel, which was clear of débris; this strengthening his belief that it was used for some practical purpose. At last, however, he was stopped by a mass of rock. Groping with his hands along the rough surface of the rock, he found an opening again on either side leading into further blackness. He sought vainly for matches. But he had already recollected leaving the box with his pouch beside Anne, when he had taken off his belt to lighten himself before starting out with his gun. Though his nerves tingled with excitement at the discovery he had made, and he longed to continue his explorations even in darkness, he knew that this would be unwise, for he was already out of reach of Anne's voice, should she call. Should evil befall him, she would be left alone with the black boy, and without a clue to his whereabouts, though he reflected that they must soon learn the direction he had taken from the position of his gun and the sight of the hole. But this passage, too, he thought, might lead to a place of death. Were he to proceed, it might be at the risk of being overcome with some poisonous exhalation such as had killed the goat, and which he would not for the world that Anne, in her search for him, should brave. Reluctantly, therefore, he retraced his steps.

Anne was in the camp where he had left her, but she had stretched herself upon the rocks in an attitude of utter weariness, and he saw that she had fallen asleep. He gazed tenderly at the strangely-clad figure, so small and girlish in its garments of fibre and feathers, and at the little pinched face, wan and marked by privation and fatigue. His heart swelled in a gush of emotion. Faithful comrade! Could ever stalwart man have been sturdier, braver, or truer mate? How cheerfully she had tramped on by his side; how uncomplainingly she had borne hardships, how dauntlessly she had faced terrors that would have subdued any spirit less finely tempered and indomitable! The moisture rose to Hansen's eyes as he looked at her. Had he had any right to bring her into this fearsome region? Ought he not to have taken her back to the coast, and there, washing his hands of the responsibility of her fate, have delivered her over to her lawful protector? He might then have returned unencumbered to pursue his journey, no doubt to his own greater advantage, and to that of the learned Society that employed him. Yet how sorely lacking in zest and savour would his explorations have been without this dear companion, who must now, if ever they returned to civilisation, share the honours of a discovery which would convulse the scientific world. And had she not refused to go back? Had she not implored him not to leave her in the clutches of Elias Bedo? No; his duty was clear; at any cost, he would serve and save her in so far as lay in his power. He would fight for her against her enemy, even though that enemy were her own husband. It should not be his fault if she were given over again into slavery. But how did he know that Elias Bedo was not even now close upon their track with a little army of troopers behind him? Well, if this were so, it behoved him— Hansen—to find as soon as might be a place of safety, and was it not possible that he had half an hour ago stumbled upon such a refuge? Thinking, however, over the position, it had sometimes seemed surprising that Elias Bedo should care to encounter danger in pursuit of a wife who had clearly shown that she hated him; for it was certain that he intended to get her back if that were possible, or he would not have come so far in search of her. On Anne's showing, he could not be deeply attached to his wife, so there must be some stronger motive actuating him than baulked love or desire for revenge. Then there came again into Hansen's mind the story he had heard of Anne's supposed lineage and inheritance of an ancient barony and of great wealth, and it struck him that here was motive to a man of the stamp of Elias Bedo. He had hardly considered whether the story was a true one—there had been so much else to occupy his mind. Now, studying Anne's high-bred face, and thinking of the courage which had sustained her, and of the grit and resource she had displayed, he could well believe that she came of some grand old race, and that there ran in her veins the blood of heroes. "Bon sang ne peut mentir," he repeated to himself, and inwardly recited some other saws of like meaning as he replenished the fire, refilled the billy which had boiled away, and raked a glowing bed of ashes ready for the cooking of whatsoever food Kombo might bring.

Anne was still sleeping when the black boy reappeared, his eyes gleaming, his dilly-bag full of spoils. Hansen checked his triumphant shout, "Yai! Yai! Mungàlu mogra" (I have brought fish), motioning him to make no noise, but to lay down quietly the fruit of his foraging expedition. Whereat Kombo emptied his dilly, and the white man's hungry mouth watered at the sight of three released crawfish slithering among the stones. Kombo related that he had come upon a pool in the little river dammed by rocks in which mud crabs abounded. He declared that they might camp here for weeks, and not starve. Evidently the poisoned breath of the Tortoise did not affect its brother crustaceans. Besides the crabs, Kombo had found two pouched mice, and a handle of beetles' larvae, as well as some edible roots. Truly, this was fare not to be flouted by gods, let alone starving humans, although they had to it neither salt nor seasoning, nor any beverage but spring water with which to wash it down.

Chapter XXI—Ave Baiamè!

WHEN Anne awoke, the crawfish were boiled, and appetisingly torn asunder; the larvae spluttered on the ashes; the pouched mice gave forth a savoury odour, and some roots, resembling parsnips, smoked on a plate of fresh cut bark. Outside, from Kombo's fire, which he had made on the other side of the buttress, came grunts and ejaculations in the aboriginal tongue, expressive of intense delectation. Kombo had been, as he would have put it, "nai-al kandu,"—extremely hungry. Nevertheless, his first care had been to dry, as expeditiously as possible, some shoots of the pituri he had gathered—the Blacks' opium. He did this in front of the fire, though, properly speaking, the process should have been longer, and carried out by the heat of the sun or in warm sand. But Kombo yearned for the drug which he knew would plunge him into a state of beatitude, and make him forget his fears. In their wanderings he had often searched for it, and had been bitterly disappointed at not finding the plant, which only grows in certain districts, and is so prized by the natives, that a man carrying it, though he belongs to a hostile tribe, is treated as a sacred messenger. Now Kombo realised that even if he should fall into the clutches of King Multuggerah, his possession of the pituri, and his knowledge of where the plant might be found, would give him an unassailable position in the Maianbar camp.

As soon as he had satisfied his first pangs of hunger, he carefully prepared the ashes of a certain wood he had found in the scrub, and having mixed them with the pituri—thus freeing its alkaloid properties—he chewed the mixture into a paste, when it was ready for use, and might be kept for any length of time. But Kombo had the full intention of making an expedition later, on his own account, and securing a quantity of the invaluable drug.

Presently Anne opened her eyes, and raised herself, staring about her bewilderedly. During sleep, her features had been contracted as if she were in pain and puzzlement. She was puzzled still, but the look of pain faded.

"Where am I? Oh! I have been dreaming. Eric, I have had such a horrible dream. I thought the Blacks were all round me again, as they were outside the cave at Kooloola, and one of them threatened me with his nulla-nulla. And he seemed to turn from a black man into a red man, and then to change again, and I saw that he was my husband."

"You are safe from your husband, at any rate," said Hansen; and yet as he spoke, doubt came over him. Might not Anne's dream be prophetic?

Why should not Elias Bedo, as well as they, have crossed the strip of desert?

"Eat, little comrade, eat!" he said. "That was the nightmare of exhaustion. Here is a beautiful meal, and you need it badly. So do I, for that matter; and as for Kombo, he is enjoying himself finely. After we have fed, I have got something to tell you."

"Nothing bad?" she exclaimed. "You said I was safe."

"No, nothing bad, but something highly interesting. I feel just now like Columbus when he sighted America, the discoverer, not of a new continent, but of a lost civilisation. But eat, little woman." And he set her the example by breaking a craw-fish's claw with a stone and handing it to her; then attacking one himself in like fashion.

Anne cried out in surprise and joy.

"Where did you get them? I thought it was carpet snake, and was wondering if I was hungry enough to manage snake. Oh! how good this is! It reminds me of old times when Etta and Kombo and I used to fish in muddy holes in the paddock for lobsters, and boil them for tea. I remember we used to think the fresh-water lobsters which we caught ourselves, much better than the crabs that the Blacks used to bring us from the sea-shore. I don't know which was the best fun— fishing for lobsters in the paddock, or knocking oysters off the rocks on the beach, and cooking them over a sea—weed fire. If we only

Fugitive Anne

had some quart-pot tea!" she sighed. "I wonder when we shall taste tea again?"

Nevertheless, they ate with gusto. The craws, as Anne called them, were delicious. The beetles' larvae when roasted was not unlike slices of omelet, but had a woody, aromatic flavour; the roots made a good substitute for bread. It was a long time since they had fared so sumptuously. When they were filled, Hansen told his tale of the tunnel he had found, and of his suspicions that it had been, if it were not now, put to human uses. He wanted Anne to go with him at once and explore the passage, and was a little vexed that she seemed somewhat unconcerned. But his heart melted at the signs of weariness on her face when she declared herself too tired to move again that afternoon, and begged that, for a few hours at least, they might rest and enjoy themselves. She suggested that they should build gunyas against the wall of rock, and make a comfortable camp for the night. On the morrow, she said, they would talk about exploring the passage; she hadn't the nerve for it now, and she echoed his thought—how did they know that it might not be another death trap, like the blue mouth of Gunida Ulàla, where the striped goat had perished? She had not yet got over her fright, and wanted to forget for the present that they were in a land of mystery. Hansen had to confess that he, too, was tired, and they decided to defer the expedition. It did not matter, he thought, since now he felt assured that they had at last reached the kingdom of the Red Men. He took out his pipe, and filled it with the few pinches of tobacco remaining in his pouch, which he had been saving, having jestingly declared some time back, that he would smoke his last pipe under shadow of the Tortoise. They were truly under its shadow here, for the sun was declining westward, and neared the bulging top of the rock carapace. A pleasant langour of repletion stole over Hansen, and for some time both were silent, while he puffed lazily, leaning back against the rock in luxurious anticipation of the wonders before them. Kombo, on the other side of the buttress, was silent too, for in the joy of a full stomach, and under the influence of pituri, he slept blissfully beside his camp fire, and dreamed not of Debil-debil nor of mythical monsters. All nature seemed hushed. There was no sound but the trickle of the brook, and a very faint murmuring in the leaves

164

of the palms and scrub trees. At this altitude it was not disagreeably hot.

The picture was a pretty one. The fire, which had burned down, sent up dreamy curls of smoke. Hansen savoured every puff of his pipe as he, too, blew cloudy rings into the quiet air. His back was set against an angle of the buttress, and he looked with lazy admiration at Anne, who had throned herself upon a ledge a little above him, her feet upon a rock, her face turned towards the scrub, as she softly hummed snatches of song. She had thrown off her cap; and her brown hair, thick and curly, grown by this time to the base of her throat, framed her face, which had now regained its original fairness. Her delicately cut features, her sensitive mouth, and large clear brown eyes, seemed, in her wanderings and hardships, to have acquired a spirituality of expression not so noticeable hitherto. She began to sing, more loudly and continuously, bits of old ballads, such as Hansen liked to hear of nights by the camp-fire.

"That's jolly, Anne," he said. "I quite agree with you. We'll rest and be thankful for to-night, and start with new spirit to-morrow. Sing on, little friend. It does me good to listen to you. Let us have something soothing and triumphant too, for this day should be memorable to both of us. If we have not actually entered the undiscovered country, at least we are upon the verge of it."

Anne gave a little shiver.

"Are you not afraid, Eric?"

"Of what, my comrade?"

"Are you not afraid of what you may find in this undiscovered country of yours—more places of death—savages—horrors? I have the sense of something strange and deadly. I seem to feel it in the air."

He bent forward, and, putting out his hand with impulsive affection, took hers, and held it close for a moment. He would have carried it to his lips, but checked himself. Never was Red Cross Knight more chivalrous in the treatment of captive maiden, than was Hansen in his manner to his comrade. Her eyes met his in a quick glance, and were averted scrubward.

"I don't want to be a kill-joy," she said, "but I cannot help the feeling I have had ever since we came among these mountains."

"And what is that?" he asked.

"It's what I told you—a sense of foreboding and danger. You know what the old Maianbar Medicine Man said of these red people. He made the Blacks dread them so that they will not come near the place. How do we know that the Red Men may not be in ambush at this moment, waiting to murder us?"

"I don't think that's likely," he answered. "Of course, little woman, nothing is more natural than that you should feel as you do. It would be strange if you weren't nervous, brave as you are; but because you're frightened, it doesn't follow that there are any live red men, or that they will murder us if there are. I will tell you the conclusion I have arrived at, for my brain has not been idle this last day or two, and everything we have seen, or rather have not seen, makes me sure it is a right one. The desolation of the country; the mass of bones—animals' bones—at the mouth of the blue cavern; the forgotten temple; the old lava streams and the formation of the rocks—all confirm my theory. It appears to me certain that in prehistoric times, as far at least as Australia is concerned, this part of the world was peopled by a highly civilised race which, improbable as it may seem to you, had some connection with the old civilisation of Central America and Peru."

She started and turned. "How could that be? The two places are an ocean apart."

"Yes, but that ocean, or a great portion of it, may once have been land. We all know that the configuration of the globe has changed more than once—is always changing. It is beginning to be realised that the world is much older than even the Egyptologists have maintained, and many scientists have believed. The general opinion is, that a vast continent once spread in the South Pacific, of which the innumerable islands that dot the ocean from Australia to near Chili are the highest remaining points. And even supposing there were no land passage," he went on, waxing warm in the interest of his theme, "we know that those ancient Americans were navigators, for it has been shown by the excavations in the buried cities of Yucatan that they knew the world was round. Therefore they must have understood the compass. In the oldest of the Peruvian sacred books, too, there is mention of a people who came in ships from the great sea and the islands in the east."

Anne gave a sympathetic exclamation. She did not understand much of what Hansen was talking about, but felt sure that he was wonderfully clever, and was quite disposed to accept without question any theory he might advance.

"Go on. Do tell me more," she said.

"It's a big subject," he answered, "and, naturally, nobody knows much about the matter. But it's proved by the ruins that have been found on the Pacific Islands, that they were once the seat of a great civilisation. Pyramids, towers, mounds that show sites of great cities, the stone-lined canals in Strong Island and Lele—these are well-known to South Sea navigators, but they have never been scientifically explored. I have often thought, Anne, what a rich virgin field lies there—what untold treasure may be buried in the Ladrones, the Marquesas, the Gilbert groups, and many others of the South Sea Islands."

"Have you seen these places?" she asked.

"No, but I know a seaman who has been over the ruins of the temple at Metallanine, and who has seen the ancient harbour and canals and the great watergates that still remain below what was once a citadel. Well! A nation must be pretty civilised to build canals and water-gates."

"But it may not have been so long ago as you think," said Anne.

"Who can say? Certainly, there was a great Malayan empire holding sway in these seas, which is within the historic period, and it has left its traces in the Islands. But the ruins I speak of are not Malayan; they are like no ruins in the world but those of Central America. The similarity between the shape of the Pyramids in the South Seas and those of ancient Mexico would go some way to prove a common origin. I myself have had some proof of the connection in the signs upon that old altar we found on the hill. I am much mistaken if I have not seen the same hieroglyphics on the monuments at Uxmal and Chichen-Itza. But I'm always boring you, dear little comrade, with archaeological lectures."

"No, no," she cried; "I'm very stupid and ignorant, but I love to hear you talk."

"Well, anyhow, you see my point—though please let me protest that there never was a more intelligent or delightful listener to a chap who's a shingle loose, as you Australians say, on old ruins and dead civilisations. I believe that in ages beyond the record of man, Australia may have been colonised by some of the Mayan race, and that we have now come upon the traces of that civilisation. I have told you that the tortoise was a sacred emblem of antiquity among the Chinese, the Mexicans, and the East Indians. Here is one of the places where it was worshipped."

Anne's eyes were full of wonder and interest.

"And the worshippers," she said. "Why have we not found them?"

"Because—as the lava drift and the volcanic evidences make clear—there has been some convulsion of nature which has destroyed the vestiges of former inhabitants. It must have been a cataclysm in which fire and water took part, for undoubtedly the desert between the ranges was once an inland sea. I have an idea that the sides of these hills, and perhaps part of the valley, were the site of a populous city. The valley may have been an inlet of the lake, which again may have had communication with the sea. Who knows, Anne, but that ships once plied along a great water-way flowing through that very desert pass in the mountains by which I crossed the first range? I am certain that its sandy bed was upheaved, for there are fossil shells in it. Very likely, too, the scrub which we found impenetrable, covers dead towns and monuments of a people that no longer exist."

"It all sounds very romantic and astonishing, and I like to hear you talk," repeated Anne. "You make everything seem quite possible. And do you think that the red men, which the Maianbar's old Karraji talked about, are the remains of that people, or do you think they are all dead and gone?"

"I cannot tell. The remnant of them may have migrated further west into the unexplored centre of Australia, or their dwellings may be hidden by the very mountain against which we are leaning. There don't seem any left on this side of the Tortoise. That old temple has long been deserted, and there isn't a sign of human habitations along the sides of the hills. But according to the Medicine Man's traditions—which bring us to comparatively recent time—there was a flourishing community of Red Men living about the Tortoise Mountain within memory of the Maianbar tribe. Perhaps there may have been another later eruption—the legends of the fire-spitting Crocodile rather suggest it—which annihilated the rest of the colony."

"How strange it seems," she said, thoughtfully, "that God should allow a race to be born, and become so great, only to die and leave no trace!"

"That's one of the problems of the world's history, Anne—how the different nations which have inhabited the globe have each sunk to nothingness after rising from barbarism, waxing mighty, and then falling into decadence. The life of the nation is but as the life of the man; it has its infancy, its manhood, and its dwindling old age. Who knows! To-morrow we may find the secret of the Red Men's fate unravelled at the other end of the tunnel I discovered. I have a presentiment that wonders await us there. To-day, however, let us eat, sleep, and be thankful to the destiny which has brought us so far in safety. Sing me a song of thanksgiving, little comrade."

"Shall it be the Ave Baiamè?" she asked. "That seems most appropriate to the occasion."

He nodded. The girl rose, from an instinct of reverence as well as from force of habit, for she had always stood at the door of her gunya in the camp of the Maianbars, when, morn and eve, she had invoked the Blacks' deity. Now, with head upraised, the eyes agaze into a world of their own beyond the topmost branches of the forest trees, whose leaves and twigs swayed gently against the blue, Anne lifted her beautiful voice in the song of praise and pleading, at this moment so truly echoed by her own heart, and by the heart of the man who listened. Her music drowned that which Nature made, in the murmuring of brook and branches beyond their rock retreat. Closed in on either side by the projections of the mountains, the two would scarcely have been visible to an intruder, except in an approach from the front. Even so, the man was almost hidden in an angle of boulder and precipice, while the girl, though raised on the ledge above him, and so, more open to view, was entirely abstracted in her song and in her thoughts of gratitude for their safe passing of the perils that had threatened them. Had there been any auditors besides Hansen and Kombo—the latter of whom, screened by a thick buttress of rock, lay steeped in happy visions of his Elysian hunting grounds—she would have been quite unconscious of their proximity.

Chapter XXII—The Red Men

NEVERTHELESS, Anne had an audience, and one that increased by driblets. While she and Hansen had been talking about the traces of an ancient civilisation still existent in the Pacific Ocean, two men of strange appearance had crept stealthily, and almost on all-fours, from the mountain's side to the ridge of rock screening their camp. Presently two heads reared themselves over the natural rampart. Strange looking heads they were, surmounted by flat caps of undyed wool or linen, in each of which stood up a tuft of feathers; the faces of a curious type—long, with high cheek-bones; the foreheads high, slightly retreating, and having a compressed appearance; the features thin, but powerfully moulded; the eyes of hazel or blue, almond-shaped and extremely piercing, beneath strongly curved brows; the hair wiry, straight, and of a dark chestnut colour; the skin reddish-brown.

Before Anne's song was quite finished, about ten of these people had assembled, and others were moving quietly but swiftly from the direction of the monolith shaped like a tortoise's head. The foremost of these, a fine—looking man, whose short cloak—worn over a jerkin of tanned leather, and crest of parrots' feathers—seemed to indicate him as a person of more importance than the rest, stood breast high against the rock rampart, and gazed with intense wonder and curiosity at the white stranger. He, as well as the others, held poised a sort of javelin of flint set in a long haft of wood; but none of them seemed to have any murderous intention, or they had forgotten it if they had, so rapt were they in the girl's music, so spell—bound by the picture she made. Never had they seen a white woman, nor one so small, and yet beautiful.

Anne stood, so far as they could see, alone on the platform of rock, her head erect, her eyes shining with emotion and enthusiasm, her arms slightly outstretched, the awe-inspiring chant pouring from her lips with unusual power and sweetness. Though the words were in a tongue unknown to them, the Red Men, peculiarly susceptible to devotional rhythm, recognised the song as an invocation to some deity. They had no notion of the meaning of what she sang. They could not account for her presence. To them it seemed of the nature of a miracle, and they were unable to decide among themselves what this surprising visitation might portend. But they had vague fancies of a supernatural fulfilment of prophecy, and for this reason the head hunter had hurriedly sent back a scout to summon one of their party—an authority on such matters—who was lagging behind them.

Meanwhile, the men waited, making no movement that might attract Anne's attention; and when for a few moments, silence followed the Ave Baiamè, they stooped, hiding their heads and whispering to each other of a strange coincidence that had struck them. For it happened that the morrow was the yearly anniversary of a Festival at which the prophecy, they now remembered, was always publicly chanted to the people.

Now, at Hansen's gesture of approval and murmured request, Anne again lifted her voice. This time she sang 'Home, Sweet Home.' As the last words died on her lips, she turned her head, and a cry of wonder and alarm escaped her. At her cry, Hansen bounded to his feet, and turned in the direction of her startled gaze. There, in the open end of the semi-circular recess, he beheld an unexpected sight.

An assemblage of some twenty persons was drawn up in rank. Heading it, stood two striking figures, evidently men of sacerdotal dignity, one of them younger than the other. They had the same large-boned, narrow—browed, and powerful cast of face as the hunters who had first appeared, but were of more majestic carriage and aspect, with grave, compelling eyes, the elder having a long white beard and white hair. Both were crowned with a three-cornered white cap, in shape somewhat resembling a bishop's mitre. They wore mantles almost touching the ground, of a yellowish stuff, looking like linen, and with a raised yellow border which was seen later to be made of the feathers of cockatoos' crests. The mantle fell away from an under vestment reaching to the knees, below which were short leggings, and shoes of roughly tanned leather. The mantle of each was fastened at the breast with a clasp in the form of a tortoise, made of gold and ornamented with opals. Behind them, ranged the circle of warriors or hunters—it was difficult to tell which. These all carried the short spears set in hafts apparently of gold, but were otherwise unarmed. They wore jerkins of some coarse material, which might have been of hemp or undressed flax, the hems fringed with fur or feathers, and leather leggings reaching to above the knee. They seemed to have no bloodthirsty inclinations, though each man held his spear levelled. On the faces of all lay a curious expression of fatality, of stony acquiescence in limitations decreed by destiny—not so much of melancholy, as of unconscious resignation. Hansen observed this, and though he had his gun in readiness, he made no sign of hostile demonstration. He gave a courteous inclination as the two priests or elders advanced, but they took small notice of him. Their piercing eyes were fixed full on Anne, and it was to her they tendered what Hansen interpreted as an act of homage. The priests first, then each man following them, extended the right arm, and drawing in the left, placed it across the breast, touching the right shoulder. The Elders bent their heads, the hunters prostrated themselves. Then the Elders spoke some words in a strange language, which yet to Hansen had familiar inflexions. The address was rhythmic, rising and falling in sing-song cadence, with a sort of refrain that sounded like an invocation. This the warriors took up and repeated, with fresh prostrations at each stanza. A word, of which he knew the meaning, struck upon Hansen's ear, and explained the familiarity of certain vocables. The word was a revelation, and set all his faculties on the alert. He had been unconsciously prepared for the revelation, yet this confirmation of his previously formed theory was so startling that he was almost overwhelmed by it. For the priests spoke a corrupt dialect of the ancient Mayan tongue, which is still in use among the Quichés and other tribes of Central America, and which Hansen had studied from the Indians and from the grammar composed by a Spanish bishop of Mexico immediately after the Conquest. The priests called themselves "Hu Aca Tehua"—Sacred guardians of the Aca people. They addressed Anne as "Zuhua Kak,"—Virgin of the Flame. They hailed her as "Ix Naaca Katuna"—She who should be for ever exalted; as "Zaac Naa"—White Mother; as "Chaac Zuhaa"—

Daughter of Fire and Flood; as Priestess, and Servant of the Tortoise God.

Hansen's knowledge of the old Mayan tongue gave him a fairly correct interpretation of this address. He mentally construed the phrases, allowing for perversion of the original, in which the derivatives were retained but the terminations slightly altered. Doubtless, he reflected, there was corruption of the old vernacular in its Quiché rendering from which his knowledge was mainly gained, and it was possible that the Red Men's version might be the more academic of the two. In his mind was no manner of doubt. Here, they had come across a colony of the ancient Mayan race, whose centre of civilisation had in ages past been the peninsula of Yucatan—that civilisation whose origin has been lost in the mists of time, but to whose magnificence, abundant testimony remains in the sculptured façades and the earth-grown temples of Uxmal, Kabah and Palenque—a civilisation that pre-dated the Aztec empire and the dynasty of the Sun, of which Montezuma and the ill-fated Atahualpha were the last representatives.

To fall upon these traces of dead-time glory, here in Australia, the oldest and also the newest of the world's continents, was at once an astounding and yet a comprehensible experience. In the wilds of Australia, as in no other corner of the globe, could that colony have settled itself, flourished and dwindled into decay, unknown to nations that had by turns inhabited the earth. That it should be reserved for him—an obscure explorer—to make this stupendous discovery, was a fact that almost robbed Hansen of his power of coherent reasoning. Yet in the medley of thoughts that rushed through his brain, he had a whimsical realisation of the irony of fate which had compelled poor Anne, from her flight into the Bush up till now, to play the part of divinity.

The Elders stood in a reverential attitude; the huntsmen continued to prostrate themselves, all waiting for a sign. Anne gazed bewilderedly from the strange faces, with their piercing eyes fixed upon her, to Hansen, who, master of himself again, lowered his gun, saluted her respectfully, and said in grave, measured tones, the sound of which to uncomprehending ears gave an effect of deferential petitioning.

"These men are well inclined. They take you for a goddess. I understand something of their language. It is as I supposed: they are an off-shoot of the ancient Mexicans—the Mayans of whom we were talking—settled here heaven knows how long back. Play the part of Cloud-Daughter. Make appropriate gestures, but do not speak, except to me. I shall do my best to interpret. Where I can't, I shall make a shot, and trust to luck. I've been in tighter places than this before now. Only trust me, Anne, and feel assured that there is no cause for alarm. Any show of fear might be fatal. Just keep calm, my comrade. Sing your replies to any question that they may seem to put to you, in recitative, or as you choose. It doesn't matter, since they will suppose your language that of the stars. This will impress them more than anything, and I will translate in the way that seems wisest. Trust me," he repeated, his voice ringing with passionate sincerity. "You know that they'll have to kill me before they harm you. But there's no danger of that."

The girl, falling into the spirit of his instructions, waved her hand to him, thus seeming to signify gracious approval of his words. She stood up straight, giving no sign of alarm, and unblenchingly regarded the Elders, who once more made a reverential obeisance.

At that moment, Kombo, awakening from his sleep, and utterly scared at the sight of the Red Men, burst through the circle of the Elders and hunters and flung himself upon the rock where his mistress stood.

"Yuro Kateena!" he cried. "Yuro Kateena! Pialla Mormodelik," and he pointed to the sky. The presence of the Red Men revived in his mind traditions of his tribe, and Kombo in thought flew for protection to his native gods.

The gesture and the cry appealed to the Red Men as a new proof of the stranger's divinity.

"Yuro Kateena!—Kateena—Mormodelik!" the chief Elder repeated. His brows knit, and a puzzled expression crossed his face. Then a light seemed to break upon him; it was evident that he dimly understood the meaning of the words, though they had long been unfamiliar to him. This was not surprising, on the theory that there had once been intercourse between the Maianbars and the Red Race; and no doubt some of the aboriginal words, especially those applying to the nature deities, had been handed down from the far back Medicine Man, who had first penetrated the fastnesses of the Tortoise worshippers.

The chief Elder spoke to his colleague some words in Mayan, which Hansen knew as signifying "Child of the Stars!" Again the Elders hailed Anne as "Chaac Zuhua!"—Daughter of Flame and Flood; and, extending their hands, showed by their gestures that they wished to lead her with them into the interior of the mountain. They had taken but little notice of Hansen, whom it was clear that they imagined to be merely an attendant of the goddess; but now he interposed commandingly, stretching out a protecting arm over the girl, while he summoned all his resources in regard to the Mayan tongue. Considerably to his own astonishment, words came to him glibly, as though some unseen influence prompted them.

"Not so, oh, men of a once mighty nation, now fallen and abased," he said, daringly. "It is for Her who is exalted, to command, for me to interpret, and for such as thee to obey. She who rose from the Shadow Land beneath, to be throned among the stars, and hath now descended to earth from the heaven that is above, knows not the speech of men, but the language of the gods only, which I, their servant, have also learned. Therefore, oh! Hu Aca Tehua,—which I interpret as guardians of the Aca people,—whatsoever petition it may be your desire to tender, I will expound it, and return the answer."

Hansen, whose speech had halted slightly at the start, gained increasing confidence as he saw the impression he produced. The Elders frowned in angry amazement at first; then, as they listened, their wrathful wonder gave place to awe.

"Thy words are bold in the utterance, and strange and somewhat unpleasing as coming from one not of our race," replied the foremost of the two, haughtily. "First, we would know who has instructed thee in the language of our people, of which this black slave and those of his kind in the forest around, are wholly ignorant; and secondly, who has given thee authority to be an interpreter between us and the messenger of our gods? It may go ill with thee, if thou art vaunting thyself unduly."

"Truly it is ye, not I, who shall suffer the ill, if ye flout the chosen of your Great Ones," answered Hansen, with assumed bravado. "According to thy ignorance will I answer thee, oh Guardian of the Aca! The world is big and old, venerable friend," he went on, with a courage and assurance that further impressed the Elders. "Generations of men have come and gone, and the graves of dead cities have given up their records to new-born nations, while this last handful of a perished people has been rotting away among the gum-trees. As for my authority, are not our presence among you and my speech in the Mayan tongue proofs that the Mayan gods have not forsaken ye? More, I cannot say, save that I am but the Interpreter. Here"—and he pointed to Anne—"Here is the messenger, come to redeem the ancient promise, that a priestess and deliverer should be sent among you."

Hansen made his shot at a venture, knowing that in all religious mythologies that have ever been, there occurs a prophecy of the re-incarnating or coming again of a divinity. In this case, he hit the mark closer than he had expected. The Elders consulted each other with their eyes, and softly uttered some sing-song words, the meaning of which Hansen did not grasp. Then there came from the mouth of the hunters a sort of answering chant, a few lines only, which rose and fell in barbaric cadence, wild and solemn, and quite unlike any music Anne or Hansen had ever heard. The girl realised from the gestures of the Red Men that she herself was the object of the chant, and in obedience to Hansen's signal gave an antistrophe in a few bars of recitative from an Italian opera. The Red Men acclaimed again, though they did not understand what she sang, and the chief Elder put his clasped hands to his forehead impressively.

"We are ready to believe, Stranger, and to do homage to the gods' messenger, for it is true as thou sayest—we have an ancient prophecy declaring that a priestess shall walk dry-shod where the sea once flowed, and coming into our City of Refuge, shall do service in the Temple of Aak, and bring prosperity to his children. Though," added the Elder, doubtfully, "there is in the prophecy something of the nature of a warning, which it is possible may apply to thee."

"And what is that warning, good friend?" asked Hansen.

"That, thou mayest perhaps learn later. It is not clear enough to be of moment," said the Elder. "Prove to us now thy knowledge of our gods."

"Of what god shall I speak to thee?" said Hansen. "Shall it be of the Nine Lords of the Night, who hold the gates of the senses, while man is wrapped in sleep? Shall it be of Viracocha Zazil, Lord of the Dawn? Or of Tohil and Huracan, Ruler of the Winds, and Wielder of Thunderbolts? Or shall it be of the Grim Lords who are named in your sacred tongue, Priests, Lord of the One Death, and Lord of the Seven Deaths, to whom the Day and the Night are one, and to whom the elements are subject? Shall it be of Xibal, Sovereign of Ximohazan, the Valley of Oblivion, where there are neither tracks nor trails, in which the body of man crumbles away and is forgotten, but whence the soul of him returns in new shape to do the will of Those who are most mighty? Say, then, Hu Aca Tehua, holy guardians of your people, have I proved to you my knowledge of your gods? Do you receive me as interpreting the will of Viracocha the Doer—Lord of Dawn; as servant of Aak, who is Intercessor of the Sun, and Supporter of earth and heaven? Say, Priests, are my words in accordance or not with your ancient faith?"

"Thou speakest well, Stranger, and Interpreter as thou hast called thyself. Verily, it would seem that thou too art a messenger from the great gods, for thou tellest glibly the sacred names, which none in these mountains, save the remnant of that once great people of Aak, have spoken since the Day of Humiliation and Terror—that day when our nation was given over to the wrath of Kàn, the Great

178

Serpent—four-footed, which sent out fire and ashes from his mouth, darkening the face of our Lord the Sun. Then did the deeps burst their boundaries, and rose and fell and were swallowed for ever into the bowels of the earth. Then was our city of old time, and all that dwelt therein, destroyed by the power of that same four-footed Serpent, whose vengeance drove Aak—our Lord and Prince—in the beginning, from his home beyond the far seas. We see, too, that thou art instructed in the doctrine that I, Naquah the Elder, Kaboc my colleague, and the five other Elders, also the Priestess and people, have learned from the writings of Those who went before. For thou dost speak of Viracocha, Builder of Forms, Minister of the Supreme One, Lord of the Lesser Light, to whom be praise. And true it is that this mortal body of man must descend into the Valley of Eternal Oblivion, into the realms of Xibal; and most certain, likewise, that it shall not for ever die, but, like the grain of corn put under the earth, shall arise and live again and bear fruit. Nevertheless, I, Naquah, have not seen nor heard of the spirit of any man that we have held converse with, returning after death, reclothed in body, to be known by his former kindred. Surely, me-seems, such a spirit would have come back to dwell with its own people; yet with us this has not been, and our hearts have grown faint in waiting for our Deliverer. Once, were we many and mighty, but now are our numbers few, and as the tale of suns goes by, fewer still do they become. In old time the wives bare children in plenty, but now are they often barren, and from generation to generation it has been handed down to us that our strength has continued to decrease. Well, it may be that the gods have seen our diminishment and the curse that lies upon us, and have sent this maiden, according to the promise of old, to lead the Children of Aak into a new land over which the great Serpent may not cast his breath, nor extend his claws, so thus shall our nation once more build cities and multiply and prosper. But of the fulfilment of that promise we can have no certainty, until the Supreme One gives the Sign, through His Minister and Doer, Viracocha, to convey His Word to Aak the Intercessor, and to be a command to the Aca people.

"Then shall it be seen if the Brightness of Him Whose Name is unutterable, Whose vesture is the Sun, shall strike into the Holy

Place, proclaiming that of a truth the Priestess, who was fore-ordained, hath been chosen from on High, and standeth in the flesh for Aak to accept as his servant, and the Aca to obey as their queen."

The Elder paused for a moment, and gazed earnestly into the face of Anne. Clear it was that he was deeply impressed, yet not wholly satisfied. "Myself, I know not," he said; "and concerning the will of the gods, my heart quakes within me, for this maiden is small, and though not ill—favoured, she hath but a child's stature, and may not find grace in the sight of Aak, being unlike the maidens of the Aca who attend the Zuhua Zak—Chief Virgin of the Flame—whose emblem is the Eye of Viracocha, and whose song is well-pleasing to Aak."

To the best of his ability, Hansen translated the speech of the Elder, assuring Anne that she had nothing to fear, though it was with some trepidation that he inquired in what the duties of a priestess of Aak consisted. Horrible visions of the Aztec rites presented themselves to his imagination; and he had made up his mind that were there any question of human sacrifice, they would all at once make a bolt for it, reflecting that his gun and Anne's revolver, with Kombo's quick wits to aid them, might be a match against the long-robed priests and the score of lightly armed warriors. But Naquah's reply to his question, which was delivered in flowery language and at considerable length, made him feel more easy. He understood sufficient of it to assure himself that this Mayan off-shoot practised no bloody rites, and that the only propitiatory offerings required by Aak, were green herbage and spring water. He gleaned, also, that the god's chief delight was in the music made by the high priestess and the other Virgins of the Flame, whose office it was to tend the sacred fire kindled by "Our Lord the Sun" once a year, and to purify the water which seemed to have a significant part in the religious observances of the people. Aak the Intercessor, and Viracocha of the Dawn, secondary deities to our Lord the Sun, were apparently peaceful divinities, taking pleasure in the fruits of the earth, and demanding not hearts nor entrails of human or animal victims.

This Hansen explained to Anne, satisfying at the same time Kombo's ejaculatory queries, for the black boy clung close to his mistress's skirt, and the aboriginal wails of "Yucca! Yucca! Eeoogh! Eeoogh!" (woe! woe! alas! alas!) sounded unceasingly. But the friendly demeanour of the Red Men gradually soothed Kombo's excited nerves, especially as he found that the strangers called down no consuming fire, and that the Thunder of the Tortoise had been but a figment of the Medicine Man's imagination. Presently, it was proposed by Naquah that the messengers of the gods should be conducted to the abode of the people of Aca, there to be given in charge of the Elders, and the High Priestess of the Flame. So once again poor Anne resigned herself to the part destiny allotted her, taking comfort in the thought that the service of Aak and the companionship of the Red Men seemed at least to offer less alarming possibilities than her residence among the Maianbars, with old Buli as her conductor to the Deep Tank, and the chance when she arrived there of being eaten by Multuggerrah the King. She saw, too, that Hansen was all alert with curiosity and interest, and that he could hardly restrain his impatience to see the dwelling-place of the Aca, though he maintained an attitude of dignified courtesy during the long speeches of Naquah, and the offering of gifts by the hunters, who, in token of homage, laid at the strangers' feet the supply of food they had brought with them, doubtless intended as light refreshment during a fishing expedition, for they carried, as well as their short spears, what seemed to be barbed tackle and fishing-nets. The food was mostly fruits of various kinds, some of which were quite unknown to Anne, and thin cakes made of maize. Kombo's mouth watered at sight of these, and they were appetizing to the two white people, though dignity forbade them to eat. No scruples, however, restrained Kombo, who, after cautiously examining one of the maize cakes and testing it between his teeth, ate with avidity.

"I believe that bujeri fellow Red Man," he observed. "Mine think-it old Medicine Man tell plenty lies to frighten black fellow. I believe all gammon long-a Kelan Yamina and Mirrein Debil-debil. Ba'al Debil-debil got-im flour; ba'al Debil-debil make-im damper. My word! This bujeri damper! I believe that fellow Red Man very kind to Missa Anne. Mine no think-it Massa Bedo come look out for Missa

Anne inside Tortoise Mountain; he no find-im road. But suppose that fellow come, then mine plenty talk to Red Men and altogether fight Massa Bedo and make him go bong. You no hear, Missa Anne? Bujeri damper! I believe Red Men plenty brother belonging to you."

Having come to this satisfactory conclusion, Kombo, being a philosopher, set his mind at ease and took stock of his surroundings, while he walked behind Anne and Hansen, munching his corn-cake with great gusto. He tried to talk to the hunters, but soon discovered that they understood neither Blacks' language nor the aboriginal pidgin English, and that they considered him quite unworthy of attention. But his keen eyes noted every stick and stone and feature of the mountain as they walked along towards the tunnel, the two Elders preceding their captives, and the hunters, as advance and rear-guard, closing the procession. In this order, but in single file, they entered the Heart of Aak.

Part II

Chapter XXIII—In the Heart of Aak

AT first, the darkness of the tunnel was dense as pitch. They came to the block of stone with the openings on either side, which Hansen rightly conjectured to be a mass of the mountain that had fallen and interrupted the passage. Then, after following one of the forks a short distance, they found themselves in a wider space, broad and high enough for two to walk comfortably abreast, and which was dimly illuminated from an unseen opening. A cool current of air flowed past them, and they could hear the rushing sound of water. As Hansen's eyes grew more accustomed to the dusk, he discovered that there was a small cascade where the other fork of the tunnel also entered this larger space, and that they were now walking along a causeway with a low parapet on one side, and a stream running at the depth of a few feet over a smooth bed of rock below it. No doubt the builders of the tunnel had taken advantage of a subterranean channel bored by a river—perhaps that very one which they had last seen above ground on the other side of the desert; but it was clear also that the greater part of the work was due to the labour of man. Herculean labour it must have been, without blasting powder or modern mechanical contrivances, and Hansen found himself marvelling how the masses of rock had been quarried and disposed of, and speculating, as many another explorer of historic remains has done, whether we are so much ahead of our forefathers as we imagine, and whether they may not have possessed secrets of science, lost, and as yet, far from being re-discovered. So excited and interested was he, that he called together all his knowledge of the Mayan vocabulary and grammar, and questioned Naquah as to how and when this extraordinary tunnel had been constructed. But the Elder either could not, or would not, give him any definite information. It had always been there, he said. It had existed since there had been any record of the Aca. The mountain had been a sacred place from the beginning. Hansen gleaned a few facts with difficulty. The Great Builders had chosen it. They had known how to cleave the rock, and to lift stones upright that were beyond the power of many men. The secret of their magic had perished with them. There had been one left from the destroying power of the Serpent. It was he who had gathered into the Heart of Aak the remnant of the Faithful who were saved in that far-off day of terror. He had written the record, and delivered his magic to his son, who in turn had given it to his son, and so on for generations. But in later times, long after he was dead, the Serpent had again waxed furious, and had once more breathed out ashes and blackness. Thus it happened that while digging for certain graven pillars which had been buried in the valley below the temple on the hill, a second cataclysm had taken place, and in it, the last of the Wise Men, the last of the Great Builders, had perished, and had taken his magic with him. This had been many suns back, and from that time the wisdom of the Ancestors had been no more written; there was none to tell it from father to first-born, and again from first-born to first-born. Thus the Aca had built no more, but had been content to dwell in their sure refuge in the Heart of Aak, where never since, had the Serpent assailed them.

It was not from Naquah that all this information was extracted. The Chief Elder grew irritated by Hansen's poor management, as he considered it, of the Mayan tongue, which was scarcely surprising, for the speech of the Aca differed somewhat from the language Hansen had learned in Yucatan, and, moreover, he was stiff in the handling of it for want of practice, and, unless spurred by danger or excitement, had some ado in remembering the vocabulary. Thus, Naquah soon relapsed into dignified silence, and Hansen had recourse to Kapoc, who was younger and more communicative. Kapoc went on to say that the natural channel had been widened, and the causeway made by the Builders—the Great Builders, as in a tone of awe he called them—they who had made the city. This, according to tradition, had been a wonder of cities, and had spread to the edge of the water, and along the sides of the hills—a city of temples and palaces, and pyramids and many carvings, all of which had been first swept by the waters, and then swallowed up when the earth had opened. Of the country surrounding the city, only the mountains of the Tortoise, and the Crocodile—or, as the Aca named it, the Four-footed Serpent—had been left unscathed. Also the remains of the great temple, the encasing of rock, and the sacred stones which the flood had not swept away. In the time before the cataclysm, said Kapoc, the Aca had been a prosperous and powerful nation, and their ships had sailed where now was land, eastward to the far seas. "How long ago," Hansen asked, "had the cataclysm happened?" He knew not, nay, for generations there had never been any wise men of the Aca who could say. The count of time was lost; the sculptured records of the ancient people were buried deep where no man could dig them; and there was nought but a certain sacred record that the first Wise Man, who was saved, had made—that Wise Man who had led the few by secret ways within the bosom of Aak.

All this time they had been following the course of the underground river, now descending by rude steps cut in the rock, or by a gentle incline, now by a level path which yet was anything but straight, for it turned and curved, leading through a labyrinth of corridors at right angles, parallel with each other, and branching in different directions so numerous and intricate, that it would have been almost impossible, without a guide, to make a way back to the opening. The place reminded Hansen of a subterranean labyrinth in Central America which he had once visited. The light continued dim, but was sufficient to enable them to pick their steps. Suddenly, however, they were again plunged in darkness for a few minutes; then the glare of torches ahead showed them a lofty circular hall, supported by rude pillars, in the centre of which was a large shallow basin of water, and round it stood a small company of men, holding aloft flaming brands. These men, who had evidently been sent to meet the returning party, were not dressed like the hunters in tunics and hide leggings, but wore a shapeless garment of yellowish white stuff, resembling the under vestments of the Elders, from which Hansen assumed that they belonged to the priestly order, and were no doubt servers or acolytes.

The torches threw flickering gleams on the water in the basin, and over the walls and floor of this place, showing dark objects moving on the ground, of different sizes and uncouth appearance. These turned out to be turtles or tortoises of various sizes crawling about the edge of the basin. Ann gave an involuntary shriek as her feet came in contact with one of these. She now saw that this rock chamber was the home of a number of these creatures, some almost gigantic in size, others still in their infancy. The elder Naquah stopped, scrutinized a family of them, and, pointing to one of the smallest, gave some directions at which the torch-bearers salaamed, and one stooped and turned the creature on his back, while another assisted him to place it in a flat basket in which they carried it away. Kombo was charmed at sight of the tortoises.

"Bujeri fellow turtle, Missa Anne," he cried, for Kombo had tasted turtle soup, and the prospect of a supper of turtle fat would have reconciled him to much devilry. He was beginning to realise that Debil-debils who made corn-cakes and provided roads through mountains which should form a barrier between his beloved Missa Anne and the pursuit of Elias Bedo, could not be such bad Debil-debils after all. He would have caught a tortoise on his own account, had not the torch-bearers rushed upon him and held him back with menacing gestures, nor did they loose their hold till the Hall of Tortoises was left some little way behind. Hansen asked Kapoc for what purpose the young tortoise was destined, and was answered oracularly that by it Aak would signify his inclinations. The Dane had heard of the ancient method of divination by means of the markings on a tortoise's back—a method still practised in parts of the East—and knowing also that the word Aak in Mayan signifies turtle, concluded that the sacred reptile had something to do with that venerable worship.

Daylight now showed through a wide archway before them, and, passing beneath the arch, they stood in what looked like an enormous amphitheatre, partly natural, and partly hollowed artificially in the mountain-side. Day was waning, and it was the rosy light of late afternoon which fell into the arena, through huge openings in an outer shell of rock closing in its south—western side, and through which a stretch of undulating cultivated land was visible. Apparently, they had completely penetrated the great hump of basalt, on the eastern side of which the wanderers had encamped. The top of this vast circle lay open to the sky; and, except in the outer wall and where side passages seemed to have been excavated into the heart of the mountain, enormous precipices towered many hundreds of feet. What gave the appearance of an amphitheatre was, that up to a considerable height the precipices shelved in terraces and balconies, and were honeycombed with large cells, evidently the dwelling-places of the tribe. The inner walls of these cells, in the recesses of which lights glimmered, glowed with colours—being painted, or hung with bright-hued tapestry—and stretched far back into impenetrable gloom. On the outside were windows and doors cut in the rock. Steps led up to these abodes, and here and there, a white—clad figure looked down from overhead. The inhabitants of this rock city seemed, for the most part, however, to have gathered in the clear space in the centre. This apparently served as a market-place, there being open stalls set about its sides spread with merchandise, and braziers here and there on which maize cakes, nuts, and plaintains were cooking, giving forth an appetising smell.

The crowd was not a large one—perhaps a hundred in all; and Hansen reflected that if it represented even a third of the numerical strength of the Aca, Naquah had good reason to complain that the wives did not bear as the fruitful vine, and that the population had dwindled. This no doubt was due to inter-breeding through centuries, of the same stock, for there was no trace of aboriginal admixture. Notwithstanding, the people did not give, as far as physique went, the suggestion of degeneration. They were all of the same type as the hunters who had surprised the wanderers' camp— large, loose-limbed, of the high-cheek-boned, strong-featured, narrow, and somewhat melancholy cast of countenance which Hansen associated with that of the Shawnee and other tribes of American Indians, though when analysed the faces of the Aca were entirely different from theirs. These men were unlike any others that Hansen had ever seen. They wore mostly the tunic and leggings of the hunters, their upper garments of coarse stuff occasionally dyed brown, blue, or dull red. Many wore a sort of mantle knotted at the breast and hanging below the middle, which was usually painted, or worked in startling patterns and brilliant colouring, and fringed with feathers or the tails of small animals. The women were hardly inferior in point of stature to the men. Anne seemed a pigmy in comparison with them; and so far as could be seen in the fast fading daylight, they were handsome, with fine eyes, and a quantity of reddish-brown hair that harmonised with their reddish complexions. They were, however, fairer than the men, probably from living more closely in their rock dwelling, and being necessarily less exposed to the air and sun. They were dressed in clinging robes—the poorer ones in coarse, shapeless garments; those who were evidently of a better class, in finer draperies, and these wore mantles much longer and more flowing than the cloaks of the men, dyed also in brilliant and fantastic designs, and fringed with feather trimmings.

The little crowd parted and congregated again in two long lines as Naquah and Kapoc advanced, preceded by the torch-bearers—the torches being, it appeared, a sign of sacerdotal rank. The Elders had Anne and Hansen between them, while Kombo walked behind. Kombo's interest in the rock-city, the booths and braziers, and above all, the Aca women, was uncontrollable and farcical in its expression. He grinned and ogled, and sniffing the roasted nuts, rubbed what he would have called his "binji," uttering ejaculations indicative of pleasure. But the ladies of the Aca regarded him scornfully as one of the black, outside race, and showed scant curiosity concerning him, so absorbed were they in the white man and woman. Hansen they admired, and he knew sufficient Mayan to understand their outspoken commendation of his fairness and his build. They did not conceal their opinion that the man was both strong and beautiful, but the woman they declared to be of little account, and so small as to be only fit for a child's doll. Whence, they asked, had the strangers come, and how had they gained admission into the Heart of Aak, the Citadel of the Saved—for it was by a name conveying this meaning that the rock town was called? The hunters scattered among their women-folk, and the lines of people broke into knots, while the men recounted their tale. But they were recalled by the voice of Naquah, as he and Kapoc stepped forward, commanding silence. Then Naquah spoke, and Hansen without much difficulty seized the gist of his address.

"Children of Aak," said the Elder,—"In the Hall of Tortoises, Hotan the hunter, returning, found us and told us of the wonder that had befallen. So, following him, we went, and, at the foot of the Great Shell—the roof of Aak's refuge—we found this woman who stood singing in a strange tongue a song of praise to the gods. With her were this man and the black slave who has served them on their way thither. In our ancient language, that of the land of Mayab, whence came our forefathers of old, did the man address us, claiming to be the maiden's protector, and a messenger from our most high gods. True it is that he knows the sacred names, and can speak of the doctrine They have delivered to us. It would appear also that among the inferior race which inhabits the forest, the maiden's divinity is established, since she is hailed by the black slave, who hath guided them across the desert, as Lady of the Clouds, and Sister of the Stars. But whence otherwise she has come, and what her earthly origin, I know not, for she understands not the tongue of the Aca, only—so the white man, her protector, declareth—that of the Spirits of Space. This too, is a thing unaccountable to me. Nevertheless, who shall dare pass judgment on the ways of the gods? And moreover, the man is acquainted with that old-time prophecy which was graven on the fallen stones, and given to us in the writing of our Saviour, the Great Ancestor, so that it hath been handed down in the Temple, from Elder to Elder, ever since there has been knowledge of hidden matters. Ye know the Prophecy—for is it not sung on each returning of the month and the Day of Humiliation and Terror, by the mouth of the Zuhua Kak, at command of the Intercessor, between the people and our Lord the Sun? Ye know how that prophecy tells of a priestess that shall, in the fulness of ages, walk dry-shod over the bed of the sea, and lead forth to new life and hope the forsaken Children of Aak. Whether this maiden, who in looks is no more than a child, be in very truth that god-sent priestess, is not for me to declare, though it doth appear to me that strange and small as arc her stature and the fashion of her face, her countenance beareth the stamp of the gods.

"This is my counsel, People of the Aca, to be delivered to the five Elders:—it is, that to-morrow the maiden be presented in the temple, when, by the mouth of the Zuhua Kak, of the Virgins of the Flame, the Elders, and the people, penance shall be said before the Symbol of Xibal, Lord of Death, and afterwards supplication beneath the

Disc of Life to Him whose raiment is the Sun, and to Viracocha, the Doer, Lord of Dawn, that our nation and our dwelling-place be no more destroyed by the Bursting Fires and Great Waters. Then shall the maiden stand within the sacred circle and await the Sign of our Lord the Sun. And if it be so that He Whose Name be not spoken, Whose utterance is the Red Beam, shall shed upon her the light of His Glory, and make manifest in her the Supreme Will—then shall the mantle of the Zuhua Kak be placed upon her, and the sacred Eye be set on her brow, and she shall be taken into the sight of Aak the Intercessor, and shall sing in his ears her wondrous song, heard by me—Naquah, and by Kapoc the Elder and the hunters of our company—which resembles no song of woman that ever before moved the souls of men. And if her song be pleasant in the ears of Aak, and he shall accept her as his priestess, henceforth shall she render service in the temple, making obeisance before the Throne of the Radiant One."

Chapter XXIV — Keorah

A BRIEF silence followed, and then came a one-throated cry:

"Keorah, Zuhua Kak! Keorah, Zuhua Kak!" And at that moment there sounded a clear ringing voice, proud and scornful in its intonation.

"I, Keorah, Zuhua Kak, High Virgin of the Flame and the Flood, answer to your call, People of the Aca."

At the sound of the voice, Anne and Hansen raised their heads in the direction whence it came. On the side of the amphitheatre facing eastward, high above them, was a wide balcony, its base and roof supported by rudely sculptured pillars hewn from the rock. Standing in a statuesque attitude on the balcony was the most beautiful woman either had ever beheld.

Behind, and at the sides of this woman, six other women were grouped, each holding aloft a flaming brand or tall lamp—it was difficult to tell which—all of them robed in white. They were younger and fairer, it seemed, than the women of their race, with long, reddish hair falling unbound, save by a white fillet that was held on the forehead by a jewelled ornament. Hansen took in their presence in a swift, comprehensive glance, which returning, was enchained by the one excelling them all who was in their midst.

The rock city was now almost in darkness. The rosy afterglow that had greeted the strangers had faded. The short Australian twilight was deepening into night, and the lights above and below, and glimmering from the depths of the cave-dwellings, shone redly in the gloom, giving a most weird effect to the vast place. Adding to this weirdness, the full moon, now risen, hung like a great electric arc above the circular opening in the mountain, and lent its radiance to the face of the woman on whom the attention of all was centred— Keorah, Zuhua Kak.

Most commanding of mien was the High Priestess of Aak. Young too, of bounteous classic proportions; her bosoms full, her neck rising like a column above her white robes, that were girdled at the waist with a glittering zone. A long mantle, bordered with raised bands of rose, fell round her shoulders, the ends held together at her breast by a jewelled clasp. A band, with plume of pink feathers, circled her forehead, and in front of it was a great opal, which, when the torch rays struck it, sent out answering flames. Her eyes were large, and of a deep blue, and they shone brilliantly beneath level, strongly marked brows, giving out gleams something like the gleams of the opal above them. These eyes, lowered upon the crowd, met the eyes of Hansen, and lingered upon his face. As they did so, the fierce fire in them died, and her look of angry defiance melted. The masses of her red-gold hair fell forward as she stooped over the balcony, making a splendid veil, out of which the opal on her brow and the wonderful eyes glowed softly. Her gaze was seductive, and a feeling of mesmeric attraction overpowered Hansen. For a moment, he seemed to lose the sense of space and time, even of the unwontedness of scene and situation. The High Priestess' eyes drew him against his will; he became conscious only of her. Anne's voice recalled him to the present, thrilling sharply in his ear.

"Eric," she said, "I am frightened. Who is that woman, and why does she look at us so strangely? Oh! what do these people want with me? I see them pointing, and I cannot understand what they say. Tell me, for I don't think I shall be able to bear it much longer. I'm obeying you, Eric. You told me not to speak or to rebel, and I have been watching, and trying to do as you wished. But, oh! I'd rather almost be with the Maianbars—for I could understand and talk to them— than with this mysterious Red Race."

Hansen turned from the gaze of the Priestess to meet Anne's pathetic eyes looking appealingly from her little white face, so child-like, and now so weary.

"Dear little comrade," he whispered, reassuring her with a sudden inborn strength and tenderness, "be brave, as you have been all along. Trust in God—and in me." He put his hand upon her shoulder, and his touch gave her new confidence. "Believe that I will let nothing harm you while I live to be your protector. I know how to deal with these people, and, by-and-by, I will explain everything that you don't understand. I'll teach you what I know of their language. Be certain, however, that they are a harmless, peaceable race, and mean good to you and not ill. That woman is, I gather, High Priestess of the god Aak—Aak means in the Mayan tongue, tortoise or turtle—a simple, innocent kind of fetish, who, it seems, only requires sacrifices of grass and water, and somebody to sing to him. I learn that to—morrow is the anniversary of some sort of religious festival, having to do with a prophecy about a priestess who was to walk over the desert and bring luck to this queer set of heathens. They have an idea that you are this priestess, and it is to be decided somehow in the temple to-morrow. I assure you there is nothing in it to make you nervous. All that you have to do is to sing, and the worst that can happen will be, that they'll turn us adrift again. But I must say, that I think it would be to the advantage of science if we could stop and study them for a bit. Only go on playing your part as I have told you, and stick to your revolver, whatever happens."

"But I cannot help their taking it from me, if they want to do so. And if I am to supplant that woman—she frightens me more than all the rest of them! Oh, Eric, I am so tired of being a goddess. I did hope there was an end of that, when we got away from the Maianbars. "

"It is better to be a goddess than to be eaten," said Hansen, trying to speak jestingly. "We must make the best of things, my dear—for the present, at any rate. There's always the chance of escape. Stay, the woman is speaking. I will translate for you what she says."

"Naquah! Kapoc! The five Elders await you in the Council-Chamber," the High Priestess' voice rang out. "Go, tell them what has come to pass, and consult with each other, if ye will, as to the prophecy of which we have heard much this day. Concerning its fulfilment, neither I, nor thou, Naquah, have aught to declare. Is it for us poor mortals to question the decree of Him whose Name may not be uttered—whose minister is Viracocha the Doer, and His Intercessor Aak—whose is the Red Flame and His Vestment the Sun.

Now, touching the prophecy—thrice, as ye all know, on the return of our great day of prayer and abasement, when unveiled are the faces of Death and Life—thrice has our Lord the Sun withheld His holy beam—and this for no fault of ours, but that all might come to pass as was written of old. So it may well be that the priestess fore-ordained, from beyond the water's bed and the far sea, has now, in the fullness of time, come among us. To-morrow, therefore, shall it be seen, in presence of the people, whether she be illumined by the glory of the Red Flame, and singled out by that Holy Sign, and if afterwards the favour of Aak be vouchsafed to her. To-morrow, then, if the sign be given, will I, Keorah, Zuhua Kak, yield to her, who is chosen of the gods, my sacred mantle and the star upon my head, which is the Eye of Viracocha that closeth not in slumber. Then, clad with the emblems of holy office, this maiden messenger from the great Ones will prostrate herself before the Discs of Death and of Life, and sing the wondrous song some of ye have already heard, to delight the Ear of Aak our Lord. Gladly will I, who have served the gods, and have been obeyed by the people, do reverence to the Will of the Supreme, and, loosed from my Priestess' vows, will I henceforth take my place among the daughters of men. Faithfully have I striven to fulfil my office, and, peradventure, I shall receive my reward. It may be that as my heart desireth, so shall the gods do unto me. And with the thought of this I am content. Yet there is a word I would say unto ye, Elders and People of the Aca. Forget not the warning that was graven on the ancient stone, and written by him who saved us in the Fire and the Flood. Divide not Beauty and Fair Strength, nor suffer them to be constrained, lest evil befall the Children of Aak, and the Curse of the Serpent be not lifted from you. Therefore entreat the Lord Aak, and supplicate Viracocha—the wise and the far-seeing—for right judgment and clear vision; and abasing yourselves, cry aloud, 'Guide us, Aak the Intercessor. Give us wisdom, Viracocha, Dweller in radiance, Builder, and Mighty Doer. Thou who hearest and dost perform, Who art stronger than Death, and defiest the Grave, Lord of the Four Winds, and Light of the Dawn!'"

The strange chant uprose, Keorah's voice leading, and all the people crying, "Guide us, Aak! Enlighten us, Viracocha, Lord of the Strong

Hand, Chief over the Night, Darkness, Death and the Waters. Hear us, Viracocha!"

When the invocation had ceased, there was silence, and all prostrated themselves. Then Naquah stepped a little nearer to the balcony, and desired to know what were the High Priestess' wishes in regard to the lodgment of these strangers.

"Give them to eat, and clothe them," commanded the High Priestess, "for truly it seems to me they are weary with travel, and their garments are earth-stained in a way unfitting for the messengers of the gods. Let them have of our best. To the child-maiden give robes of linen—this shall be the care of my virgins. And to the man who is Beautiful Strength, do not furnish priests' vestments, but manly habiliments such as are worn by the noblest and most valorous among you. Let the maiden be brought at once into the Virgins' House for refreshment and rest until the hour of our vigil be past. Then will I myself see that she is clad and prepared for the Festival of Death and Life on which to-morrow's dawn shall rise, and for presentation to our gods. For the man of Beauty and Strength, thou, Hotan the hunter, art responsible. Lead him to thy dwelling, feast him and do him honour, awaiting the counsel of the Elders, and my pleasure concerning him. And now, peradventure, it is the last time that I, Keorah, Zuhua Kak, charge you in virtue of my office, for before moonrise to-morrow, another may reign in my stead. Nay! I mourn not, nor do ye mourn if it be the Supreme Will that I descent to the level of ordinary womanhood; for bethink ye that the lower life has joys which to the Priestess are forbidden, and it may be that these shall be my recompense. Ill would it beseem me, then, to show ingratitude to the gods if, for the dignity and honour of the priestess-ship, they give me in exchange those simple and yet sweeter joys of which I have not dared to dream. To-morrow, then, our Lord shall make known his will, to which I, with you, will bow. We shall meet in the temple. Till that time, my bidding be done."

She moved back, and disappeared through the arch behind, the band of virgins parting for her to pass, then with torches uplifted, they followed her within.

A hoarse murmur, partly of dissatisfaction, partly of excitement and surprise, swept through the crowd. It was not clear whether the Aca people regretted or desired the dethronement of Keorah, their present Zuhua Kak.

It seemed strange to them, as it also did to Hansen, that she should herself refer to the prospect with such remarkable equanimity, even giving a suggestion that release from her vows might not be wholly unwelcome. While she was speaking, he felt the spell of her eyes still upon him, and as he looked up and met their gaze, the heart of the woman leaping beneath the priestly band that reined it, became evident to him. A thrill of understanding ran like fire through his blood, and flashed upon his face, bringing a glow to Keorah's as she spoke her last words. When she turned, the spell seemed broken, and Hansen steadied his reeling senses, and responded warmly to the pressure of Anne's little cold hand, which slid trustfully into his, while the shouts of the populace were raised to Viracocha and Aak. He hurriedly interpreted to her the speech of the High Priestess, and again bade her be of good courage. But there was little time for talk. The hunter Hotan—he who had been foremost of the band outside the mountain—now approached, and with a deep obeisance pointed to the street, if it could be called so, that opened at a right angle with the balcony on which the Priestess had stood, signifying that Hansen must accompany him thither. At the same time, three of the linen-clad torch-bearers, Naquah's attendants, led poor bewildered Anne to a flight of steps cut in the rock at the right of the Priestess's balcony, and thence through a low arch into the dwelling of the Virgins of the Flame.

Kombo followed his mistress to the small portico at the head of the staircase. He was not permitted to go further in spite of his signs and protestations, and his mistress's dumb entreaties. Men, even black slaves, were not admitted into this nunnery. On the threshold of the inner doorway, the acolytes made reverence, turned, and descended into the street. But Kombo unslung his blanket, put down the tin billy and pint-pots, the tomahawk and pointed stick that he carried, and disposing of his properties in a corner, made it clear that not for all the Virgins nor the acolytes did he intend to budge.

"All right, Missa Anne, mine make it camp like-it this place," he announced, cheerfully. And in truth, to Kombo, after his recent perils and privations, this sheltered porch, with the busy market-place below and all its array of lamps and braziers, with the chance of corn-cakes and roast plantains being handed up to him, presented a most desirable resting-place. He frowned on the acolytes at last when they persisted too long in trying to make him go.

"Ba'al mine yan," said he. "Mine no go long-a you. Mine sit down close—up Yuro Kateena. You look out. I believe that fellow Cloud-Daughter pialla Mormodelik, suppose you take Kombo." And he pointed first to Anne, then heavenward, then to himself, at which the acolytes prostrated once more, and hurried down quickly, being more than ever convinced of the divinity of the small stranger.

The Virgins met Anne with more curiosity than reverence, for till Aak and Viracocha confirmed her pretensions, they could not be sure that she was really the priestess who was to bring prosperity to the people of the Aca.

There were three of these maidens waiting to receive her, young, handsome, tall and stately, and curiously attractive with their long peculiarly expressioned faces, their russet hair, and graceful robes. All wore on their breasts what was evidently an insignia of the order, a tortoise in gold set with opals; and Anne noticed in wonder that what she had imagined to be a metal clasp on the left shoulder of each of them, was in reality a small living tortoise fastened by a chain. The little creatures appeared to be semi-comatose, but occasionally a weird wee head protruded itself, and showed two blinking pin-point eyes.

The Virgins led her through two ante-chambers lighted by oil lamps oddly shaped, like frogs and birds, made in earthenware. The walls of these rooms were painted in hieroglyphs or small barbaric-looking designs, and the floor was covered with a sort of matting. There were low stools of wood set about, and projecting from the walls, were several altar-like tables. Beyond was a larger apartment almost circular in shape, with cells branching from it. In this, the stone walls were rudely sculptured; opossum rugs and kangaroo skins strewed the floor, and a table in the centre was spread with a linen cloth on which were fruits, cakes, and earthenware bowls, some containing a mess of maize porridge, others a foamy brown liquid, which Anne discovered to be chocolate. In this room stood three more priestesses, making the number six. One of these was evidently more important than the others, and this lady advancing, greeted Anne with the same salutation that the hunters and Elders had made—crossing the left arm over the breast, with the left hand touching the right shoulder. She motioned Anne to a seat at the head of the table next herself, and after a grace incomprehensible to her guest and the pouring of a libation of chocolate into a hollow in the floor, the meal began with a bowl of porridge placed before each. Other dishes followed, simple but palatable. There were hot cakes of different kinds made of Indian corn, dipped in a sauce of chilies and tomatoes, fried beans, and plantains cooked in various fashions, together with chocolate which, though oily and flavoured with spice, seemed to Anne, unaccustomed now to anything but water, a most delicious beverage. The Virgins talked among themselves, but their talk was of course not understood by Anne. She was beginning, however, to pick up already one or two Mayan words, and one of the priestesses found amusement in making her say the English equivalent of the names of the dishes, and in endeavouring to imitate the pronunciation of what they believed to be the language of the gods.

Anne's spirits rose. There was certainly nothing alarming, so far, in the aspect and manners of this simple community of women like herself. She ate and was strengthened, and almost felt herself to be amongst friends. But she was glad that the High Priestess was not present, for Keorah, Zuhua Kak, had inspired her with a superstitious terror. She hoped, however, that it would wear off on closer acquaintance. At any rate, it was clear that these under-priestesses were amiably disposed to her. By-and-by, the eldest of the Virgins rose and motioned her to follow through a corridor cut in the rock. This passage appeared to end in a sleeping chamber, for the room they came to, held a raised couch covered with a feather rug; while in a semi-circular recess was a large basin scooped in the rock floor, let into the ground, and filled with bubbling water. The Virgin pointed to this and then to the couch, giving Anne to understand that she might bathe and sleep. Then she left her alone, and drawing a curtain over the doorway, Anne undressed and stepped into the bath, which was tepid, most exhilarating, and evidently a natural spring with some peculiarly invigorating mineral qualities. Afterwards, she wrapped herself in a linen garment placed in readiness on the couch, and, creeping under the feather blanket, was soon enjoying the most luxurious sleep she had known for many days.

Chapter XXV — "By the Shining Blue Death-Stone"

ANNE was awakened by a sound of monotonous chanting that seemed to come from a curtained arch at the head of her couch. She rose, and peering through an opening in the heavily embroidered mats, discovered that these divided her from a kind of chapel in which the seven Priestesses of the Flame were engaged in praying. She concluded that one, slightly in advance of the rest, was the High Priestess, but it was impossible to distinguish any one in particular, for each was shrouded in a mantle of black, with a deep hood that overshadowed the features. All were kneeling with heads bowed, and the object of their devotion appeared to be a tripod on a slightly raised dais at one end of the chapel, from the basin of which issued a pale blue illumination. This ghastly light could not be described as a flame, for it was perfectly stationary except for a certain intermittency in its degrees of radiance. It waxed and waned like the throbbings of a pulse, and at once, Anne was reminded of a like effect which she and Eric had seen in that triangular patch of phosphorescence on the mountain's side at the spot they had afterwards identified as the Place of Death. The tripod, too, was triangular in shape.

But for this strange blue light, the chapel was in complete darkness; and as far as Anne could see, no other altar, nor any statue, nor picture accounted for the nuns' reverential attitude. They beat their breasts, and grovelled in extreme abasement before the tripod, while their voices were raised in a monotonous chant, meaningless to Anne as Abracadabra, in which she could only clearly make out certain phrases that recurred over and over again like the burden of an incantation: —

"Holi! Huqui! Xibal Xibalba!

Holi! Huqui! Xibal Xibalba!"

It was not till some time afterwards that she learned their interpretation: —

"We call thee! We beseech thee!

Xibal, Lord of the Dead!"

Anne crept back to her couch, and waited for an hour or more, as she fancied, while the chant droned on. Then she must have gone to sleep again, for suddenly, without preparation, she knew that the singing had ceased, and became conscious of the glare of lights where darkness had been. Looking towards the curtained doorway by which she had entered from the corridor, Anne now saw Keorah, the High Priestess, standing with two of her Virgins, one on each side of her, holding lighted lamps; while within the chamber, at the head and foot of her couch, were the four other Virgins of the Flame—foremost among them she who had received her at the banquet, bearing robes of white linen. Another held a veil of gossamer material, while the remaining two carried bottles containing unguents and essences.

Anne, dazed with sleep, stared vacantly around her. The High Priestess gave a command in her own tongue to the Virgins, and signed Anne to rise. The girl did so, and stood before Keorah. They made an interesting picture, these two rivals, if that could be called rivalry in which one had declared herself willing to yield, and the other desired not to take.

Unevenly matched they seemed: Anne comparatively diminutive—even insignificant; the insignificance redeemed only by the unconscious dignity of her expression; unformed, childlike, shrinking, with the linen garment provided by the priestesses drawn closely round her thin shoulders, her short hair ruffled over her brow, her delicately featured face, worn and pale to the whiteness of milk; her spirit, appealing yet indomitable, shining from the large dark eyes, that seemed as the eyes of another breed of woman, in contrast with the glittering almond-shaped orbs of the Priestess. So she stood, a pathetic yet forceful figure. Keorah towered above Anne, majestic in her proportions, magnificent in colouring and array, her red hair framing the strange, long, fascinating face, with its gleaming blue eyes and crimson mouth. Upon her forehead, the

Eye of Viracocha shone dully beneath her pink feather head-dress, and her mantle of office with its curious feather border and designs—an eye and heart, a hand and a cross, embroidered in shades of red and blue—swept in ample folds round her splendid form, and was held in place by the jewelled tortoise at her breast.

Was the High Priestess so willing after all to exchange for human joys the privileges of her exalted position? There was nothing of the womanly submissiveness of her address to the people to be read now in her bearing and expression. It was as the upholder of saccrdotal authority that she came into the presence of this usurper of her rights.

She eyed Anne silently from head to foot. It seemed to the girl that Keorah was appraising her own points of vantage, and measuring weapons with the scanty armoury of her foe. But there was no possibility of words between them. Anne did not understand Keorah's language, and both women were too proud to descend to the common medium of signs. Thus they stood facing each other for a minute or two, neither uttering a sound.

Keorah, addressing her Virgins, broke the silence. It was not till later that Anne understood what she said.

"Time shortens. Dress the maid in fine white robes, as befits a suppliant of the gods. Veil her so that in the hour of abasement Xibal, Lord of Death, may not blight her by his baleful ray. Place upon her the black mantle without which none dare approach the Blue Stone. Then lead her last in my following, and let her kneel in the Circle of Virgins beneath the Disc of Death, till the moment when she must stand in the appointed place before the altar of Viracocha, Lord of Dawn, and receive the verdict of the most high god."

The Chief of the Virgins now came forward, attended by those carrying perfumes, with which Anne was first anointed. Then they combed out and sprayed with essence her short curls; contemptuous, as she clearly saw, of the meagreness of her adornment in this respect, compared with their own masses of red-gold hair—in which, however, all were inferior to the High Priestess herself.

They bound a narrow white fillet upon Anne's forehead, then dressed her in the loose linen robe carried by the eldest Virgin, leaving it ungirdled, save by a thin cord of twisted strands of flax. Then they threw the muslin veil upon her head, letting it fall in front, and fastening it with bone pins at the shoulders; and over all, they put the long black mantle, with a large hood which completely covered her head and form.

After having thus apparelled her, and at a word from Keorah, who led the way, the Virgins conducted Anne into the chapel and left her standing at a little distance from the raised tripod, with its strange basin of phosphorescent light, while, in a sort of robing recess opening off the chapel, each donned a shrouding black cloak and hood similar to that worn by Anne, except that while hers was quite plain, those of the Virgins had a design in the centre of the back, none alike, but varying, doubtless, according to the rank held by its wearer. Keorah's mantle was more elaborately embroidered than those of the others, and she was robed with considerable ceremony by three of her attendants. Finally, she was given a long staff tipped with the same phosphorescent substance as that enclosed by the curved edge of the tripod, which glimmered palely in the half darkness of the chapel. This staff the priestesses handled reverently and with great care, presenting it on bended knee, while they chanted the words of the refrain, "Holi! Huqui! Xibal Xibalba!"

Now the nuns moved in procession, singing as they went, Keorah heading the band, alone. Her eyes were fixed on the staff, which she held upright a little way from her; and she led in a clear high-pitched, but somewhat thin, mezzo-soprano, the invocational hymn.

Anne was at first jarred by the strains, with their long monotonous cadences and strange harmonies, composed, it seemed to her, on a different musical scale from that common in Europe. Nevertheless, curious as was the diapason, she found the music affecting her after a few minutes almost to fascination.

After Keorah, the other six priestesses walked in pairs, the last two having Anne between them, and all of them, except the High Priestess, carrying torches. They went along winding passages hewn in the mountain, Keorah's staff shining like a dim star in the darkness at any point where the abutting rock momentarily intercepted the light of the torches. For it seemed a peculiarity of the phosphorescent stone, that it was absolutely dull in sunlight, and only emitted its full radiance in total darkness, though by lamp-light it was not entirely eclipsed.

Anne's dulled senses and exhausted nerves had been quickened and recuperated by food and sleep. She felt more herself again; her spirits had risen, and her brain was alert, taking in everything around her with curiosity, interest, and a feeling of awakening awe. Yet though keenly alive, she had still the sensation of living in an intensely real dream. The nuns walked on, chanting for perhaps ten minutes, then halted before an archway draped with heavy feather-embroidered curtains. Here, the torches were extinguished, only the ghastly blue flame of Keorah's death-stone staff shining in the blackness. The two foremost virgins drew the curtains apart. Keorah passed through, the others followed, and Anne now found herself in a vast shadowy hall, standing in a kind of chancel raised several steps above the body of the building, from which it was partly divided by a row of slender pillars. The chancel was illuminated only by a triangular object set in the wall, somewhat higher than a tall man's head, and protected by a stone balustrade reaching from the ground to within a few inches of its lower edge. This triangular object emitted a pale blue light, swelling and diminishing with wave-like regularity—the light which Anne already associated with that of the mysterious Death-Stone of Gunida Ulàla—the same light as that of the tripod in the Priestess' chapel, and of the staff Keorah bore.

At this end of the temple there was no other illumination; but far away in the blackness beyond, showing the vast extent of this rock-hewn hall, a few torches glimmered feebly. All else was shadow. The gloom seemed even denser within the weird radius of the Death-Stone, where, to right and left, with an empty space between, was gathered a concourse of black shrouded figures, all bowed towards the ground, and wailing the same monotonous chant that Anne had heard in the chapel, with its ever-recurring burden, "Holi! Huqui! Xibal Xibalba!"

The doorway by which the procession of priestesses had entered was near the triangle of the Death-Stone. Before it, forming a line round the protecting balustrade, were the Seven Elders, who called themselves Hu Aca Tehua—Sacred Guardians of the Aca people. Naquah stood in the centre of the line; but as Keorah advanced, it parted, and the Elders re—formed in two rows, one on each side of the triangle, thus giving place in the centre to her and her maidens. Keorah immediately prostrated herself, the others following her example, they kneeling in a semi-circle with Anne in the middle, so that as she knelt in line with them, she was behind the figure of the High Priestess, and in front of the Death-Stone.

Anne dimly perceived that there was now some elaborate ritual in which the Elders assisted, connected with the placing of the staff Keorah had carried inside the stone balustrade. There, it glowed like a corpse candle below the witch-like flame aloft. All that Anne could see of Keorah and the Virgins on either side of the High Priestess, was the shapeless outlines of their concealing cloaks and hoods; but of the Elders who who were in profile to her, she could discern, by the blue light of the Death-Stone, cadaverous features, and in four of them, long grey beards, the other three, of whom one was Kapoc, being apparently younger. Of the congregation, Anne could only catch, as her eyes roved sideways over her shoulders, partial glimpses; and in the uniform mass of black, it was impossible for her to conjecture the whereabouts of Hansen. She wondered whether he were present, and what had become of Kombo, who in face of the Death—Stone, must be a prey to the direst terror. But even these speculations regarding her only protectors relaxed their hold upon her attention as the service proceeded in motet and antiphon, Keorah's voice leading, the Elders and Virgins returning the phrase, which again was echoed in muffled tone by the bowed congregation. Anne had not prostrated herself after the manner of the Virgins upon either side of her, each of whom kept upon her arm a warning and detaining hand. She kneeled upright, a small stiff figure, staring about her, at first as best she could, beneath her overhanging hood, then with her gaze becoming gradually fixed in the direction of the Death-Stone in front of her. She tried not to look at it, but a feeling as though she were being mesmerized was gradually overpowering her. For, in the position in which she was placed, the blue light seemed to converge upon her, sweeping over the heads of the Virgins and Elders, and enveloping her head and shoulders as the ray passed and spread, growing wider till it was merged in the further darkness of the temple. And now, as the chant went on, an increasing sense of awe stole over Anne; she became more and more controlled by the pageant and its atmospheric conditions, and by something stronger and more compelling—the spirit, perchance, of this barbaric worship at which she was assisting. She felt herself at the feet of Xibal, Ruler of the Shades, and her heart went out in the supplicatory expressions of his ritual. All seemed grimly appropriate, terrifically real—the darkness of the temple, the black shrouds of the devotees, the absence of any altar or propitiatory offering beneath the bare triangular symbol—for what offering short of life itself can be acceptable to the Lord of Death? Everything impressed the novice painfully, and carried her beyond herself. Nothing but a curious upbounding of her heart within her as the thought of her companions crossed her mind, seemed left of the original blithesome Anne. Yet she was not afraid, nor did she even feel herself a lonely stranger in the midst of an adverse crowd, alien to herself though it was, in nature and in faith, but rather the momentary centre of primal elements, for which she had always in her bush wanderings been vaguely conscious. There were powers, she knew, which had in the beginning created order out of chaos, and who presided still over the appointments they had made, and the Faiths which served them. To their mighty aid, Anne trusted, lifting, amid her strange surroundings, her wordless petition for courage and support, with the appealing voices of the Aca. Involuntarily, then, she covered her head and bent her body in reverence, while the Hymn to Xibal rose and fell in ear-piercing cadences. At the time the strange, and, as they seemed to her, uncouth phrases, conveyed no meaning to her mind, but later on, she learned the interpretation of them.

HYMN TO XIBAL.

(Lord of Death.)

God of Shadows! Breath of Night!
Wielder of the dreadful might.
Quencher of our life and light.
Hear us, oh! Xibalba.

We are kneeling at thy throne.
By the shining blue Death-Stone;
List! the Aca make their moan
Unto thee, Xibalba.

Thou who hast so strong a hand.
That the face of all the land
Darkened is at thy command.
Spare us, Lord Xibalba.

Thou who leapest in the waves.
Thou who lurkest in the caves.
Thou who diggest deep our graves.
Slay us not, Xibalba.

Thou who makest ghosts of men;
Who may call, we know not when.
Man or maid from mortal ken, —
Hush thee, Lord Xibalba.

Thou who drawest in the breath.
Who art Lord of every death.
List to what the Aca saith; —
Rest thee now, Xibalba.

Sing we softly unto thee
Prayer and praise on bended knee.
That thy people may go free;
Waken not, Xibalba!

Sleep, Xibalba, sleep in peace!
Here, thy worship shall not cease
If thou lettest us increase;
We are thine, Xibalba.

When thou wakest, men must weep.
Therefore lull thee into sleep.
While thy slaves their vigil keep
Tremblingly, Xibalba.

We at length shall long for rest.
And creep, thankful, to thy breast.
Knowing that what is, is best;
Life or Death, Xibalba.

Which the greater mystery
Matters not; for we shall see
All that was, or that will be.
When we wake, Xibalba.

Though the night be dark and drear.
Yet the morning shall appear
Which shall make all meanings clear.
Even thine, Xibalba.

When our journeyings are past.
In one vision strange and vast
We shall understand at last
Death and Life, Xibalba.

Therefore sleep, oh! sleep in peace.
For thy worship shall not cease
Till we win from thee release

Eternally, Xibalba. Now in the half mesmeric condition in which the
blue light of the Death—Stone and the weird music had plunged her,
Anne became aware that the final invocation, repeated three times in
strains growing gradually fainter, was dying in a last long echo

through the vast hall, and with its expiring sigh, absolute silence reigned in the temple. The Virgins and the Elders were mute, with bowed forms, before the Death-Stone; the worshippers remained soundless and prostrate. Not a movement, not a breath fluttered the black, shrouded mass. The silence was deep and profound as the silence of the grave—the grave, no longer empty of life and given over to corruption, but filled with the spirit that is in itself all-being. Thus did the silence which spread through the place seem to Anne. How long it lasted she did not know. The awesome stillness, and the sense of an overpowering Presence that pervaded it, were to her the only realities of time and place. She was aroused at last by a faint stir, and a sound as of a long in-drawn sigh, telling her that the tension was relaxed. The priestesses kneeling on either side of her, pressed their hands again upon her arms, and, as they rose swiftly and noiselessly to their feet, she rose also. They turned, and Anne turned with them, facing the opposite end of the temple, where, in the far distance, she perceived a faint glimmering light coming, as she at first fancied, through a round window.

The nuns leading her, she descended the steps into the nave of the temple, which she now traversed along a broad clear space, between the rows of kneeling black-robed worshippers. Immediately after she and her conductors had passed, the people in each row rose and reversed their positions. Now in the rear, she heard music sounding again, not this time that of human voices, but the muffled clash of cymbals, and the rhythmic beat of some peculiar kind of drum, which gave back a curious hollow rumbling, and blended with the subdued tramp of feet upon the stone pavement. Anne dared not look behind her; she was too spell-bound to show curiosity, but she guessed that the Priestesses and Elders and others of the congregation were following her towards the glimmering round, which grew larger as she approached it, while the faint light it shed expanded and became clearer. A beautiful silvery radiance seemed struggling out of moving shadows like that of a full moon lightly veiled by clouds. She now saw that this end of the temple was also a sort of chancel, approached by steps, and partly screened by a row of pillars set at a considerable distance apart. The round window, as she had at first fancied it to be, was placed high—but not so high as the Death-Stone triangle opposite—in what appeared the terminal wall of the temple. But now she saw that it was not a window. It looked more like a disc of burnished metal, from the surface of which there leaped up pale little flames and white points of light, among which were brilliant, coloured specks, that shifted and changed like the multi-tinted fires in an opal. It was, in fact, an immense shield encrusted with opals of peculiar brilliancy.

Chapter XXVI—The Red Ray

PRESENTLY, they mounted the three deep steps leading to this second chancel, which she dimly perceived to be cut longitudinally by two rows of massive pillars showing cavernous recesses on either side. But the light was so faint, and the veil hanging over her eyes so impeded her vision, that Anne could form no definite conception of the place.

Suddenly, she was brought to a standstill upon a circular piece of pavement that showed light upon the dark stone flooring a few feet distant from, and slightly sideways to, the luminous disc. With swift, silent movements the two priestesses divested her of her shrouding mantle and hood, and threw back the veil which had covered her face, and which now hung from her shoulders over the simple robe of white linen in which they had dressed her for the ceremony. She saw that the priestesses had likewise taken off their outer black garments, and wore only the white dress of their order, and the gold tortoise studded with opals which clasped it on the breast.

Now that her veil was lifted, Anne could see more clearly in the milky light, which was like the early radiance of a summer dawn. Lifting her eyes, she was able to trace the moulding and projections in the high vaulted roof of the temple, which, though cut in the solid mountain, was elaborately carved in curious figures and hieroglyphs. A pale shaft of light gleamed down through a deep circular aperture in the ceiling directly over her, and she saw that the little tunnel slanted at such an angle, that the column of light issuing from it, struck directly the centre of the disc and accounted for the glimmering radiance which the burnished plate gave out, and which intensified as the dawn lightened. But there was not yet a beam of sunshine to kindle the milky luminosity of the disc. And now Anne saw that these were indeed opal fires, and that the great circular shield was literally a mass of these precious stones closely encrusting it, with one enormous opal of special purity in the exact centre. It seemed to Anne that on this stone the light was focussed.

Full of wonder and admiration, the girl lowered her dazed eyes to the body of the temple. Where, a little while ago, all had been blackness, there now showed a mass of white and colour. The dark coverings were shed, and the whole congregation stood clad in festal array facing the opal disc, and with backs turned to the Death-Stone, the blue light of which grew duller and duller as the dawn-light increased.

The clash and beat of cymbals and drums played in the rear by a band of acolytes, marked the advance up the broad open space of a procession of the Virgins and Elders, who were following Anne from the Triangle of Death to the Disc of Life. Keorah, at its head, walked alone with stately tread, her arms outstretched, bearing no longer the Staff of Death, but the golden Globe of Life, emblem of the Sun. Her russet hair fell over her shoulders upon her gorgeous mantle of office, and the Eye of Viracocha shone upon her forehead.

Very slowly, very solemnly, the procession came, moving to the rhythm of the cymbals and the drum's hollow beat, till, at a distance of three or four yards from the spot where Anne was stationed, Keorah halted. Then drums and cymbals ceased. The Virgins and the Elders stood motionless. The people fell on their knees again in silence. Three times the High Priestess raised and lowered the holy emblem she bore, in salutation to the Lord of Life. Then her shrill, sweet voice rang out in the opening phrases of a chant of which as before, the Virgins took up alternate stanzas. This hymn was less monotonous and dismal in character than the one they had sung before the Emblem of Death; but Anne, as she listened, not understanding the words, realized that it was of deep and solemn significance. It was, in fact, the prophecy of which the Priestess and the Elders had already spoken. Roughly translated into rhyme by Hansen later, it ran thus:—

THE PROPHECY.

When the night of our darkness is over at last.
When the light of the morning shall rise and appear.
When the time of our travail is finished and past.

Then the Daughter of Dawn, our Deliv'rer, draws near.
Viracocha shall send her, and guide her fair feet
Dry shod o'er the plain where the great seas have been;
And the People of Aca her coming shall greet.
Who shall serve as their Priestess, and rule as their Queen.
Fair Strength is her Sceptre, and Beauty her Crown:
By their mystical might, by the Sign that is true.
She shall lead forth the Aca in ancient renown.
From flame and from flood to a land that is new.
Then seek ye her smile; of her frown be afraid.
Lest alone ye are left in bereavement to mourn.
Hail! Hail to the Priestess, the Wonderful Maid.

To the Chosen of Aak, and the Daughter of Dawn. Anne listened intently, studying the expression of the chief singer in the hope that she might gain some clue to the meaning of the song. Keorah's long, oddly attractive face, with its peaked chin and strange eyes, enchained her attention for a time; then her gaze wandered to the shaft of light as it descended in a diagonal course from the opening overhead. Its beams did not touch the Priestess; but as they travelled towards the opal disc, Anne felt that her own head fell within their radius, and had the sensation of being bathed in light. It was as though a grey veil had fallen from Heaven upon her, a veil lit up momentarily by a myriad dancing sparks. As the brightness intensified, she became aware that the silvery column had faint flecks of gold, and knew that the sun must have risen, and was travelling in the heavens to a point where it would strike the opening, and pierce to the heart of the great Disc. She watched the column of light as it spread and deepened, with a child-like interest, wondering what it portended, and why it happened that she had been so placed as to directly intercept the blue ray of the Death-Stone and the glorious beam of the Giver of Life.

And now, caught by the phrasing of the chant, she looked again towards the singers, and the scene in the temple becoming gradually more broadly illuminated, she was conscious with a shock of surprise that all eyes were fixed upon her in an interest and anticipation, the sincerity of which was unmistakable. For the first time she realised that she herself was the centre of action and drama, and that upon her, and upon the great irradiated disc with which she was connected by that broad band of silvery light, all the thoughts and desires of the multitude were concentrated. Her mind scarcely took in what it all meant. Hansen had told her of the prophecy, and she had had a vague understanding of important issues at stake, of some ceremony and ordeal upon which her future would depend. But she had not expected that in this barbaric rite, as she had supposed it, there would come to her any deep religious awe, any sense of the working of unseen spiritual agencies. Yet this was what now came over her. The impression of something solemn and supernatural which had for the time overwhelmed her while she knelt before the Death-Stone, and which had passed away during her progress towards the Disc of Life, now returned with double force, and she stood as one in a dream, to whom has been vouch-safed a revelation from on high. Again, she was recalled to the scene in the temple by the dying down of the music, as it had been so far rendered in alternate stanzas by the Zuhua Kak and the Virgins of the Flame. The hymn closed with an invocation to the Deity, delivered first in another key by Keorah, and then chorussed by the whole assemblage. It was the Hallelujah to Viracocha, with which later, Anne became fully familiar.

"Uol Viracocha!" (Hail Viracocha!) "Oyoya Ku" (Thou art the Lord) "Zazil Huaca" (Thou Breath of Dawn) "Lahuna Ku" (Thou Lord of the Universe)

"Uol Viracocha!" And with a mighty shout, the congregation thundered once more.

"Uol Viracocha!"

Following upon the one-throated acclamation came silence—silence profound and all-embracing as that which had come after the Death-Stone chant—silence quick with possibility, a-thrill with long-deferred hope, on the very verge of fulfilment.

Anne's eyes went to the great disc, which now seemed to have become a circle of changing fire. The opal in its middle gleamed with a superb white light, and trembling in its heart was a small deep spark of red. Now she saw that a ray of pure sunlight had been caught and been imprisoned in the opening overhead. Just then the beam flashed down, almost blinding her with its glory. It moved direct to the centre of the disc, and there it kindled into flame the red spark which leaped up to meet it, till that which had been as a drop of rose-red blood became like the heart of a rose. Swiftly, tremulously, as the glow of sunrise spreads in the sky, the effulgence deepened and expanded till the dusky head and the pale shining face of Anne was lit up by the heavenly fire. Hushed were the eager people as they gazed, hushed were the Virgins and Elders, while Anne stood motionless amid the roseate light which lingered caressingly about her till the whole of the slender girlish form was bathed in unearthly brilliance. For several seconds did this illumination last, and then the magical rose-red radiance vanished, leaving only the silver light of morning, through which filtered the golden rays of the early sun.

A low murmur broke among the throng, gaining in volume till it seemed to shake the rock out of which the temple was cut. It was no invocation, chant, or acclamation of the gods, but the voicing of a people's emotion.

"Viracocha has spoken. It is the Sign! The prophecy is fulfilled. Behold our Priestess—the heaven-sent one. Daughter of the Dawn! Sister of the Stars. Beloved of the Highest. Server of Aak. Ix Nacan Katuna (May she be exalted). Chaac Zuhua Nakul! (White maiden for ever worshipped!") they cried, one and another, in many different keys, all stirred completely out of the characteristic apathy of the race. They waved their right arms towards the small erect form of the girl, whose pale face grew paler, and her dark eyes wider, as she realised the meaning of the gesture, and the act of homage which was implied, when simultaneously, each extended right arm was drawn back across the breast to the left shoulder, and everybody was bent in obeisance to her. She felt frightened, and yet an odd thrill of triumph went through her. She was glad that she had so successfully passed the ordeal; glad that she was chosen by the gods and by the people.

The hunter Hotan stepped forward and spoke the High Priestess' name, indicating that she also should do reverence to her newly-elected successor. Keorah's eyes blazed for a moment. She laughed harshly, drawing up her tall form, and rearing her stately head; then ignoring Anne, she turned and made a formal act of submission to Naquah, who stood at the group of Elders. The people applauded. There was a shout of "Hu Aca Tehua." Then Naquah, as spokesman of the Sacred Guardians, addressed Keorah.

"Thou hast seen the Sign, my daughter. Thou hast beheld the Red Ray descend upon the head of this stranger maiden. Thou knowest that the ancient prophecy is now made manifest, and that She for whom we have long waited has come among us. This is by the Will of Him the Unnameable, Who kindled the Eternal Fire, Who set the Wheel of Life revolving, Whose Doer is Viracocha, and His Intercesssor Aak.

"Not in wrath hast thou been set down, my daughter, from thy high place, but perchance in honour, that through thee and thy seed may the nation be blest. Since if thou who art surely Beauty dost mate thee with Fair Strength, from the twain of ye may spring a new race who perchance will give back to the people their ancient renown. I call upon thee, therefore, Keorah, who wast Zuhua Kak, to yield up the Sacred Emblems of thine office to her who has been chosen by the gods to serve in thy stead."

Again the High Priestess made formal submission.

"I hear thee, Naquah, and most willingly do I obey."

So saying, she passed out of the half-circle of Virgins and Elders into the vacant space which intervened between it and Anne, but halted half way and turned, facing the crowd with superb disdain.

"Hear me, ye people of the Aca! Did ye think that Our Lord of Dawn, and Aak the Intercessor, have withheld counsel from their servant? Of a surety it was revealed to me before the Flame descended, making known His Will, Who is Ku of the unutterable Name, and Whose vesture is the Sun. Of a surety, I say, was it shown to me that the priestess fore-ordained had come amongst ye. Was it for me to declare before the appointed time that which had been given unto me? Nevertheless, did these eyes behold and this tongue bear witness when I said to ye that gladly would I deliver the sacred symbols to her upon whom the sign should rest. For this did I cause the maiden to be placed within the Circle of Life, where, by the decree anciently graved, no woman born of the Aca may set her feet, save the High Priestess only—knowing as I knew full well, that this day should the Red Ray descend, and the Glory of our Lord the Sun be made manifest upon his chosen one. Therefore"—and she turned with outstretched arms towards the Disc of Life, and as she uttered the words of homage, raised and lowered the golden orb she carried as she had done before, in the act of salutation,—"Therefore, I, Keorah, Woman of the Aak, do give thanks to thee, oh! Moulder of Forms, Builder of the Universe, who doest the will of the Supreme, and art for ever to be obeyed by these thy children and thy servants. Worshipping, we beseech thee, Lord Viracocha."

Now she walked with stately gliding tread across the bare space, and standing before Anne, who was watching her with wondering eyes, she gave into the girl's trembling hands the golden globe, symbol of her own sacerdotal sovereignty. Then, loosening her gorgeous mantle of office, she laid it deftly on Anne's shoulders, whence it fell spreading on the ground, and quite enveloping the slender form. Afterwards, and always with the same quick, rhythmic movements, Keorah took the opal star from her forehead, and fastened it in the linen fillet that bound back Anne's short curls. There, reflecting a fuller ray of sunshine that suddenly struck and flashed back from the central opal of the disc, the Eye of Viracocha, as it was called, gave forth a brilliant beam of ruby fire from Anne's pale brow. Whereat the High Priestess bowed her head, and the Virgins, the Elders, and the congregation prostrated themselves anew, acclaiming yet louder the priestess marked out by the gods.

When the clamour had died down, Keorah, her eyes fixed upon the Disc, continued her prayer:—

"Oh! Viracocha Zazil, Lord of the Lower Light, thou who wast created in the beginning, and shalt exist unto the end; powerful and pitiful; who preservest our life and strength! Thou who art in the sky and in the earth, in the clouds and in the depths, hear the voice of thy servant, and grant this petition—the last which I shall make in the name of those gathered here.

"We beseech thee, oh Viracocha, on behalf of the maiden whom thou hast sent as thy messenger, to declare thy will to these thy people. Quicken, we pray thee, with thy spirit, the soul of her who is now thy priestess, to whom I have delivered this, the Emblem of thy greatness." She touched the golden ball as she spoke. "Clothe her in the garment of thy wisdom, even as I, thy server, have covered her with the vestment of my holy office. Lighten her eyes by the flame of thy glory, and kindle in her heart thy heavenly fire, even as thou hast kindled it in this jewel which thou didst fashion in the deeps of the earth, to be while the universe endures as an emblem of That which is unspeakable. Hear us, Viracocha!"

And the Hosanna echoed once more through the temple:—

"Uol Viracocha! Oyoya Ku; Zazil Huraca, Lahuna Ku: Uol Viracocha!"

Chapter XXVII—The Judgment of Aak

DEEPLY impressed by the solemnity of the scene, grasping imperfectly the meaning of Keorah's gestures, and her own investiture with the priestess' dignities, though of her words she understood scarcely anything, Anne stood dazed, wishful to comport herself befittingly, but wholly uncertain of what might now be expected of her.

From the people she heard a cry of "Aak!"—a vague tumultuous murmur, the exact drift of which was of course unintelligible to her. It was rendered by Naquah the Elder in a short address to Keorah, who bowed her head, and made a sign to Anne, which the girl interpreted as a command to her to move into the presence of the god. Horrible thoughts of something she had read concerning the Aztec rites occurred to her. She wondered if it could be possible that she was to be led out for sacrifice to the god Aak. A frightened cry escaped her, but was stifled. At least, whatever destiny might be in store for her, she would confront it bravely.

She looked round and down the temple, like a trapped and helpless child, who yet will not show that it is afraid. Oh! she thought anxiously, if only Eric were near to give her courage and to tell her what it all meant. There was a rift in the half circle of Virgins and Elders. The nuns were advancing up the chancel, the Elders following them. And now she saw that in the crowd below some stir was taking place—a break in the ranks, and a man pressing forward, while those behind tried to hold him back. This was a man dressed richly in the Aca costume, with a short feather-trimmed cloak and a head-dress of feathers. Anne did not realise till their eyes met, that the man was Hansen, whom Hotan had apparelled, according to the orders of Keorah, in the best his wardrobe furnished.

Anne's alarm changed to gladness. She stretched out her hands with the golden ball between them, signing him to approach. The men who were holding him back desisted from their efforts, but still kept their hold upon him, evidently considering that he had no right to advance beyond the line of pillars, into the space reserved for the priestly officials. Yet, according to the law of the order, when the High Priestess commanded she must be obeyed, and Anne was now practically speaking, High Priestess. For the ratification of her appointment, there remained only that she should be presented to and approved by Aak. For this the multitude waited, but there was little doubt in their minds as to the issue. The difficulty was settled by Keorah, who, becoming aware of the commotion, and also seeing Hansen, beckoned to him and bade him approach alone. As he did so, she motioned to him to stand at the rear of the Virgins, slightly before the Elders who had formed themselves into two lines between which he passed.

"Our Priestess needs instruction in the Aca tongue," said Keorah. "Till she has learned sufficient for the duties our Law requires of her, thy services as interpreter will be welcome. Wait and follow us in the order in which thou standest."

So saying, she stepped to Anne's left side, and, laying her hand on the girl's arm, pointed to a wide archway, elaborately sculptured, between the pillars, on the left of the Disc. Within, was a recess that seemed to be less dark and to stretch much further back than the corresponding ones nearer to her on the right. Anne saw, too, that the opening had a stone fretwork screen, and she wondered if this could be the sanctuary of Aak.

The small procession re-formed, while the populace in the body of the temple remained, pressing as closely as possible to the chancel steps with heads craned forward, so as to get as advantageous a view as possible of the presentation to Aak. The two Virgins who had conducted Anne walked in front, carrying lighted tapers which had been brought to them by one of the acolytes in waiting at the side of the Chancel. Next came Keorah leading Anne, and followed by the other four Virgins; next, Hansen, prepared to act as interpreter, and watching Anne with deep interest and anxiety as she walked very erect, an imposing little figure, with the golden globe in her hands and her mantle sweeping the pavement. Last, came the seven Elders.

Thus, they crossed the Chancel, all bending low before the Disc of Life as they passed, till Keorah stopped about a couple of yards from the screen of fretwork. Anne now saw that it had wide apertures, and that the tracery was entirely covered with raised hieroglyphic figures; also that the frame of the arch was extremely massive, and was elaborately sculptured in bold relief.

Keorah motioned to Anne that she must kneel, and she herself and all her following, devoutly bent the knee, except the two foremost priestesses, who advanced with their tapers close to the screen, and proceeded to light a series of earthenware lamps placed in niches at different heights behind the arch. At first, Anne's attention was entirely occupied with the carvings—some grotesque in design, some of great beauty, which showed strikingly against the softly diffused light of the oil-lamps. Then she became aware of a monstrous shape behind the screen—something huge, dark, indefinable of outline, which made her forget everything else, so that she would have risen from her knees had not Keorah's firm hand held her down, and she could only stare wonder-stricken through the wide apertures of the fretwork into the further dimness of the cavern. The enormous shape seemed to shake slightly, as, one by one, the lamps flickered and flamed, but it did not rise. Very slowly it stirred, and when the light became clearer, Anne descried an immense and ponderous oval, and fancied that she saw something like a head bend from side to side at one end of the great mass, which she now made out to be a gigantic, land turtle.

Hansen, peering between the kneeling Virgins—who, joined by the taper-bearers, had ranged themselves behind Keorah and Anne in two segments of a half circle with a space between—could hardly repress an exclamation of astonishment and delight. Here he beheld a living specimen of one of the antediluvian turtles, the fossil remains of which are to be found with those of the Icthyosarus and the Plesiosaurus in the great cretacean graveyard of Central Australia, that mighty ocean of the Mesozoic age. He longed for the Thing to come closer, but the monster remained motionless. Now Keorah pressed Anne's wrist, and said something in her ear, which the girl did not understand, nor the imperative gesture which accompanied the words. Keorah impatiently looked over her shoulder, and signed Hansen to approach.

As he came up between the kneeling maidens, Keorah spoke to him in low rapid tones, desiring that he would convey her directions to Anne. Kneeling on one knee behind the two, he whispered to his comrade rather more lengthily than Keorah's communication demanded.

"She says that you must sing to the great god Aak. Don't be frightened; he's quite harmless. Mercy on us—what a monster! From the look of his shell I should think he was born before the Flood. Little friend, you've done magnificently, and you're safe now. This is the end of the ordeal. Aak will accept you. Turtles are extremely sensitive to music." Anne's eyes spoke her gratitude and her joy at the sound of Hansen's voice again. But voice of her own she had none: it died in her throat. Keorah spoke again in authoritative tones. Hansen translated.

"She says that you are to hail the great god Aak as your Lord and Master, and to beseech him to signify his approval of you as his new priestess. You can't do better than copy her manner when she gave that prayer to Viracocha. It was very fine. I never expected that we should come across anything like this when I told you that we should find wonders at the other end of the tunnel."

Somehow, Hansen's exhortation, and his praise of Keorah's declamatory powers did not inspirit Anne as he had intended. She felt out of tune with the situation, and at her wits' end to know what she should sing that would be pleasing to Aak, the Tortoise-god.

"The Ave Baiamè," Hansen suggested. "Only—stay, let me think of a Mayan word that will scan, and give the right meaning. Ah! I have one! Itzàla. It means supporter of the earth. Ave Itzàla."

"Itzàla!" Keorah repeated the word suspiciously. He had to explain.

Evidently, Itzàla had no place in the Pantheon of the Red Men. She nodded acquiescently. Seeing her comrade's anxiety, and conscious of Keorah's cold bright eyes reading her face and darting glances first at her and then at Hansen, Anne found voice. Her notes were tremulous at starting, the "Itzàla" quavered, but as she went on, her voice gained volume and dramatic force. Notwithstanding, it was a spiritless performance, and neither Keorah, nor apparently Aak, as satisfied. The monstrous shape was scarcely agitated. Undoubtedly, the god gave no significant sign of approbation.

Keorah bent backward, and remonstrated in low sharp accents with the interpreter. He nodded, and again whispered to Anne.

"She says that is not enough. Aak is accustomed to loud singing and to violent gesticulation. You should raise your arms and act the suppliant. Screech. Do anything to pierce the Pachyderm senses. I know the creatures. They are vulnerable especially to sound, and they are curiously capable of attachment to humans. Little friend, throw yourself into the business. So much depends — for all of us — for science — on your success."

His words fired the girl to enthusiasm. Her dramatic instinct came to her help. She lifted her arms and swayed her lithe body in harmonious gesticulations. Her voice leaped to a higher key, to more ear-rending intonations. "Ave Itzàla," in the latest of its time-worn invocatory changes, would have melted the traditional rock. Anne's eyes grew larger and brighter as they strained into the cavernous depths of Aak's sanctuary.

She succeeded in making an impression. The great curved back of Leviathan shook like a world in convulsion. Slowy, slowly, the Thing upheaved itself. The ponderous mass rose higher, and gradually higher. Elephantine projections revealed themselves beneath, showing clubbed feet on short limbs uncouthly bent, which balanced the bulk with difficulty. Anne sang on as one inspired. She straightened her throat, letting her voice out to its full compass. She threw herself thoroughly into the part, forgetting that it was but a tortoise which she was straining every nerve to captivate.

Now the reptile's head, which had been partially indrawn, was protruded, thrust well out from under the mountain of shell, the slender horns, like those of an enormous snail, protruding; the face grotesque, yet strangely human, like that of a shrivelled old man in his dotage, with its sunken nostrils, its deep-set beady eyes, and heavy wrinkled lids. The thick creases of the throat smoothed as the telescopic neck lengthened itself. With restless movements the head darted blunderingly from side to side as the huge mass swayed, while the great feet slithered through the sand with which the floor of the cavern was thickly strewed.

So with its head facing the screen, its brilliant eyes flashing, as it seemed to the girl, answering glances to her own gaze, its small nostrils emitting a thin vapour, the Tortoise-god approached his new priestess. Placing one great foot heavily and carefully before the other, it came till it was within a few inches of the fret-work. Here it sank again, an inert mass, upon the sand, only its head moving, a smile of senile satisfaction upon its face. The eyes blinked ecstatically; the neck was thrust still further forward in Anne's direction.

With her heart beating high against the linen garment she wore, Anne sang on. In her soul was a strange blend of loathing, yet of fascination for the creature before her, and of pity for the ignorance of its worshippers. Was it possible that Keorah could believe this thing to be a god? She glanced sideways at the beautiful face with the inscrutable eyes that told her nothing. The High Priestess' gaze was fixed upon her, and Keorah's lips made a faint sound of approval. It seemed wonderful to Anne that Keorah should be glad to resign her place and power among the Aca people, though not so wonderful, perhaps, that she should be willing for another to supplant her in the favour of the beast. It must become monotonous, thought Anne, this singing to Aak—this travesty of worship. For a moment, Anne's soul quaked within her. Was she doomed to be hence—forth cooped up with the Tortoise, while Keorah enjoyed life, light, and freedom? If so, no wonder that Keorah was glad to escape. But she remembered Keorah's appearance on the balcony, how her word had been law, and how the people and the Elders had treated her almost as a queen. Then she—Anne—who was now Priestess, was to rule in Keorah's stead, and a burning desire came over her to master the situation, to show herself no mere puppet of circumstance, but a keenwitted ruler able to dominate events, and to turn her sovereignty to her own and Eric Hansen's advantage.

While these thoughts passed through her mind, her voice swelled louder in the concluding bars of her song; and the Tortoise, charmed by the melody, stretched his neck still further, and placed his nose upon the ledge of a piece of carving on the screen so near to Anne that his breath, rising in a little cloud from the dilated nostrils, stirred the feather trimmings of her cloak. The glittering eyes gazed into her face; then slowly, the creased lids closed over them, and the Tortoise remained motionless in a rapture of enjoyment. Horrible as was the shrivelled face on its snaky neck coming out of the great body, there was something even pathetic in the monster's abject subjugation by the voice of this small, proud, frightened girl.

As the last strains of the Ave died away, the breathless suspense of the crowd which waited below in the temple, found vent in a long low murmur, gathering in sound like the break of a wave on the shore. It was now for Keorah to inform the people that Aak had unmistakably signified his approval of the new priestess. She had drawn slightly to the rear, and was kneeling beside Hansen, watching him from between her narrowed eyelids. He seemed unaware of the scrutiny, so intently was his attention fixed upon the Tortoise and upon the result of the ordeal. Yet he felt in a subconscious way the magnetic influence she exercised over him and chafed against it, sensing emotional disturbance in her which must work for ill. In truth, Keorah's heart had been beating as wildly as that of Anne, though for a different reason. The nerve tension in her had been extreme. For her, too, the issue was momentous, although not in the manner that might have been supposed. She had been rejected, set aside in favour of a stranger, but she was by no means crestfallen. Rather did she seem the victor than vanquished.

She rose to her feet, and the other worshippers did so likewise. All made an obeisance to the Tortoise, which, at the conclusion of the song, had drawn in its head and was again lying, an inert mass, upon the floor of the cavern.

Naquah, at a few rapid words spoken by Keorah, motioned to Anne to come forward in the procession which now began to move. Keorah swept in advance of it to the edge of the chancel steps, and stood for a moment or two without speaking—a most striking figure in her plain linen robes with no mantle but her splendid hair; no jewels but those on the zone which clasped her waist. Nevertheless, she seemed more beautiful in her simple attire than in all her former panoply. And, unaccountable though it appeared, Keorah's face wore an irrepressible look of elation, and there was a ring of triumph in her voice, as she cried out three times:—"Manel! Manel! It is done. At the Will of Viracocha, the Flame burned. Aak beheld the Sign, and bowed before it. The gods have chosen their Priestess. Behold the Zuhua Kak!"

Chapter XXVIII—Ix Naacan Katuna

THE new Priestess of Aak had, for the present at least, done all that was required of her in regard of the Tortoise-god, and for the remainder of the day was released from duty. She had been initiated in her office by Keorah, who afterwards, formally renounced her sacerdotal functions. Then the late High Priestess quitted the temple by the public entrance and went to her own house inherited from her father, there to retire into private life so far as might be possible in the case of one who was secularly, the richest and most important lady in the Aca community. For it had till now been the custom that she who was chosen among the Virgins of the Flame to be High Priestess, should be an orphan belonging to the wealthy and ruling class. Keorah, therefore, was a woman of distinction and property, and her apartments in the nunnery, where Anne was now to be installed, had been occupied merely officially, her actual residence being one of the largest of the cave dwellings which looked out upon the market-place, and was connected by a private corridor with that in which other six Virgins lived.

Thus Anne, some little time after her presentation as the Zuhua Kak, was returning from the temple, escorted by the maidens bearing their lighted torches, along the passage she had traversed a few hours before, behind Keorah and the Staff of Death. Neither this mysterious symbol nor the golden Globe of Life was carried in the returning procession. Each was laid in its appointed place beneath the triangular Death-Stone and the opal Disc. Anne was now parted from Hansen. He had tried to remain near her on plea of acting as interpreter, but Keorah, in a last exercise of authority, had dismissed him under charge of Hotan, when the crowd dispersed on conclusion of the religious ceremony, to prepare for the games and banquet which were always part of this annual festival of the Aca.

Anne felt very much the loneliness of her position, but she was still eager and interested. She greatly regretted that she had not Hansen's knowledge of Mayan, so as to be able to talk with the nuns and understand what was going on around her. Her only friend seemed the young priestess who, on the previous evening, had taught her a few Mayan words, and laughed over their English equivalents. There was a natural sympathy between herself and this girl, who was bright and attractive. Her name, Anne learned, was Semaara — signifying arrow — and she was very pretty, with merry grey eyes and a dimple at the corner of her rosy lips. She reminded Anne a little of her own sister Etta.

The procession halted before a wide stone archway hung with feather—embroidered curtains. Two of the maidens drew these apart, and all six ranging themselves, made obeisance, and indicated that the Zuhua Kak should pass between them into the abode which was now her own. Anne found herself in a large, low room, hollowed out of the rock, and with a great opening in front which gave upon a balcony — the same balcony whence Keorah had spoken to the people on the previous afternoon. She at once grasped the fact that these were the High Priestess' quarters, and was not ill-pleased with their aspect. From the larger room, opened an inner one, evidently a sleeping chamber, the curtains of which were also drawn aside by the Virgins. This appeared to be sumptuously furnished in barbaric fashion; so, too, the room in which she stood. The stone floor was strewn with rugs of skin and feathers, the walls were partly painted in bold designs, partly hung with feather tapestry. There were divans with fine skins and handsome cushions; sideboards jutting from the rock walls, and sculptured and adorned with lamps and utensils in a metal Anne imagined to be gold; some stools there were, too, and small tables, on one of which to Anne's delight, stood a large earthenware bowl filled with tastefully arranged flowers. Dishes of fruit and cakes were laid upon a side table; and when she saw them, Anne realised that she was hungry, and might have echoed Kombo's formula "Niai Kandu," invariably uttered at the end of a march. Semaara saw her glance and laughed, saying something to one of the other nuns, who clapped her hands loudly. Whereat, a tall maiden clad in a scanty gown of rough linen, appeared, and after receiving her orders, went out again, returning presently with a dish of pasties which were made of some kind of meat—kid, Anne thought—wrapped in maize dough, fried and flavoured with chilies—exceedingly appetizing, as the new High

Priestess found when she tasted them. Meanwhile, with much ceremony, Semaara had divested Anne of the Zuhua Kak's gorgeous mantle, had brought water in a pottery basin, and a fringed towel, and washed the Priestess' feet, shoeing them with delicate sandals. The novelty of being so waited on delighted poor Anne after her long wanderings and rough sojournings among the blacks; while to be clad in cool fresh garments of linen in contrast with her cast-off fibre petticoats and shreds of underclothing, was joy beyond compare. It was extremely pleasant to have a meal set before her that had not been cooked over a camp fire, and to which she had the seasoning of pounded rock salt. She found the various condiments in which the Acans seemed to indulge, as well as their culinary methods, excellent, and she greatly enjoyed a drink which Semaara poured from a metal jug—an effervescing mixture that was slightly alcoholic. On the whole, Anne began to think that her lot as High Priestess of the Aca would prove fairly endurable.

The other priestesses did not eat with her, but attended to her wants, busying themselves otherwise in the arrangement of her chamber. Anne found them stiff and silent, till she discovered that it was not etiquette for them to speak till addressed by her. She then tried by signs to encourage them to talk, but without much success. The eldest Virgin, who had received Anne on her arrival in the house, and whose name was Ishtal, seemed rather a formidable person, much more sedate than the rest. Anne had the impression that this woman resented the deposition of Keorah, and was scandalized at her own unavoidable outrages of Acan decorum. Semaara was certainly the one whom Anne liked best, and who, she proposed to herself, should teach her the Acan language. Already she was learning the names of different objects in the room.

Presently the maidens all retired, leaving Anne alone to rest for an hour. Coming back about noon, they re-robed her in the gorgeous mantle which the poor Priestess would gladly have left behind, it was so cumbersome, and ill-suited to her little figure. But Ishtal was aghast at the suggestion, and Anne gathered that the mantle was an outward sign of the dignity she had to maintain. She was also decked in a head-dress of rose-coloured feathers, in the front of which was fastened the sacred opal.

Now they passed through the outer room, and descended the rock-hewn staircase. Down in the market-place a well-dressed crowd was gathered, and hilarity of a subdued kind prevailed—the Aca were not apparently a frolicsome race. At sight of the new High Priestess all became on the alert, but there was less curiosity than might have been supposed. The procession of Virgins crossed the space, Anne as Zuhua Kak, according to etiquette, walking alone, with the other maidens immediately behind. She was uncertain what to do or where to go, and violated custom again by calling Semaara to her side.

From Semaara she gleaned by means of signs something of what was going on, and what was expected of her. Thus she dimly ascertained that outside the temple and the nunnery—from which abode men were excluded—the High Priestess was more or less her own mistress, and by no means debarred from secular amusements, though compelled always to keep up a certain state and dignity. Now she discovered that games and feats of skill were to be performed beyond the walls of the city, and that to this entertainment she and her maidens, as well as the crowd were bound. Anne, though a little bewildered, was pleased at the prospect, for now she saw an opportunity of talking to Hansen, and getting him to explain to her the exact significance of the temple rites, and the extent of her power, which she was beginning to think might be considerable. She also wanted to know what had become of Kombo.

The black boy himself answered that question. At the corner of the temple street he darted from beside a booth, where he had been regaling himself on maize cakes and fried plantains, given him at the expense of a small crowd which was amused at his antics. The Priestess' procession had now been joined by the seven Elders and their attendant acolytes, who formed a sort of guard round the Virgins of the Flame. Bursting through them, Kombo, a ragged

Bacchanalian figure—for it had not been considered necessary to provide him with fresh garments—accosted his mistress.

"Yai! Yai! Missa Anne!" he cried out. "Where you been sit down all night? What for you no look out for Kombo? Mine been stop long-a verandah. Ba'al mine sleep. Plenty tugra (cold) this fellow. Ba'al mine been have-im supper—ba'al breakfast. Ba'al mine find-im Massa Hansen. Mine want-im go long-a church, like-it Red Man, but that fellow make Kombo yan (go away). Cobbon woolla (much talk). Plenty angry long-a Kombo. Ba'al me pidney. Mine no understand. Missa Anne, you tell Red Man that Kombo brother belonging to you."

Then a sudden sense of incongruity seemed to strike Kombo. He stopped, uttered long-drawn ejaculations, and stared in wonder and delight at Anne's magnificent array.

"My word! Bujeri you, Yuro Kateena! Bujeri dress belonging to you! Where you got-im that fellow? Tsck! Tsck! What that big stone with fire inside, like-it crown? I b'lieve you Queen same as big Missus long-a water. Yai! Bujeri feather! Bujeri blanket!" and Kombo stretched out a black sacriligious hand and stroked Anne's mantle of office. Whereat the Priestesses exclaimed, but tittered the while, and the Elders, frowning, spoke angrily in their own language.

Anne mollified them by a gentle smile and a bar or two of recitative—which produced obeisances from the seven Guardians and the acolytes—then waved Kombo a little to one side. But as she did so, she murmured—

"You been see Massa Hansen, Kombo?"

"Yoai," (yes), replied the black boy. "You look out, Missa Anne. I b'lieve big Red Mary want-im that fellow for Benjamin belonging to her." Which was Kombo's manner of reporting that Keorah had begun the wooing of Hansen.

"My word! He got-im bujeri blanket too! Poor fellow me!" went on Kombo discontentedly. "Ba'al mine got-im blanket—ba'al coat— ba'al trouser!" He gazed down ruefully at his naked legs over which hung the tattered remains of his grey flannel shirt. "Mine want-im blanket; mine want-im Red Mary like-it, Massa Hansen."

Kombo's gestures were eloquent; his need of clothes evident.

Anne signed to Semaara, who gave an order in which Anne recognised the words Zuhua Kak, and knew that it purported to come from herself. A booth-keeper, dressed in the dun coloured linen and short cloak worn by middle-class Acans, ran forward with a bundle of garments from his stall, such as were supplied to the common folk. Kombo speedily grasped the situation, and chose the brightest coloured of the tunics—a dull red one, which he put on forthwith amid the amused comments of the Acans. The tunic descended to Kombo's knees, and pleased him vastly, but the short cloak was not to his liking. He wanted a mantle like those worn by Anne and the Elders; and when one made of coarse linen with a feather fringe was at last provided for him, he donned it with supreme satisfaction, folding it round him, and strutting proudly as the camp blacks used to do when they were presented with red and blue blankets on the Queen's birthday. The booth-keeper brought him a bowl of water to wash himself in, and a flat red cap, like those worn by the huntsmen. He then took his place calmly in the High Priestess's procession, Anne signifying by commanding gestures that he was her slave and must attend her. She now saw that her word would be considered law, though it was clear that the Elders did not approve of Kombo as her body servant, and that the Virgins were a little shocked. Ishtal looked severe, but Semaara laughed as Kombo openly ogled the young priestesses, and made diffident overtures to one whom he specially admired, but who rebuffed him with haughty astonishment. Presently, the great natural portals in the rock wall of the city were passed, and the country on the north-western side of the Tortoise Hump opened out before Anne's view. It seemed to her like an immense garden enclosed by walls of basalt, which must have been a thousand feet in height. Nothing could be imagined more different than this cultivated earth-basin; from the barren fastnesses, the desert tract, and the valley of desolation which they had traversed on the other side of the Acan territory. For some way beyond the overhanging rock carapace of the Tortoise, the ground spread in a broad level terrace, part of which was artificially raised. Then the land dipped gradually to a round plain, like the bottom of a platter, which was covered with fields and farms. The inaccessible precipice walled it on all sides, except for a narrow gap, that seemed to have been cut by Nature's hand to admit the passage of a river which watered the plain, and here boiling up in impassable rapids flowed between the cleft barrier out into the country beyond. It was the same river that had forced its subterranean way beneath the desert sands, and had reappeared in the heart of Aak. Now it emerged into daylight a little way from the great head of the Tortoise, where, falling down miniature precipices and over beds of water-worn stones, it wandered through fields of Indian corn, hemp, flax, and vegetables, and irrigated plantations of cocoa, bananas, palms, and many other tropical products, including a species of aloe, from which the wanderers learned later that fibre cloth and a spirituous liquor, similar to the Mexican mescal, were obtained. On the downs, and where the land was uncultivated, it was covered with the natural Australian forest. Yet even this seemed unlike ordinary bush; the gum-trees were larger and more spreading, and among them were palms and other varieties of vegetation. Along the river banks were belts of scrub, and in the clearings nestled wooden homesteads, the dwellings of goatherds and farmers, for Anne distinguished many flocks of the same species of chamois that had lured Hansen to the Place of Death. These animals appeared to be the only ones domesticated among the Aca, for of horses and cattle there were none to be seen.

But such characteristic features of the place were not then fully borne in upon Anne, as in truth she had no time for more than a sweeping survey of this fertile champaign. Before and behind her own procession, the crowd was pressing onward to a point on the terrace where the mountain hollowed inward, and again gave the effect of an amphitheatre. In the semi-circular curve banked up by the precipice, seats had been hewn in stages up to a certain height in the rock, while at the other end, only a low wall and abutting platform interfered with the splendid view of plain and distant hills to the horizon line. No more perfect situation could have been chosen for an out-of-door theatre.

The arena was level, and strewn with fine sand. At one point in the circle was an erection which appeared to be a judges' stand. Here, amid a group of Acans, the chief of which was Hotan, Anne saw Hansen seated. He looked extremely well, she thought, in his Acan dress, and was conversing cheerfully with Hotan. It was a relief to her, though she would hardly have confessed this to herself, that at least he was not a captive in the train of Keorah. She expected that he would at once descend and take his place beside her, but etiquette evidently forbade such a proceeding, and he merely followed the example of Hotan and his friends, who all rose and made a ceremonious obeisance, standing while she passed.

A burst of strange music from a row of performers beneath the stand greeted the priestesses on their entrance. It was scarcely harmonious, and Anne eyed curiously the instruments of the musicians. These seemed mostly of the nature of drums; some huge, and made of skin stretched over the hollowed segment of a tree trunk, which stood between the knees of the players, and when beaten, gave out a wild reverberating note; others were smaller and tinkling in sound. There were also flutes, and an instrument like the Egyptian sistrum, as well as a very primitive kind of violin, also made from a hollow stem of a tree, with catgut strings, the wail of which was uncanny, but not unpleasant. To the accompaniment of this strange orchestra, an anthem was sung by the populace all standing—a hymn specially dedicated, it seemed, to the Zuhua Kak, this title recurring continually in the refrain with the phrase, "Ix naacan katuna!" (May she be for ever exalted!).

The spectators spread themselves in two rows round the upper end of the amphitheatre, the empty rock seats rising in tiers behind them, showing that the place had been originally constructed for the accommodation of a much greater number. In the very centre of the half circle, a wide deep space seemed to be reserved for the people of highest rank and importance. Here was a raised dais, approached by rock steps, carpeted with skins and having cushioned seats. About fifty smiling well-dressed men and women occupied the dais—the rank and fashion, no doubt, of the Acans—who all rose and formally saluted the Zuhua Kak and her train. From this dais, three or four more steps led to a higher platform, in the middle of which was a stone arm-chair projecting from the other seats—the throne of the High Priestess—and into this Anne was inducted with considerable pomp. The Virgins ranged themselves behind her; the Elders had their places at the sides immediately below; and Kombo, who would have stationed himself among the ladies beside his mistress, was sternly motioned by Naquah to squat on the lowest step at her feet.

Anne's eyes, wandering on either side of the lower dais, were not long in discovering Keorah. The late High Priestess was seated in a private compartment which had its own approach by a small flight of steps, and was surrounded by a goodly company of attendant men and maidens. She was certainly, with the exception of Anne herself, the most important lady present; and though she had resigned the fenced-in state of the Zuhua Kak, it was in favour of a splendid and probably more enjoyable dignity.

Her appearance was magnificent. Though the Eye of Viracocha no longer blazed on her forehead, she wore a coronet of very fine opals, and the pale yellow and bright orange plumes above it were even more becoming than those of the sacred rose. Her mantle was a gorgeous work of art, being like her linen robes—these not now of the virginal white—richly embroidered in a design of variously coloured feathers, which gave the suggestion of some wonderful tropical flower. Her hair, unbound, rippled over her shoulder in waves of ruddy gold; her waist was girdled with opals; and to protect her face from the sun's rays she carried a large fan of lyre birds' feathers, set in a golden handle.

She smiled at Anne, but there was nothing cordial about the smile. There seemed, indeed, to be mockery in her salutation; and to Anne, who had been amused and interested at the whole spectacle, and was enjoying the honour paid her, this reminder of her rival's presence came disagreeably.

Though Keorah had yielded the sacerdotal palm, it was plain that she intended rivalry in more mundane matters, and her look seemed to say that Anne should pay dearly for the dignities thrust upon her. Momentarily dismayed, her girlish pleasure sharply checked, Anne stood without movement, gazing gravely at Keorah's taunting loveliness; then the Marley blood reasserted itself, her natural pride arose, and with a sufficiently gracious, but decidedly condescending bend of the head, she signified her acceptance of and response to Keorah's salute.

Chapter XXIX—Zaac Tepal

BUT now a clangour of the drums announced the commencement of the games. The first of these was very pretty, a sort of Queen of the May dance round a tall pole ornamented with many garlands of differently coloured flowers, the object of the dancers, who were men and girls fancifully attired, being to entwine and disentangle the garlands in so deft a manner that in the last figure all remained in the hands of one performer, to whom was adjudged the prize. After this, came games of ball in which the women also joined. But Anne was less interested than she might have been in the exhibition of their skill, for she was wondering all the time when Eric would come and speak to her; and though she scarcely liked to send for him, she had a doubt lest, because of her semi-royal position, he would wait for her to summon him. She made surreptitious signs to Semaara, anxious to ascertain whether the social conventions of the Acans would permit her to do so. But Kombo's agile wits had already jumped to the situation, and before he could be restrained, the black boy had dashed down the rock stairway and along the arena to the judges' stand, shouting as he went:

"Yai! Yai! Massa Hansen! Yuro Kateena want to pialla white brother belonging to her. You come along, Massa Hansen. You tell Missa Anne what Red Men say. Kombo plenty stupid. Ba'al me pidney— me no understand. My word! Plenty coola (angry) that old man Naquah long-a me. Ba'al that fellow brother belonging to Kombo."

Kombo in his trailing blanket and Acan cap, in which he had contrived to stick an emu's straggling feather, the expression of his face a blend of cunning, vanity, and consternation, was a sufficiently comical figure to draw some exclamations of amusement from the Acans; and when he pointed to Naquah and mimicked the Sacred Guardian's wrathful demeanour, the people laughed outright, though they lowered their heads immediately afterwards, shocked at their own temerity. Hansen, choking with merriment, came down from beside Hotan, and made his way to where Anne sat enthroned. But he was not prepared for her adroit wielding of the reins. He had expected to find her bewildered and uncertain how to act, and he was surprised to see the winning yet authoritative gesture by which she soothed Naquah's wounded pride, and while rebuking Kombo, made it evident that, as her personal attendant, she required that consideration should be shown to him.

Hansen realised with a start that this splendidly arrayed and extremely regal little person was a different Anne from his brave but draggled "Chummy," in fibre petticoats and opossum-skin mocassins, who, tired, hungry, and sometimes despondent, had trudged by his side over the ranges and across the desert. Again he told himself that the Marley stuff was showing in her; and it pleased him to observe how her western polish and air of stately courtesy were, unconsciously to themselves, impressing the people among whom she had dropped so strangely.

He uncovered and bowed, standing in a respectful attitude before her. She motioned to Semaara to bring forward a stool, upon which he placed himself, and they talked in low tones while the games went on, their voices drowned by the roll of the drums and the shrieks of the flutes and stringed instruments. Hansen was intensely interested in the sports and manners of the people.

"Not so very far behind us, are they," he said, "for the remains of a civilisation that was started here, perhaps, about the time that the Phoenicians discovered tin in Cornwall, and which has never moved out of this corner since? It's wonderful, Anne. They haven't the remotest idea of any other country in the world beyond the traditions of an earthly paradise from which their first progenitors were expelled about the Adam and Eve period. I wonder if Le Plongeon is right, and if this is the origin of the story of Cain and Abel? They keep asking me whether you have come from that Eden, and if you are going to lead them back there."

"I should encourage that idea," said Anne, calmly. "It will further our chances of escape. By all means study the Children of Aak as much as you please, Eric. Personally, I should like to find the mine from which these opals were dug."

"I've been talking to Hotan," rejoined Hansen, "and getting him to tell me everything he can about the history of the race. Hotan is not a bad chap, but he has got the hump, because when we were coming along here, Keorah—your predecessor in the priestly line—snubbed him finely."

"Ah!" said Anne, softly.

Hansen might have augured a good deal from the tone of her voice, but on this occasion he was singularly lacking in perception.

"That's a queer study of a woman, Chummy," he went on, "considering that she has been evolved from what one might call barbarism. She is a consummate woman of the world, and I don't think that Europe would have much to teach her in the art of flirtation."

"And so you find her attractive, Eric!" laughed Anne.

"Don't you?" he counter-queried.

Anne laughed again in a way that puzzled him.

"I imagine that as a study, the lady would naturally prove more interesting to you," she answered. "I am not a man, and so I have not the masculine admiration of a flirtatious woman. Besides, you forget, I don't understand the language."

"Do you mean the language of flirtation, Chummy? No; you're a deal too simple and sincere for that!" Anne flushed.

"I meant the language of the Acan people, of course," she replied.

"That's not so difficult. I can teach you that, at all events. We must find a way of meeting that is not in public. Unfortunately, Hotan gives me to understand that no men are allowed in the house of the Virgins of the Flame."

"Virgins of the Flame!" repeated Anne. "Is that what they are called? It is a pretty title."

"That is the meaning of Zuhua Kak," he answered.

Anne crimsoned again. "But I—" she began.

"You are the chief of the Zuhua Kak, but you are a married woman—is that what you are thinking? Well, we needn't announce the fact; it might upset things. And we must have time to learn everything we can about this delightfully odd race. Think of the lecture I shall give before my college! We shall be the most famous persons in the world, Anne, when we get back."

"We have got to get back first," she said, philosophically. "Tell me, Eric—I want to know the exact meaning of the prophecy that relates to me, and which evidently induced them to choose me as priestess to that horrible tortoise."

"Horrible! It is a living specimen of the fossil Mewlania—the great horned turtle now extinct but for this monster. Aak may not be beautiful, but he is a stupendous fact in natural history. I have been questioning Hotan, but there is no record of the age of Aak. They say, 'He has always been, and there is no other of his kind.' Oh! If I could transport him bodily to Europe!"

Anne smiled at the idea of Aak dragging his gigantic bulk across the desert and over the ranges through the scrub.

"If I am to lead the people to a new land," she said, "what is to become of Aak?"

"I don't know. I am afraid the prophecy doesn't mention how we are to deal with such a difficulty."

"Tell me what the prophecy says," she asked again.

"I'll translate it roughly. I've been jotting it down, and amusing myself by trying to turn it into verse. Here it is," and he gave her his version of Keorah's song. Anne repeated some of the lines after him.

"Fair Strength is her sceptre, and Beauty her crown." She thought to herself that in both these things Keorah greatly excelled her. Like most small dark women, Anne admired the blonde Junoesque type, and placed no store upon the fashion of her own comeliness.

"I am not beautiful," she said, and glanced involuntarily towards Keorah, whose eyes were watching her and Hansen. An idea struck her.

"Are you `Fair Strength?" she exclaimed, suddenly.

He smiled in a slightly embarrassed manner.

"Do you know that is what they already call me. I have been christened Zaac Tepal, meaning literally, the white, strong man."

Anne was silent, pondering his words. In her mind, she went over the prophecy. The phrase, "She shall serve as their priestess, and rule as their queen," gave her pause.

"Since they have made me queen," she said to herself, "I must rule as one—if we are ever to get away from here." Aloud she repeated, "Zaac Tepal! They give curious names, these people. Do you not hear, Eric—they are calling it down there—they are calling for you. We ought to have been watching the games; it is rude to talk. What is it they want?"

Hansen listened to the hoarse roar of the crowd. Above it, shouts arose of "Zaac Tepal!" A spokesman, standing in the arena just below Keorah's box, was making a little speech in Mayan.

The spokesman was Hotan. He appeared defiant and excited. When he had finished his speech, he looked towards Anne's dais, and called also upon Zaac Tepal. Hansen rose. Then Keorah's shrill, sweet voice sounded high, hushing the clamour. She stood in front of her box, and addressed Hansen by his new name, evidently putting forth a proposition that brooked no denial. Hansen made a courtly salutation, and replied as fluently as he was able.

"They have delivered a challenge," he hurriedly explained to Anne. "This is the High Priestess' prize, to be competed for by the two strongest men chosen by the people. They've selected Hotan and me as the combatants. It is a wrestling match."

"But can you wrestle, Eric?" asked Anne, anxiously. "It won't do for you to be defeated."

"I think I may be a match for Hotan," he replied, grimly. "I know something about it, at all events. Of course, I must accept the challenge. Wish me well, Chummy."

He went down the steps into the arena, and Anne watched him stop on the way and speak to Keorah. No doubt he was receiving directions from the donor of the prize. Presently, he and Hotan disappeared. Anne supposed that preliminaries of the contest were being arranged. The drums blared once more. Two acolytes meanwhile approached her, bearing banners worked in feathers, and some small metal boxes. To her surprise she saw that they contained a kind of bean of a bright crimson, speckled with black, which she knew very well, though every year it is growing rarer in the Australian scrub. These beans are hard, and bright as precious stones, and are much esteemed as ornaments among the blacks. Semaara tried to convey to her that the Acans used them instead of money; but Anne only understood that the boxes containing them, also the banners, were to be presented as prizes to the winners in the maypole dance and the game of ball. She realised that she was to give the prizes, and presently the recipients appeared.

Two were youths, and two, women, of the Aca, wearing the fanciful attire of the performers in the dance and games—a combination of feathers and flowers adorning the tunics of the men and the linen drapery of the women. They prostrated themselves upon the steps of the dais, and then kneeled before Anne in a reverential attitude, with hands outstretched, the palms open. Semaara took the gifts from the acolytes, and handed them to the High Priestess, signifying their destination. It was an awkward moment for the poor untrained High Priestess, who did not know the Acan formula for such occasions, and who saw that the spectators were gazing expectant, at once curious and dissatisfied. It flashed into Anne's mind that Keorah would have acquitted herself admirably, and she was suddenly stimulated by the desire to emulate her rival. She determined to resort once more to melody, the charm of which never failed her. She sat very erect upon her throne, a small but stately stage-queen, and as she waved each banner over the head of its winner, and laid the box of beans on each extended palm with slow impressive gestures, she sang a few lines of such operatic airs as, on the spur of the emergency, occurred to her. Her voice was strong and clear, and the music was so unlike that to which the Acans were accustomed, that the crowd was at first startled and then enthralled. Hansen too was startled as he listened and watched, standing by Keorah's box. But his surprise was at this fresh exhibition of Anne's readiness and power. He had not even an impulse to laugh at the incongruity of many of the operatic words with the scene, so soul-stirring was Anne's delivery of them. He caught the infection of the multitude, and joined heartily in the "Uol, Zuhua Kak!" (Hail! Great Virgin of the Flame!) which echoed from the rock walls of the amphitheatre, as the winners of the prizes retired backward from the dais, and the brief ceremony was concluded.

His own turn had now come, and, throwing off his mantle, he stood, clad in the tight-fitting Acan jerkin, facing his opponent Hotan, in the sand—strewn space of the arena.

It was an exciting contest; horrible, Anne thought, to witness, as the two powerful bodies writhed and struggled, closing upon and entwining each other like two pythons in deadly embrace. Nevertheless, she could not turn away her eyes for a second, though her face went white as chalk. Keorah, on the contrary, flushed with excitement and pleasure, was watching with the fierce zest of some old-time Roman lady who had staked her jewels on her pet gladiator.

The men were evenly matched in point of muscle, but Eric was the better skilled of the two. So it came about that Hotan was overthrown, and that Hansen advanced amid the shouts of the populace to receive his guerdon from Keorah. The Acans were not wholly pleased. Hotan was a favourite, and had been their acknowledged champion. For several years past Keorah had clasped on his arm the golden bracelet which, by Acan custom, was the High Priestess' prize at this special annual festival. Therefore there was some feeling of resentment that it had been won by a stranger, repressed only on account of the general belief that the new Priestess and her interpreter were favoured by the gods. Keorah, however, was scarcely applauded when her fingers placed the armlet below Hansen's elbow.

With one knee on the ground, the Dane bent his head and kissed the hand that had decked him. This courtesy, so common in Europe, was quite unknown among the Acans, as it is among many so-called savage nations to-day. Its effect upon Keorah was sudden and unexpected. As Hansen's lips pressed her skin, he instantly felt the nerve-thrill that ran through her. The blood rushed to her face; her wild nature was set aflame. With difficulty she commanded herself. Looking up, he saw the blush, and his eyes met hers. Again he was affected by their odd fascination. She said some words in a low voice.

"It is well that we speak the same tongue, Zaac Tepal—white lord of the strong arm. By right of this token, I may claim thy fair strength in my service if I require it. Say, then, that we are friends."

"I am deeply honoured, Priestess," replied Hansen. "Since thou accordest me thy friendship, the strength of my arm is assuredly thine, though in this peaceful community, and seeing in how great esteem thou art held, it seems to me that there will be small need of such service."

Keorah smiled slowly, her eyes narrowing between their thick-fringed lids, which, with the slight uplifting of her pointed chin, gave a most attractive and yet malign expression to her long face.

"How know we what may come, Zaac Tepal?" she answered. "Since yesterday even the order of things has greatly changed amongst the Acan people. And thou art wrong to call me 'Priestess.' Yonder sits thy Priestess. I am no longer Zuhua Kak, but a simple woman with no claim to honour but that of woman-hood."

"To the most beautiful of women, then, I tender my homage," said Hansen, with thoughtless gallantry, but he almost repented the words when he saw the flush mount anew to Keorah's cheeks. Yet he was a man, and he felt flattered. Besides, as he looked at her, he could not help feeling that the compliment was not an exaggeration. She was beautiful; he really had never seen a woman with so strange a power of fascination. And he liked her thin sweet voice, which resembled certain high-pitched notes of a stringed instrument, and seemed to suit so well the language she spoke.

"I thank thee, my lord stranger," she said. "It is well that thy heart inclines thee, for according to custom of my people, the winner of this prize," — and she touched the bracelet on his arm, — "is specially bound to do the giver's bidding until the Festival of the Sun returns again. For some time past it has been Hotan's part to render me such small services as a woman may need, but now the office is transferred to thee. Tonight, therefore, thou shalt sit by my side, and in our converse together we will become better friends. I would learn somewhat of the land thou hast left, and if it irk thee not, I would have thee talk to me of the world beyond the seas, and of the men and women who dwell therein. For I am weary, oh! Zaac Tepal, of the shut-in homes and the narrow thoughts of my people of the Aca. Fain would I hear what earth holds beyond the walls of our City of Refuge, wherein, ages back, the Great Builders imprisoned our race, for fear of Kàn, the venomous serpent; though it seems to me," and she laughed derisively, "that the venom of that rock monster hath long since departed. I confess to thee that my body craves and my soul yearns for that which it is not in the power of the Aca people to bestow. Perchance it hath been reserved for thee to supply my need for knowledge, and truly with rejoicing will I feed my hungry heart upon thy wisdom."

The charmer charmed deftly, appealing to the immemorial sense of supremacy in the animal man. Hansen, moreover, reasoned subtly that intercourse with Keorah would further all his scientific aims, since through her he could acquaint himself with Acan customs and history, and thus be enabled to shape his course to advantage, besides, all the better qualifying himself as Anne's instructor. He therefore took the seat to which Keorah waved him, and the two were soon absorbed in conversation, while they viewed together some feats of tumbling and spear throwing, and an archery contest among the huntsmen.

Anne, throned in lonely state, had seen Hansen kiss Keorah's hand, and now watched the pair as they conversed in obvious enjoyment of each other's society. At sight of that kiss, a sharp stab had pierced Anne. It was not caused by envy nor by wounded pride. She shrank from analysing the feeling; she only knew that it was pain. Nevertheless, Hansen's conduct gave her strength, for it lashed her spirit, always daring and quick to respond. She saw how necessary it was that she should become mistress of the situation, and determined to lose no time in learning to speak Acan. On the spot, she began to take lessons from Semaara, and was rapidly enlarging her vocabulary. Ishtal scowled upon her preference for the younger Priestess, and talked aside to Naquah and another of the more ancient Elders who was named Zel-Zie. Anne began to suspect that Ishtal had designs upon the Priestess-ship for herself. It seemed clear, however, that the new Zuhua Kak was establishing herself in the favour of the people, probably because of the strangeness of her appearance and ways. Anne was quick-witted enough to realise that as she knew no precedents, it would be wiser to start innovations. She resolved therefore to keep eyes and ears open, and to strike out a line of her own; and failing Hansen's assistance, she thought that it would be well to turn Kombo to account.

She looked round for the black boy, but he too had deserted her. As a matter of fact, Kombo's amorous inclinations having been severely checked by the Virgins of the Flame, he had been busy casting his eyes over the ladies of humbler degree in search of a suitable "Red Mary." Among Keorah's servants, he had found one who condescended to smile upon his antics, and now he was perched like a monkey upon the edge of the lower platform behind Keorah and Hansen, and, taking example by his master, he was to the best of his ability paying court to the maid.

Anne smiled, not without bitterness, but reflected philosophically that to be lonely is the penalty of greatness. She was not sorry when the games ended, and when, after she had presented the last banners and boxes of red beans, the crowd began to circulate among the booths set about the terrace on the east side of the amphitheatre, and the Zuhua Kak's procession was reformed for an adjournment to the great banqueting hall.

Chapter XXX—The Banquet

THE scene of the banquet was an enormous rock hall facing due west.

It was a natural cavern, as, indeed, were many of the dwellings and passages that made the Heart of Aak a huge human burrow. This one had been greatly enlarged by the prehistoric builders. To them were due the sculptures and vaultings of the ceilings, and the carving into symmetry of the great archway—the width of the cave itself which gave upon the terrace and the plain.

By prescribed rule, the banquet began two hours before sunset: and as the orb dipped westward, his rays filled the vast place, illuminating dark recesses, showing up barbaric paintings and reliefs, and bathing in a flood of yellow light the seven massive tables, which extended inward from the great opening. The tables were placed in slightly converging lines, and with such regard to astronomic conditions that at this particular season of the year the person seated at the head of the central one would exactly face the setting sun as it sank below the horizon. This person was always the Zuhua Kak.

The banqueting hall had no doubt, in the days of Acan prosperity, been exclusively for the priestly and aristocratic members of the community. Now three tables at most sufficed to accommodate these, and the remaining four tables, as well as a space on the terrace outside, were given up to the common folk who scrambled for the leavings of their betters. Wooden benches, with at stated distances a chair or stool of honour, were ranged along the three centre tables, which were covered with bright coloured cloths, and loaded with fruits, cakes, and cold viands—the hot meats being brought in separately, smoking from the fire.

The banqueting hall was already filled when the Zuhua Kak and her attendants came in to the peculiar orchestral accompaniment of the Acans, which sounded at their appearance, Anne and her maidens marching up the cleared gangway on one side of the chief table; the Elders and acolytes along the other.

All present rose as she entered, and she perceived that about fifteen paces down the middle table, Hansen was stationed at the side of Keorah. Now Anne's spirit arose—for she had plenty of grit in her—and though she knew nothing of the customs of the Aca at this religious feast, she determined to make her influence felt by the people and by Keorah. She had not lived among the Australian blacks for nothing, and was a quick judge of persons, and keen to perceive points of vantage.

She was ushered by Naquah to the place reserved for her; her Virgins of the Flame ranged themselves on either hand below her, and the Elders seated themselves, according to seniority, in places of dignity. The rest of the company, eager to attack their food, then settled down without regard to precedence. No great ceremony, it appeared, was observed at the Acan feasts, which were distinctly barbaric in kind. Anne's advent occasioned a slight displacement of the order of things, but of this she was not aware. Usually, a master of the ceremonies was appointed, who regulated proceedings, calling the guests' attention by striking a small drum placed before him, with a gold baton provided for the purpose. This office had, of late, been held by Hotan as winner of the "High Priestess' prize," and he had always sat by Keorah's side. Now it devolved upon Hansen. Hotan, sitting opposite, somewhat lower down the table, scowled at his successful rival, and tried to carry off his discomfiture by an air of bravado, and a violent flirtation with a pretty Acan woman. Attendants, scantily clad, were bearing along great dishes of meat, bowls of chocolate, and jugs of pulque and other intoxicating drinks made from the pressed juice of the agave, and from certain roots and berries extremely potent in quality. A kind of beer made from crushed maize was being freely distributed among the common crowd, who were jostling each other at the outer tables. Even in the more select company, disorder prevailed, as corn-cakes, condiments provocative of appetite, and cooked birds, were handed rudely from one to another, and torn between the guests' fingers.

Anne's natural refinement revolted against the coarse prodigality of the feast, and the free and easy manners of those present. It was as though primitive instincts, excited by the games, and the suggestion of new-given vitality conveyed in the morning's religious rites, were unleashed, entirely altering the character and demeanour of the people. Even the grave, dignified cast of the Acan countenances had changed to an expression of almost brutal hilarity. For the first time, Anne realised, that in spite of the wonderful civilisation of the Aca, in some respects she might still be among savages.

It had been supposed that the Zuhua Kak, who had received her due meed of honour, would now seat herself and fall in with the general tone of license. No doubt this had been Keorah's way. Anne resolved that it should not be hers. Therefore the guests were surprised, when, after a noisy interval of several minutes, they perceived that she was still standing. Very upright was the small form of their new High Priestess, her head thrown back, her eyes sending a strongly disapproving gaze down the long table, while the Eye of Viracocha, on her forehead, leaped in answering flame to the reddening sun. Hansen caught Anne's look, and was even more surprised than the rest. Keorah saw it too, and smiled in sartirical courtesy while affecting consideration for the stranger's ignorance of Acan customs. She motioned Anne to seat herself and join in the banquet. But Anne took no notice of Keorah's hint. She, on the contrary, signed commandingly to her maidens, who, amid glances of astonishment, rose to their feet; and then Anne, turning, beckoned to Kombo, who, though he eyed longingly the feasting at the further tables, had not dared to disobey his mistress's orders, that he should be at hand in case she wanted him. She spoke sharply to him now, bidding him go and tell Hansen that it was her intention to sing a grace before the feast proceeded, and that she desired silence. All the company looked taken aback, not knowing what was about to happen. There was a lull, above which Keorah's shrill tones might be heard ordering that wine should be brought her.

Kombo leaned over Hansen's shoulder, a grin on his face, but faint awe in his voice.

"Massa Hansen! Missa Anne want to say grace—you know, like-it white man with shirt outside of trouser—clergyman belonging to you. Missa Anne say Red Man ba'al woolla (must not talk). Mine tell you, Massa Hansen, you look out. I b'lieve Missa Anne no like that fellow Red Mary long-a you."

Hansen laughed, but the reproach struck home. Yet he thought Anne ought to know that it was not his fault if Keorah insisted upon monopolising him. He got up, slightly confused, and striking the gong before him, according to the directions he had received, made known the High Priestess' wishes.

Keorah looked angry.

"My successor is over zealous," she remarked, contemptuously. "At dawn we supplicate the gods. But when noon is over, we play and feast till the setting of the Sun, when we again offer our Lord praise. Do thou inform the new Zuhua Kak that this is the Acan custom, and bid her deliver herself now to mirth."

But something in Anne's look told Hansen that Acan custom or no, Anne meant to assert her dignity. He again gave the announcement, but in his effort to collect himself, his Mayan faltered—he, too, had tasted pulque, and the laughter and unseemly movement of the company were not altogether stilled. Hotan came to the rescue, crying "Uol, Zuhua Kak!" at which all eyes turned towards Anne, and noise was hushed.

Then out burst the glorious voice, in what the Acans believed was the language of the gods. Was ever operatic Italian set to nobler use? The grace was sung—its literal meaning small matter, yet dramatically appropriate, as Hansen gladly owned. His heart filled with admiration of the girl, and he joined enthusiastically in the renewed shouts led by Hotan of "Uol, Zuhua Kak!" Anne majestically acknowledged the salute, and took her place, the rest of the people who had risen now reseating themselves.

Keorah's hand, oddly magnetic, touched Hansen's bare arm where her golden bracelet clasped it. She was pledging him in her own cup—a goblet of gold set with opals, and most curiously wrought in shape of two serpents intertwined, their open jaws forming a double mouth.

"It is thine," she said, handing it to him, with a gracious smile, after her lips had touched the brim. "Keep it in remembrance of thy championship this day." He sipped. The wine was sweet and strong. "Drink with me, Zaac Tepal," said she, "and renew the vow of service thou hast made me. Nay! Start not. I exact no heavy dues. It is the Zuhua Kak who binds with chains of gold. Keorah, the woman, weaves only ropes of flowers."

As she spoke she drew from across her bosom, where it lightly hung, a garland of orchids—pink, spotted with red and brown—shaped like some strange insect, a species Hansen had never seen, most uncanny but very beautiful. Lifting her finely moulded arms, rosily tawny, she threw the wreath over his head.

"Pledge me," she said, her eyes gleaming on him intoxicatingly, and they drank, he clinking the cups to her amusement and delight.

"It is a way of my people," he explained.

"And its meaning, white lord?"

"Friendship and fealty," he answered. The Mayan words rendered the signification poorly, and she affected to misunderstand it, and made him explain more elaborately, clinking and drinking again. He now saw that the lady next to Hotan had taken off her garland also, and placed it over the shoulders of her cavalier, and that many of the Acan men were so decorated, by which he concluded that Keorah was merely following an Acan custom, thus robbing her act of special significance. Nevertheless, a guilty pang shot through Hansen. He felt vaguely that something was not as it should be, but the strong wine was coursing through his veins, and Keorah's voice sounded wooingly.

"What thinkest thou of the blossoms?" she interrogated, coquettishly. "They are grown with much care, for we love flowers— we women of Aca. Tell me, Zaac Tepal—in the feasts of thine own land have thy women a delight in thus honouring the men who please their fancy?"

"Do I please thy fancy, Keorah?" asked Hansen, recklessly.

"That will I tell thee later, when thou hast satisfied my desire for knowledge," answered she. "Have I not said to thee that body and brain and soul of me yearn alike for the life and the wisdom beyond that which is closed in the heart of Aak? But thou shalt visit me in thy house, Zaac Tepal. There will we talk at ease, and thou shalt say wherein I am different from the women of thine own kind. Perchance we have each something to learn from the other, for if thou hast knowledge of the outer world, I have power in the present. Now eat and drink, and disport thyself contentedly. Dost thou approve of our Acan dainties? This is boar, spiced and prepared after a fashion taught by the Builders of old; and this—nay, thou surely knowest Iguana flesh? But let me tell thee that since the sun last set on our Feast of Life, these great lizards have been kept and fed on plants of special properties under favour of the gods to whom the festival is dedicated. Thou wilt find the meat tasty. Wilt thou not pledge me again, Zaac Tepal? The wine is soft and mellow, and of a certainty cannot hurt thee, seeing that it is kept apart for the Virgins of the Flame."

Keorah drank freely, and Hansen reckoned that it would be rudeness to refuse her. And she was right in saying that the wine was soft and mellow. Yet, in spite of her assurance, Hansen was compelled to think that the Virgins of the Flame must possess strong heads. He felt his own brain getting confused. He knew that his laughter was vacuous, and had a dim consciousness that there was pain—perhaps contempt—in Anne's grave eyes which regarded him from the end of the table. Yet Keorah's gaze had a witch-like effect upon him. So, too, the strange beauty of her long narrow face, and the splendour of her amber hair, the threads of which thrilled him with an electric charm as she bent towards him, almost leaning at times against his bare arms and shoulder.

The hall and the assemblage swayed before him, and the revelry rang to its height. Anne's face became a blur. The din of talk, and the unfamiliar sound of the Mayan syllables which differed somewhat from the language he had studied, increased the sense of bedazzlement. Most of the people were chattering shrilly, the men and women lolling in pairs. At the great table only the Zuhua Kak and her Virgins had chosen no swains.

More than once, when the revelry was passing the bounds of decorum, Anne sent some message by Kombo, a request that Hansen would make known her wishes on certain matters—the manner of serving, a demand for information—anything that she thought might create a diversion, or curtail the banquet. Occasionally, one of the Elders, who maintained their priestly dignity throughout, in quaint contrast to the license permitted the revellers—would remind Hansen of his duties as Master of the Ceremonies. Then the young man would spring uncertainly to his feet, and, striking feebly with his baton, give out a stammering announcement.

At this part of the table a little drama was going on, and though Hansen did not seize its full import, he knew himself to be a chief actor in it. Hotan, opposite to him, was another. The Acan was drinking deeply, but unlike Hansen, accustomed to the beverages, he was enabled to keep a clearer head. Hopeless of piquing Keorah, he took no more notice of the lady seated beside him, who was forced to content herself with her other neighbour, while Hotan directed all his attention to the late High Priestess and her companion. The muscles of his bare arm, on which were four of Keorah's golden armlets—signs of championship—stood out as he clenched his hands stormily, while his copper-red skin took a tinge of vermilion. Mad with jealousy, he threw taunts at the white stranger, and, but for Keorah's interposition, there must have been a quarrel between the two men. But this Acan woman—semi-savage though she might be—was well versed in feminine wiles. She made herself a buffer between the antagonists, turning a thrust with the rapier edge of her wit; amusing herself now by leading on Hotan, then by laughing at him; provoking Hotan's jealousy by her open favour of Hansen, and again spurring Hansen to fresh demonstrations of gallantry by pitting him against his rival.

"Is thy fair strength so great a thing after all?" she murmured. "Lies it in thy wits, or in thine arm alone? It has been enough, I know, to bring thee hither, and to serve thee, with the black slave's aid, in guiding our Priestess yonder, over mountain and sea-bed to her destined place in the Temple of Aak. By it, too, thou hast robbed Hotan of his prize, but will it suffice thee against such woman's weapons as I may choose to wield for one of my race against a stranger?"

"I challenge thy weapons, Priestess," he cried, inflamed by the mockery of her voice. "But to thee only will I yield back Hotan's prize, since thou dost desire him again for thy champion. Test my strength, then, in warfare of wit or muscle as seemeth good to thee."

"Said I that I desired Hotan again for my champion?" She laughed softly. "To all women change is pleasant. But wilt thou never forget that I am no longer Priestess? Perchance, Zaac Tepal, the contest will be between thee and me alone, and mayhap I am testing thee already. Drink to my success!" And again she filled the goblet she had given him.

The banquet lasted more than an hour. As it proceeded, noise and license increased, so that the feast seemed likely to end in an orgie. Anne sat, stately and pale, eating little, and drinking only chocolate. A feeling of illusion came over her. The whole scene was like a dream, and the one thing in it that seemed real was the sun. Now the great orb was shining a fiery ball low in heaven and right in front of the cave. It drew Anne's eyes insensibly, seeming to lift her soul from her body, and rekindling in her the religious enthusiasm she had felt at the flaming forth of the Red Ray in the temple. She might have been a Pagan stirred to Nature worship, and put back by Time to the infancy of the world. Truly the sun appeared to her as the very outward emblem of Deity—the immortal visible symbol of Supreme

Creative Force. Beams of glory streamed from him, which penetrated the place, and, in the half obscurity of the cavern, deepening to a luminous purple, filled with moving motes of brilliant light.

The rays swept down along the great tables—impalpable golden bars that were cut short, Anne fancied, at the Zuhua Kak's chair of state. It seemed to her that the sun was stretching forth the welcoming arms, and thus ratifying the choice of herself as his Priestess. At this moment there came a beating of the hollow-sounding drums, and a slow shrieking from the primitive fiddles.

The Elders rose to their feet, and the band of acolytes filed up from the lower part of the hall to the upper end, where the priestesses and guardians had their places. Semaara leaned towards Anne, and, pointing to the setting sun, crossed her right arm on her breast in the Acan act of homage. Anne quickly understood that a parting salutation was to be delivered to the Lord of Light. The crowd of feasters had risen; a hush had fallen upon their merriment. Naquah and Zel-Zie, who were heading the tables on either side of the High Priestess, signed to her that she should lead the song of praise. Anne saw Keorah looking at her, and signalling in a patronizing manner. Then an inspiration came to the girl. She would conduct the rite in a fashion that she guessed was unprecedented—breaking up the feast, and leading out the people for a valediction in the open.

She rose from her chair, commanded pause by an authoritative gesture, and summoning Kombo, bade him deliver a message to Hansen. The Dane, muddled by wine, and supporting himself by a hand on the table, only vaguely took in its import.

"Missa Anne—you know, Yuro Kateena"—for Kombo made a distinction between Anne the wanderer, and Anne in official capacity as a goddess—"that fellow say everybody go outside see sun lie down. Yure Kateena go first long-a Red Maries belonging to Tortoise; then old men, and by'm-by Massa Hansen and big fellow Red Mary. Missa Anne want to pialla sun before he go to bed. Missa Anne say you makeim Red Man pidney (understand)."

Hansen blinked amiably, and gave a vacuous smile. Kombo, who recollected his own past experience, uttered a grunt of deep commiseration.

"Poor fellow you, Massa Hansen! I b'lieve you drunk. Ba'al mine like grog belonging to Red Mary. I b'lieve that make white man plenty sick. You no drink any more, Massa. All right now—Kombo look out long-a you. Mine no tell Missa Anne you drunk."

Kombo's plain speaking sobered his master. Hansen assured himself that he was certainly not the worse for liquor. It was that red witch Keorah who had confused his faculties by her mad talk. But he saw that Hotan was jeering. He straightened himself, struck the gong with his baton, and made the announcement, but it was only half audible. Keorah took the words from his mouth, and repeated them in sweet high-pitched tones. The Zuhua Kak was about to introduce a new custom among the Acans. She desired that the feast should end, and that all should follow her outside the banqueting hall, where she would sing to his rest, our Lord the Sun. Keorah's manner was scornful. She ostentatiously quaffed the last drops of her goblet, and bade Hansen and Hotan do likewise. Now all eyes were turned on Anne. The little form reared itself regally, shoulders back, head raised, arms lifted at first as in adoration, then folded upon the breast, not in the Acan mode, but as in the picture of Murillo's Madonna.

So Anne stood till all sound, save the music, was stilled. Then, with her gorgeous mantle floating behind her, and followed closely by her Virgins, she swept slowly down the hall between the rows of feasters who had turned, and remained standing for her to pass. She looked neither to right nor left, but with rapt eyes fixed upon the dying sun, moved out through the great arch of the cave, and took her station upon the terrace facing the orb, which sank slowly to the level gap in the ramparts of hills closing in the plain. All before her, steeped in evening light, spread the wide garden—land of the Aca with its natural fortifications and river gateway, over which the sun hung poised, a blood-red ball, resting on a sea of molten gold. Above it, lines of fire faded into an expanse of purplish pink, which was flecked by tiny cloudlets, like the rosy finger of a babe.

Anne stood motionless for several minutes as the Elders, the acolytes, the musicians, and the throng following them, passed out through the arch, and made two semi-circular bands from the cavern's mouth to the edge of the terrace. Now, as the red globe neared the horizon line, Anne stretched out her arms in an attitude of invocation. The drums ceased their rhythmic beat. There was no shout. Not for the common multitude was it to cry. "Uol!" to the Lord of the Universe. But all the people bowed themselves, and there was silence in which every ear was strained. Then, as the sun sank behind the earth, Anne began her chant.

"Rocked in the Cradle of the Deep" was the lullaby she chose for its magnificent melody. Poured forth from her lips, it rose and swelled, to fall and rise again in sound waves of wonderful grandeur and sweetness, over the wide expanse of sky and plain, throbbing through the listening air in exquisite cadences from above the bowed heads of the worshippers, right away into the golden west. Never, surely, had the Sun-god of the Acans been hymned in strains so majestic.

Chapter XXXI—The Lighting of the Lamp

SILENCE followed Anne's song. The sun had disappeared; the red and gold of the heavens were being slowly veiled by the star-spangled purple of night, for twilight was short in these regions.

The ceremony was over. With the Acans, there always seemed an abrupt transition from religious to mundane interests, and a cross murmuring had arisen among the revellers, who were displeased that their feast had been curtailed even a little. Anne turned, not knowing what might happen. She had expected to be acclaimed, but evidently her share in the day's pleasure was considered to be over, and none seemed inclined to trouble themselves about her. They were a queer people, she thought, these Acans; even their enthusiasm was doled according to rule. The poor little High Priestess was glad at least that nothing more was required of her, and signified to Semaara that she would go back to the nun's house. She saw that the young priestess' eyes were wandering, and that her attention was distracted by some conversation near. Anne fancied that she recognised the voice of Keorah, as well as certain masculine inflexions at once familiar and strange. She followed the direction of Semaara's eyes. Hansen was leaning against a rock column roughly carved in the shape of two entwined snakes. Keorah, beside him, thrust forward her oddly fascinating face from between her somewhat disordered locks of waving amber. "Sabul kak yutz?" she pouted, and Semaara gave a slight meaning laugh. Anne knew that Kak meant flame in Mayan, and determined to ask later for a further translation. Hansen smiled indulgently. "Mà," he said, shaking his head.

"Yalcab u kak!" pleaded Keorah. She touched the armlet on his arm, as though claiming by it his acquiescence to her wishes.

A look, half of flattered vanity, half of puzzlement, came over Hansen's face. He spoke some faltering words in Acan. He seemed to yield. He nodded. Keorah pressed her point. He nodded again. She laughed triumphantly. "Chichan u cha kak," she said, impressively. "Chichan yacol ahtoc!" Anne heard an odd little exclamation from Semaara, and the young priestess' eyes gleamed curiously. It was clear to Anne that the words had a signification out of the ordinary.

"Chichan—u—cha—kak," Hansen repeated, slowly, as though he were doubtful of the meaning of the phrase, and were trying to fix it in his mind. "Chichan yacol ahtoc," added Keorah with marked emphasis. She pointed towards the wall of the city, and then to the sky.

"Chichan u cha kak," Hansen said again. Keorah moved away, her tinkling laugh pealing back like an invitation to follow, but Hansen still supported himself against the column, and stared vacantly into the dusk. He might easily have distinguished Anne, but the dizziness of his brain made him unconscious of her presence. As she, too, moved along the terrace by Semaara's side, with her Virgins closing in behind her, she heard him muttering to himself "Chichan u cha kak!"

The High Priestess' apartments seemed wonderfully attractive and even home-like to tired Anne as she entered the rooms. They were lighted by barbaric-looking, yet graceful, lamps of coloured earthenware, the flax wicks burning in oil of a particular purity, so that the light was soft and pleasant as any which modern civilisation could have furnished. It threw up the designs of the feather tapestry, and the glint of metal upon the furniture in the front room; while in her bed-chamber the young priestesses made a special illumination that pleased Anne, for it gave her a grateful sense of importance. At each corner of the couch was a metal stand supporting a golden lamp in the shape of a tortoise, evidently emblematic of the Zuhua Kak's high calling, the light of these being more brilliant and of an even greater purity than those in the other room. Nothing more dainty in its way could be imagined than the sleeping chamber, the luxury of which was due, no doubt, to Keorah's taste, though she had but rarely occupied her official residence. Anne eyed longingly the low soft bed that seemed wholly modern, with its downy pillows and linen sheets spread by Semaara's deft hands.

The Virgins would have disrobed their High Priestess with ceremony, but Anne courteously dismissed all except Semaara. They retired, making the formal Acan salutation—Ishtal stiffly disapproving—and the two girls—for they were no more—were left together. Semaara at once took off the state mantle, the feather head-dress, and the out-door sandals. She would have proceeded to comb Anne's short curls with an implement made of a hard kind of wood, somewhat in the shape of a curry comb, but Anne bade her desist, conveying that she preferred to wait upon herself.

Semaara, interpreting this as a dismissal, was about to follow her sister nuns, performing the ceremonious Acan obeisance. But a freakish impulse seized her. She laughed like a child who wants to show off a new trick. Returning, she kneeled before Anne, took the High Priestess' hand and kissed it, reproducing Hansen's air and gestures as he had kissed the hand of Keorah. The manner of the girl, her mischievous laugh, and the significant gleam in her eyes, suggested to Anne that she might then and there take another lesson from Semaara in the Acan language. So she signed to the girl to remain, and began touching one by one the things around her, giving the Acan form of interrogation, which she had already learned. Whereat Semaara told her the name of each object, and Anne repeating it, wrote down phonetically in one of Hansen's note-books that he had given her, with a worn piece of lead pencil preserved during their wanderings. Seeing this, Semaara gleefully fetched a brush and pigments, with a yard or two of the bark paper used in long narrow sheets by the Acans. This she folded into the shape of a book, and being smooth and shiny, it made an excellent surface for picture-writing—an accomplishment Semaara was eager to display, making Anne understand that it formed part of the education of the Virgins of the Flame, and was not common among the laity, who employed the hieroglyphic alphabet.

Semaara was no mean draughtswoman, and put considerable realistic expression into her pictures. Anne saw her own opportunity. It was but a step from the concrete fact to the abstract idea. She repeated with distinctness, as well as she could remember it, the conversation they had overheard between Keorah and

Hansen, indicating that she desired a translation. Again the meaning look came into Semaara's eyes. She laughed, blushed, put her hands modestly over her face; then pointing to Anne and to herself, exclaimed "Zuhua Kak?—Mà!—Mà!" shaking her head, and showing clearly enough that as Virgins of the Flame they had, neither of them, any concern with such matters. There was no doubt that she meant by this all that pertained to love-making.

"But Keorah—" objected Anne; "she also was a Virgin of the Flame."

Semaara negatived the assumption animatedly. There could not be two Zuhua Kaks. Anne herself was Zuhua Kak—Aak had chosen her. Therefore Keorah was released from her vows. Keorah might marry—Keorah was losing no time in taking advantage of her freedom; she had already, according to Acan custom, chosen her spouse. This in a series of rough but expressive sketches, perhaps not quite in conformity with western notions of propriety, but clearly indicating the life-long union of man and woman. The Acans, if crude in their forms, had evidently jealously preserved from their first teachers, the Great Builders, conventional principles of morality and monogamy. One of the drawings represented Hansen—Zaac Tepal—in the act of setting alight a lamp of peculiar form. It resembled the Greek caduceus, two serpents intertwined, a flame bursting from between their mouths. Anne recollected the column in front of the banqueting cave; the embracing serpents had appeared elsewhere in the frescoes on the rock walls. She had noticed, too, with wonder at the feast, that some of the men and women had drunk to each other in a cup with two mouths thus shaped, and she had felt jarred by the coarse laughter which she now guessed to have been ribald allusion accompanying the pledge. Semaara confirmed her instinctive understanding that the intertwined serpents were the Acan symbol for marriage. The priestess held up her drawing of Hansen lighting a lamp—equivalent, as she pantomimically explained, to the declaring of himself as a suitor, and roguishly reiterated, "Chichan u cha kak. Yacol ahtoc."

So this had been the meaning of Keorah's words! Thus had the former High Priestess boldly wooed Eric as her lover! But had he really consented? Did he know what the formula implied? ... How dared she? Shameless woman! Anne's small frame shook with indignation. Her eyes blazed upon innocent Semaara. She signed abruptly to the girl to leave her, and the young priestess, puzzled and a little frightened, gathered up her picture writings and departed.

Anne threw herself upon her couch in the middle of the four emblematic lamps. Their light worried her. She buried her head in the pillows, half angry, half disconsolate, and a few dry sobs shook her, the outcome of fatigue, and lack of courage to face this new and most difficult of all contingencies. She was honest enough not to hide from herself that Hansen's defalcation was the real cause of her distress and emotion, which, she felt, was totally unbefitting her position as Elias Bedo's wife; and she had a comical realisation that her present attitude was still more unbefitting her dignity as Zuhua Kak, High Virgin of the Flame, Daughter of Dawn, and Priestess of the Sun.

Something of the afterglow of that Pagan glory of a few hours back now lightened her gloom, and made her almost ashamed of giving way in this manner. She got up impatiently, and opening the closed curtain of her bed—chamber, passed into the outer room, which was in darkness, for the Virgins, before leaving, had extinguished the lamps. The heavy curtains dropped behind her, and the darkness, as she stepped slowly through it, felt like a living oppression. It seemed to envelope and choke her. Here, the curtains were drawn too across the opening to the balcony, making the gloom denser. She groped her way along the chamber. Never had she felt so lonely in the bush nights, when Hansen, wrapped in his blanket, and the faithful Kombo were slumbering near her. She wondered what had become of the black boy, whom she had lost sight of after the banquet, whether he was still camping at the head of the steps leading to the nuns' house, or whether the seductions of the Acan city had proved too great a strain upon his fidelity.

Anne drew aside the hangings and went out into the balcony. It was a relief to escape from the oppression of her rock chamber. Outside, the darkness had, if the term may be used, a sort of pale luminosity. In the circular space overhead, the sky was gemmed with stars, but she could not tell whether the moon, now on the wane, had risen behind the cloven mass of the mountain which towered eastward, riddled with the burrowings of the rock streets. Only the feeble glimmer of a lamp or two in the cave dwellings relieved the blackness of the precipice. In the market-place below all was quiet: the booths were empty and silent, and every sign of business had disappeared. Occasionally from a distance came the sound of some belated traveller. But the Acans seemed to take even their amusements as decreed by Fate, and subject to certain limitations of time and circumstance, and were doubtless already sleeping off the effects of pulque and other such potent intoxicants.

Anne leaned over the rock balustrade in front of her window, whence she had a glimpse both of her own stairway and of the winding steps leading to the adjoining balcony. She was pleased to see that on the little square platform outside the nuns' entrance door, and in its most sheltered corner, Kombo had stretched himself—a blanket-wrapped mummy, indistinguishable as a thing human, save for his stertorous breathing. The sight of Kombo gave her a sense of stay and comfort, though, as a matter of fact, the drums of the Aca would scarcely have awakened him from his heavy sleep.

To left of the nuns' house, and in a more protruding line, there jutted another balcony, separated from hers by a rough-hewn partition, and approached at the furthest end by a flight of steps cut slantwise in the cliff. This stairway forked at the top, a small flight leading to the door of an entrance into the cave dwelling, while two or three steps branched outward to a ledge skirting the stone balustrade of the balcony. Anne had already been told that this dwelling, adjoining that of the Virgins of the Flame, was Keorah's ancestral property, her private residence, connected by a back tunnel in the rock with the official quarters of the Zuhua Kak.

Now Anne became aware of a faint rustling near her, of the drawing of curtains, a shadow projected upon the balustrade, and a stealthy step upon the adjoining balcony. The girl drew back sharply into the shelter of a pillar, but was still able to see what went on. A figure bent close to the balustrade—a female figure, either closely veiled, or with the upper part of her form concealed by falling hair. Anne fancied that the form was that of Keorah. The woman was adjusting some fixture, a metal abutment—for the object gave a faint glint of starlight—to the stone coping of the balcony. The fixture, whatever it was, stood out a vague convoluted blur against the emptiness beyond. Having done her work, the woman retreated, moving across the balcony within range of the watcher's vision, into the deeper shadow of the adjacent window—an opening corresponding with that through which Anne, on her side, had passed. There the woman withdrew behind a curtain, but Anne felt confident that she had not moved altogether away.

Just then came a sound upon the rock pavement of the market-place,—the heavy and slightly uncertain pad-pad of two sandal-shod feet. It was one person walking alone. The steps slackened. They halted immediately below; then shuffled on for a moment or two, and stopped again, as though the pedestrian was not sure of his destination. Anne peered from behind her sheltering pillar, and in the dimness discerned the figure of a man in Acan costume. She almost laughed under her breath as she found herself noting the details of his dress. Of course! What else should anyone wear here among the people of Aca? The whole world, for all practical purposes, as far as concerned Hansen and herself, was narrowed down just now to the kingdom of the Aca. Even Eric was apparelled as an Acan. Her heart beast faster at the thought. Could it be that this man was Eric?—that he was keeping a tryst?

The darkness was too dense for her to distinguish the man's face, and besides, the stairway curved, and his back was towards her. He mounted stumblingly. The long Acan cloak concealed his figure, and was bunched up at the throat, hiding his hair. He did not go in at the door of the house, but turned sideways along the ledge below the balustrade, stopping at the object which had been fastened by the woman to the coping of the balcony. Anne waited in suspense. Presently she heard the scrape of a lucifer match. That told her that it was Eric, for the Acans used flint and tinder. She crept closer to the rock partition between the two balconies, and bent cautiously forward. He was fumbling still with his back to her, but the lighted match showed her his hand, which was certainly the hand of Eric. The lighted match revealed also the shape of the twisted thing standing up above the rim of the balustrade. There could be no manner of doubt as to its meaning in Anne's mind. The metal gleamed in the spluttering light, and now she had no difficulty in recognising the hand-wrought convolutions of two snakes' bodies coiled round the stem of an earthenware bowl, upon the brim of which twin snakes' heads rested. The match went out as it touched the wick floating in the bowl—the lighter's hand was unsteady. Another match was struck, and the second attempt proved more successful. The lamp now burned up brilliantly, and, as Hansen moved a little, it shone full upon his face. He was leaning over the narrow ledge, holding the balustrade with his left hand, and staring across it at the curtained doorway into Keorah's house as though he expected the curtains to part, and some acknowledgment of his presence, and of the act which he was evidently rather proud of, to be vouchsafed. His face still wore a vacuous look, but it was also marked by an air of complacency, the appearance of one who has accomplished under difficult conditions an unusual and only half comprehended feat. He gave a chuckle of somnolent satisfaction, and gurgled out half audibly, "Chichah u cha kak!" But there came no response. Hansen waited a minute or two, and then, gravely regarding the beacon lamp as though it had failed in the result expected of it, he crept along the ledge again, and unsteadily descended the stairway. Anne saw him look up at the emblematic lamp as he passed, with a glance of such comical dissatisfaction that she would have laughed outright at any other time; but now she held her breath and remained silent, her soul filled with an odd mixture of revulsion and pity, while he went on his way across the deserted market-place, and up the narrow rock street leading into the heart of Aak. She could hear the pad-pad of his feet as he went, and had a sudden impulse to call after him, and bid him return and extinguish the lamp, for she felt quite sure that he had not fully grasped the significance of what he had done. The maternal instinct that lurks in every woman's breast moved her to defend him against himself, but she could not forget how readily he seemed to succumb to Keorah's fascinations, and pride kept her from speaking. Thus the appeal she longed to utter died on her lips, and she was turning back to her own chamber, when a soft, indescribable sound of mirth caught her attention, and she saw on Keorah's balcony, framed within the now parted hangings, the figure of Keorah herself. Her opal coronet and feather plumes, her glittering belt and resplendent robes had been removed; and the woman now stood, clad in simple linen draperies like those of Anne herself, with no touch of colour about her save in the masses of her red-gold hair, upon which the lamp-light leaped. In her long, clever face, her brilliant eyes shone like fire, and kindled to an expression of intense satisfaction. It was to Anne, who had thought she knew Keorah, as though a strange and sumptuous animal was gazing through these windows of the red woman's soul. The elementary instincts of that sex so long held in unnatural subjection, had arisen triumphantly and were wantoning in their emancipation.

Keorah looked at Anne and smiled, but it was not a smile of animosity, nor even of derision. At the moment, Keorah felt neither one nor the other. She was too secure in her own sense of possession and of gratification—in the knowledge that not for a small thing had she bartered the barren dignity of Zuhua Kak. The two women faced each other, in a silence more significant than speech, a minute. Then Anne, never lowering her eyes, passed like a shadow into the darkness of her own room.

Amid her luxurious surroundings, the poor little High Priestess lay down, feeling more hopeless and desolate than she had ever been during her sojourn among the Maianbars, and gave her bitter thoughts rein. They were very broken and disjointed, most of them, for she was too tired to think clearly. She only fancied that the web of a cruel fate was closing round her, and that she was friendless indeed. The camp of the Maianbars appeared as freedom in comparison; though her only friends there had been savages and cannibals, they had somehow made her conscious of a certain sympathy which—at all events latterly—they had frankly extended to her. Even old Buli had been kind to her in his primitive fashion, and had there been need, they would all have fought for her—

unless, indeed, they had been commanded to eat her by Multuggerah the King. In any case, they would have been true to their own code of loyalty, which she understood as she could not understand the code of this Aca people.

The Maianbars had revered her as divine, but befriended her humanity. To these people, from Keorah downwards, Anne began to realise that she was nothing more than a symbol, the embodiment of a prophecy, and even in that not greatly to their taste, being built on a different, and in their eyes, less attractive mould from their own. On the other hand, there was about them, Anne felt, something essentially alien to her instinctively modern ideas—the very type of countenance, with its fatalistic expression, the mingling amongst them of civilisation and barbarism, the beauty and coarseness, the ignorance and yet culture of a primitive sort, the superstition which for ages had dominated the nation, confining it within the narrow precincts of this rock refuge—all revolted her. Anne knew that she had successfully impressed the Acans, but she knew too that the threads of government lay loosely in her hand, and that it would require effort to hold them. She saw that she must contrive by bold dealing to establish her supremacy, for it was her only hope of escape. But whatever she might succeed in bringing about, there would be Keorah to reckon with. To mollify Keorah would mean giving up Eric. And how could she escape without Eric? How, too, could she leave him in Keorah's power?

The scene in the balcony had created a tumult in her mind. She felt again the woman's pity and the woman's contempt for man's weakness. The Eric to-night had revealed to her was a new Eric—not the chivalrous, self—contained companion of her wanderings, whose chief characteristics had seemed brotherly consideration for her, and scientific enthusiasm in his explorations—but a man like any other man, easily turned off his balance by the wiles of a designing woman, and the vulgar temptation of strong drink. She judged unfairly, as women do, but her pain was deeper than she dared acknowledge. The suggestion of Eric Hansen as another woman's lover—half savage though she were—showed Anne a chamber in her own heart which, while Elias Bedo lived, she might not enter.

But as brother and friend she bewailed her chum, for had she not had his companionship in the interval between the present time and her departure from Maianbar's camp, her solitary position would not have appeared so overwhelming. She could have called forth her natural courage with a lighter heart, and might have tackled her fate as she had done before, bravely, with only the aid of Kombo.

True, Kombo still remained to her. But had not Unda, the black gin, lured him into the camp of the Maianbars; and was it not extremely likely that some yet more bewitching "Red Mary" would make him unwilling to quit this land of women and maize cakes? Whether white or black, men were all alike, thought poor Anne. The excitement of the day, which so far had buoyed her up, was followed by reaction in which she saw everything darkly, and presently the tension of her tired spirit gave way, and she buried her face among the pillows, and wept like a weary child.

Never had she felt so desolate, not even in those nights under the stars, near Cooktown, or in the cave at Kooloola, when she had known that all her relations in Australia were murdered; and when she had been frightened even of Kombo, and had sung her evening hymn in trembling faith, casting herself upon the protection of unseen powers before closing her eyes in sleep. She would have liked to sing the simple hymn again, but was afraid to raise her voice lest some of the Virgins might break in upon her. She could only lift her heart in dumb supplication, and, as she did so, a curtain of peace seemed to fall upon her. She crossed her hands upon her breast as she had done in her invocation of the Sun Spirit whom the Aca adored. Perhaps the great Pagan deity would overshadow her, and draw her within his protection. This was her last waking thought. The rays of the four lamps at the corners of the Zuhua Kak's bed seemed to blend into a shining disc—the symbol of eternal life and love, and with a long, soft sigh she fell asleep.

Chapter XXXII—Aak Breakfasts

DAWN peered feebly into Anne's rock chamber, for she had left her curtains apart, and the morning light paled that of the lamps which still burned at the four corners of her bed. These lamps, emblematic of her lonely priestess-ship, brought back sharply to her mind the remembrance of last night's events, and she wondered whether Eric's torch of love shone yet upon Keorah's balcony. Half dazed she sat up, the veils of sleep falling from her eyes and brain, and the thought of the serpent-lamp uppermost in her mind. She sprang out of bed, her bare feet scarcely touching the skins and feather mats which strewed the floor, as she ran to the front opening, and, just as she was, stepped out upon the balcony.

She peeped round the partition. Yes, there in the pearly light, Anne saw the metal snakes rearing their open jaws, with the flax wick flaming brightly between them. The sun was not yet risen, but a faint pinkish radiance showed above the great back of the Tortoise hump, shedding a pale glow down upon the market-place, where already were some signs of life. Anne noticed that she was not the only person whose attention was attracted by the lamp on Keorah's balcony. Several booth-keepers had paused in the business of setting out their wares, and were standing with eyes upraised; while some herdsmen and labourers, evidently on their way to the fields, had halted too, and were laughing together and talking with jocose gestures, not altogether seemly, as they pointed to the emblematic serpents and the little flame they guarded. Anne hastily drew back, afraid lest these people had seen her, but she soon satisfied herself that it was the lamp and not she herself which had provoked their mirth. The girl blushed hotly. If she had been a little uncertain before as to the meaning of the lamp, she could no longer have the least doubt on the subject.

She went back to her bedroom, wide awake, her faculties brisk and alert. For so long had she been accustomed to wake in the small hours, and under curious conditions, that now her senses quickened naturally to activity, as they might have done aroused in an emergency by starlight, to continue her march through the bush.

Tucking her naked feet under her, she sat down on the edge of the bed. Near her was a miniature drum, like that put before Hansen at the feast, which she concluded was for the summoning of her maidens. But she determined not to call Semaara yet. She wanted to think out things in relation to her morning discovery. On a small table by her bed, the Virgins had placed, before leaving her the night before, a bowl of goats' milk, and some fruit and cakes. Anne drank the milk, and ate a little, glad of the early breakfast. It stimulated her brain, and helped her in forming a plan of action by which she resolved to guide herself. On the whole, Anne was a level-headed young woman, and, having once made up her mind what she would do, was not given to sentiment or vain regret.

After her little meal she dressed herself. Then her first care was to write up her vocabulary, committing to memory the words she had already put down, and practising herself in elementary phrases that she had picked up from Semaara. Next, she took stock of everything around her, with a view to further lessons. From her balcony she watched the Acans setting about their day's employments, and, bethinking herself of Kombo, looked to see if he were astir. But Kombo's blanket lay in an untidy heap, and it was not till she had peered about for some minutes that she espied him in the street that wound round the temple, apparently receiving hard usage at the hands of an Acan woman. He was vociferating loudly, and calling upon Yuro Kateena to pialla Mormodelik for his protection. Anne reflected that his thieving, or possibly his amorous propensities, had got him into trouble, and that a lesson might do him good. In any case, he escaped the clutches of the Red Mary, and disappeared in the dimness of the rock street. Anne looked up at the precipice with its many caves, and the wall closing in the market-place, and realised afresh with a shudder that she was a prisoner. The delicious morning air streaming down through the opening above the market-place came to her like a breath of liberty, and made her long for the old Bush days of hardship when she and Hansen and Kombo had tramped together, and at least had been free; when, too, there had been no other woman to come between Eric and herself. But that last thought she resolutely quelled. She had no time nor strength to spare for repining. Action was what was needed, and that of the wisest.

Before long the Virgins entered to pay their morning respects, and were surprised to find their High Priestess sitting dressed, calm and ready for whatever official duty she might be called on to perform. It was made clear to her that she would shortly have to go in procession to the temple, and by-and-by the stage mantle and the roseate head-dress, with the Eye of Viracocha, were brought forth. Ishtal performed the ceremony of robing. Poor Semaara hung back shy, and evidently frightened after her abrupt dismissal the previous evening. But Anne called her to her side, and found a few moments to talk to her alone, playfully chiding her in such phrases as she could put together, and re-winning the girl's confidence by her graciousness. She even commanded herself sufficiently to show Semaara the lamp on Keorah's balcony—now extinguished—and to try to ascertain what would be the order of proceedings in the wooing of Eric. Semaara hung her head and laughed, conveying that it would be as Keorah pleased. She also volunteered the information—signified by signs and more picture—writing—that Keorah was organising a pleasure party outside the city in honour of Zaac Tepal. Oh! dear no, she added; the Virgins of the Flame did not go hunting, though Keorah, when Zuhua Kak, had sometimes indulged herself in this manner. Naquah and Zel-Zie, however, had not approved of her passion for out-door amusements. And, as for the rest of the nuns, after the service to Aak was over, they mostly remained indoors weaving linen for the sacred robes, and preparing certain beverages used at festivals. Only occasionally did they walk, accompanied by the Elders and Acolytes, in the garden domain below the great terrace.

Semaara's pantomimic confidences were pathetic. She too would have liked to amuse herself. For her own part, Anne was much too proud to suggest forcing herself upon Keorah's party, but she privately resolved that if the privilege had been accorded to the last Zuhua Kak, she would claim it forthwith, and organise a hunting party to which Keorah should not be invited. Furthermore, she registered a mental vow to command Zaac Tepal's attendance upon herself as interpreter, whenever this was conformable with the dignity she intended to assume.

Before long, the procession of Virgins went again by the passage in the mountain to the temple, there to do service to Aak. The great place was now lighted by openings in the roof that had been closed at the celebration of the Feast of Life and Death. The Life Disc shone dazzlingly with prismatic colours, but the Death Stone triangle showed, in the presence of the sun, only a sinister blueness.

The Virgins passed up the huge aisle to the Chapel of Aak, and, at one side of the fretwork screen, paused before a small postern door wide enough to admit one at a time, which turned upon a pivot in the centre and gave admission to the sanctuary of Aak. Ishtal signed to the High Priestess to enter; and Anne, scarcely able to control her terror of the creature, went in, and found herself in the presence of the Tortoise-god.

It was a large cave strewn with fine sand, and lighted from the top as well as by a great archway that led out of the mountain itself into a space enclosed by a low wall—the pleasure-ground of Aak. This Anne saw but vaguely, for at first she was conscious of nothing but the monster who reposed his enormous bulk in the middle of the cave. He stirred slightly, and the round head, with its two horns erect, protruded sideways from beneath the mighty shell. Anne was relieved to find that the creature was sufficiently far from her to make it a matter of time before the unwieldy mass could be dragged in her direction. But at this moment the beat of the Acan drums sounded in the distance. There was a confused murmur of steps and voices, as a crowd came into the temple to attend the daily worship of their god. Aak stirred again as if expectantly; and now in the archway Anne saw a band of acolytes bearing large stoups of water, and open baskets containing green vegetables and herbage of different kinds. They did not enter the sanctuary, but stood waiting, while two of the priestesses went past the Tortoise, ranging themselves one on each side of the arch, as though to guard the sanctuary from profane intruders on that side. Two others stood at the temple entrance, and the remaining two began in a methodical manner certain operations for the comfort of Aak, such as scooping out the liquid left in a large flat dish shaped like a tortoise's shell— possibly the shell of some departed antediluvian monster—with scoops made of the backs of young tortoises, then wiping the water vessel with linen cloths ready for refilling. They also raked the sand of the cave, removing shreds of green stuff and strewing the ground afresh with fine sand that emitted a pleasant odour. This was taken, as well as the implements with which they performed their offices, from the acolytes in the outer court.

All the time the drums beat, and the great creature showed elephantine signs of agitation. But Anne took heart of grace from the unconcerned manner in which the Virgins did their work, approaching their deity with formal reverence, but certainly without fear. Each time they passed the beast, the two ministering Virgins made a quick obeisance, and the other four, as well as those acolytes whose hands were not employed in the bearing of water and herbage, stood with their right arm folded across the breast in the Acan act of homage.

Now, their homely services rendered, the two Virgins came to Anne and conducted her with much ceremony towards the Tortoise, signing to her that she should make a genuflexion as they themselves did. Anxious to omit no necessary and harmless formula, Anne complied, though with difficulty repressing nervous laughter the while. Then the maidens brought forward a basket of lettuce, from which Anne understood it was her duty to feed the monster. Anne took the basket, staggering slightly in her nervousness under its weight, for it was a large one and well filled. Aak evidently possessed a healthy appetite. With head eagerly protruding, Aak was awaiting his meal in the full relish of anticipation. Inwardly quaking, Anne went nearer. The calm demeanour of the attendant Virgins made her feel ashamed of her own terror, and summoning all her courage, she broke the lettuce leaf by leaf, and held it towards Aak. The god stretched himself enjoyably; his snake-like neck swayed; the creases of his throat straightened; his nostrils dilated as he delicately smelt at the herbage; then the slit-like mouth opened, and in a mumbling fashion Aak chewed his lettuce. He was a deliberate feeder, and took time over his breakfast, but presently the contents of the basket were swallowed, and another was handed to Anne, who went on feeding the monster till he began to show signs of satisfaction. Then she proceeded to fill the water vessel from the stoups handed her by the acolytes, but there was an un-priestesslike celerity in her movements as she stepped gingerly to and fro past the monster. Aak seemed to be conscious of her personality, and extended his head each time as she went by, elevating his horns, which twinkled at the tips like little eyes watching her. He had obviously some remembrance of the fascination she had exercised over him on the previous day, and was ruminating upon it.

At last the Great Aak's appetite was appeased. He had eaten and drunk, and the telescopic lids drooped over the small glittering eyes, and the odd wrinkled face, so like that of an aged man, wore an expression of senile complacency. The acolytes withdrew by the outer gateway, Anne having deposited several baskets of green stuff within the cave for Aak to regale himself with when he felt so disposed.

Now the Virgins led Anne out through the archway in the rear of the cave into a sanded court bounded by a low wall outside which a number of spectators had gathered in the hope of seeing their god take his morning exercise. In the middle of the enclosure, which was of great extent, was a large tank hollowed in the rock, artificially shelved at the sides, so that Aak might have less difficulty in dragging his unwieldy bulk up and down, when he chose to lie in the water or to bask near it in the sun. Beneath the wall, all round the court, was a carefully tended wide border of grass with beds of the vegetation that Aak specially enjoyed. In places, the rock ground showed; in others, there were drifts of sand in which the reptile might almost bury himself if he desired. It was a paradise for tortoises, though it had but one gigantic occupant. Anne found herself wondering whether Aak sometimes felt lonely, and sighed for an antediluvian spouse.

Having been conducted round the god's domain, she was taken back to the temple, and quitted Aak's sanctuary with no small feeling of thankfulness that her personal ministrations were over for that day at least. She had still to sing to the monster, and this constituted part of the morning worship for which the people in the temple were assembled. They were anxious to hear whether the new Zuhua Kak would continue to acquit herself creditably, but they were soon satisfied on that point. The procession passed through the revolving door, and the Virgins, all kneeling, ranged themselves in a semicircle behind Anne before the fretwork screen, after the order of the previous day, only that the Elders did not come up to the chapel of Aak, but remained in the nave of the temple.

As before, at the sound of Anne's voice, the Tortoise awoke from his stupor of repletion, and the same process of fascination went on. The great thing stirred and heaved; then, putting one foot slowly before the other, advanced towards the opening with its carved partition. There he again rested his head upon the stone work; the strange old man's face reared itself; the diminutive nostrils puffed breath in agitated clouds; and the shining eyes, like enormous beads, blinked repeatedly, and at last closed in an ecstasy of delight.

Anne sang on while the congregation listened. The influences of the temple again enveloped her, so that to herself her voice came forth as in a dream. Turbulent emotions filled her; loathing of the whole ceremonial and of the monster whom she had fed and served, yet with this a curious pity both for the huge helpless creature, and for the ignorant people who worshipped it as a god. Then, too, the trapped feeling of being a captive in the heart of a mountain among a strange race which seemed a survival of some forgotten phase of evolution, alien to her in every ordinary bond of human sympathy, and revolt against being compelled to join in such a travesty of religion, while underlying the disgust, was some subtle recognition of primal godhead, caged and dwarfed since the beginning of the world, nevertheless asserting itself in these dumb symbols of a barbaric worship.

The service in the temple over, Anne had scarcely reentered the nuns' house, when a message reached her, sent through one of the acolytes and rendered intelligible by Semaara, to the effect that a deputation of the Elders desired to wait upon the Zuhua Kak in the audience chamber to confer with her upon a matter of importance.

As soon as she had grasped what was required of her, Anne realised instinctively that the occasion was a crucial one, so ceremoniously was the message delivered, and with such evident awe on Semaara's part, that she felt sure it had some definite purport, and resolved to commit herself to nothing without being fully aware of what she was doing. She saw here, too, an opportunity of asserting herself in regard to Hansen, and, woman—like, made the most of it. So after a minute's rapid thought she signified her gracious assent to the Elders' wishes, but demanded the presence of Zaac Tepal at the interview to act as interpreter. Her request was a perfectly natural one; but Semaara's diffident manner, and the glance of amused consternation on some of the maidens' faces as they glanced in the direction of Keorah's balcony, showed that it was likely to clash with the arrangements of the former Zuhua Kak. Anne let it be seen that she divined their thoughts, and loftily dismissed the question of Keorah's pleasure by commanding that a messenger should be sent at once to find Zaac Tepal. She also desired that Kombo should be found, and bidden attend her in the audience chamber, which she learned from Semaara was immediately below the nuns' dwelling, with an entrance from the market-place, a sort of neutral ground where the High Priestess might hold state receptions of both sexes, which it was contrary to Acan usage that she should do in the nunnery itself.

In a short time the messenger—an acolyte—returned, and Semaara brought the information that Zaac Tepal was below, awaiting the pleasure of the High Priestess. Anne scribbled a few brief lines on a page of her notebook, saying that she expected shortly to receive certain of the Sacred Guardians in the audience hall below the nuns' house, and required his presence as interpreter. The note puzzled Hansen a little as he read it, for he scarcely recognised in this autocratic High Priestess his little friend Anne. She seemed to have doffed with her fibre petticoats her old charming simplicity. Moreover, he found himself in a predicament: he was now on his way to join the hunting party, and had been looking forward with some amusement to astonishing the Acans by his use of firearms. And then he knew that Keorah was not the sort of woman who tamely submits to interference with her plans by other people.

Hansen had vague, uncomfortable recollections of his sayings and doings the previous evening, though no one had told him plainly the meaning of that mystic lamp that he had lighted. He made a good guess, from the hints and suggestive looks of the Acans, as well as from Hotan's scowling dejection, that it was something compromising, and he had trusted to smoothing matters with Keorah on this day's excursion. There was no help for it, however. Anne was High Priestess, and Anne seemed to have discovered that the High Priestess'word was law. He thought it odd, and unlike Anne, that she had not come out herself to explain things, but supposed that this would be contrary to Acan etiquette, and with a shrug he turned to go back to Hotan's house, in which he lodged, to leave his gun and get ready for the audience. The sound of voices, and sight of a gay crowd issuing from Keorah's house made him pause. His enchantress greeted him with an arch air of appropriation, the men in her train pointedly made way for him, and the women looked shyly up at the lamp attached to the balcony, and made him significant salutations. Hotan, in full hunter's garb, appeared just then from another direction, and tauntingly challenged the stranger to show his skill in the chase. Here Hotan felt sure of excelling his rival, and had dreamed wild dreams of reinstating himself again in the favour of Keorah.

The sorceress laughingly chided her new lover.

"Hast thou forgotten thy vow of service, Zaac Tepal, that thou dost not offer to carry my bow, which in truth is heavy for a woman's arm. Where, too, are thy weapons? For thee, Hotan, before challenging thy foe, it would have been generous to give him choice of thy bow and spear. Thou hast but ill obeyed my directions to show hospitality to the White Lord. Perchance thou didst remember that I am no longer Zuhua Kak, and have not now the power to enforce obedience."

Hotan insolently threw down his bow and quiver and the short spear he carried on the pavement at Hansen's feet.

"At Keorah's command my best is thine, Stranger, but it shall advantage thee nothing," he said rudely. "Yesterday thou didst conquer me. To-day I have my turn. And to-morrow, mayhap, thou, Keorah, wilt claim my service again for the chastisement of this impostor who has publicly insulted thee by making a jest of that which among the people of Aca is held sacred. 'Twas in jest, not in earnest, as I know well, that the lamp on thy balcony was lighted last evening."

Keorah's face paled with anger, and she thrust out her arm as though she would have struck Hotan, but recollecting herself, she made a feint of misunderstanding his speech. Turning a strange smile upon Hansen, she said with acid sweetness: "Nay, it is not I who am now in charge of the sacred symbols of Aak. I rob not our new Priestess of her office. Let me pray thee, White Lord, to pardon the unmannerliness of one who hath overvaunted his prowess, and is angered at the victory of another. Do not, in thy turn, mistake jest for insult."

"Willingly do I excuse my host, to whom I owe hearty thanks for his generous entertainment," replied Hansen courteously. "Yet, since I but did thy bidding, Lady, I would gladly understand wherein lies the difference, according to Acan prejudices, between jest and insult."

A little titter went round the group, and Hotan gave a triumphant jeer.

"Said I not the truth?" he cried. "And may it not happen that, to-morrow or later, vengeance will be taken upon these impostors? Were they true messengers of the gods—this Zaac Tepal, as thou callest him, and the small white woman in rags whom he brought hither, and whom, thou, Keorah, for thine own purposes, hast suffered to usurp thy place—were they messengers of the gods, I say, would they need instruction concerning a time-honoured custom among the children of Aak?"

Keorah's eyes flashed fire.

"Silence!" she cried, the sonorous Mayan word dropping like a bomb from her lips. "No more of thy jealous gibes, Hotan, if thou would'st keep my favour and be my guest to-day. Zaac Tepal, look to thy weapons. We start at once."

Hansen bowed, and stammered his apologies.

"A thousand regrets, Lady. I had hoped to show thee a more potent weapon than these that mine host has obligingly thrown at me. But I have received a counter command, which forbids me to accompany thy party in the chase."

"There can be no counter command to outweigh mine," said Keorah, haughtily. "Whence comes it, fair Lord? 'Twill be easily set aside."

Kombo, in tow of the acolyte who had been sent to find him, burst just then upon the scene, and immediately began pouring forth his woes.

"Massa Hansen! Massa Hansen! Ba'al you go out long-a big fellow Red Mary," he cried, his sharp wits at once comprehending Hansen's dilemma. "I believe Missa Anne plenty coola (angry) like-it that fellow," he went on. "Mine go look out Missa Anne. Mine tell Missa Anne red man take waddy (stick) long-a Kombo. Poor fellow me! Red man been hit Kombo—Red Mary been hit Kombo. What for? Ba'al me pidney. Mine no like-it this place. Mine want to go back long-a bush. Mine want-im brother belonging to me. Ba'al mine got-im brother—ba'al mine got-im gin. I b'lieve mine go back and find-im Unda."

At the remembrance of his deserted wife, whose worst fault had been her devotion to him, Kombo wept. He looked a pitiful object; and indeed it would appear that not only had the Red Mary, but the Red Mary's brothers and cousins, punished him for his presumption. There was a weal across his face; he had lost his emu's feather; his cloak was torn, and his arms and legs were bleeding.

Keorah was exceeding wroth at the interruption.

"Let the black slave be driven back into the forest," she cried. "He belongs to the barbarians, and his presence among us is forbidden by law. Beat him, and lead him out into the desert." She signed to the acolyte who was in charge of Kombo.

The youth, accustomed of old to render her strict obedience, hesitated, torn by contending fears.

"The Zuhua Kak claims him as her slave, and bids him attend her in the audience room," stammered the acolyte. Keorah laughed in angry scorn.

"The Zuhua Kak, it seems, hath small respect for Acan dignity to choose a black barbarian for her body-servant," she said. "And thee—?" She turned imperiously to Hansen. "Perhaps thou too, wilt tell me that it is the Zuhua Kak who orders thy presence. Art thou also the slave of this strange woman?"

"Not so, Lady; I am the friend and interpreter of her whom the gods have sent," replied Hansen, again bowing courteously, but already somewhat disenamoured of his enchantress, whose primitive instincts were getting the better of her, and whose want of self-control compared unfavourably with Anne's quiet dignity. "The Zuhua Kak, who, I have been given to understand, is sovereign among the Aca, has bidden me be present to make known her will to the Sacred Guardians when she receives them. They have demanded an audience of her. Already I see them approaching. In my country, the Queen's invitation is a command superseding all others. Therefore, craving thy pardon, I may not consult my own wishes, but must obey those of the High Priestess, to whom thou hast resigned thy throne."

This was indeed an unwelcome way of putting things to Keorah, but Hansen saw that the situation necessitated plain speech.

At that moment the deputation of Elders, arrayed in ceremonial mantles, halted close by on their road to the audience chamber. Naquah, Kapoc, and Zil-Zie represented the Sacred Guardians. Zil-Zie, with his long white beard and fatherly expression, seemed to Hansen a more prepossessing person than crusty Naquah, and he at once addressed him, making known the difficulty, and commending Kombo to his protection.

Zil-Zie gave the black boy into charge of the acolytes, bidding them dress Kombo's wounds before taking him to the audience room, then diplomatically attempted to soothe Keorah's wrath.

"'Tis no common barbarian," he said, "but the guide who led our Priestess's feet across the sand where once was sea, and who may perchance have received commission from the gods to aid her when she again leads forth the people. Remember, too, that the maiden does not yet speak our tongue, and needs both her interpreter and the slave. But if thou desire it, thou shalt enter with us, my daughter, by virtue of thy recent office. So shalt thou hear what passes between us and the Chosen of Viracocha, and give thy counsel thereon. Thou wilt not need long to defer thy chase."

But this invitation Keorah proudly and sullenly declined, much to Hansen's relief. He felt it would be extremely difficult to act as he should do in Anne's service, before those keenly flashing eyes. Keorah vouchsafed him no farewell, but, making a scant courtesy to the Elders, swept round and back to her own house, her guests following her with some diffidence. Evidently her wrath was acknowledged a dreaded thing. Hansen smiled grimly to himself, recognising that he had but temporarily escaped it.

Meanwhile, in the audience chamber, Anne and her maidens were gathered, awaiting their august visitors. It was a long, low hall, hollowed, like all the rest, in the heart of the mountain, open in front, and adorned with frescoes and anaglyphs of curious design. It was lighted up by lamps placed upon ledges in the walls. A dais at the end of the room was raised by one step; it was spread with skins, and upon it a great carved chair was set for the Zuhua Kak. Other seats were placed about the room. All was in readiness before Anne appeared, descending the short flight of stairs leading from the nuns' apartments, and followed at equal distances by her Virgins. She had of set purpose insisted upon all the accessories of her new rank, and looked quite a queenly little person, with her long mantle sweeping behind her, the rose-coloured plumes, and the Eye of Viracocha upon her forehead.

She rose at the entrance of the Sacred Guardians, and with much graciousness bowed separately to the three. Kombo somewhat spoilt the effect of this reception by rushing forward with an irrepressible cry, "Missa Anne! Plenty mine want-im you. My word! Cobbon bujeri fellow you! Altogether like-it big Missus long-a water. You tell Red Mary Kombo brother belonging to you."

He would have precipitated himself on the platform and seized her hand, but Anne restrained him with a gesture, seeing the necessity of inculcating in Kombo a proper sense of her dignity.

"Ba'al you come alongside of me," she said. "You pidney. Now mine like-it queen. Outside, ba'al mine brother belonging to black fellow. Inside, plenty mine brother to Kombo. But when Red Men look out, Kombo sit down close-up floor, and make-it bow to Yuro Kateena like-it Red Men." This injunction Anne delivered with a grandiloquent air, in measured tones which impressed alike Kombo and the Acans. Hansen was deeply amused, but his respect for his little comrade's cleverness and resource was rapidly increasing. Kombo's eyes twinkled; he jumped to the situation. There was nothing Kombo enjoyed more than acting a part, and to "take in" the Red Men was indeed a salve to his wounded pride and his bruised limbs. He promptly squatted on the step of the dais, and first looking to see that the eyes of the assembly were upon him, made a half somersault at Anne's feet, knocking his head with great solemnity three times on the ground.

Anne with difficulty restrained a smile. She dared not meet Hansen's eyes, lest she should break into a laugh, but she had the comforting reflection that, at a pinch, she might safely rely upon Kombo's native intelligence.

Chapter XXXIII — The Audience Chamber

KNOWING nothing of Acan precedents, Anne had thought it best to model her demeanour on what she supposed to be the usages of European courts, though her acquaintance with these was limited to the operatic boards. She condescendingly motioned the Elders to three chairs which had been set in front of the dais, and, as she re-seated herself, she signed Hansen to stand near her, a little to one side. Her maidens were ranged behind her.

"I must congratulate you upon the manner in which you have risen to circumstances," murmured Hansen. "It's perfectly splendid. But have you any idea of the part you've just now got to play?"

"I've been trying to study it as well as I could without the words," she answered composedly, "and I think I know what to do. Will you please translate for the old men everything I say, and give me back their answer?" Then turning at once to the Sacred Guardians, she smiled winningly, and addressed them in English, pointedly keeping her attention upon them, as Hansen translated her words.

"I am very glad to receive you, and to thank you for the welcome you have given me. I trust that the favour of the gods by which I am honoured seems to you worthily bestowed."

She spoke with a sweet superiority, and again made them a charming salutation. The Elders bowed their right arms across their breasts in response. Kombo, his ears strained to catch the speeches, and his eyes alert, did likewise in solemn mimicry. The Elders looked slightly disconcerted. Zil-Zie smiled, Naquah scowled, and Kapoc made an angry movement, but they were propitiated by the black boy's ingenious pride in his own performance.

"I believe, Missa Anne, that all right now," he remarked, squatting in his place once more. The corners of Anne's mouth twitched, and Hansen stifled a guffaw in an elaborate cough before he took up the Elders' reply. Said Naquah surlily—

"The gods distribute their favours as seemeth good to them, and though we hold it somewhat strange that the Daughter of Dawn should not speak our ancient language, nor be acquainted with our ancient customs, we have no will but the will of Viracocha, and of the intercessor Aak."

"And thou, Daughter of Dawn, and Deliverer, hast made that will clear to us," gently put in old Zilzie. "For in thee is the fulfilment of our old-time prophecy which tells of one, fair as thou art, who should walk across the sea-sands as thou hast walked, to bring tidings of joy to the Children of Aak."

"Well do I know thy prophecy, Hu Aca Tehua," answered Anne proudly, "for am I not verily she of whom it was said that she shall serve as your Priestess, and reign as your queen?"

Hansen duly rendered the emphasis of these words, though the extraordinary aplomb with which Anne made the amazing statement somewhat staggered him.

Kombo, the irrepressible, resentful of Naquah's tone to his beloved mistress, struck in—

"Yoai! Bujeri queen! Yuro Kateena! Suppose old fellow Red Man saucy, I b'lieve queen make-im altogether bong."

Kapoc could not this time restrain his wrath.

"Was it the Zuhua Kak's pleasure that her black slave should thus break in with unseemly chatter?"

"Kombo, be quiet, or I'll tell Debil-debil to come down long-a you, and stop that ridiculous bowing," murmured Hansen, chokingly.

Kombo subsided with meekness.

"All right, Massa Hansen. Mine no make a noise."

And Anne loftily craved indulgence for the zeal of her servant, who had not any wish to offend. He was no slave, she said, but had been especially commissioned by the gods to lead her and the interpreter hither; and to that end had the gods endowed him with knowledge of the land, while resembling that of the savages around, so that he had been enabled to preserve them through many dangers. Whereat, when Anne's speech had been interpreted, Zilzie's old eyes gleamed kindly, and he assured the High Priestess that no ill should happen one so wise and faithful.

"Perchance," he added, "the gods have yet work in store for him, in the mission which thou, oh Daughter of Dawn, art called here to accomplish, and of which we would now speak with thee."

"Speak on, my fathers," said Anne sweetly, concealing beneath her mask of condescension the sudden sense she had of something brooding in the minds of the Guardians, and which might present a difficulty not quite easy to overcome on the spur of the moment. "Say what thou wilt. Doubtless the Spirit of great Aak will enable me to answer thee to thy satisfaction. But thou hast need, oh Zilzie, to remember that it is but a few hours since I came here, and that I have scarce seen thy land and thy city. It were well, perhaps, to wait before asking my opinion of the country and habits of the Acans till I have a better knowledge concerning them."

Zilzie nodded considerately, but Naquah gruffly rejoined—

"Thy opinion of our country and its customs, Priestess, is not what we dost desire from thee, since in truth, as thou sayest, there is much for thee to learn concerning them. We would speak with thee of the mission which it is foretold thou shalt perform—that of which the prophecy telleth. Thou knowest that it is for thee to lead forth the people of the Aca to a land made ready for them beyond the Flame and the Flood, where they shall increase and once more become mighty, as in the days of their ancient renown. We would ask thee where that land lies, and the road, along which thou wilt guide us. For in this matter, no doubt, the gods have fully instructed thee."

Hansen's heart quailed as he interpreted Naquah's address. How would Anne reply to it? How get out of the dilemma without losing the Elders' confidence, and bringing about disaster to them both? He thought uneasily of Hotan's insinuation that the new Zuhua Kak and Keorah's "White Lord" were no better than ragged impostors. For his own part, he had a shrewd suspicion that unless he gave himself up entirely to Keorah's wishes, she would prove a ruthless enemy. It would be bad enough to be chased out of the mountain before he had an opportunity of deciphering the hieroglyphics on the monuments, and of learning something more about this wonderful pre-Adamite survival, but who could say what worse might not befall them? He longed to make some sign to Anne, warning her of a danger she perhaps had not foreseen, but all through the audience she had kept her eyes steadily away from him. Now, however, he was reassured by her manner of grappling with the situation, and led to wonder anew at the powers of strategy she had so unexpectedly developed.

Anne turned on Naquah a surprised look, that with her readiness — for she did not hesitate a moment—contrived to check any suspicion that had arisen in the Elders' mind, and to make Hansen admire even more fervently her courage and adroitness. She threw evident astonishment into her voice as she answered the old man, in plain and simple words, which Hansen duly elaborated into more flowery but none the less decided Mayan terms.

"Nay, sacred fathers, methinks 'tis not I alone who am unversed in Acan lore. For in truth the manner of thy questioning would show that ye of the temple have become rusty in thy prison of stone, and being long unused to converse with thy Great Ones, canst not tell the way of working when they stoop to arrange the affairs of men. Shall I, then, who, though ignorant may be of the customs that have grown up among ye Acans, have learned something of the wisdom of the gods, instruct ye therein, Hu Aca Tehua? Know that now, as in olden time, the High God decrees; the Doer rough—shapes; the Instrument carves the lines. Know, too, that in their dealings is neither haste nor impatience, but all cometh to pass in its due time. Yonder, to the west, in the House of our Lord the Sun, lieth that place of delight to which the gods of their favour call ye. There shall the Flame devour not, nor the Flood drown. There doth everlasting Life reign, and the Red Ray eternally shine. There are palaces got ready for ye, and temples with which those of the Great Builders' fashioning may not compare. But the first steps from thy prison must needs be arduous, and the magic of the Four-footed Serpent Kàn may, even in slumber, be vigilant. Therefore counsel and fore—thought are needed, that the way chosen may be smoothest to thy feet, and that ye escape the vengeance which for many ages hath slept, but that may awaken at sound of alarm. To me, the Instrument, has been given this task, and I have been bidden by the light of my own understanding, and by the aid of Zaac Tepal, Lord of Fair Strength, and of the black guide whom the gods have specially endowed with knowledge of the wilderness stretching around ye, to choose and prepare the road by which ye shall travel, so that ye faint not, and that no mischance happen to obstruct the purpose of Viracocha, delivered through me, his servant."

Anne paused, waiting with an appearance of lofty unconcern while Hansen translated her speech, to see the effect it produced on the Elders. Zilzie smiled benignantly. Naquah gazed dourly from his heavy brows, and seemed to be pondering her words, while Kapoc looked puzzled but pleased. It was Zilzie who replied.

"Thou speakest wisely, Daughter of Dawn. And I, who am old, and leap not quickly to adventurous enterprise, agree with thy holy counsel to do naught in haste. Moreover, hast thou considered that Aak himself hath a voice in this matter, for surely unless the gods aid in his transport, he would find it difficult to drag the great burden of his sacred flesh over the rocks and through the forest we must needs traverse to seek safety from the Four-footed Serpent?"

"Am I not, oh! Zilzie, chosen Priestess of Aak? And thinkest thou that his wisdom is hidden from me? Knowest thou not that it is the spirit of a god that is immortal, and that the outward form is but the prison-house which may be burst at will of the All Great? In countless returnings of the Sun, hath Aak worn impatiently his fetters of flesh. What if for him, too, the hour of deliverance is nigh?

And is it for us to question the power of the Supreme? Be ye certain that, in spirit or in form, Aak will go with his children."

Kapoc, intent on practical considerations, broke in almost before Hansen had rendered Anne's haughty utterance.

"I would gladly know, Priestess, by what means thou wilt set about choosing the road over which we are to travel."

Anne laughed lightly, and made a gesture, conveying, that having dismissed the weightier subject, this point was easy to deal with, and indeed a reason for terminating the interview.

"Surely, good father, there is but one answer to thy question. The gods do not waste time and strength in providing supernatural means, when there are those at hand for which ordinary limbs and intelligence suffice. Does one choose a way out of a mountain by remaining closed up within it? Mine eyes of this body do not see through stone, and I would gladly take a survey in the open of thy country and the cliffs that surround it. I propose then that thou dost take me forth at once—thou, and such of the Sacred Guardians as will pleasure me with their company. My black friend shall go with us, and of my Virgins, Semaara must attend me during our walk."

Anne turned, and with a graceful and gracious hand, drew the girl, blushing, to her side.

"I find this maiden hath an exceeding aptitude in reading my wishes, and interpreting them into the Acan language," she said, "so that by converse with her, my knowledge of thy tongue is like to increase the more quickly. Therefore do I now dispense with the further service of my interpreter, who is free to join the hunting party from which I regret to have detained him. I wish thee good sport, Zaac Tepal."

Thus, with a courteous gesture, Anne dismissed Hansen, who, greatly surprised, and by no means wholly pleased, left the audience-chamber. Then the High Priestess, after affable bows to the three Elders—each of which was solemnly reproduced by Kombo—told the black boy to wait for her outside, and departed with her Virgins to the mid-day repast, before starting out to explore the neighbourhood, an excursion which she promised herself should prove both useful and interesting.

Anne, and her little party of Virgins and Elders passed outside the natural wall of rock, and descending the terrace by rough-hewn steps, entered the cultivated basin which was at once garden, granary and live-stock farm to the people of Aca. It almost seemed that the earth depression had been, in some far back period, a volcanic lake—drained perhaps in the great cataclysm; or else a stupendous crater. This last theory was somewhat corroborated by the formation of the cliffs, which rounded the hollow from each side of the Tortoise Mountain and closed the basin, except for the abrupt break, through which the river flowed outward to empty itself no doubt into the Gulf of Carpentaria.

The surface of the ground was irregular. Here and there small hillocks stood up, and there were also enormous boulders of stone, some of which had been hewn into obelisks, and were rudely sculptured into hieroglyphics.

Passing a row of these, Anne questioned Semaara after her fashion, and gleaned that they had a religious significance, and were in some way connected with the computation of time. Would Eric, thought Anne, succeed in getting tracings of the hieroglyphics, and if so, how should they carry them away? She thought, too, what interest Eric would have found in this tour of inspection she was making. She wondered in which direction he had gone hunting, and concluded, as she could see no signs of the party, that it must be on the other side of the encircling ridges. Looking towards these, she perceived large goat-yards divided by walls of loose stones from the cornfields and cacao and other plantations. A great number of these animals appeared to be kept by the Acans, and no doubt it was one more adventurous than the rest, which, clearing the ridge, had strayed down towards the Valley of Death. Anne, whose instinct of locality had been considerably sharpened during her wanderings, tried to place that grim gorge, and decided that it must lie almost at an angle with the market—place, south of the great rock forming the head of the Tortoise. She longed to get the bearings of the whole place with a view to ultimate escape, and inwardly determined to explore it on every opportunity that offered, and, if possible, alone with Kombo. That, she feared, would not be permitted, but at any rate she could impress upon the black boy to keep his eyes and his ears open. He had already, she discovered, learned a few words of Acan, and now she bade him "look out plenty sharp," and tell her by-and-by all that he noticed. Her great desire was to ascertain what the country was like beyond the river outlet—whether desert or wooded, and if it offered facilities for escape. It might be that there was a gap in the high mountains which stretched northward up Cape York Peninsula, and if so, they might still gain the Port of Somerset, according to her original intention. She knew that on the Gulf side of the Peninsula there was no settlement nearer than Port Darwin, and to reach that without horses would be an impossibility, even if they escaped being murdered by savage blacks. These thoughts ran as an undercurrent in Anne's mind, while outwardly she gave her attention to everything about her, finding indeed much to interest her on all sides.

Conversation, unfortunately, was limited, and she half regretted not having made Hansen come with them. She wanted to ask questions, but could only do so by signs, which the Elders were slow in understanding. Naquah was still morose, but Zilzie and Kapoc pointed out the objects they fancied would please her. She would have liked to linger at the farms where scrub-turkeys and jungle-hens seemed to take the place of barn-door fowls, and where, in enormous aviaries, closed in by wide-meshed netting of an agave fibre, were hundreds of tame birds, some with very beautiful plumage. Specially did she notice one compartment devoted to those furnishing feathers of the sacred pink. Emus here seemed to resemble the ostrich, and there was a large bird with snowy breast, the skin of which Anne recognised as that supplying the bed coverings of the nunnery.

Of animals she saw none of those—if the striped goats could be
excepted—which are domesticated in other countries. Horses and
cattle seemed unknown; the Acans had, however, a dog of the dingo
breed used by the goat-herds. They kept wild hogs penned, to be
fattened for the table. The kangaroo tribe was no doubt considered
worthless, but a kind of marsupial platypus appeared to be regarded
with favour, either for cooking purposes, or for the sake of its soft
fur. Anne wondered if this was the creature that Eric had been so
anxious to find. Various small animals cooped, or running in yards,
were preserved for eating, and to this use also were put certain
reptiles and insects; while some delicacies indicated by Semaara,
such as frog spawn, a species of fly and a worm infesting the aloe,
made Anne feel that the Blacks' feasts of larvae, snakes, and grubs,
were clean and wholesome by comparison.

One farm was devoted entirely to the rearing of iguanas, which, after
having been fed on an aromatic diet, were much esteemed as food by
the Aca.

In the maize fields, husbandmen were busy, for it was the time of
threshing the golden grain upon a primitive floor of crossed
saplings. The pods on cacao trees hung ripe; so too the pepper
berries and fruits and spices were ready for gathering. The great
millstones crushed roots and nuts. Flour was being ground from the
yucca plant, and young shoots of agave and bamboo were being
prepared into a vegetable pickle. All seemed prosperous, though on
the faces of the labourers—men and women—was the same look of
stolid resignation, which brightened, however, into a gleam of
curiosity as the High Priestess passed. Anne wondered how the
Acans could bear to think of leaving so well-ordered and fertilised
an abode, to wander through desert and forest in search of the new
land promised them in the prophecy. Then she reflected that the
dwindling race imprisoned during untold centuries within rock
walls, and watching its own decay, might welcome at any cost the
chance of infusing new life into its sluggish veins, and might indeed
long to enlarge its activities. Perhaps she ought rather to feel surprise
that there was any energy left in the Acans, and that their intellects
and wills had not atrophied under the conditions of an existence

which, however interesting to a stranger, must to them by this time have become exceedingly monotonous. The greater marvel was that a character like that of Keorah should have been produced from such a stock.

There was no time to-day, Semaara explained, to see the sheds where flax was got ready for the weavers, or the work of the tanners, or the pottery manufacturers and workers in metal. The mines from which gold and opals were procured lay some distance away in the mountains, she replied, when Anne questioned her on that subject, pointing to the stones on her forehead and at her breast. The opal was considered sacred, and Anne learned that only the priestly class was permitted to wear it; but gold, except for the manufacturer of implements or ornaments, seemed to be of as little account among the Acans as it was in the day of Solomon. The money currency was represented by certain kinds of beans, of which the little red ones with black spots were the rarest and most valuable. If only, Anne thought, Hansen could find and take away gold and opals sufficient to make him rich for life! But that she plainly foresaw would be difficult.

The path which they took back led near the wall of the earth-basin, where the cliff dipped down from the rock head of the Tortoise. This reared itself, a gigantic monolith, above them. There were two ways of returning—the other being a road through a garden tract, where grew many brilliant flowers and blossom-bearing trees and shrubs. The atmosphere there was laden with perfume, and after the free air of the country outside Anne felt it heady and enervating. The Elders chose the low road, but Kombo had darted up a track towards the cliffs, calling out "Bujeri look-out, Missa Anne!" and Anne, imagining that he was directing her attention to some feature of the place likely to serve her own purposes, insisted upon following him. The fact was, however, that Kombo had espied a rude stairway going up the monolith, from which he knew there would be a fine view, and an opportunity, perhaps, for finding out what was going on in the world they had left. The fear of Massa Bedo and the black troopers was always before Kombo's eyes, and he would have been glad to assure himself that Anne had not been tracked to her refuge.

But his intention of climbing the Head was frustrated by the acolytes, who raised their voices warningly, and made menacing movements with their arms; and Kombo, having received one severe drubbing at the hands of the red-folk, had no desire for another, so slunk back to the protection of his mistress.

Anne noticed that there was surprise and dissatisfaction on the Elders' faces when she pointed to the raised road below the precipice, which, extending like a rampart round the monolith, finally descended by a short flight of steps to the broad terrace outside the market-place and theatre. It was clear that they did not like the suggestion, and she soon saw that this was a path not greatly frequented, and suspected that there must be some reason, of course inexplicable to her, for her companions' hesitation to accede to this simple desire of hers. But she had already discovered that it was the High Priestess' prerogative to do as she pleased in such matters, and the line of conduct she had resolved upon was to assert that prerogative on all possible occasions.

Therefore she signed imperiously that her wish was to be obeyed, and moved on, following the black boy. She saw that Ishtal and Naquah exchanged sinister glances, that Zilzie's face was sad as at an ill omen, and that Kapoc's expression was craftily exultant. Semaara walked dejectedly by the High Priestess' side, and made no attempt, as before, to enlighten her upon points of interest. An ominous hush fell upon the party, and there seemed indeed something unusually forbidding in the aspect of the precipice, black from ancient volcanic fires, and that of the grass and lichen-covered pavement upon which they trod. Great holes, like burst bubbles, showed in the face of the cliff, and Anne fancied that a subterranean tunnel was hollowed in the ridge, in which certain borings, that appeared at intervals above their heads, might be supposed to admit air and light. Kombo eyed these curiously, and only terror of the Red Men kept him from scaling the rocks and exploring them. Occasionally, a bat or a flying fox flew out of one of them; and once an eagle hawk swooped down with an angry screech, and circled above their heads. Looking aloft towards the summit of the monolith, the rough stairway led to one side of the similitude of a mouth, and on to the caves which were hollowed into the shape of eyes. Protruding from the open mouth of the rock monster, appeared a little platform. It seemed a regular conning-tower, from which one might well watch the approach of any foe. The same thought which disturbed Kombo was also in Anne's mind. Instinctively, her thoughts flew to her husband. Had Elias Bedo got across the strip of desert, and was he even now lying in wait outside this mountain prison? What if he should discover a means of entering, and denounce her as an impostor—his wife, masquerading as a Virgin Priestess! In such case, how would the people of the Aca punish her for what they might justly consider an act of sacrilege? She had no reason to suppose that a terrible fate would await her at the hands of this people who were apparently gentle, and not addicated to bloody ritual. Nevertheless she shuddered, and for the moment the whole aspect of life seemed to become grim and terrifying. The gloomy visages of Naquah and Ishtal frightened her; in Kapoc, too, she scented distrust and dislike. It was as though she was walking in a nightmare. The grimness of the situation oppressed her as it had not done since her entrance into the Heart of Aak.

Suddenly, after rounding a slight projection in the precipice, and just before gaining the stairway to the Tortoise's mouth, the procession halted, and all, with the exception of Anne and the black boy, drew a corner of their mantles over their faces, while muttering a few words in their own language—a prayer or an incantation; then made a deep obeisance, and passed on in trembling and fear. Anne alone remained upright and unmoved, for even Kombo, catching the infection, called "Debil-debil," gabbled the aboriginal form of exorcism, "Ibbi-ri-bita Wanga!" and went by crouchingly like the rest.

Anne perceived in the face of the precipice a patch of deeper blackness, a triangular opening, perhaps into the tunnel of which she suspected the existence, perhaps into a cavern, associated it might be with some deadly and mysterious rite in the Acan religion. The triangle, she knew, was for some occult reason among them connected with the Death Stone, and she saw round the doorway — which resembled an inverted V—a narrow border of that uncanny-looking blue marble of which the symbol of death in the temple was composed. On each side of the blue line were rows of hieroglyphics, which would probably, she thought, give Eric the clue to the mystery, were he able to decipher them.

When they had gone on a few steps, the Virgins, Elders, and acolytes uncovered their faces, and Anne saw all eyes fixed upon her with, she fancied, amazement and horror. It flashed upon her mind, that as Zuhua Kak, she too, should have been overcome with awe before the triangle instead of exhibiting unconcern. The angry suspicion in the eyes of Ishtal and Naquah, and the vague pity in those of Zilzie, made her conscious of her mistake, but she tried to retrieve it by holding her head high and returning fearlessly the gaze of her companions. She was guilty, however, of the weakness of asking Semaara by a sign the meaning of the triangular doorway. Semaara shrank and would not answer, throwing a timid glance backward at the Elders, which seemed to warn Anne against indiscreet questioning. The girl looked troubled, and also a little suspicious, but Anne knew intuitively that the affection she had inspired in Semaara's heart would outweigh distrust, and so she merely kept silence for the present, waiting till a favourable opportunity should occur for gaining the information she desired. But notwithstanding her high spirit, the poor little fate-decreed Priestess felt her heart sink within her, and the nightmare oppression deepened.

She had recovered herself somewhat before reaching the nunnery, where she graciously saluted the Elders, dismissing them with an appropriate gesture towards the setting sun, and chanting a few bars of recitative, which she was glad to see had some effect in removing the impression her ignorance had made.

Chapter XXXIV — The Conning Tower

THINGS went on for about a week much in the order of the first day. The early part of the forenoon was invariably devoted to the service of Aak, the remainder to secular occupations, and to studying the language, with which Anne made such quick progress that she could soon talk to Semaara, ungrammatically it was true, for the Mayan is one of the most complicated as well as the richest of tongues, but still fairly intelligibly. The lessons were a source of considerable amusement, and lightened the solemn decorum of the nuns' house, for Semaara in her turn attacked English with avidity, and playfully made a point of knowing the equivalent of the words she taught Anne, in what she called the speech of the gods. The other Virgins caught Semaara's spirit, and even Ishtal seized every opportunity of making herself acquainted with English words. Anne unsuspectingly took a pleasure in gratifying the elder Virgin's sudden thirst for knowledge, glad that anything should relax her stiff, unfriendly demeanour. It was not till one day when conversing with Hansen in the audience chamber, that, glancing towards the group of Virgins attending her, the High Priestess was struck by a peculiar expression, a look of crafty alertness on Ishtal's face, which, when she found herself observed, changed to its usual stolid calm. An uncomfortable feeling came over Anne. Was it possible that Ishtal had been picking up English for the purpose of playing the spy upon Anne and Hansen, and reporting to the enemy Naquah? For Anne, Eric, and even Kombo in his elementary fashion, were conscious of warring forces and divided sympathies among the Elders and more important Acans of the aristocratic and sacerdotal classes. Hotan made no secret of his animosity, especially since Hansen, at the instance of Keorah, had removed his quarters from Hotan's house, and established himself in a cave dwelling with an Acan attendant of Keorah's providing. Anne wondered within herself whether this man might not be a spy too, and her misgivings were not lessened when she heard Keorah address Hansen, on some occasion when the High Priestess was within hearing, in a curious but captivating medley of English and Mayan. It was a pretty jest, thought Anne bitterly, but might have unpleasant consequences, and after this she was wary in her manner of imparting information. But the mischief, alas, was done.

Kapoc, too, was inimical to the strangers, and there were many others of the wealthy Acans who were not altogether inclined to abandon their gardens and granaries and rock palaces on the strength of an ancient prophecy, and at the bidding of a little white girl, of whom it was already whispered that she was an impostor.

In the meantime, Anne took care to impress upon the people that she was diligently considering the question of the Exodus, conferring on the subject with Aak, and searching out the most convenient path. She cleverly played upon the hesitation of the citizens, knowing that they were ashamed to confess unwillingness to obey the gods, and would not venture, lest the people should judge them harshly, to put hindrances in her way. She boldly proposed exploring excursions in company of Kombo, with Semaara, who was agile and useful in the way of giving information, as the only Virgin in attendance. In this manner she searched the garden basin for a convenient outlet, finding none but the river, truly a water-gate, for it foamed in impassable rapids between high cliffs. The subterranean passage by which they had entered the mountain Anne did not care to attempt, nor would it have been possible without surer guidance than that of Semaara, so intricate was the labyrinth of tunnels. Hansen had passed out of it upon his hunting expedition with Keorah, but to find his way again would be beyond even his power. Moreover, it was only by a ruse that he contrived one day to meet and accompany the others. Keorah frowned upon any desire that he showed for Anne's society, and Keorah's wishes had, he felt, to be considered. Partly from politic motives, partly from a man's natural weakness, he feared to oppose the handsome red woman, who in truth attracted him. Anne did not believe in the motives of policy when he explained them to her. Hansen's enslavement to the red enchantress seemed to her too evident. She avoided the subject of Keorah; and a certain restraint crept up between the two, so that Hansen sometimes fancied that Anne was a little spoiled by the homage paid her as Zuhua Kak, and Anne, her heart sore within her, told herself that a strange woman had come between them, and that the old familiar friendship could never be again.

There was another very powerful charm to Hansen in the Acan city, and this was the tantalising study of the hieroglyphics. Some were totally unintelligible to him; others he could translate very imperfectly from the studies he had made at Copan and Palenque; but here memory failed him; he had no notes, no means of comparing signs, and all he could do was to draw the figures laboriously and clumsily with Acan brushes and pigments on the long strips of prepared bark which served the Acans as paper, in the hope of one day carrying his treasure away with him. But that dream he had of reading a paper before the scientists of his country, or the Royal Geographical Society of London, seemed every hour to become more distant.

It was one day, when Anne had started forth with the unacknowledged object of discovering the secret of the upper tunnel and the triangular doorway, that he joined her, and they mounted the rude stairway to the rock head of the Tortoise.

They found it a more difficult climb than they had anticipated. The steps were broken away, and here and there were yawning gaps in the rock itself, across which Hansen had to leap first, and then, with the help of a staff, assist Anne to pass. These very crevasses gave food for speculation. Clearly, they were due to the forces of nature, and the rock must have been riven after the building of the staircase. This either put the making of the stair back to the cataclysm that had swallowed up the city of the Aca, or it showed that there had been volcanic convulsions since that epoch. Hansen was of opinion that the clefts were of comparatively recent formation. In that case, there must have been an earthquake, perhaps an eruption, probably several of them in the intervening time; and no doubt it was the sense of insecurity continually present which had kept alive in the people's minds their ancient dread of the Four-footed Serpent Kàn.

"Otherwise," said Hansen, "I can't see why they should always have stopped, shut up inside the Tortoise, so to speak, for they don't seem, within the memory of man, to have ventured even as far as the bit of desert on that side, or more than a few miles of the other. It must have been a pretty powerful superstition to make them so deadly afraid of a stone crocodile, that had been quiet and harmless for a thousand years or so. I should say that he had given them frequent frights to account for it. I wish I could find out when the last eruption happened." But there was no one whom he or Anne could question concerning the records of the Aca, for Semaara had positively declined to ascend the monolith. She had not liked coming that way at all, and when Anne left her she asked permission to retrace her steps and return to the city by the lower route. Anne knew that this was in order to avoid passing the triangular opening in the face of the precipice, and spoke of the matter now to Hansen while they were resting after jumping one of the rifts, and climbing a steep bit where the stairway had been broken away. She asked if, in his talks with the Acans, he had heard anything to throw light on the subject. But it had never been mentioned, and the mystery of the doorway remained unsolved.

The sun was getting low, and they mounted as quickly as possible, considering the difficulties of the climb. The broken stairway— hardly now to be called a stairway, with the chasms that yawned between many of the steps—went up on the Acan side of the mountain, so that no view could be obtained of the outside country till, near the top, the staircase divided; one rude flight almost unscaleable, mounting to the extreme summit of the monolith, the other branching through a small cleft in the rock into a round cave that gave upon the Valley of Desolation through which they had approached the Tortoise region.

Kombo chose the more difficult ascent to the crown of the Head, creeping on hands and knees when he reached it, for he was afraid lest the Elders should see him from below, and resent with violence his ascent into a holy place. But whatever had been the use of this natural tower, clearly no foot, profane or other, now trod the sacred stair, and probably the Acans would have considered it a proof of divinity that the small white woman had accomplished the feat.

The mouth of the Tortoise was a long narrow cave, looking less like a mouth, now that they stood within it, than it had done from a little distance.

Round the cave into which Anne and Hansen entered was an inner rim, serving as parapet at the bottom edge, but cunningly designed to represent from the outside part of the eye-ball of the tortoise, for now Hansen realised that they must be in the eye-socket of the stone monster; and looking across over the parapet he perceived that to his left was a similar opening, making the other eye of the image. Glancing downward, he could see below the cavern mouth, of which the under lip projected in a triangular curve, over a deep gulley below. A glint of bluish stone caught his eye; he could see, also, beneath the abutting lip on the floor of the gully, flecks of white, spreading outward. He recognised the gruesome spot. It was Gunida Ulalà—the Place of Death.

He did not call Anne's attention to the fact, fearing to alarm her, and seeing that she was occupied in examining the rough sculptures and frescoes on the walls of the cavern. These were emblematical and in a fair state of preservation, and Hansen determined to come again and examine them at his leisure. It was clear that there was a connecting passage between this and the other eye-socket—probably with the mouth as well—indeed, the presumption was that the whole interior of the Tortoise's head was, like its body, burrowed by secret passages. Presently, Anne came forward to the parapet, and in a puzzled way located the gorge. She thought, but was not quite sure, that this was the fateful spot of the Blacks' traditions, and he only vaguely enlightened her. Gazing beyond, he made her look at the strange landscape, illuminated by the reflection of the lowering sun, and with an unnatural stillness upon its every feature. Still, there was not a trace of animal or human life in the valley or upon the ridges surrounding it. All was utterly wild and desolate.

Now Hansen saw that they might have considerably shortened the journey up the gorge could they have come in a straight line, instead of having to take curves, to ascend and descend in order to avoid ravines and precipices. The sulphurous patch he had likened to the

Big Hell of Japan seemed quite close; so, too, the strange Druidic circle where they had found the Tortoise Altar. The Place of Death, he concluded, must be immediately below, as he could not trace its where-abouts. The red reflection of the lowering sun gave an effect of nearness, and he might have imagined the Crocodile Mountain, bathed in a red glow, standing sentinal at the opening to the gorge, and to be but at the distance of half-an hour's walk. It stood out against a glimmering span of desert and a brassy sky, the veritable image of a gigantic petrified saurian, with long scaly back, distended jaws, and even the grotesque similitude of a clawed foot, formed by a projecting ridge of rock cloven in three places. Small wonder was it that fearsome myths had woven themselves around a freak of nature so extraordinary. Within the crater mouth of the monster were jagged points like teeth; and as Hansen looked a sudden fancy struck him, and he bent eagerly forward, straining his eyes through the field-glasses he still carried with him. Had a drifting cloud been caught and imprisoned, or could it be that the monster's lips emitted a thin trail of smoke? He altered the focus of his glasses, and looked again. Did imagination deceive him? Could it be that the volcano was once more showing signs of activity? Was the Four-footed Serpent, mysteriously warned of the contemplated Acan exodus, gathering up his dormant energies for a last outburst of wrath, whereby he might annihilate the remaining handful of victims whom he had held in abject terror for so long?

Hansen handed the glasses to Anne.

"Look!" he said excitedly. "I can't make this out. Is it cloud or smoke?"

Anne had been watching him. Now she too, scanned the mountain.

"I don't know," she answered doubtfully. "There's something—but the sun is shining on the rock, and I can't tell properly. Eric, do you think—can it be that there's going to be an eruption?"

At that moment Kombo scuttled down from the Tortoise's forehead, full of alarm. "Massa Hansen," he cried, "I believe Munduala, Fire

Debil-debil, sit down and make-im smoke inside Kelan Yamina—old man Crocodile. Mine plenty frightened. Mine want-im run away other side of Mirrein."

"You one fellow big fool," said Hansen unceremoniously, for it did not fall in with his plans that Kombo should make a commotion among the Aca people. "Ba'al that smoke long-a Crocodile. That cloud like-it sky. Suppose you say that fire-debil, Red Man plenty coola, and take it waddy long-a Kombo. Then Kombo altogether sore—plenty sick like-it kobra," and Hansen feelingly stroked his own head at a spot where the black boy's woolly pate had suffered recent damage. "You pidney—no fire long-a Kelan Yamina. Suppose you think it fire, no say. Keep-it mouth shut."

"All right, Massa Hansen," returned Kombo, demurely. "Mine no want—im waddy. But mine lookout sharp. Suppose mine see Fire Debil-debil sit down long-a Crocodile, then mine run quick, tell Massa Hansen and Missa Anne. Then we burra-burra quick yan. I b'lieve mine find-im road inside of mountain long-a river. Then Red Man no catch Kombo. My word!" The black boy heaved a deep sigh. "Plenty mine sorry me no been catch-im yarraman (horses) belonging to Massa Bedo and black policeman, when that fellow close-up camp. Suppose mine catch-im yarraman, mine plant him long-a cave. Then altogether we been run away. I b'lieve afterwards lose-im Massa Bedo—lose-im Red Man—lose-im Red Mary!" Kombo brought out the last words sadly, his face puckered into a grotesque mask of melancholy. He did not like to give up his dream of replacing black Unda with a handsome red woman, though so far his amorous pursuit had brought him nothing but contumely. And it needed another drubbing yet to complete the disillusionment. Anne wondered if Hansen was in like case, and whether for him the spell of the Red Mary was still unbroken. The thought brought its own bitterness. Hansen gave an odd little laugh, as though he followed what was passing in her mind.

"Come, Anne," he said, "it is getting late, and we've got to climb down. In a double sense, may be. I don't know that we shall be able to live up to this god and goddess-ship much longer. Some of them are beginning to suspect us of being ordinary mortals. We must be humble and diplomatic, and humour the children of Aak—bearing in mind that there are still several hieroglyphics to be copied somehow, and the opal mine to be found."

"I am not thinking of either the hieroglyphics or the opals," said Anne gravely. "I am thinking of the best way to escape."

"Well, we've discovered to-day that there's no chance of doing so by the river, unless we shoot the rapids in a barrel, as they do at Niagara. But Kombo swears to the tunnel going right round inside the cliff, and maybe there's an opening outside, beyond the river mouth. I wonder if that mysterious grating leads to the passage."

"I don't know. I've tried several times to find out from Semaara what it means, but nobody will speak of the Death-Stone door."

"The Death-Stone door!" he repeated. "Queer, isn't it? I'd like to chip off a bit of that blue marble from the gorge where our goat was killed, but when the red men go out hunting, they carefully avoid that direction. I've a notion that the Place of Death is a store-house of electricity. The other day I got round here by myself, and took a look at the triangular opening. I put my hand on the narrow line of blue round it, and each time I did so, had the sensation of a strong electric shock."

"Did you go in?" exclaimed Anne.

"Yes, but there's a grating of stone a few paces up, quite immovable, though clearly it must be meant to move. I tried to find out how, and came to the conclusion that it must be worked on the ancient method by counterweights."

There was silence for a minute; then Hansen went on—

"If it were not for the distrust of these people, which may prove dangerous, and the uncertainty about getting away from them, I'd like immensely to spend six months in the place. It's enormously interesting. But you're right, we must secure a line of retreat. I wish it might be a straight one, and not a labyrinth to which we have no clue. Kombo,"—he turned to the black boy,—"You say plenty cave sit down all about?"

"Yoai, Massa," returned Kombo. "Yesterday mine find-im big fellow cave over there." He pointed to the lower end of the earth-basin in a south—westerly direction. "I believe that hole go long-a mountain all the way, come out other side close-up where I find-im mogra (fish) when Red Man look out first time."

"That's the way we came," said Anne, shrinking at the suggestion. "I should not dare to go back by it—now."

She was thinking of her pursuer. Hansen was thinking, too, of the possibility of a route round the back of the southern range, which Bedo and the black troopers on good horses might have taken instead of crossing the desert in their quest of Anne. This would mean that after tracking Kombo, when the black boy had dragged himself back to give warning of her husband's nearness, Bedo and the troopers would have had to retrace their road in part before taking the longer and circular route, which, although much easier for mounted men, would occasion considerable delay in their pursuit.

"It's a choice of evils," said Hansen, gloomily. "East—the desert, the scrubs, the Maianbars, and Elias Bedo; West—the Gulf, wild Blacks, and the very remote possibility of striking some explorers' camp, and of finally getting to Burketown. On the other hand, the almost certainty, without horses, of being captured by the natives. North— South, the same rocks! And there are my priceless specimens buried at the edge of the desert! Well, we must trust to time and chance. Meanwhile, as I said, let us humour the Acans, and watch the Crocodile. An eruption just now, provided it wasn't a dangerous one, might serve us well. I believe that's smoke, and I shall come up here again and keep a look out. But it would be fatal to upset either Kombo or the Elders, who would want to fly at once; and what would become of my investigations? Bear up, Chummy. Keep a brave heart, and the Providence aloft, which has guided us so far, will lead us safely back again." So saying, he took Anne's hand in his, and guided her out of the Eye-cavern, to where the stairway with its yawning crevasses descended to the terrace.

That night, when the other Virgins had left her, Anne succeeded at last in drawing from Semaara, in part at least, the information she wanted about the mysterious doorway. Semaara appeared greatly depressed. On returning from the walk, Anne had found her in converse with Ishtal, and there were tears in the younger Virgin's eyes, a display of emotion rare among the Acans. Indeed, Anne sometimes wondered to herself whether this strange impassive people knew what love was—whether that fatalistic calm was ever broken by the deeper human feelings.

She questioned Semaara as to the cause of her disquietude. Semaara only shook her head; but suddenly, drooping upon her knees, she kissed Anne's hand with almost impassioned fervour. Then Anne put her arm round the girl, and, drawing her close, the two wept together. Anne, touched to weakness and to the momentary forgetting of her sovereign part, confessed her own sense of loneliness, her dread lest evil should befall Hansen and herself, her suspicions of emnity against them on the part of Keorah, Naquah, Hotan and others of the ruling persons. Motives of policy kept her from including Ishtal in the list of her enemies.

Tears were at first Semaara's sole answer, confirming Anne's guess that there was a plot against her. Semaara faintly shook her head when Zaac Tepal was mentioned, indicating clearly enough that Keorah had no grudge against him. The plot was against Anne. So much she admitted. Keorah was the instigator, Hotan and Ishtal willing accomplices. For the wily Keorah, though bent on subjugating Hansen, was at the same time coquetting with Hotan, and in fact playing a double part all round. This Anne knew from instinct as well as from Semaara's hesitating confidences. She had already realised that they were surrounded with spies, and that this was the reason of Ishtal's assiduity in learning the language of the gods. Now she knew that Keorah had not wasted her opportunities either. Semaara ingenuously related how that lady had been taking lessons from Zaac Tepal, doubtless with the object of understanding any conversation between the Zuhua Kak, Zaac Tepal, and even the black slave. Semaara, her tongue loosened under Anne's influence, confessed that she had unwittingly lent herself to these aims. She, who was more frequently with her mistress, had better opportunities for learning English words and phrases, and had in playful pride taught these back again to Ishtal. Only this afternoon had Ishtal aroused the younger girl's suspicions by becoming vaguely confidential, hinting that Keorah had some deep-laid scheme, though what that was Semaara could not guess, though she had cudgelled her brains severely over the matter. All she knew was that Keorah and Ishtal had been in close consultation that very afternoon. Was the Daughter of Dawn aware that a passage connected the nuns' house with that of the former High Priestess, which had been invariably used by Keorah during her reign of office, and was so still whenever she chose to take advantage of it? Semaara feared that some talk between Anne and Hansen in the audience chamber had been overheard. At all events, it was suspected that the two were not, as they alleged, messengers of the gods, but merely strayed wanderers who had imposed upon the credulity of the Children of Aak. Oh! If by any machinations the Elders and the people were to be induced to believe this—! Semaara had no words wherewith to continue. She shuddered and wept.

"And if the people believed me false," Anne asked calmly, "what then, Semaara?"

The Virgin gazed at her aghast, and trembled anew.

"Dost thou not know?" she cried: "Thou, Daughter of Dawn, to whom the gods have revealed their wisdom, thou who art in the counsel of Aak! Art thou then ignorant of the ancient custom which has been from the beginning?"

Anne, pulling herself together, was silent a moment or two. At last she said:

"Am I then so ignorant, Semaara, as thou seemest ready to believe? May it not be the will of Viracocha, that through me, his chosen one, the cunning of Keorah, Ishtal, and Naquah, unworthy servants of the gods, be brought to naught, and turned to their own undoing?"

During her service in the temple and her official intercourse with the Elders and Virgins, Anne had acquired many of the Mayan turns of speech, and the lofty-sounding phrases peculiar to that ancient tongue were beginning to fall gibly from her lips. Even in speaking English she sometimes found herself unconsciously fashioning her language upon the ancient Mayan model, which the people of the Aca followed. There was about it a rhythm that pleased her musical ear. Now she spoke with the solemnity of one inspired; and in truth the part she was called upon to fulfil was, by sheer force of the conditions surrounding her, rendered painfully real. Only by upholding their verisimilitude could she hope to escape from them.

"Hast thou so little faith in me, Semaara," she proceeded, "and not in me alone, but in the divine Red Ray by which That of the Unutterable Name did show me to the assembled people as their fore-ordained Priestess and Deliverer?"

Semaara flung her arm across her breast, and bowed herself after the Acan manner of rendering homage.

"Thou art indeed the Priestess chosen by the gods," she cried. "That I well know. I could not doubt thee. And yet,"—the girl stammered,— "Naquah said, in truth thou didst appear to be ignorant—"

"Of what, Semaara?" asked Anne, softly caressing the bent head. "Nay, I can read thy mind; and this would I say to thee:—Has thou not heard that a decree delivered by the gods is sometimes ill-translated by men, so that in the passing of ages, by reason of man's lust and cruelty and self-seeking wile, They who are all-wise and merciful would scarce recognise their own again? Then is it that They seeing from above appoint a deliverer to undo the evil. To this end am I come, and for this purpose have I beheld and made no sign. Nevertheless, for the searching of hearts, would I hear from thy lips of that ancient custom among the Acans—of the doom of sacrilege, and of the opening of the Door of Death."

She spoke at a venture, her thoughts instinctively turning to the mystery of the triangular opening, and the perils of her own situation, should she—Priestess of Prophecy, and elected Zuhua Kak—be denounced as an impostor. The effect of her words upon Semaara was surprising. The girl lifted her face, wet from weeping, but radiant with relief.

"Ah! Thou dost know! Thou canst save thyself. It was but to try our faith that thou didst pretend to be ignorant. Oh! Forgive me. Never again will I doubt thee!"

Anne kissed Semaara, deeply moved. She felt that she could trust this one of the Virgins at least, even though all the others and the whole Acan tribe were treacherous.

"Thou art brave and true, Semaara, and I love thee," she said. "Speak, and fear not. Tell me when last the Death Door was opened."

Semaara shook her head.

"When? I know not. I am not learned, nor can I read the records. I am but the youngest of the Virgins, to whom has not yet been committed the hidden knowledge of the Elders. It was a long time back—before my mother was born—before the last time when the Serpent arose and shook the earth. But I have heard Ishtal tell that in those days the black barbarians were suffered to enter our land, and that with one of them—a mighty chief—the Zuhua Kak was in league that she might flee from our City of Refuge to where the hills rise beyond that sand which once was sea."

"And was it for this that she suffered the doom?"

"For this, and because through her the black barbarians caused our land to become corrupt, and evil to enter the holy place. Then did the

Chief Elder give forth a decree made in old times by one of the Great Builders and..." Semaara's voice fell to a whisper. "And the Door was opened."

Instinctively Semaara drew a corner of her mantle across her face as in the act of worship before the death symbol.

"And then?" asked Anne, eagerly, not having wholly followed the sonorous Mayan words, which, as the Virgin's awe deepened in approaching a sacred subject, fell undiluted from Semaara's lips, instead of the medley of English and more colloquial Acan in which the two had begun to talk.

"Did the High Priestess go through it? What happened to her? What was there—beyond the Door?"

Anne shook Semaara in her anxiety as she bent forward, her two hands upon the girl's shoulders. But Semaara drooped her head lower, and covered her face more closely still. Anne had to stoop down to catch her faltering accents.

"Beyond it...was the end. The Lord Xibalba...awoke."

Chapter XXXV—Kombo's Discovery.

THE High Priestess was alone with Aak in his garden. The western sun was shining full upon the Tortoise-god's domain, reddening the water in his bath, and making the ground round it glow with warmth. The monster had scooped a hole in the mass of heated sand, and lay basking luxuriously, his head indrawn, showing only the enormous bulk of his shell, which, as the light struck it, gave out fiery glints somewhat dulled by the age and opaqueness of the great carapace.

Usually, a little crowd collected in the afternoon outside the wall to see the god take his exercise; but to-day Aak was lazy, and the people, tired of waiting, had gone away some time since.

Anne was seated in an angle of an upstanding mass of rock, one of many huge boulders that had fallen from the cliff and been utilised in the construction of the wall, and which consequently was irregular both in height and shape. Her head leaned, supported by her two hands; her elbows rested on her knees, which were drawn up with her feet upon a stone which poked up out of the sand. She was half crouching on a ledge of the boulder, and from the outside of the enclosure would not have been easily seen. Any chance passer-by observing her would have supposed that she was absorbed in religious meditation. It had become her habit, now that her dread of the Tortoise-god was wearing-off, to seek the seclusion of Aak's pleasure-ground while the monster slept in the afternoon sun, ostensibly that she might commune with the god on matters relating to the Acan exodus, in reality to have some time to herself for quiet thought over the one question that filled her mind—how to escape from this rock prison. Daily did it seem more oppressive. Even the hours she spent out of doors could not reconcile her to the cave dwellings, the dark rock streets, and worse than all, the constant espionage to which she was subjected. Since her last walk with Hansen, when they ascended the monolith, she had been condemned in her excursions to the company of Kapoc and Ishtal, and had never again found an opportunity for any private conversation with Eric. In those days she scarcely saw him except when he crossed the market-place in the train of Keorah, bent upon a hunting expedition, or at the public banquets seated beside that enchantress. No doubt he was improving his knowledge of Acan customs and records, and he was apparently not ill—pleased with the present conditions of his lot. Keorah certainly seemed happy and triumphant, and was too evidently learning how to flirt in English.

A once familiar sound broke the thread of Anne's sorrowful meditations. It was the aboriginal note of warning.

"Wirra! Wirra! Kolle mal. Missa Anne—Missa Anne!"

Anne lifted her head, and peered cautiously round the boulder, looking to right and left. No one was in sight upon the terrace, but close to her, in the breach where a stone had been broken out of the wall, she saw Kombo's black face and glittering eyes. The boy was trembling with excitement. There was an ominous note in his voice; and indeed the ejaculation "Wirra! Wirra!" which is "Bad! Bad" in the native tongue, meant ill-tidings.

"Tsch'k! Tsch'k! Mine look out plenty long time for you. Mine frightened long-a red man. Ee-oogh!" Kombo cast an apprehensive glance at Aak. "Ibbui-bita-wanga! Ba'al mine see Mirrein (the Tortoise) sit down there. You believe that one big Debil-debil no hurt Kombo?"

"That one have big fellow sleep—no look out long-a Kombo," replied Anne re-assuringly. "You come sit down close-up long-a me, and tell me what you got to say."

Kombo glanced rapidly round to make sure that he was unobserved, and vaulted like lightning over the wall, precipitating himself in the shadow at Anne's feet.

"Plenty mine frightened long-a Red Man," said he. "That fellow always take waddy to Kombo. Ba'al mine want-im stop long-a Red Man. Nalla yan burra burri (Let us go away quickly), Missa Anne.

To-day I go look out road inside of mountain. I find-im hole close-up river where that fellow make big noise, and fight long-a rocks. Big fellow rock go up, big fellow water go down." Such was Kombo's description of the rapids and impassable water-way. "I find-im road—all dark—bujeri road, come out other side of mountain; plenty big for yarraman to come through. Missa Anne!..." Kombo dropped his voice mysteriously, his eyes and his whole countenance teeming with news—evidently great news, which his dramatic instinct bade him work up to a climax. "Missa Anne!" he whispered, "Mine been go long-a road. Mine been come out other side of mountain. Mine been look about; mine been see—yarraman!" (horses).

"Yarraman!" Anne exclaimed, fully alive to the importance of the information. "Do you mean white man's yarraman, Kombo? Not brumby?" (wild horse).

"Ba'al that one brumby, Missa Anne," replied Kombo. "That one yarraman belonging to white man; yarraman belonging to Murnian (black trooper). Plenty mine want-im marra (steal) that fellow yarraman, and plant-im long-a cave. Mine think by-'m-by, Kombo, Missa Anne, Massa Hansen—suppose that fellow no want-im stop long-a Red Mary—man-im yarraman; make-im track and altogether yan. Yai! You pidney!" And Kombo gave the black's expressive gesture that signifies "Do you understand?"

Anne was deeply disturbed.

"What for you no man-im yarraman to-day, and plant-im long-a cave?" she asked, restraining her impatience so that Kombo might tell his tale in his own way, by which she knew that she would get at particulars all the sooner.

"Murnian been look out," replied Kombo laconically. "I been see two fellow Murnian in camp belonging to white man."

"You been see white man?" queried Anne, her heart bounding against her chest in the anxiety she felt.

"Yo-ai (yes). Mine been see white man. Mine been see Massa Bedo."

The bolt had fallen. It seemed to Anne that she had known all along what Kombo had now come to tell her. Elias Bedo was encamped outside the Tortoise Mountain. Sooner or later he would be discovered by the red men, and brought into the Heart of Aak, where he would most assuredly be confronted with his runaway wife.

"You been see Massa Bedo?" she repeated dully.

"Yo-ai," returned the black, and Anne added —

"You been let Massa Bedo see you?"

"Bal!" retorted Kombo contemptuously. "Ba'al mine let-im Massa Bedo know where Kombo sit down. Massa Hansen, he say, `Kombo, you one big dam fool.' Ba'al mine one big dam fool. Plenty mine look out inside kobra (head) belonging to me. Mine think inside kobra." Kombo tapped his forehead. "By-'m-by, when Massa Bedo go to sleep, Murnian lie down and go to sleep too. Then mine marra (steal) yarraman, mine swim across river and plant-im long-a cave. Yai! You pidney!"

"Yo-ai," assented Anne, but there was a hopeless note in her voice. It would not be so easy, she thought, to catch black troopers asleep, and to steal horses and conceal them in a cave. "Oh! Kombo," she cried, "Mine plenty frightened. What are we to do?"

"Yan!" promptly answered Kombo. "Mine see about that. What for you jerrun?" (afraid). The boy roughly tried to console his mistress, seeing that she was discouraged, heartsore, and well-nigh broken in spirit. He stroked her sandalled feet with his black hands. "Missa Anne, I b'lieve Kombo one good fellow boy. Mine no one big fool. I believe that big fellow Red Mary make fool of Massa Hansen."

Anne winced at Kombo's blunt summing up of the situation, but she said nothing. It might indeed be true that Keorah was making a fool of Hansen. Kombo went on, his face brightening—

"You see—mine no let Massa Bedo catch Missa Anne. What for run away from steamer? What for stop long-a Maianbars, suppose all no good, and Massa Bedo catch Missa Anne? I b'lieve that fellow cobbon woolla (very angry) long-a Missa Anne. I b'lieve that fellow take waddy, mumkull (kill) Missa Anne, and put Kombo long-a gaol. Ba'al mine let him do that."

Anne nodded sadly. She felt it was not unlikely that Elias Bedo would beat her and perhaps kill her if he got her into his power, especially if it happened that he was plied with the strong drink of the Acans. He had beaten her before when he was drunk, and several times on board the steamer he had threatened to shoot her if he could only get her alone in the bush. Here, far from the law's jurisdiction, there would be nothing to prevent him from working his will upon her.

"Kombo," she said desperately, "Ba'al mine know what to do. How can you? No time—no horses. Suppose to-morrow Red Man find Massa Bedo, that fellow say, 'this wife belonging to me.' Then Red Man plenty coolla. Red Man no believe any more that Yuro Kateena one big queen,—sister belonging to Mormodelik. No believe any more that Yuro Kateena pialla big debil-debil Mirrein,—Aak." She pointed to the Tortoise-god which lay immovable in the sand. "Red Man take away this"—she lifted a fold of her Zuhua Kak's mantle; "take away fire-stone,"—she touched the opal on her forehead,— "and send away poor fellow me, outside of mountain long-a Massa Bedo."

Kombo knocked his head upon the sand, and muttered mournfully, "Wirra-wirra! (bad! bad!) Red Men altogether like-it Buli. Mine want-im run away from red men, same as run away from Buli. Mine know what to do," he went on more cheerfully. "You no fear. You believe mine look after you. Mine know how to get yarraman—you see. Suppose Massa Hansen want to stop long-a big Red Mary, all right. Me brother belonging to Missa Anne. Me no one big dam fool."

Kombo chuckled malignly. He had his human weaknesses. Never in his inner consciousness—his kobra, as he would have put it—had he quite reconciled himself to Hansen's domination. There was always in him a lurking notion that he himself would have managed much better for Anne than to lead her into this devil-haunted region. Only weariness of Unda's savage charms, and dread lest he should be eaten by Multuggerah the king had caused him to fly from the Maianbars' camp. Often since, it had seemed to him that he was fallen between the devil and the deep sea. The Crocodile, Mirrein— or Aak—and the Red Men representing debil-debil, and Multuggerah the deep sea. His hide was sore from flagellations administered by Acan men, and his self love wounded by the snubbings he had received from Acan women. That a Red Mary would ever permit him to make love to her he had proved an illusive hope. And, man-like, he resented the fact that Hansen had secured to himself the biggest, the most beautiful, and the wealthiest of the Red Maries, while he, Kombo, was scornfully denied the favour of her waiting maid. Not only, too, was he flouted by Red Maries and beaten by their men-kind, but the booth—keepers, having suffered from his thieving propensities, had also risen up against him, so that in the entire Heart of Aak there was now small joy for Kombo beyond the legitimate satisfaction of his appetite by the food provided for him, and this was thrown at him as though he had been a pariah dog. The red race had a rooted prejudice against the barbarians of the bush, founded upon ancient dealings with the Maianbar tribe; and although Kombo was the specially commissioned servant of the High—Priestess, he had not succeeded in making himself popular with the Acans. Consequently, he had already determined to quit the place as soon as he possibly could, and was delighted at the prospect of having Anne to himself again, shrewdly suspecting that Hansen would be loth to leave either Keorah, or the hieroglyphics that entranced him, at a moment's notice.

Kombo was nothing if not dramatic. He did not immediately unfold his scheme, but point by point told the story of that day's doings in his queer mixture of pidgin-English and blacks' language, which would have been almost unintelligible to an outsider.

First he had essayed a passage that in his wanderings he had discovered through the wall of rock encircling the earth-basin wherein the Acans had their farms and gardens. This was a tunnel piercing the cliff diagonally and giving upon the alluvial tract beyond the rapids and the breach in the wall where the river widened and shallowed on its way westward. But Kombo found that this alluvial belt was bounded on one side by a continuation of the ridge-wall, on the other, where he stood, by, as it were, a second line of fortification—another mighty wall of rock cutting down from the higher level at the head of the Valley of Desolation by which the wanderers had entered the Heart of Aak. As may often be seen in Australia, an enormous slice seemed to have been cut out of the land below the Tortoise hump, leaving a V-shaped, flat-bottomed gorge like the end of a long flat trough with unscaleable sides and no visible end. That was how Anne pictured the place from Kombo's description, after its own queer fashion, sufficiently graphic.

The black boy's idea had been that he would round the Tortoise mountain and see what possibilities for escape the country offered by heading the range and striking southward. So he had clambered up in the angle of the gorge, and had finally come upon an opening in the rock at the head of a slanting fissure encumbered with stones, but still practicable for a man, and even for a sure-footed beast. He had gone into the hole, which was high enough for him to stand upright inside, and there found another tunnel. Indeed, this whole mountainous region seemed burrowed with caverns and passages, and Anne wondered, as she listened, whether the Great Builders of Acan tradition had made them all, or if some, at least, were due to the action of internal forces. Kombo could not enlighten her on this point. He could only describe how he had walked along the tunnel, which inclined upward, and in parts was cut in steps making a subterranean stairway. He explained that he had been "plenty frightened lest he should altogether lose-im road," but this underground way seemed to be both shorter and straighter than that by which the Red Men had led the travellers into the City of Refuge, and Kombo had eventually found daylight beneath the stone carapace of the Tortoise mountain, not very far from the original entrance. A desire for mogra (fish) had now seized Kombo, as he remembered the muddy pool in which he had caught the craw-fish of that delicious repast which had been followed by the arrival of the Red Men. He was making for the bit of scrub and the stream meandering through it, when he heard the clank of hobbles, and saw at a little distance, three horses grazing. He recognised the brands of the horses, and knew that they belonged to the company of native police commanded by Captain Cunninghame. At this point, Kombo squirmed on the ground at Anne's feet, speaking in a hoarse whisper, and illustrating his tale with appropriate gestures, as he told how in breathless excitement he had crawled noiselessly, "like-it snake," among the rocks and undergrowth, and had presently sighted a white man's camp. There, engaged on their mid-day meal, he had seen two of the black troopers and Elias Bedo.

"Massa Bedo smoke and talk long-a Murnian. One fellow policeman very good tracker, and that one tell Massa Bedo he find track long-side of mountain. Mine think ba'al that fellow been see hole where Red Men come out. I believe only make camp yesterday. That one policeman find fire—stick and shell belonging to crab. He find, too, one billy that mine been forget when Red Man made me plenty frightened. That one Murnian tell Massa Bedo white man make-it camp like-it that place. He say very soon track white Missus. Then Massa Bedo jump up, and go look out camp. My word! He plenty swear! Mine stop little while till camp altogether quiet. S'st! S'st! Ba'al mine make a noise. Mine crawl close-up fire; mine see billy where tea sit down. My word! That bujeri tea! Mine been think, suppose pituri long-a tea, then Massa Bedo and Murnian drink when come back and sleep—altogether like-it that fellow bong. Massa Hansen no say Kombo one big fool that time!" The boy laughed impishly. "Mine been take out bag, and put pituri long-a tea. Then mine jump up and yan quick long-a hole. Mine want to tell Missa Anne to look out,—Massa Bedo close-up. No time to lose. I believe one day—two day—that fellow find out where Red Man sit down."

Yes, there was no doubt that Elias Bedo had tracked his quarry to the lair. Anne sat overwhelmed, staring in a dazed manner at the huge shell of Aak, as he lay in the sand. She had not taken in the import of Kombo's operations at the camp fire, and even felt a dull irritation at the triumphant gleam in the black boy's eyes, as, his first terror gone, he went back in thought to what he had achieved. Anne could not realise that the native's quick wits had already conceived and partly executed a plan of escape. She herself could see nothing but disaster hemming them on every side. For a day or two, as Kombo pointed out, Elias Bedo would certainly be discovered by the Red Men. It remained a question how the Acans would receive the stranger; but from their peaceful proclivities it might be supposed that they would greet him without enmity, and listen to his story, which would now be more easy of comprehension by the Acans from the knowledge of English acquired by Keorah and Ishtal. Alas! what in this case would be her own and Hansen's fate? Anne shudderingly recollected Semaara's dark hints concerning the Door of Death.

"Kombo! Oh, what shall we do?" she said again in hapless consternation. The black boy gave the same answer as before.

"Man-im horse and yan. Look here, Missa Anne, mine been tell you, mine been put-in pituri long-a tea!"

"Pituri!" said Anne vaguely. It was the first she had heard of Kombo's find among the ridges near Gunida Ulala.

"Yo-ai," said Kombo. "Mine been find-im close-up Tortoise Mountain. Ba'al mine been eat-im pituri, because that fellow make black-fellow plenty sleep—altogether stupid."

It argued force of character on Kombo's part that he had understood the temptation. No doubt, he had feared the consequences of giving himself up in a drugged condition to the tender mercies of the Acans; probably also in this land of cakes and ale the desire for that potent drug—a stimulant in small quantities, a powerful narcotic when freely taken—had been less insistant than when he had been enduring the hardships of the bush. Seeing that still she did not quite

understand, the black boy opened his Acan jerkin and showed her
lying upon his chest, which was most hideously wealed, a little bag
that he had made himself out of opossum fur,—the kind of bag that
is recognised at once among aboriginal tribes as containing the
precious pituri, and the possession of which ensures safety to its
bearer, no matter how hostile the people among whom he travels.
He loosened the string of plaited grass by which the bag hung from
his neck, and showed her a small lump of greyish-black dough,—
pituri which had been prepared with ashes of the gidya tree, and
chewed into a thick paste after the manner of the blacks.

Anne knew that the plant, extremely rare, for it grows only in a
certain soil, is so highly prized among Australian natives, that
sometimes messengers carry it for hundreds of miles, bartering it for
food, weapons, and various valuable commodities. She began to
understand Kombo's scheme. Now she grasped the black boy's
hand, and patted it, saying—

"Bujeri you, Kombo! Plenty you brother belonging to me."

"You see, Missa Anne, that all right now," the boy cried, exultingly.
"No fear! Pituri like-it debil-debil—no can wake up. You pidney?
Mine go quick now long-a camp. While Massa Bedo and Murnian
fast asleep, mine take saddle, bridle, swag. Mine put-im long-a
yarraman. Mine drive three fellow yarraman inside mountain. Mine
plant-im long-a cave—put plenty stone outside door—make-im
fence, so no can run away. That take long time. I believe then sun
jump up. Mine come back—look-out a ration and hide long-a cave.
When Red Man no see, I catch little fellow iguana. Mine want-im
take plenty cake; plenty corn; plenty tucker. By-'m-by, moon look
out of sky—little fellow moon; mine come up long-a verandah;
Missa Anne look out all ready. Missa Anne bring baby gun, and
suppose Red Man saucy, Missa shoot. But I believe Red Man all
sleep like Massa Bedo. Mine show Missa Anne where cave sit down;
then man-im yarraman and make track long-a big water, where Red
Man no can find."

Such was Kombo's plan of campaign. It seemed practical, and was certainly ingenious. Once on horse-back, they might consider themselves free; the great difficulty in the enterprise had been got over by Kombo's cunning use of the pituri—that was, if Elias Bedo and the troopers had drunk of the drugged tea, and if the drug had duly taken effect, so that they were in a sleep deep for a time as that of death—as Kombo had put it, "altogether like-it bong." But there was a chance that they might not drink the drugged tea—that the pituri might not act as was intended. Then—what if a rifle shot should act as was not intended—put an end to Kombo's daring scheme—perhaps to himself?

"Kombo," said Anne, "ba'al you frightened that Massa Bedo wake up?"

"Yo-ai, Missa Anne. Plenty mine frightened suppose Massa Bedo wake up. I believe that fellow shoot Kombo. But mine no frightened when Massa Bedo drunk long-a pituri. Mine look out first. I believe Massa no wake up till sun walk long way. Then he feel bad like-it kobra; he no want to get up. By-'m-by he look out yarraman. No find! Suppose no yarraman, no can ride. Missa Anne get good start. Kombo and Missa Anne long way in the bush. Red Mary no good; mine no like-it Red Man; mine no like-it that one big god. Mine think debil-debil sit down inside. Mine like best Missa Anne pialla Mormodelik; sing song to Baiamè; and say prayer like-it white man." Kombo rose from his crouching posture, stretched himself against the boulder, while after one apprehensive glance at the slumbering Aak, he gazed yearningly out over the wall of their mountain prison. Anne's breast throbbed too with the passion for liberty. Oh! to think that in two days they might be riding through gum-forest along the banks of the river, down towards the Gulf and Burke-town and ships and civilisation. She could scarcely believe in the possibility of such joy. Yet if Kombo could only contrive to secrete the horses and all went well with their scheme, it was more than possible.

She was longing to see Hansen and to tell him the news, and her mind was working with the thought of how she could manage to get some words with him in private. There was not in her mind, as in

Kombo's, any idea of leaving Hansen behind. She got up, telling Kombo that she must go back to the nuns' house at once, and bade him be off and do his work well, giving him some parting injunctions as to the need for caution. The boy vaulted like a kangaroo over the low wall, and she retraced her steps to the temple, where Ishtal and another of the priestesses were waiting.

Anne desired that the Virgins would remain until Aak saw fit to bestir himself, saying that she would walk back by the market-place alone. Ishtal remonstrated. "It was not well that the Zuhua Kak should be seen in the city unattended," and she was preparing to follow, but Anne haughtily waved her back in a way that brooked no denial, and passing through the door of Aak's sanctuary went down the long aisle of the temple and out into the rock street.

It was in this street, a little higher up, that Hansen had his lodging. In Anne's mind during all the latter part of her interview with Kombo there had been one dominant thought—how should she inform Eric of what had happened, and of their proposed flight? Kombo had suggested that he should not be told, had more than suggested that he would desire to remain with Keorah. Anne's heart sank like lead as she realised the possibility of this. Well, if he preferred what she considered slavery with Keorah to freedom with herself, so let it be, but at least he should have the chance of making a choice, and she resolved at all risks to give it him. Whatever might be his personal inclination in the matter, she knew that he would never betray them, and that he would help them to the best of his power. See him, therefore, she must without delay. So close was Keorah's watch upon him that there was danger as well as difficulty in the attempt, but she determined to make it, and that at once. She could not sleep knowing that he was in ignorance of the events of the day.

So, emerging from the temple, Anne mounted the narrow way, which at this hour was unfrequented and dim in the gathering dusk. She had a faint hope that chance might befriend her, and give her a sight of Eric. In this she was not disappointed. Her quick eyes perceived him before he saw her, standing on the rock steps which led to his cave dwelling. He was alone, and had evidently just returned from the chase, for his gun was in his hand—that wondrous weapon which was the envy of Hotan, and the terror and delight of the Acan huntsman. He started at the sound of Anne's low `Coo-ee' uttered timorously, scarcely above her breath, and seeing the small figure in its feather-trimmed mantle of deep rose, that looked almost black in the evening light, he stepped briskly forward and saluted her. But she made a movement enjoining reticence, and walking quickly past, gave him a furtive sign to follow her.

The street was a cul de sac, and at the end of it shelved inward, making a recess, in the dimness of which they might exchange a few words secure, comparatively speaking, from observation. Anne went towards this spot, and drawing close into the shadow of the cliff, waited for him to join her. He sauntered leisurely along, making a feint of turning up a narrow alley which connected the street with one parallel to it, then gliding swiftly beneath the rock, was at her side.

Her mantle was partly drawn over her face; he could only see her dark eyes shining with excitement.

"What is it?" he whispered. "Do you want to speak to me?"

"Yes," she answered shortly; "I have something very important to tell you, but I can't say it here. I am afraid that I may be watched. I left Ishtal in the temple behind, but she will certainly follow me if she dares. She is always at my elbow. I want to say that you must—." She stopped suddenly, and her dark eyes avoided his. He was not sure whether the rosy red that flashed upon her cheeks where the mantle was drawn aside, was due to the reflection of the rose-coloured garment, or to a red gleam of the dying sun piercing the narrow opening of the street; or—could it be—to some hesitation in herself? But it was not like his little comrade to be deterred by conventional considerations. "I will do anything you wish," he said hastily. "Only tell me what it is."

She went on with an effort. "You must come to my rooms this evening—when it is quite dark, and the nuns have left me. I can't ask you to come openly, for that is against the rules, as you know, and there would be a fuss. I think you could climb the balcony. You—" She was going to say, "You have climbed the adjoining one," remembering the occasion when he had lighted Keorah's lamp; but she hesitated again. He caught her up, perhaps reading her thoughts.

"Yes, yes, it is quite easy. I will manage it,—about ten o'clock. Will that do?"

"Thank you. I will be waiting. Now I mustn't stop. As it is, I am breaking rules by walking alone. But I must see you, and that's the only plan I can think of. Don't let anything prevent it. Every chance of escape—every hope—at least for me—hinges upon it. Be sure that you come."

She clasped tightly on her breast the slight nervous hands which held together the folds of her mantle, and looked up at him, her large eyes bright with—he could hardly tell what. Never had he seen fear in Anne's eyes, yet now something like it seemed to look out from them, and appealed to his heart.

"Of course I will come, Chummy," he said, and a sudden longing came over him to put his own hand upon those nervously clasped ones, but she made a warning sign. A stealthy footfall sounded in the street a few paces from them, and a dark shrouded form disappeared up the side alley.

"I must go," she said. "To-night I shall expect you. Take care you are not followed. Look behind you; watch your own footsteps. Eric! We have been through a good deal of danger together—though in some ways it has seemed to us like a holiday trip—but we have never been in so great danger as now."

She turned. One upward flash of her eyes, and she was gone, the small form in its heavy mantle vanishing silently into the darkness of the rock street, for the afterglow was wiped out, and night had set in.

Hansen stood still, troubled and anxious. He already knew two Annes—the cheery comrade of his adventurous journey, the queenly and resourceful priestess, but this was a new Anne whom he did not know. She had sometimes seemed to him tantalisingly devoid of womanly weakness, and its consequent charm. Now, though loyal, courageous and enduring as ever, there was that about her that, while thrilling his pulses in human fashion, deeply stirred his inner being. He made a movement to follow her, but checked himself. She had bidden him be cautious. He peered out of the recess, making sure that the upper part of the street was empty, then he walked down the intervening space, and quietly entered his cave-lodging.

Chapter XXXVI—The Tryst

IT was now the Acan supper hour, and the thorough-fares were deserted. Later, business would be in swing at the booths in the market-place; and Hansen hoped, under cover of the throng of people who would be making their purchases for the next day, and the noise of their talk, to gain unnoticed the stairway to Anne's balcony, and swing himself up into the shelter of a pillar where he might wait quietly the hour of the tryst. There would be less likelihood of detection then than if he waited till the city was still, with the chance that his movements might attract attention from some windows looking on the market-place, or from some belated passer-by.

Meanwhile he occupied himself with his own evening meal, served by the impassive Acan whom Keorah had provided for him. The man stood gravely as Hansen poured himself a bowl of chocolate and attacked the roast kid and maize cakes, for which in truth he had now small appetite.

He felt shaken by his meeting with Anne, though he could not tell what her hurried words portended. Her small pale face and shining eyes seemed to meet his gaze wherever he looked about the room. She was very dear to him, this little Chummy, dearer than he had before realised, and he knew that strange and strong as had been Keorah's power of fascination, it needed but a word from Anne to break the spell of that enchantress. And yet, though he felt Anne's uneasiness and distrust of his loyalty—he dared not even to himself call it jealousy—he could not lay bare his heart to her. For was she not alone, and committed to his care, and was she not still Elias Bedo's wife? His code of honour was a strenuous one, and to speak one word of love to Anne in these conditions would be to violate it.

His food choked him, but he forced himself to eat, knowing that he might need all his strength. He was irked by the presence of the serving-man and bade him go and amuse himself for the rest of the evening, as he required him no more. The man departed, and

Hansen, looking at his watch, saw that it still wanted an hour to the time Anne had named. He leaned his head on his hands, and gave rein to his thoughts, frankly wishing Keorah, in company with Elias Bedo, and the whole Acan community, at a safe distance—in the maw of the Crocodile for all he cared—so long as he were left alone with Anne and the prehistoric records. This reminded him that only that day he had fancied out hunting, that there was a certain lurid reddening of that spiral cloud which hung as far as he could make out—for the mountain had not come prominently in view—over the open jaws of the Crocodile, and he made a mental note that upon the morrow he would, if circumstances permitted, ascend the monolith and take an observation from that vantage point.

He pulled himself together, and now ate vigorously, discovering that, apart from sentiment, his long day in the Acan hunting-ground had left him hungry. After all, man is nothing but a piece of machinery. Oil him, and he runs easily. Five minutes after he had swallowed his mess of kid, and drunk a glass or two of Acan liqueur—a special concoction from certain berries cultivated for the purpose—Hansen, who had badly needed his supper, felt a different being. He got up from the table, shaking back his shoulders, and his fair head with its untrimmed locks like those of a great shaggy dog; and humming unmelodiously enough a few bars of one of Anne's songs, he went into the adjoining cavern, which was lighted by one of the curious Acan lamps, and performed some sort of toilet, putting on the darkest cloak he could find in the wardrobe with which the forethought of Keorah or Hotan had furnished him during his residence in the huntsman's house. He then considered how he should arm himself in view of possible emergencies, and perhaps sudden flight, but decided that his gun being cumbersome, he had better leave it behind, and content himself with the revolver which he stuck in his belt.

He pulled the curtains of his rock doorway together behind—nearly all the cave houses opened thus on to a ledge and a stairway—and stood on the threshold, peering from side to side before he passed into the street.

A good deal of business of a kind was done after nightfall in the city
of the Aca, but it mostly concentrated in the market-place. Here the
great precipices, faintly dotted with specks and streaks of light from
the windows of the cave dwellings, loomed darkly. Down below
were ghostly grey patches, around which the torches flared upon the
booths, making the blackness deeper beneath the projecting
balconies and in places not given up to stall-keepers and their wares.
In the market, the crowd was busy huckstering and packing up and
carrying away their purchases before the booths closed and the Acan
population took itself off to bed.

Nobody seemed to take any notice of Hansen, though every now
and then he threw a glance over his shoulder to make sure that he
was not being followed. All went well so far, and presently he found
himself beneath Anne's balcony. He looked for Kombo on the small
platform outside the entrance to the Priestess' house, but there was
no sign of the black boy. From this platform Hansen, watching his
opportunity, swung himself up to the ledge outside the stone railing,
and then waited, crouching in the angle where it joined an abutting
pillar—one of those which had framed Keorah and her Virgins when
she had for the first time exercised upon him the magic of her
beauty. The Zuhua Kak's rooms were curtained close, and all in
darkness, but from Keorah's house next door there came gleams of
light through the window hangings, a sound of laughter, and the
secular music of the Acans. Hansen wondered, if she were giving an
entertainment, why he had not been invited. He was thankful,
however, that he had not, and before long the music ceased, and a
figure went down the stairway, that he recognised as that of Hotan—
apparently Keorah's only guest. Hansen crouched lower, afraid lest
his presence should be noticed, but Hotan went on his way without
looking up. Peering round the pillar and the partition wall, Hansen
could see the staircase by which he had mounted that memorable
night when he had lighted the mystic lamp on Keorah's balcony. The
two serpents were still there intertwined, but there was no flame in
the vessel between their jaws. Hansen had often since that night
thought of his action, but he did not yet fully realise its meaning,
though he suspected that it was some pledge of betrothal. Keorah,
however, had not directly alluded to it, and Hansen did not care to

run the risk of questioning her. He was aware that Keorah was not a woman whom it was safe to thwart, and he could only hope that she was not like the four-footed serpent, nursing wrath in order to pour it forth later upon himself and hapless Anne. He could never understand why Keorah had so willingly allowed a stranger to supplant her in the important office of Zuhua Kak. He shrank from explaining it on the theory that Keorah had ulterior motives and passionate yearnings which had found their centre in himself, and in which as Virgin High Priestess she was not permitted to indulge. And yet this would have been plainly apparent to a less interested observer.

Gradually the lights below were extinguished, the bustle subsided, and the market-place became silent and deserted. Hansen watched anxiously. The hour of the tryst was passed; the curtains at the back of the balcony remained unstirred. At last from behind them a faint voice whispered, "Eric!" He moved nearer at the call.

"Hush! Step softly. I am here. Give me your hand," and as the hangings parted, he felt Anne's fingers quiver within his own. She drew him into the rock chamber. No lover could have found more romantic prospect of adventure. But the business of to-night was not love-making. Hansen felt instinctively that nothing was further from Anne's mind. The room was in darkness, except for a pale radiance cast through the curtained doorway of the inner chamber by the four emblematic lamps that the Virgins had lighted round Zuhua Kak's bed, and by the red glow of one or two torches still burning in the market-place. The other doorway, leading into the entrance corridor, was draped with feathered tapestry, and through the meshes of the foundation in the interstices of the pattern, there showed also a feeble glimmer from a lamp placed some way down the passage. The small form of the girl in her white linen robe seemed like a wraith in the gloom. He could see her face dimly, and knew that it was agitated. She trembled from head to foot, and he also saw that she had not control over the muscles of her throat. Anne hysterical! That was strange indeed.

"Chummy!" he said tenderly, "what is the matter? Were you afraid I shouldn't come?"

She took no notice of the question beyond drawing back when he put out his hands as though to place them upon her shoulders.

"Well," he said, "what is it?"

"My husband is here," she exclaimed bluntly.

"Here!" he cried, starting, and looking round. "Impossible!"

"Oh! I don't mean in this room—though I daresay it won't be long before he is down there," and she pointed towards the market-place. "He is outside the mountain. Kombo saw him to-day."

"You poor little soul! So that's the trouble." His voice broke, but it was in pity for her. And his pity seemed just the thing Anne could not bear. She shook again, and a dry sob choked her.

"They will find him; they will bring him in—and then—"

"Then you who are Zuhua Kak, and queen among the Aca, will order him to be driven out again. Where's the use of wearing a magnificent High Priestess' mantle, and what Kombo calls a 'fire-stone' on your forehead, if it doesn't mean that your orders are to be obeyed? Have no fear, Chummy! You and I together can deal with this business. After all, it is only what we expected."

His tone jarred upon her rasped nerves. She could not realise that its lightness was affected as a cover to his real feeling.

"That is easy to say," she answered; "but if you had"—she paused, commanding herself with an effort—"if you had had opportunities for weighing the responsibilities of my position,"—she laughed hysterically at her own stilted way of putting things.—"I mean, if you were me, you would know that the office of Zuhua Kak is not without its dangers."

Fugitive Anne

"Its dangers!" he echoed; "do you suppose I haven't thought of that? But I'm in the dark, Anne. Tell me exactly what you are thinking."

"I am thinking," she returned slowly, "that if it were proved I was Elias Bedo's wife, and not the messenger of the gods, not the daughter of Viracocha, my influence over the Acans would be gone. I should no longer be Zuhua Kak, and there would be some terrible punishment in store for me. Not that it would matter much," she added bitterly. "The worst penalty would be that I should be given back to my lawful protector. I would risk anything to avoid that. I would try to escape, even if it meant death in the trying."

His mouth twitched; he bit his lip. For a moment or two he did not speak, but her eyes were turned away. She had them fixed at the end of the room, near the entrance door to the corridor, upon a piece of feather tapestry, the pattern of which—a barbaric medley—seemed to stand out upon the lighter ground as though there were a light behind it.

"Anne!" he said, earnestly, "I see that you have some plan in your mind. Now will you tell me exactly what it is—all that Kombo has given you to understand about your husband's movements—and let me have a voice in the matter? If it's an idea of escaping at once, nothing rash must be ventured. I shall not allow you to do anything by which you run any risk of your life."

She was unreasonably exasperated by his words, which seemed to her to indicate unwillingness to leave the city of the Acans.

"You have no power to prevent me," she answered, "unless you were to betray my plan to the Elders and to Keorah."

"What! You can think that of me!" he exclaimed, surprise and pain in his face and in his voice. "How have I deserved this of you, Anne? If you had had any thought of that kind, why did you tell me to come here this evening? Give me your confidence freely, or else let me leave you." He turned as if to go. He was wounded to the heart, and

332

intuitively she felt this, yet with a woman's perversity would not acknowledge that she had wronged him.

"No, don't go," she said, but with no great warmth in her tone. "I'll tell you what Kombo said to me, and the plan he has worked out. It is your right to hear it, and to choose what you will do. Of course, I know that even if you don't care to follow it, you will keep silence and help us as far as you can. I spoke hastily. I do not distrust you in that sense."

"In what sense, then?" he asked, resentfully, but she did not seem to hear him. A sudden look of apprehension had come over her face; he could tell that by the way she strained forward, her eyes fixed intently upon a piece of feather tapestry that hid a portion of the rock wall. His tone changed. "What is the matter? Has anything startled you?"

She did not answer at once; then her gaze turned slowly from the feather—wrought monsters on the wall.

"No. I thought I saw that bit of embroidery move. I fancied there was a gleam of light behind it, and I was afraid."

His eyes followed the direction of hers.

"I don't think it's anything. That's only one of their feather pictures. Here's another survival of the ancient Mexicans—another corroboration of my theory, if I wanted one. It's an Aztec art. I'll strike a match and look if you like whether there's a door behind it. But matches are precious in these days."

"No, don't waste one. That's not a doorway. The entrance to these rooms is over there." She pointed to the heavily draped archway. "But it seems to me that the whole of the rock is undermined with secret caves and passages, and I'm always fancying that I'm being spied upon. Never mind. I must have been mistaken. You shall hear now all that Kombo told me this afternoon."

So, unaware that, hidden behind the feather monster, Keorah was listening eagerly, and piecing together as far as she was able the English words of which she understood the meaning, Anne related the substance of her interview with Kombo in Aak's garden. She told Eric how the black boy had discovered a passage in the double wall of rock, how he had seen Elias Bedo, her husband—Keorah knew the word husband—encamped close to the spot where the Red Men had first found them; how Kombo's sharp wits had grasped the whole situation; how the black boy had put pituri in the white man's and the troopers' tea, and how he had planned returning that night, and while the men slept a drugged sleep, stealing the horses and concealing them in the cave, ready for flight upon the following evening. All this she set before Hansen quietly and distinctly—the very calmness to which she forced herself, though every nerve in her was tingling, and the clearness of her enunciation making the eavesdropper's task easier. Hansen deliberated gravely, pointing out dangers, weighing possibilities,—the risks of taking that route through unknown country where the explorer Burke had met his death, and where a similar fate might befall them at the hands of cannibal blacks—the unlikelihood of their reaching Burketown—that one point of civilisation in the middle of the Bight of Carpentaria—the doubt whether it would not be wiser to trust to the chances of the Acan Exodus, and the question of being able thus to secure valuable spoils which would materially aid scientific investigation, and be a benefit to the world at large.

Anne chafed. His arguments seemed cold-blooded. In them she read the desire to remain, the disinclination to abandon Keorah, and with her the opportunity for study of the Acan hieroglyphics. In comparison with these delights she thought that her peace of mind, her deliverance from the clutches of Elias Bedo, counted as nothing. At last she cried passionately—

"What do I care for all that? What does it matter to me whether you can find a key or not to the hieroglyphics? That is nothing in comparison with chances of safety, it seems to me. All I know is this—I cannot stay to face my husband. Kombo and I are of one mind about our escape. He is only a black boy, but I have trusted

Fugitive Anne

him before, and I shall trust him again. Poor Kombo! He has his own reasons for wanting to be quit of the Red Men. His experience has been less fortunate than yours." She laughed unsteadily. "Anyhow I have made up my mind that if Kombo can get hold of the horses, I should be foolish to delay. It remains to be seen, Eric, what you desire to do."

"Since you have made up your mind, there is only one thing for me to do," he replied, and to her sensitive fancy there was something very uncompromising in his voice. "You came to this place under my protection, and under my protection, if you so choose, you shall leave it. I am at your service absolutely. All I wish is, that you should realise the risks you may be running. For the rest"—he faltered, and his eyes sought hers in the dimness pleadingly, but Anne's look was averted—"you seem to me to have changed, Anne, since you became Zuhua Kak. A sort of barrier has arisen between us. I don't quite understand you."

"Nor I you," she returned impetuously, now turning to him, her voice and mien showing a lofty disregard of convention—if, indeed, as he grimly thought, there could be any idea of the conventionalities in their present situation. The man and woman stood facing each other, each seeing the face of the other as a glimmering white patch in the dusk.

"From what I have observed," she went on, "I can only infer that you would prefer to remain here, where there is, I am sure, much to interest you, and where you are very welcome among the chief of the people, until it suits you to go back to Europe, with the result of your investigation. For me, of course, things are different."

Hansen stared at her bewilderedly. Man is an obtuse animal, and he was only beginning to understand the workings of the feminine mind.

"You thought I cared about deciphering the hieroglyphics and the rest of that scientific rubbish more than I care for your safety!" he said. "Anne! Anne! I can only say again, how have I deserved this?"

335

He put out his hands once more and took hers. But though their strong grasp was a denial to her feeble asseveration, she shook them off and drew back as before.

"No, Eric, I did not think it was the hieroglyphics and the scientific rubbish, as you call it, that you cared for more than my safety," she answered, her voice cutting like a diamond edge. "I thought you cared more for that other woman than for anything which concerned me."

There was something very childlike and very feminine about Anne as she said these words, which a little while before she would have thought it impossible she could utter. But something stronger than pride had leaped in her bosom, and turned the stately little priestess into a mere ordinary woman with a woman's weaknesses, a woman's inconsistency; and through his anger and his hurt, Hansen felt a sudden joy, though he stood stiffly, making no sign.

"It is quite natural," Anne went on, borne away by the flood of feeling. "You and I have been good friends, but at best I have been but a burden to you. You have been very chivalrous in not letting me see it, and I thank you for all your kindness. I was foolish not to realise that I must be a hindrance in your plans when I almost asked you to take me with you. But it's not too late now for you to carry them out without me, for you will have that woman's help, and you need be in no anxiety on my behalf. Kombo and I got on very well before, and you can trust him to take care of me again. We went through a good deal, you know, before we met you. Once free of this people, we can fight our way to the coast. That is the plan we propose."

"And may I ask," said Hansen huskily, "what plan you propose for me?"

"I should not presume to make plans for you," answered Anne. "I conclude that you want to go on with your scientific discoveries, and I don't imagine that now you will find any lack of advantages in that respect."

"Chief of these being Keorah," he said; and she might have seen in the twilight of the room, had she been watching his face, the flicker of a smile, but she kept her eyes steadily away from him. Now he had regained something of his composure.

"Anne! Anne!" he said, "it rejoices me to see that you are after all, but yet a woman. You have tried to be cold and judicial, and in spite of everything your heart has spoken."

He was close to her. She could feel his breath upon her cheek. She could see the flame of passion scintil-late in his eyes. Her nerves thrilled, and her body shook with suppressed emotion. She made a valiant but ineffectual stand.

"How could you—how dare you think that I'm jealous of Keorah? What right have you? You know it is not that. How could it be that?"

"I should never dare to suppose such a thing," he replied humbly. "As you say, what right have I—and how could it be that? But, my child, nevertheless, I think you are a little mistaken in your thoughts of me, and that's where you prove yourself a woman after all. You fancied that I cared more for Keorah and for science than for you. I could not show you—how was it possible?—what you are to me. You must know how I am tied and bound by the conditions under which we have been thrown together. But the old friendship was very precious. And now this strange red woman has stepped in and spoiled it all."

"But has she spoiled it?" Anne cried, proving herself even more a woman by her anxiety to retrieve that which a few minutes back she had been so ready to cast away. "Has she come between us in that? I don't think, Eric, that the old friendship is 'altogether bong,' as Kombo would say." She laughed a soft laugh that was music in his ears, for there was a ring of happiness in it, and when Hansen's fingers again closed on hers, she did not draw herself away.

"Chummy!"—and the man's voice deepened and faltered—"it is not only friendship that I want of you. Only, it's all that I dare ask of you as things are, my dear. You must know—you must understand. Won't you trust me, child—even though—"

"Even though Keorah may appear singularly attractive in your eyes, and no matter how freely she lavishes her blandishments upon you, or how pleased you may seem to be at them! Is that how it is, Eric?" returned Anne lightly, with the old cheery note he had known so well in the bush. "I suppose that I must trust you, for, indeed, to tell you the truth—" She hung her head and hesitated for a moment, but then went on bravely, "To tell you the truth, Eric, I think something in me would have gone 'altogether bong' if you had said that you meant to stay behind."

He crushed the little hands in his; then raised one passionately to his lips. But he did not stoop to kiss her face, nor would he even put his arm around her. Anne realised in that moment, perhaps more fully than ever before, the loyalty of the man—in spite of his many manly imperfections—with whom she had to deal.

Chapter XXXVII—My Lover and my Lord!

AS they stood thus, hands clasped in hands, eyes meeting eyes through the gloom of the chamber, a low laugh sounded behind them,—a silvery laugh, high pitched, sweet but soulless, so empty of human feeling, unless it were malignant feeling, that it would have been difficult to believe the laugh was uttered by a woman. But Anne and Hansen both knew the voice; both dreaded it. They started and turned, and he made a movement of recoil—afterwards she remembered that he had done so—but she instinctively drew nearer to him, her heart warm yet with the glow of his tenderness, his presence giving her courage so that she felt strong enough to do battle even with Keorah.

For it was indeed Keorah who had laughed that tinkling scornful laugh, and who stood now framed in the entrance arch between the drawn curtains—a splendid figure illuminated by the torches that a pair of women held upraised behind her, and which drew glints of coloured light from the opal ornaments she still wore in right of her past priestess-ship, and which made her ruddy hair seem likewise a flame.

"Thou art all in the dark, oh! Zuhua Kak," said the mocking voice, "in darkness of earth only, since through virtue of thine office, thine inner eyes must ever be lighted by that lamp of the Spirit which illumines not the ways of common humanity. Thou art in truth High Virgin of the Flame, and I who, at the will of the Eternal didst in outward seeming resign my privileges to thee, may not presume to question thy spiritual illumination. Nevertheless, I bring thee light, oh! Holy Virgin of the Flame. For where I am, there Light must follow me."

She laughed again with shrill sweetness, and sailed into the room, her heavily embroidered draperies sweeping round her, while at a sign her women placed their torches in niches provided for the purpose at either side of the doorway, and disappeared into the darkness of the corridor. "We do not want listeners to our talk," went on Keorah, affecting not to observe Hansen, who had relinquished Anne's hand and withdrawn towards the window. "I, who but a short time since was Zuhua Kak, come to thee, who art installed by decree of Viracocha in the place I held, to take counsel with thee in distress that is a penalty of ordinary womanhood. I know that as Daughter of the Gods, and foreordained messenger to the people of Aca, thou art skilled in deep lore, and in knowledge of the mind of man transcending that of a mere child of earth, and so I come to thee, oh! Zuhua Kak, in the hope that thou mayest be able to ease the heart of thy suffering sister. For was not I Zuhua Kak before thee, and am I not therefore thy sister? And in truth my heart is heavy to-night and my spirit sore within me."

She paused and seemed to wait for Anne's reply, but the girl only bowed her head coldly, saying nothing. Keorah resumed.

"Thou who art set so high above thy kind, doubtless knowest naught by experience of the temptations which assail weaker women. Nevertheless, it seems to me that by the light of thy inner wisdom thou mayest see more clearly than thy humbler sister in what manner it were best to deal with human heart-burnings and perplexities, and mayest guide me, perchance, to those calm heights above the surges of passion in which thou thyself dost dwell. Well do I, who was ever faithful to my vows, know in what royal peace, by aid of power divinely vouchsafed, the High Priestess may maintain herself. But I—when in obedience to the Sign of the Red Ray, I delivered to thee the Symbols of my holy office—ceased to be thus mysteriously immune from the glamour of love and the strivings of my womanhood. Unlike to thee, oh! Child of Dawn, to whom men can never have seemed other than flitting shadows, I acknowledge my thraldom to him who by tender wooing has gained my heart, and I plead with thee, who dost so nobly hold thyself, for guidance, that in stooping to love I may comport myself as befits one who but a few weeks ago was as thou art, Zuhua Kak."

Anne stood motionless, save for a slight heaving of her bosom and a nervous twitch of the muscles of her throat, listening to Keorah's words. She understood their drift, for in these weeks she had studied the Mayan language with success, and was sufficiently versed in its ornate phraseology to follow Keorah's clearly enunciated speech. As was its wont, her brain worked quickly, and she was rapidly weighing arguments that should decide for her the best course to pursue. Turning deliberately to where Hansen stood in the shadow of the window curtains, she motioned him forward towards the light.

"I have heard thee, Keorah, and I gather from thy words that thou dost desire advice from me upon some weighty matter that troubleth thee. But clearly, conversation is difficult between thee and me, since thou hast not been instructed in any language which is familiar to me, and I, though I understand somewhat of the Acan tongue, am not learned in its subtleties. First, then, I would say to thee that, as thou seest, I am not alone. Here is Zaac Tepal—as thou dost name him—the Interpreter commissioned by the gods. He will assist my imperfect understanding of thy tongue by translating to me what thou dost wish to say."

Keorah gave a well-feigned start of surprise and virtuous dismay.

"Zaac Tepal—here! At this hour—and in the private apartment of the Zuhua Kak! Nay, I learn with astonishment, messenger of Viracocha, that thou dost hold thyself superior to the rules of the Acan Priestess-ship, decreed by our gods, and from the foundation of our community kept sacred. It is the law of our order that this chamber be held secure from masculine intrusion."

Hansen broke in ill-advisedly—

"For this intrusion I would crave pardon. I would explain that my mistress, the Zuhua Kak, required my presence in view of the transporting of the great Aak."

Keorah's lip curled disdainfully.

"Methinks," she said, "that the great Aak, who is himself interpreter between gods and men, should be able to give his own counsel to his high priestess. I spoke not to thee, Zaac Tepal. No doubt thou art here, as thou sayest, at thy mistress' orders, and it is the Zuhua Kak who is accountable for thy presence. The great Aak supplies but a badly needed excuse."

Anne looked confusedly at Hansen. She had not quite followed the rapid interchange of Mayan, for Keorah spoke excitedly, and at her request he was forced to give a clumsy translation of what had passed. Anne's lips grew white, and she stood very erect as she answered him steadily: "Repeat to the woman that you are here by my orders, and for the reason that I required to consult with my interpreter. Say to her, also, that since I gave no permission for the admittance of a visitor into my private rooms, I enquire by what right she has forced her way here."

Hansen hesitated. He felt himself between two opposing forces, and though he did not greatly care what happened to him individually, he feared that serious damage might result from the clash against each other of these two floods of feminine passion. Then, too, though Anne had certainly proved herself capable of holding her own among the Acans in any ordinary emergency, she had not yet been pitted in actual personal combat against Keorah. The beautiful red woman was a formidable enemy, and one whom it would be wiser to tranquillize rather than exasperate. Therefore he gave Keorah a somewhat modified version of Anne's remarks. Both women watched him closely; neither was deceived. Keorah sneered contemptuously and glared at her rival; the savage suddenly unveiled. Anne reared herself in yet more stately fashion, and summoning all her resources in the Mayan tongue, addressed the red woman with a frigid courtesy that would have done credit to a great lady in some European drawing-room.

"I have asked by what right you confer upon me the honour of your presence unannounced?"

Keorah scented a refinement of social warfare in which she must be worsted, and completely dropped her mask of civilisation. She made a threatening gesture; her eyes sent out lightnings of rage. Her

342

sinuous form quivered like that of a panther gathering strength before it springs. Then she suddenly swerved to Hansen's side. The furious look changed to one of cunning. "Reply for me to the Zuhua Kak, oh! Zaac Tepal. Tell her that Keorah will stoop no more to dissimulate, and that she shall know of a truth why I forced my way hither. Tell her that an Acan woman has the right to follow her future lord even into the chamber of the Zuhua Kak, and that it is to claim thee, my lover and my betrothed husband, that I am come. Nay, feign not surprise like some coy maiden, Zaac Tepal, for by thine own lips have the binding words been said, and thou art surely mine, White Strength, my lover and my lord, since the night when thou didst first pledge me in the betrothal cup, and when according to ancient usage among the Acans thou didst light the marriage lamp upon my balcony."

She stopped, her glittering eyes fixed upon his face with that odd magnetic power in them which, when she chose to exert it in its full force, affected him against his reason and his will. It was like the spell of a witch, he often thought to himself. There were times when he had the power to struggle against it, and there had been other times when she had taken him in his weaker moments, and he had yielded to its seductive attraction. To—night he had no mind to yield, yet a certain native chivalry in him, the presence of Anne, the remembrance of past weakness and something in the woman herself, made it impossible for him to give her the lie direct. He reddened, and stirred awkwardly. His embarrassment appeared to the indignant Anne almost a confession. Keorah saw her advantage. There had been a note of appeal in her voice, but it was the appeal of one who holds a yet stronger weapon hidden.

Hansen at length stammered out, "That's all a mistake, Keorah—a foolish prank performed in ignorance."

The savage element in Keorah blazed forth at once. She cut short his excuse with an indignant wave of her hand.

"Thou dost call thyself a lord of men and wouldst deny thine own deed and speech! Thinkest thou that the meanest Acan hind would play double to a woman? I command thee by thy manhood to interpret to her the words I have said."

"How can I interpret them, oh! Keorah?" he answered, totally at a loss before her. "Let that matter remain between thee and me. The Zuhua Kak knows nothing of what thou art pleased to call our betrothal."

Keorah smiled in malicious triumph.

"Then is it the more needful that she should learn the truth, Zaac Tepal. Tell her, oh! husband of my choice, whom the gods have sent to reward me for loss of greatness given to her in my stead—tell her of the bond of union between us, soon to be confirmed by the marriage rite. Bid her be glad with our gladness, and rejoice with us that her hand hath led thee to me. For had not the gods ordained her to that high loneliness in which I must have dwelt for ever unmated, never should I have known thee, my beloved; never should I have tasted of the fulness of life."

Her accents had regained their silveriness, and there was in them a deeper note of genuine emotion. She extended her arms in a movement extraordinarily graceful and enticing. It was the passionate woman pleading for and with her lover. And Anne could not have doubted that Hansen was indeed Keorah's lover, but for that which had passed between herself and him a few minutes back. Even then, in those moments of exquisite assurance, the dagger of distrust was only just withdrawn from her breast. Now the wound reopened. She gazed at Hansen, a whole world of anxious tenderness, of enquiring reproach in her brown eyes; then withdrawing them, for his were lowered, she met Keorah's exultant gaze. The red woman went closer to him and laid her outstretched hands upon his arm.

"Speak, Zaac Tepal,—my conqueror, my lord!"

"Thou dost ask too much," he muttered. "I have said—this thing, if it were true, is not one with which to trouble the Zuhua Kak."

"If it were true? Perjurer! Thou art but jesting with me to try my faith. Was it not only last night that thou didst solemnly pledge me in my wine—cup—that thou didst whisper sweet vows to me both in thy tongue and in mine? Didst thou not call me most beautiful of all the women thou hast ever known? Didst thou not salute me after the manner of lovers in thine own land? Didst thou not kiss me, Zaac Tepal?"

Keorah uttered the English syllable archly and with dulcet sweetness.

Anne heard and understood. It was evident that Keorah had been an apt pupil to a willing instructor. Hansen's laugh—harsh, contemptuous, but truth-telling—dispelled all doubt in Anne's mind. She turned away and stared vacantly at the wall beyond; but there she still seemed to see Keorah, clinging now unrebuked to Hansen's side, her fingers stroking proudly the gold trophy he had carried off at the games, and which she had then clasped below his elbow, and which he had worn ever since. Her round rosy arm stole up slowly, with a suggestion of delicious enjoyment, till it circled his shoulder. Anne saw it all, even though her eyes were turned away—saw his shame-faced acceptance of the caress; knew that Keorah had not lied; made no allowance for the fact that wine is a potent factor, and that man thinks little of snatching a proffered kiss. She turned suddenly upon him, able to bear no more.

"Zaac Tepal, I dismiss thee! To-night I have no further need of thy services," she said, retaining sufficient possession of her faculties to speak in her studiously acquired Mayan, so that Keorah might also understand. Her own voice sounded to Anne far away, and the shadowy room seemed to rock around her, and become dimmer still, only those two figures standing out stationary and distant.

"Zaac Tepal!" she cried, her voice in Hansen's ears sounding like the voice of an animal in pain. "Dost thou not hear me? I have no further need of thee. Go!"

He started as if from a dream, and roughly shook himself free from Keorah's hold.

"Come," he said to her gruffly. "Our presence is an insult to the Zuhua Kak."

Keorah cringed mockingly, and made as though she would plead with Anne.

"I pray thee, grant us grace, oh! Zuhua Kak. Fain would I stand in thy favour, for as thou knowest, it will be thy office to hold forth to us the holy orb which, kneeling' before thee on our marriage day, we shall solemnly touch with our right hands, making to each other the vows that are binding, till Xibal, Lord of Death, calls us to the Place of Sleep. And seeing that by the will of the gods thou must join us in union, I know not wherein we have deserved thine anger, nor what insult there can be in the humble suing of a highborn Acan woman and of him who is to be her husband."

Keorah spoke in her own language, but paused a moment, and then bending backward with a swaying movement of her lithe form, she took Hansen's right hand in hers, and drawing him to her side, said in English, with halting but exquisite intonation, "My husband!"

Anne knew that Eric must have taught her the words. She waved the two imperiously aside.

"Begone, woman! Mr Hansen, take her away."

For a moment of tragic issue, the three stood, Keorah's and Hansen's eyes fixed upon Anne; the red woman's full of elation, his deeply sorrowful as they searched Anne's face for some sign of relenting. But there was none; the small features were rigid, and her right arm, motionless as marble, was extended, pointing to the doorway.

Keorah gave her cruel laugh.

"I obey thee, Zuhua Kak, but ere long it may be, thou wilt repent this ungracious dismissal. Come, Zaac Tepal, we will depart."

She drew his arm within her own, and he allowed her to lead him. She covered his grim acquiescence by her proud complacency, her rapt eyes dwelling on his moody face, her every movement towards him as she walked, a caress. Thus the two passed through the archway, and were swallowed up in the gloom of the rock corridor.

Now, forgetting everything but her pain, Anne gave a long shuddering moan. Her tense form collapsed, and she sank in a heap on the floor, her face hidden in her linen robe, her curly head resting upon her drawn up knees. There, Keorah's women saw her, as with silent footsteps they came back to remove their torches. They were obeying their mistress's orders, and like well-drilled servants exchanged no word. They only glanced from the bowed form of the High Priestess meaningly at each other, and went out, leaving the room in darkness.

Chapter XXXVIII—The Subjugation of Elias Bedo

IT was the next morning, and the sun was not yet high in the east. Outside the Tortoise Mountain, his rays poured upon the great grey precipice with its natural buttresses, its clefts and caverns beneath the jagged edge of the rock carapace, near to where the wanderers had camped upon the day of their entrance into the Heart of Aak.

The tunnel Hansen had then discovered, and by which the red men had emerged, showed a dusky patch, half concealed by bushes and scarcely distinguishable on the face of the cliff from many another hole made by time and weather. Outside the opening, her back to the mountain, Keorah stood enveloped in her Acan mantle, pale yellow in colour, and bordered and patterned with feathers of a contrasting orange. Her russet hair, even more brilliant in tint than her cloak, flowed down her back, flaming where the sun touched it, and thinning into feathery strands as the wind, which swept in small gusts up from the valley below, caught it playfully, spreading it on each side of her face.

The air was curiously oppressive for that time of year, even in this tropical region; and above the intersecting hills on the south coast, there hung a roll of lurid-looking clouds seeming to tell of a gathering storm. But overhead, the sky was of a brilliant blue, and here the breeze, though warm at mid-day, beating against the mountain through the moist belt of scrub which sloped down below the untimbered space at the foot of the precipice, was laden with pleasant odours. Whiffs from eucalyptus forests, and from the resinous Australian pine, the scent of scrub flowers and aromatic shrubs, and through all, as seemed to the red woman, whose nostrils savoured these perfumes, a breath of wide expanses and untrodden wastes from the distant sea and the world of men.

Both Keorah and Anne, though women of different types and conditions, were consumed by the same desire to escape from their luxurious Acan prison, even though it might be to risk death among the blacks. In Anne, it was the yearning for freedom; in Keorah, an unconquerable craving, inbred in her, for pleasure and power, and for a fuller and more magnificent world which she had learned at last from her talks with Hansen really existed beyond these fastnesses. Hitherto, her knowledge had been limited to the vague traditions preserved among the people of Aca, of a mighty civilisation in the far-back past, from which the race had sprung. Now she knew there were other grand civilisations, other countries and other peoples who were not all red like her own. To gain experience of these, and possession of the strangerman who had captivated her fancy, was the end and aim of Keorah's intrigues.

In pursuance of these, Keorah had risen with the dawn, and made her way to the outskirts of the mountain. All night her busy brain had worked, connecting and translating the shreds of talk she had overheard from behind the tapestry in Anne's chamber, and which, though imperfectly understood, had furnished her with a sufficiently direct clue to the terror dogging her rival and the means by which matters might be hurried to a crisis, the flight prevented, the High Priestess disgraced, and the White Lord secured for herself as a lover, and guide to the outer world. She knew the power of her wonderful eyes, the fascination of her long narrow face, and had no fear of not being able to mould Hansen to her purposes. And, in truth, seldom had the sun looked upon a woman more beautiful than Keorah as she lifted her face to his, and throwing back her mantle from her shoulder, drew into her chest through the red parted lips long inhalations of the morning fragrance. She had, with her craving for subtle and sophisticated experience, an almost animal delight in air and sunshine, the free indulgence of her senses and exercise of her body which her cramped life as Zuhua Kak had only inflamed. At this moment her heart was throbbing and her pulses tingling with wild hope at the prospect, however uncertain, of accomplishing her desire, and satisfying the passionate impulses within herself which clamoured to be in harmony with the common laws of nature. At last, at last, she might do this, and in her fancy, the radiance of the sun, and all the fresh scents of the bush which she was taking into her being, seemed harbingers of success.

But Keorah was not one to waste time in romantic imaginings, though the warm flutter of the wind as it crept up her bare arm and played upon her face seemed to her like a lover's fervid kisses and intoxicated her with the foretaste of future joy. Drawing her mantle again about her shoulders, she stepped carefully among the rocks and shrubs, and rounded the natural buttresses of the cliff in the direction where she expected to find signs of a stranger's camp.

"E-li-as Be-do!" She pronounced the syllables slowly to herself as she had heard Anne and Hansen speak them; for that there was a strange man in pursuit of the High Priestess she was quite sure, and also that this was his name. Of his whereabouts she had learnt sufficient from Anne's account of Kombo's discovery to guide her in her quest. Hansen, in the few minutes she had spent alone with him after leaving Anne's presence upon the previous night, had sternly declined to gratify her curiosity, had indeed done all he could to refute her suspicions, but Keorah was too clever to doubt that something very serious and prejudicial to Anne lay behind the appearance on the scene of this new actor in the drama — something which would greatly simplify her own procedure for the ruin of the High Priestess. It was not Keorah's habit to dally in her workings, nor to take counsel with anybody. She knew that she must first satisfy herself of the truth of what she suspected, and till she had done this — a task she would not entrust to another — not one of her allies could be of much use to her. Once assured of Elias Bedo's relations with Anne, it would be time enough to instruct Naquah, Kapoc, Ishtal and the rest in the parts they were to play. Hotan was like a dog ready to do her bidding; she already had him in leash. He was at hand awaiting her further commands.

Keorah went on, her head bent towards the ground like a black tracker, though every now and then, she would give a quick glance in front and to the side, her eyes shining with the gleam in those of a panther in search of prey. And yet she meant no direct ill to Elias Bedo should she find him. Had it been her intention to secure him by force she would not have ventured thus, a woman alone, within his reach. She dealt in woman's weapons, fully alive to their efficacy. Meanwhile, below her breath, she practised herself in the English phrases she had picked up. They were mostly of an amatory character.

Suddenly, as she went round a projection of rock, she came upon the man she sought. He was lying half wrapped in his blanket, his head propped against his tilted saddle, and his face exposed to the full rays of the sun, which beat down and were reflected back from the shining surface of the precipice, focussing upon a locket that hung open from his pouch, and sending glints from the mounting of his rifle, which lay a little way from him, flung carelessly against a stone. He would have been an easy target for a black's spear or a red man's javelin, so profound was his slumber. Evidently Kombo's trick had succeeded, and the pituri had done its work. Beside him, in the ashes of the dead fire, with a half-consumed damper and a piece of roasted bandicoot, stood the empty billy which had held the drugged tea. He must have been asleep a long time, for there was not a spark among the ashes, and the piece of meat was covered with soldier ants. Were he to remain so till after noonday he would undoubtedly get sunstroke, and death would free Anne from his pursuit.

Keorah's eyes roved about, and lighted upon another camp a few paces off, where, stretched in the same heavy stupor, were the two native policemen who had accompanied Bedo. She stepped across, and looked with disgust at the black barbarians, kicking a pinch or two of gravel upon the out-stretched hand of one of them to see if he would stir, but he and his mate had drunk freely; possibly they had, like Kombo, gathered some pituri on their won account among the hills. Anyhow, it appeared as though nothing short of the last trump would waken them, and Keorah, peering round first to satisfy herself that there were no other human beings about, went back to the side of Bedo.

He was not a prepossessing object, and Keorah thought it was not surprising that Anne should run away from him; but she wondered that he, having come so far to regain her, and being within the precincts of possible enemies, should be content to lie there in a lethargy like that of a gorged python. She spurned him scornfully with the toe of her arched foot, and noticing that he stirred slightly, reminded herself that she had come to captivate and not to flout this singularly repulsive person. Her heart felt no temptation to swerve from its allegiance to Eric, however, as she compared the only two white men of her acquaintance. Very different from Hansen's clean-limbed, clear-skinned, and wholly attractive personality, was this corpulent, brutalised man, with his bull-throat, bulky trunk, and dark heavy face on which was a stubbly growth of black hair streaked with grey. Keorah did not like men who were black or red either, and Hansen's chief claim to her admiration lay in his Viking-like fairness.

Keorah felt a supreme contempt for Bedo. Yet she bent closer over him, so that her long hair swept his shoulder, and fluttered against his cheek while she pulled the little locket away from the pouch, and without much difficulty, detached it from a chain to which it was fastened. As she turned the open side upward, she started, and gave a low exultant laugh, for here was full confirmation of her suspicions. The locket held a coloured photograph of a woman's face, and Keorah instantly recognised the face as that of Anne, the reigning Zuhua Kak—Anne in her girlish days before the shadow of Elias Bedo had clouded her youth—a brighter, younger Anne, yet nevertheless bearing a likeness incontestable.

But how should the Daughter of Dawn, the messenger of the gods, the immaculate Virgin of the Flame, come to be pictured here in an amulet that this coarse son of earth carried about his person?

It was clear to Keorah's quick understanding that the owner of the locket must consider Anne in some sort of way his property; that undoubtedly he must stand to her in the position of either lover or husband—probably the latter, for had he been merely her lover, why should she not have discarded him without taking the trouble to put so great a distance between them? And the garments of these white people gave on arrival evidence that they had travelled far. Why, too, should she be in so great trepidation at the mere thought of his finding and claiming her? As Keorah stood with the trinket in her hand, gazing at the portrait, her senses all on the alert, her heart thrilling with the thought that success in her schemes was now almost a certainty, she did not consider the risk she might be running in thus exposing herself unprotected to the power of such a man as now lay before her. She looked down from Anne's portrait to the recumbent form, and her wonderful eyes seemed to gather in and emit force as she fixed them intently upon the face of the sleeper. Whether consciously or otherwise, she certainly sent forth a magnetic current which had the effect of rousing him from his stupor. His eyelids flickered and slowly lifted, his lips moved, the sound of a muttered oath came from between them. His limbs stirred; he partly raised himself and stared bewilderedly at the unexpected vision before him, his drugged brain not yet clear enough to decide whether it were reality or hallucination.

Like many materially-minded men Bedo was strongly given to superstition, and though he would have knocked any one down who called him a coward, he had a horror of anything bordering on the supernatural. Consequently, his first thought, when he beheld Keorah, was that she had come from another world. A howl of terror burst from him, that in other conditions must have immediately awakened the troopers and called them to arms, but they slept on undisturbed. Bedo gathered up his thick limbs and crouched back of a sudden upon his haunches, drawing himself away from her, while he looked up at her with an expression of fear and astonishment so comically blended, that Keorah laughed aloud.

"Damn you! What are you?" cried Elias Bedo, still shaking, but slightly reassured by the sound of her laughter.

Keorah smiled bewitchingly, and stretched out her arms, her mantle falling back so that the bare throat and part of her soft rounded neck showed above the generous curves of her bosom, draped in her close—fitting linen robe. Bedo's oath might have been a term of endearment for all she knew, for Hansen was not given to swearing at women. Eager to learn a new phrase, in her sweet high-pitched voice, with the most fascinating foreign accent, and an air of coquetry, she repeated the objurgation after him. "D—damn—you!" said she, making a little cooing sound, and stroking his rough, hairy hands clasped round his knees with her pretty pink fingers. The touch convinced Bedo that she was at least flesh and blood. His look of terror relaxed. His jaws broadened into a grin. He stared at her excitedly.

"What the dickens are you?" he exclaimed. Keorah did not understand, but, satisfied with the result of the newly-acquired phrase, cooed it again. "D—damn—you!"

"The devil!" ejaculated Bedo.

Keorah seized upon the word. She had heard Kombo talk of debil-debil: she knew what that meant.

"Debil-debil? Ma (No)." She shook her head and pointed to herself. "Keorah," she said.

"Keorah!" repeated Bedo, recovering himself. "A very pretty name, and you're an uncommonly pretty woman, my dear, though you aren't quite white. I suppose you're one of those famous red people the blacks talk about—eh?"

Keorah laughed and showed her white teeth and a dimple on one side of her narrow attractive face. She could not comprehend him much so far, but she felt that matters were progressing satisfactorily.

"You mustn't damn people," Bedo went on. "That's not pretty for a woman."

"Pretty woman," she repeated with her slow captivating smile, having previously learned the appropriateness of the words as applied to herself. Seeing that she did not altogether follow him, he tried black talk.

"Look here, Keorah, where camp belonging to you? You got him brother? Cobbon bujeri chief this fellow. Mine sit down long-a you."

Keorah laughed on, but he could not feel sure that she understood black talk.

"Pretty wo-man," irrelevantly pronounced Keorah. "Pret-ty man—Ma!" Her lip curled in coquettish disdain. She laughed meaningly into his face. "Husband—E-li-as—Be-do!"

"By Jove! How the dickens does she know my name?" He jumped to his feet and came close, leering at her.

"Husband—eh? You want-im husband belonging to you? All right, my dear. Bujeri gin you belonging to me," and he made as though to kiss her. But with a quick movement Keorah evaded him. Lightnings flashed from her eyes. All the majesty of the late unapproachable Zuhua Kak sat upon her brow. Perhaps it was well for Elias Bedo at that moment that she was not in her own city as Zuhua Kak, among her guarding acolytes, or his shrift would have been a short one.

Bedo stood, checked and appalled.

"The deuce! What a spitfire! I've a good mind to force a kiss, you handsome demon."

Keorah saw her danger. She leaned towards him deprecatingly, and smiled in her seductive way, subduing him by the magic of her eyes. She really understood a good deal of his speech by this time, but wished him to believe that she did not do so. Now she pointed to the mountain behind her, and along the unwooded space beneath it.

"Keorah...be-au-ti-ful...wo-man!" she stammered with dulcet expression. She did not know quite what to say in the emergency, but she remembered that when Hansen had been most kind and pleasant to her, he had called her a beautiful woman, and she thought the phrase might re—establish safe and friendly relations with this too familiar stranger. Bedo chuckled coarsely.

"Beautiful woman! I believe you—a doosid sight better looking, though you are red, than most white ones. And I don't know that I like you any the worse for putting a good value on yourself. You aren't going to let yourself be caught by chaff, eh, my fine bird?"

Steadying himself against a boulder, for the drug had left him not quite master of either his limbs or his brain, he gazed at her in open-mouthed admiration, taking in confusedly the details of her attire, from the cream—coloured, fine-woven underdress, to the feathered mantle and sandalled feet. His cupidity was aroused at sight of the gold and opal belt round her shapely waist.

"Hullo!" he cried, "what's that? Have you more of the same kind where that came from?" and he would have snatched at the cincture, had not Keorah's compelling gaze kept him at a distance. She still pointed to the mountain, and her gesture seemed to him to signify that there the treasure lay.

"Inside there, my pretty? But how are we to get at 'em? You'll show me the road—eh? But I must make sure of that. No killings and roastings and eatings—being eaten it would be—for me! Not if I know it! No hanky panky, Miss Keorah. We'll see first how you came to know my name—whether it was Anne that told you. By Jingo! I see it now. It must have been Anne that told it you. And if you haven't eaten Anne, the odds are you won't want to eat me." He swayed himself to and fro, chuckling still, and again leering at her. Keorah caught at the name.

"Anne!" she said, and his eyes, following hers, fell upon the open locket which she had let drop on the ground when he had tried to kiss her. He lurched forward, and stooping picked it up.

"So you've been robbing me? You're a nice baggage! And you know who it is—do you? Now I'm seeing daylight. Yes, that's Anne, sure enough; and the devil take her—after I've done with her. You—you devilish fine woman—d'you know where she is? Here—" and he tapped the locket. "White Mary like-it this. You pidney where that fellow sit down?"

"Yo-ai!" Keorah laughed again like a pleased child. In the course of her assiduous attention to the white people's talk she had picked up even a smattering of Kombo's queer jumble of English and Aboriginese. She tossed her head now, with its wealth of red hair, back towards the mountain. "Come," she said again, "E-lias—Be-do—Hus-band... Anne—Wife... Keorah—be-au-ti-ful woman... Anne—be-au-ti-ful—wife."

"By the Lord Harry, you're wrong there, Miss Keorah," exclaimed Bedo, with a harsh guffaw. "She don't hold a candle to you. And I'm sick of her—damned sick of her and the chase she's led me."

The infuriated husband fired forth a volley of profanity which irritated even Keorah's uncomprehending ears, and she gave an angry frown, which changed, as she recollected herself, to a brilliant smile, the piquancy of the transformation completing Bedo's enslavement.

"Well, you are—!" he began, and words failed for the moment. "Stunning," he added, as Keorah's tinkling laugh echoed among the rocks. "You'd keep a chap alive—you would. Now if you were only Baroness Marley, with a fortune at your back, and I'd married you for it, and run you up half way through Australia, and got you yarded and roped at last, and the flashness whipped out of you, why, we'd have a high old time of it, Miss Keorah. We'd make tracks for the old country, and go on the burst, that we would. And I ain't so sure that I shan't do it. I'll yard in and rope the two of you. And I ain't so sure that I won't chuck the other by-and-by—if you can put me on to where those opals and the gold comes from."

Keorah did not make much out of this tirade. It was uttered too rapidly, and the ex-bullock driver's vernacular was not the language employed by Hansen when, after the banquets at which he had sat by her side, the White Lord had indulged his hostess' fancy for learning the "speech of the gods." But she wanted to humour him, and to secure beyond a shadow of doubt the incriminating testimony against Anne. So she still cooed in his face, and stroked his sleeve with one hand, while with the other, she touched the picture in the locket.

"Anne—wife—belonging to you?" she queried insinuatingly. "Tell Keorah."

"Yes, bad luck to her! Yo-ai, Keorah, that wife belonging to me."

"You—hus-band?" There was a whole volume of questioning in her shrill sweet voice.

Bedo snarled assent. The fact was clear. Keorah had gained her point. He began to regret having been so explicit; possibly a stringent code of morals might be in force among the red people. At once he endeavoured to convey, partly in words, partly by pantomimic expression, that though Anne was his wife, though he desired above all things to know her where—abouts, it was only with a view to punishing and repudiating her, and that henceforward, Keorah should reign alone in his affections.

She nodded as if she understood, and smiled on, poking forward her chin and throwing aslant at him through her narrowed eyelids, a gleam of daring between the red lashes that entirely captivated him. With snake-like grace she sidled closer, laying one hand upon his arm as she began to lead him away from his camp towards the opening in the mountain. He moved on obediently; her half closed eyes were magnets drawing him. He had thought a moment before that he would take his gun and wake up the troopers, but now the gun and the troopers were alike forgotten. Suddenly, when they had gone several paces, she opened her eyes to their fullest extent, and turned her head round to him as she walked, while she softly pulled him by the hand. The effect was mesmeric. Bedo was like a man bewitched. He followed stupidly where she led him, forgetting everything but that fascinating face. Only before the dark hole in the mountain side did he draw back, refusing with an oath to go further.

But Keorah's touch was electric. Her voice lured him, her voice, purring caressingly in that enchanting foreign accent, "Come...Come." Her eyes were like stars shining before him till he was well within the tunnel. There the darkness swallowed them; but what did it matter, thought he. She held his hand, and what danger could there be in a woman alone and unarmed?

Suddenly her soft clasp relaxed. The hands she had held were seized by stronger ones, and prisoned behind. He heard Keorah speak in a strange tongue,—she was addressing someone as Hotan. She had glided ahead, and a great burly man taller than Bedo, was by his side, gripping his arm, while two other men behind him tied a linen cloth over his mouth effectually gagging him, and stifling the oaths which came from his throat. Then a glimmer of light showed through an aperture overhead, and Elias Bedo heard the rush of the river over its subterranean bed. He was being led into the Heart of Aak.

Chapter XXXIX—The Death-Door

HANSEN awoke late that morning. He had passed a troubled night. Visions of Keorah, scornful, cajoling, triumphant, disturbed his slumbers, and Anne's pale, pained face rose repeatedly before him in his waking moments. Rivalry between these two had now become a terribly serious matter, and Hansen saw plainly that the only way out of the dilemma was by prompt escape, if that were possible. To-day would show how Kombo's plan had prospered, and if they could avail themselves of it. Should that fail, nothing short of a cataclysm would be likely to help them. And a cataclysm, if it came, might engulf them also. Reflecting upon the events of the previous day, Hansen remembered the heavy redness of the sky, which he had noticed in the direction of the Crocodile Mountain, and the lurid-looking clouds which had gathered towards sunset. He determined to climb the monolith as he had planned, and to take observations. True, it was considerably later than he usually rose, a heavy sleep into which, after much tossing and tumbling, he had at length fallen towards dawn, having lasted some hours, but there would still be sufficient time for him to make the excursion and return by mid-day. It was unlikely that Kombo would seek him out to report matters before then. The boy would need sleep himself after being up all night, and he had told Anne that he meant to pilfer from the booths in order to stock their saddle-bags—a process that would certainly require time and care. Hansen shrank from this deliberate despoiling of the Acans, but felt that Kombo in his generation was wiser than he. At all events, Anne must not be permitted to suffer more than was necessary; and in order to make sure of their liabilities as far as the Crocodile was concerned, Hansen hurried on his clothes, and prepared to climb the monolith.

Anne meanwhile was singularly irritable and restless. She no longer exhibited the serene calm of the High Priestess which had become her so well, and had sustained her in the difficult part she had to play. Her faculty for dramatic personation seemed to have deserted her, and with it, she knew too surely, her influence over the people of Aca would depart. But she had no spirit to pull herself together in so far as concerned her demeanour as Zuhua Kak. It did not seem worth while. In a few hours' time, provided all went well with Kombo's schemes, she would be quit of Aak and his children for ever. That hope inspired her with courage, and even secret joy of a tempered sort.

Among the Virgins, Ishtal was not slow to observe Anne's attitude, and to attribute it, in part at least, to its true cause. Her orders in regard to the supervision of her chief were strict, and she scarcely for a moment left Anne's presence—an intense aggravation of the girl's distress. Yet in Ishtal she felt that she had an almost acknowledged enemy, and such antagonism was, in her present mood, less painful than the sweet friendliness of Semaara which she found less easy to deal with.

Already Ishtal saw herself in fancy the successor of this little white usurper, and a worthy wearer of the Zuhua Kak's insignia of office. All her life she had coveted the position, and was in truth much better fitted to hold it than either Keorah or Anne. Her ascetic temperament found nothing to irk it in the restrictions of a priestess' life, and her flawless dignity of manner secured her respect from all classes.

Poor little Anne, cowed by the calm, steely gaze of Ishtal's grey eyes, tried to repress the eager anticipation of liberty which in spite of all would bubble up within her, lest the elder Virgin should suspect and frustrate. It was true that Anne's sweetest hope in the thought of escape—friendly reunion with Eric—was miserably clouded by what had passed the previous evening,—the hope that had flamed on high for a minute or two under the restrained tenderness of his avowal and had been unduly dashed away by Keorah's intrusion and triumphant claiming of—as she had put it—her betrothed husband.

Could that be true, Anne thought? Had Eric ever really made love to Keorah? Was it possible, in such case, that he could have so spoken, so looked at Anne herself, as to make her feel certain that his whole loyal devotion was hers, though while she remained Elias Bedo's wife honour forbade him to own it? In spite of appearances, in spite of his own damaging half admission, Anne's trust in him burned up again and would not be quenched.

She could not believe that he had been altogether false. Weak certainly he was in allowing himself to be swayed by Keorah's undoubted powers of fascination; culpable even towards her after the manner of men towards women whom they hold lightly—but not altogether inexcusable.

Young as she was, this small Anne had long cast her childhood behind her. She had not been married to Elias Bedo for nothing; nor had she drifted from her original home in the Australian wilds through the experiences of a musical student in London and back again to the Bush, without learning something of the world and its ways. She had seen a good deal of men and of their vices and follies during her short, varied existence, and had stored up the knowledge in her astute little brain. On sober reflection she was therefore able to make some allowance for her errant friend, and to realise that as man is constituted, the temptation to flirt with a woman of Keorah's character and charms, who advanced more than half the way herself, would have been difficult for a stronger male nature than Eric Hansen's to resist. Last night Anne had been indignant, outraged, her heart wounded to the quick. This morning, the solemn tender words that Eric had spoken just before Keorah's entrance came back to Anne, and now in the depth of her soul, she knew that he loved her. She felt that, notwithstanding all, she could put her hand in his again and renew her faith to him. That he would join her and Kombo in their escape she did not doubt, and escape seemed breathlessly near. As Anne stood at the wide window of what she called her prison-house and watched the first rays of the eastern sun glint over the frowning face of the mountain across the market-place, she felt almost in her nostrils the wild breath of the Bush, for which she, like Kombo, so ardently longed.

The scent of eucalyptus seemed wafted to her through the multifarious odours from the stalls beneath, where the vendors of cooked meat and fruit were displaying their goods. She, too, here in the shadow of the Tortoise rock, sensed as her rival was sensing the burning wastes of desert, the tangled stretches of scrub, the distant sea, and the world beyond. It was at this very moment that Keorah, standing outside the fortress of Aak, lifted her face to the sky and savoured love and freedom—another of Nature's children, though of so different a mould, clamouring for the mother-gifts she felt were her right.

Little did Anne dream, keenly alive though she was to the perils that beset her, how close would be the race between Keorah and herself. If she thought of Keorah at all at this moment, it was as a treacherous enemy, plotting in the darkness of the caves against her, to rob her of her lover and her life—not as one whose foot was even now placed upon the road leading to the outer world, whose one desire was like her own to leave the prison walls of Aak behind. Her thoughts, just then, were chiefly of the possibilities of Kombo's success; of her own chances of avoiding detection when it became time to answer the black boy's signal for flight; and of how Hansen would contrive to meet them. She thought, too, of the joy of being on horseback again, and of the wild ride down the gorge and along by the river to the unknown country at the head of the great gulf. It was from this picture that she was recalled by the voice of Ishtal, who demanded rather than requested that the High Priestess should prepare for attendance in the temple. Anne had, amid her preoccupation, forgotten that this was a day of religious ceremony among the Acans upon which she, as Zuhua Kak, had to go with the Virgins, Elders, and Acolytes, first in state to the temple, and thence to bless, in presence of the people, the storage of threshed corn and the harvesting of certain berries used for the compounding of that potent sacred beverage that had wrought Hansen's undoing. She had excused herself on plea of indisposition from the early offering of food and water to Aak, and had instructed Semaara to tend the god in her stead. This she had done partly to avoid the company of the girl, for her heart had been touched by Semaara's affection, and smote her at the thought that she was soon about to leave her only friend among the Acans without a farewell. If Semaara were occupied with the various duties that the High Priestess planned to delegate to her subordinate, she would, Anne hoped, have but little opportunity for noticing anything out of the common in the manner of her chief. Perhaps the fuss and the ceremonial of the festival, upon which Ishtal expatiated, would serve this purpose, thought Anne; and though her spirits sank upon hearing that as was usual on these occasions, there was going to be a banquet when the blessing of the corn was over, she reflected that, as the population of Aca would probably be heavy with drink, she and Hansen and Kombo might more easily get away unseen.

So she allowed herself to be dressed in her most gorgeous robe of office with the plume of rose-coloured feathers on her head and the sacred opal glittering on her brow, and prepared to descend, with her retinue, the rock stairs that led down to the market-place.

It was now about noon. High in the sky, the sun hung just over the City of Refuge like a blinding, metallic disk, pouring hot rays down even into the usually cool recesses of the rock streets. In the Heart of Aak the atmosphere indeed was stifling. It had been strangely hot all that morning, a heaviness that increased hour by hour, varied only by occasional gusts of warm wind that circled round the subterranean spaces and died down as suddenly as it arose. In the intervening stillness, the heat grew more intense. Nevertheless, all was activity here amongst the people. The whole population of Aca had turned out of their rock dwellings, and were thronging the thoroughfares, while the goat-herds and husbandmen had all come up from the fertile earth-basin in which the fruit and corn were grown. It was customary on these agricultural festivals for the Zuhua Kak and her train to walk in procession round the public places and along the outer terrace by a more circuitous route to the temple. Presently, therefore, the semi-circular space where the great wall of the mountain riddled with caverns curved towards the garden hollow was filled with spectators dressed in grey feathered garments with plumes on their heads, who awaited the passing of the High Priestess.

The oppression of the atmosphere made Anne feel faint and dizzy, and the weight of her magnificent mantle trailing behind her was almost more than she could bear. But she managed to look quite regal at the head of her train of Virgins, though each one overtopped her by several inches. This was the last time, she thought to herself, that she would ever appear in this splendid panoply; and, woman-like, she regretted somewhat that she could not take with her these gorgeous robes with their rose-coloured trimmings, her opal clasps and girdle, and the specially perfect stone which held the feathers above her forehead. She looked round for some sign of Kombo that might assure her of the success of his venture, and at least of his safety, but could catch no glimpse of the black boy among that multi-hued throng. How grotesque and strange it all was! She felt like a woman in a dream; and in dream fashion, among various trivial incidents and objects stood out the animated face of a child held up in the arms of a goat-herd, which contrasted with the usual impassive Acan countenance; the ludicrous solemnity of a money-changer giving red beans for gold dust, and the antics of a tame emu which thrust its long neck from side to side among the booths. Then as she turned at the foot of the stairway from the nuns' house, and thus caught a direct view of the Virgins descending in pairs above her, Anne was struck by a peculiar alertness in the tiny live tortoises that the Virgins always wore on their breasts attached to a chain. The queer little things were moving restlessly over the shoulders and bosoms of their guardians, drawing sharply in and out their wee snakish heads and darting gleams from pin-point eyes. They seemed to feel something unusual and alarming in the air, which was in truth full of electrical disturbance. Always sensitive to the magnetism of a number of people, Anne was conscious of a spirit of unrest in the crowd, of lightly leashed emotion that might break forth at a touch, and transform these ordinarily phlegmatic folk into a very rabble of avengers, should they learn the truth about her whom they now hailed as half divine. The wild strains of the Acan orchestra, the hollow reverberations of the drums, the shrieking of the uncouth fiddles, and clashing of sistra, now preluded the uplifted voices of the choir in the hymn to the Zuhua Kak. Anne herself was more impressed than ever by this strange music, remembering that never again should she hear that song of praise ring out, the refrain echoing clearly back from the rock walls:—

Ix nacan katuna

Uol Zubua Kak!

A vague regret swelled in Anne's breast. It was so nearly over—the Priestess life, the Pagan worship. And in that worship, how much there was which appealed to certain religious instincts born in her, that had grown with her growth, and were interlinked by every fibre of her being with the primeval mysticism of the Australian Bush. So real to Anne was this nature faith, that often as she had kneeled before the sun's effigy—the shining disc of life—it had seemed to her that here was the purest and most expressive symbol of That which is unutterable—according to the Acan formula—ever given to man. And when by right of her office as Head Virgin of the Flame, she sang in the temple service the anthem

Uol Viracocha!
Oyoya KU
Zazil Huraca
Lahuna KU
Uol Viracocha!

she did verily feel herself in some inexplicable bond of unity with the Ancient Spirit of Earth, Herald of the Greater Light; and at such moments she was in truth Priestess—Child of Viracocha, Daughter of the Dawn. As these thoughts passed through Anne's mind, Semaara, walking with Ishtal behind, was puzzled by the expression of her chief's face, for it seemed incongruous with the High Priestess' depression, even irritability of the morning. Ishtal, too, could not understand the change. The elder Virgin's crafty eyes turned from right to left scanning the approaches into the market-place as though she were on the watch for something that she expected to happen. She also had noticed Keorah's absence from the scene, though not aware of its cause. Keorah had not taken Ishtal wholly into her confidence, for Keorah was too wary to confide wholly in anyone, at all events, in any other woman. But Ishtal knew enough to be sure that Keorah would strike home when the fitting opportunity occurred, and that at any moment, chance might bring the opportunity, Ishtal fully realised.

She was right. The moment came, and with it Keorah and Elias Bedo.

Keorah and Hotan had led the man down by the intricate, subterranean passage, and through the hall of tortoises and along the short rock corridor to the top of the flight of steps leading into the market-place.

Keorah had soothed Bedo's alarms as best she could, by smiles and such reassuring English words as she had at command; and, when they got into the light—dim though it was in the clearer part of the tunnel—had caused the gag to be removed and his arms unbound. The two serving-men, Acans of huge stature and girth, walked on each side of him, holding his hands; and behind, stepped Hotan, whose eyes continually followed Keorah as she moved in front, the pride of possession lighting them, for she had cleverly beguiled him, and he hoped now to gain the reward of his service.

Bedo's brain was still confused with the unaccustomed drug, and he made no attempt to escape, useless though it would have been. Besides, Keorah's eyes turning back continually in his direction were like magnets drawing him, and her tinkling laugh like the ghost-bell which, according to Indian superstition, lures the willing listener to his doom. His wife's name, too, was part of the spell. Pointing onward, Keorah said many times "Anne... wife... hus-band," so that one idea impressed itself upon Bedo's dulled understanding—his chase had not been in vain; at the end of the passage he would find his prey.

The strains of the Acan hymn reached Keorah's ears, and told her that her operations had been well calculated. This was the time at which the Zuhua Kak and her Virgins were marching in procession to the temple.

The platform at the top of the little flight of steps looked down upon the market-place, and peeping round the archway that gave upon it,

Keorah saw that on one side, the train of Virgins was approaching, while descending a narrow street on the other, came the seven Elders in full canonical array, Naquah, the chief, at their head, Zilzie and Kapoc following, the others in twos bringing up the rear. The platform on to which Keorah was about to advance, stood at an intersecting angle so that here, the three lines converged, making a central point of action in the drama.

An open roadway round the edge of the amphitheatre was reserved for the procession, the rest of the space being filled with the Acan crowd which a little while before buzzing like a swarm of bees, was now waiting in respectful silence for the Zuhua Kak to pass.

Keorah beckoned to Bedo, pointing with his other hand to the small figure of Anne nearing them with slow, stately tread. Bewildered by the sound of the music, the maze of colour and the whole novel scene that was presented to his astonished gaze, he did not at first recognise his runaway wife, and sent his eyes roving over the heads of the people in search of her whom he had been given to understand that he should see. Keorah spoke a few hurried words to Hotan, bidding him watch but not bind their prisoner; then, as the two streams of Elders and Virgins approached each other, she went forward and stood in view of the multitude at the front of the platform.

Looking up, Kapoc first caught sight of her with Hotan, and the stranger, craning forward between his two guards, a foot or two behind. Then Kapoc felt sure that serious business was in train and whispered to Naquah, who halted, and gazed up also at the newcomers.

Meanwhile, Anne proceeded unthinkingly, wrapped in her own musings, and almost a mechanical actor in the scene. She had not noticed the gestures of Kapoc and Naquah; she had not seen Keorah nor the dreaded figure of Bedo, nor did she notice the suspicious glances started by Ishtal, that from all sides were directed towards herself. She might have gone on past the platform, observing nothing and giving the lie to all those accusing glances by the simple indifference and unconsciousness of her manner, had not one of those freakish impulses made her look up at the critical moment when she came opposite the platform.

Keorah she saw standing with one arm outstretched towards her, the other pointing to Bedo, an embodiment of remorseless fate. But her eyes went past Keorah and were transfixed by that ungainly form in bushman's garb, which had now moved, pressing forward from the rear, the eager unkempt head thrust out, the furious blood-shot eyes meeting hers in a stare of triumphant recognition.

The man gave a malignant shout of "Anne! Anne!" He shook his clenched fist at her, and would have cleared the steps and burst down among the crowd to confront her, but for Keorah's warning exclamation to Hotan, and the restraining hold of the Acan keepers.

"Just wait till I can get at you!" Bedo cried furiously. "I shall not let you escape me now. You've led me a pretty chase, and by—I don't mean to let you go again. You're my wife, Anne, remember, whatever you may call yourself here, dressed up in that toggery. I'll unmask you. I'll have the law on you. I'll force you to come back with me." He raved at her. His very utterance of her name was condemnation in the ears of the Elders and Virgins, for they had heard Hansen call her Anne. Indeed, the looks of husband and wife gave too sure evidence that they were closely connected with each other. Stern words of reprobation broke from Naquah, and all through the crowd, went a hoarse murmur like the growl of an angry beast. Keorah alone stood scornful and unmoved. It was part of her scheme to pose as champion of the outraged gods, showing no personal animus against the impostor.

All Anne's customary presence of mind forsook her. She had never been brave in presence of this man. Probably she would not have married Bedo, had he not physically cowed her. There are women upon whom certain men have such an effect. A sharp moan broke from her lips. She stared back at him, her eyes wide with horror, her face going white as chalk. She had stopped dead, her form rigid for a moment or two. Then, seized with a great trembling, she swayed dizzily, and might have fallen, but for Semaara's sustaining arm. Not expecting this sudden pause, Anne's maidens, pressed by the crowd, broke their line, separating on either side of her while she, shorn already of the pomp of procession, stood like some helpless, hapless creature caught in a snare. She looked wildly round in search of Hansen or Kombo, but there was no sign of either.

Now there rose a tumult among the people. She heard cries in which the words "Zuhua Kak" sounded above a shrill confusion of Mayan. It seemed to her that they were demanding an explanation. Then old Naquah's voice uprose, she supposed in arraignment, and above the noise, came Bedo's wrathful asseverations while he pointed at her, at himself, and at Keorah, who only smiled, biding her time to speak, but by her darting gaze, her cold and scornful attitude inflaming the crowd to fiercer imprecations.

By uncouth pantomimic gestures, Bedo appeared to be conveying the fact that the High Priestess was his wife; and it was clear that the Acans fully grasped his meaning, and that they believed him, and were madly exasperated at the imposture practised upon them, and the sacrilege against their ancient traditions. The deep-mouthed roar swelled louder. This people, which a short time before had acclaimed their High Priestess as a divinity, now wanted to rush upon her and destroy her. In the tumult of speech that followed, Anne lost all hold upon the language she had acquired so laboriously. She did not know what was said. She only knew that her fate rested with Keorah and that Keorah was pitiless. For now as by common consent, and under the sway of old habitude, the populace called upon their former High Priestess.

"Keorah, Zuhua Kak! Keorah, Zuhua Kak!" as they had done upon that evening of the wanderer's entrance into the Heart of Aak—so long ago, it seemed—when in the paling afterglow the flaming torches of the Virgins had illumined Keorah's statuesque form and oddly beautiful face, above which the Eye of Viracocha gleamed, and the then High Priestess had replied as she did now, though in slightly varying terms:

"I, Keorah, who may not again be Zuhua Kak, High Virgin of the Flame, do nevertheless answer to your call, oh! People of the Aca."

Chapter XL—The Wrath of Kan

IT was over. The trial, such as it was, had been gone through then and there in the market-place, hurried on by the vindictive jealousy of Keorah, and the fanatic rage of Naquah, who saw the altars of his gods desecrated and the holy traditions of his race violated, and who, refusing to listen to the deprecatory plea for delay from Zilzie, demanded loudly summary retribution for the insult.

The people seconded him in their hoarse-throated cries for vengeance on the impostor. The honour of their religion was the strongest passion of which they were capable, and the sin of sacrilege was consequently rare in their annals. According to their understanding this quondam priestess was judged, and found guilty of it, and she must die. Their elementary minds could grasp no possible middle course. Desire for bloodshed once awakened within them, so changed these mild-mannered Acans as to seemingly revolutionise their whole nature. And Anne stood, the butt of their fury, self-convicted, white with inward terror, but once more outwardly composed, her native courage feebly re-asserting itself, and struggling to meet her fate unshrinkingly, whatever it might be. Hansen was still absent, and so was Kombo, and there was not one person to say a word in her behalf, except indeed Semaara, who incoherently remonstrated and entreated, in her efforts to shield her mistress from the wrath of the mob. A strange trial it was, in which the prisoner had no defending counsel, in which the accuser—her husband—did not understand the language of pleaders and judges, or anything but the vaguest outline of the situation; and in which the accused, found guilty on evidence that was practically unprovable, since there could be no examination of witnesses, was unable to follow the words of her condemnation. But Anne knew well, if only by the awe-stricken and pitiful looks of Semaara, that a doom had been pronounced against her; and she knew also that it must have to do with the symbol of death and the triangular door, for at certain phrases uttered with great solemnity by Naquah, every man and woman in the assemblage, with the exception of herself and Elias Bedo, bent their bodies and drew the corners of their mantles over their faces, as the Elders and Virgins had done on passing the mysterious opening below the Tortoise's Head.

Oh! If Eric were but here to tell her what it all meant, thought poor Anne, to speak for her to the people in their own tongue, and to rescue her from the frightful penalty of a Zuhua Kak's transgression, at which Semaara had darkly hinted. Had Keorah planned that he should be away when she struck the blow? Would she—Anne—be killed before there was time for her to see Eric again, even to bid him farewell?

It seemed that this was to be. Evidently, no respite would be granted. At command of Naquah, the Virgins stripped her of her splendid mantle, and outer embroidered robe. They took away the rose-coloured head-dress, and the glittering Eye of Viracocha, and left her, a forlorn figure clad only in the plain white linen dress that, except for its fineness, had no distinctive mark of dignity. There was a movement to offer to Keorah the insignia of Zuhua Kak, and to re-instal her in her former office. But Keorah waved the emblems aside, and pointed to Ishtal as their rightful wearer. Not upon a woman who, by grace of the gods, had resigned the Priestess-ship, and betrothed herself in marriage, might the mantle of the Zuhua Kak again descend. To Zaac Tepal was she vowed—Zaac Tepal, whom yonder usurper had, by lying words, enticed into her service, but who was guiltless of wilful outrage upon the Acan sanctities. As wife of Zaac Tepal would Keorah give counsel to her people, even instructing in the closer mysteries Ishtal, her lawful successor. But as Zuhua Kak could she reign no more.

Thus it happened that Ishtal attained her long-cherished ambition, and they put upon her tall angular form the gorgeous mantle Anne had worn so regally, and set upon her head the rose-coloured plumes, and the sacred opal upon her brow. Now the people clamoured that their eyes should be no longer offended at sight of the impostor, and that the ancient decree made by the Great Builders should be forthwith put into execution.

The mob divided, and reclosed in more orderly file. The Virgins ranged themselves in pairs behind Ishtal—all but Semaara, who had to be forcibly separated from her former mistress, and, weeping bitterly, took her place last in the train. The Elders followed at a little distance; and at Naquah's order the musicians recommenced, and the choir raised their voices again, but this time it was not the anthem to the Zuhua Kak that they sang, but the hymn to Xibal, Lord of Death. Immediately behind the band of Virgins, and a little in front of the Elders, was led the small, white figure of Anne between two stalwart acolytes, her hands bound by a linen cord; while further back, Keorah, who with her following had come down from the platform, walked in company of Hotan, still keeping watch over Elias Bedo. Hotan, enlightened at last by Keorah's open declaration of her betrothal to Zaac Tepal, and realising that notwithstanding all he had done for her, his own cause was hopeless, was too disappointed to care much what happened next. He had become moody and silent, and walked along, his gaze fixed on the ground, paying small attention to Bedo. Amused and scornful, but not caring to press his services still further, Keorah kept a keen look-out over the prisoner herself.

Sharply as Hotan was suffering, his feelings were slight in comparison with those of the unhappy Bedo. Though he was now perfectly sure that he had done a very bad thing for himself in denouncing Anne as his wife, Bedo did not yet fully realise the depths of the disaster into which he was plunged. He had not, of course, understood a word of the speeches made by the Sacred Guardians, Keorah, and the rest, but he had observed the angry looks of the populace, had seen Anne stripped of her fine robes and outward marks of sovereignty, and had already come to the conclusion that he had better have held his tongue. He did not at all like the attitude of Keorah, who, from the moment upon which they had entered upon this scene of magnificence, had bestowed upon him no more smiles or blandishments. His uneasiness became abject terror when he found himself dragged down from the platform, surrounded by an increased guard of burly Acans, and, at command of Keorah, again gagged and bound, while he was forced into the procession and so surrounded by these big, red men that he could

see nothing of what was going on. He had heard some short, sharp
sentences in what he thought a very queer language, interchanged
between his enchantress—no longer, it seemed, inclined to
enchant—and the strange old bearded men whom he perceived to be
persons of authority. These remarks, it was quite apparent to him,
related to himself; and he had not at all liked the gesture of Keorah
and the expression of her face as she closed the discussion, having,
he inferred, made her will clear concerning him. It was very evident
that her intentions were not benevolent, and he sought in vain to
propitiate her by vociferations of gallantry. It was then that she had
bidden her serving-men gag him, and he was now led along in the
wake of this relentless Circe, who remained impervious to his
distress, while a horrible uncertainty was coming over him as to
what might be in store.

The procession passed out of the city through one of the openings in
the rock-shell, and turned along the terrace in the direction of the
Tortoise's Head. As it advanced, a faint trembling shook the ground
beneath. It lasted but a moment, and the multitude moved on
unheeding. Following this, came a low rumbling, like the roar of
distant thunder, which reverberated from one side to the other of the
cultivated basin lying below. The rock walls enclosing the great
hollow looked strangely forbidding. They were of a livid greyness;
every fissure and projection showed on the steep escarpments; and
their jagged tops, with old gnarled gum trees, some lightning-
blasted, stretching eldritch arms over the precipices, stood out
portentously distinct against a brassy sky. It was the sort of sky that
may be seen when bush fires are raging. Behind the Tortoise's Head
a thick cloud was rising, spreading upward to the sun, an oddly-
shaped cloud with branching arms of vapour and a dull redness at
the base. Everywhere, brooding hush prevailed. All nature seemed
awaiting the march of death.

Keorah murmured to Hotan that a storm was nigh, but he, occupied
with his own thoughts, did not hear her, and for the most part, the
people were too absorbed with the business in hand to pay attention
to atmospheric warnings.

Along the broad terrace the procession filed, while the crowd pressed behind and beside it, and scattered forward down the slope and into the fields and gardens where men climbed the dividing walls, and even the roofs of goat-herds' dwellings, to obtain a better view of what was passing. But all halted at one particular point, above which the monolith towered. They went no further, but waited, crouching slightly, and drawing partly over their faces the folds of their mantles, behind which eager eyes peered upward.

Anne, who was walking as in a dream, not having yet realised her impending fate, was straining her eyes this way and that, in the wild hope that Hansen might appear. But at sight of that ominous shrouding movement she remembered the spot, and now knew whither she was being led.. Cold horror clutched her heart. She tried to speak, but all the words she had known of Mayan forsook her; and of what use to appeal in English since none could understand her? It suddenly occurred to her that she might try her hitherto unfailing resource in moments of danger. She straightened herself, reared her head, bravely struggled to get the pitch of her voice, brought up a few quavering notes, and then sent forth, pathetically rich and clear, the opening bars of her Ave. But the high rock on one side of her, the human wall on the other, seemed to force her voice back, and stifle it in her throat. Still she might have struggled on, but Keorah laughed shrilly in the rear, and that laugh killed poor Anne's pitiful endeavour. And now the Acan drums, which had stopped during a short interval, beat again in hollow clangour. The fiddles shrieked in direful strain, and above the instruments, rose a solemn swell of sound as Ishtal and her Virgins led the choir, and all the people joining in, there was poured forth the invocation before the Death Stone which had first broken Anne's slumbers in the nuns' house,—"Holi, Huqui, Xibal Xibalba!" The slow rhythm was awesome, and the peculiar harmony of the anthem made it seem truly a dirge of death.

While this chant was being sung, the Virgins and the Elders who had wheeled and divided, were standing in rows of four—two Virgins in the centre, and an Elder on either side of them,—their shrouded faces turned to the cliff. Then—with the ending of the chant came an impressive silence, in which all remained standing, but with heads bowed on their breasts. Anne alone continued upright, her face uncovered, her eyes lifted to the precipice frowning in front of her above the tall forms which, placed as she was, a little distance behind, hid the base of the rock from her view. An irony it was that this small white woman, so frail and helpless in her bonds, should be thus closely guarded by the band of lusty acolytes; for she was literally hemmed in beyond hope of deliverance by the multitude of her enemies. The people were massed around her at the back and upon either side, spreading over the wide terrace, every soul of them keenly on the alert and breathless with anticipation, though they now preserved an extraordinary quietude. Through the stillness Anne could hear Semaara's sobs, which went to her heart. Then another sound broke the silence. It was Keorah's high voice giving an order, which a slight scuffle and movement in the throng showed was being immediately obeyed.

Two vigorous Acans in Keorah's livery of yellow and brown pushed their way forward, dragging with them a human bundle—no other than Elias Bedo, flaccid from terror, gagged by a coarse linen cloth stuffed into his mouth and secured at the back of his head, his arms tied to his sides, and even his legs hobbled to prevent any chance of his escaping, so that he could only limp in maimed fashion after his warders. They placed him in a line with Anne, an acolyte and a warder between. And so at last, husband and wife, pursuer and prey, came almost within touch of each other. Anne turned upon him a glance of horrified pity, quickly averting her eyes, and saying nothing. But Bedo, with cold sweat upon his forehead, his features convulsed in rage and fear, his black eyes starting from their sockets, writhed in his bonds, and made ineffectual efforts to speak.

At a long, deep-drawn note from the musicians, the Virgins and Elders prostrated themselves for a moment or two and rose again. In those moments, on a level with the kneeling forms, Anne had seen herself confronted by the mysterious triangular opening in the mountain which was rimmed with the blue Death Stone. As they rose, Ishtal and Naquah went forward together—Kapoc, Zilzie, and the other Virgins following—Semaara's agonized gaze shooting back at the condemned High Priestess. Then Anne felt herself being pushed forward by the acolytes guarding her, and knew that Elias Bedo was being brought after her. She heard the grating on its rock pivot of a ponderous door within the entrance. She heard Keorah's mocking laugh at her shoulder; and turning her head, saw the long narrow face in its frame of red hair with the pointed chin tilted upward, close to her, and the cruel eyes gleaming upon her with exultant hatred. Then a darkness spread before Anne; it was the darkness of the dungeon into which she was being thrust. Her imagination leaped to the picture of a more horrible fate even than that designed for her. Was she to be buried alive in the mountain?

There was a crepitating sound, a fizzle of flints striking fire, and a tiny forest of torches flared, illuminating the dark recesses of a wide vaulted corridor hewn in the rock, the walls of which were frescoed and sculptured. At the further end of the passage, showed a three-cornered glimmer that widened gradually, as, chanting the death hymn, the procession moved on with solemn tread nearer and nearer to the aperture.

The patch of light soon grew into a great triangular mouth of which the lips curled down at the edges. The lower lip curved outward, making a platform that abutted at the height of perhaps a hundred feet upon a sinister-looking gorge below.

Beyond, the landscape was formed of barren hills where gaunt, almost naked eucalyptus trees of an immense age reared their twisted limbs among boulders of basalt. The lines of these hills seemed to intersect each other in the zig-zags of a widening valley— that valley of desolation into which the wanderers had entered from the desert. North-eastwards on the horizon, above the down-sloping spaces, appeared the ends of two monstrous fangs, the open jaws of Kelan Yamina—the old-man Crocodile Mountain of the Blacks. Resting upon the petrified snout, and caught in the jagged teeth, was a lurid cloud, flame-coloured at its base, and raising aloft dusky branching arms menacingly to the darkened face of the sky. The whole sweep of the heavens seemed to have suddenly lowered. Grim shadows, caused by the straying vapour, flitted among the distant hills. High in mid—heaven, the luminous disc of the sun, paled to a strange whiteness amid its inky setting, hung majestic and remote, as though unwilling to look upon the dreadful scene. A purple mist shrouded the ravine below the Tortoise mouth, but through this, at the bottom of the gorge, could be discerned white patches like streaks of gypsum.

Anne knew the spot. Twice had she been close to it. It was the gorge strewn with bones into which the chamois had leaped on the day when they had entered into the Heart of Aak. And she and Hansen had looked down upon it from the cave Eye-Socket in the Tortoise's Head. It was Gunida Ulàla of the Blacks' tradition—the Place of Death. Well, if her doom was to be that of the hunted chamois, Anne felt glad to think that she would be killed outright.

The two prisoners were at once brought forward to the edge of the platform, the Virgins and Elders with Keorah and Hotan and others of the chief personages in the Acan community, ranging themselves in a half—circle, while the multitude pressed up the corridor at the back. Looking down shudderingly Anne saw beneath her a space of the shining blue floor of the gorge unencumbered with bones, and guessed that death would be instantaneous at contact with the life-destroying stone. She turned her eyes compassionately on the huddled form of Bedo, bound hand and foot, with the gag covering his mouth, and shivering in the most abject terror, though he had no idea of what was to come.

"It will not hurt, Elias," she said. "Very soon all will be over. Try to be brave, and make all the delay you can. God may save us yet. But at least, let us forgive each other if we are to die together."

The beating of the drums drowned her words. Bedo strained to make out the syllables, and his features were contorted with the wild effort to speak, while his eyes sought hers in dumb, frenzied appeal. Then at a sign from Keorah the men in charge removed him to the further end of the platform, placing themselves between him and Anne so that she should hold no communication with him.

Her thoughts, however, it must be confessed, were chiefly of Eric. She had hoped till the last that he might come and save her, and now gazed desperately up the sides of the gorge where the precipice shelved towards the great head, in the mouth of which she knew she must be standing. The eye-sockets were above her. Oh! If by some blessed chance he had gone up there and could look down and see the horrible thing impending, and descend—she knew not how—to her deliverance! But there was no glimpse nor sound of him. How could there be in this awful death-trap? She was alone, helpless, at the mercy of her enemies, with not even Kombo nigh to give her aid. Why, on this day of all days, should it happen that the two were away from her? It was as though the insulted gods of Aca had carefully planned her destruction, and were offering her up as a propitiatory victim to the dread Four-Footed Serpent, whose hideous presence seemed to dominate this scene of sacrifice. As though in answer to her thought, there came the sound of a sharp concussion somewhere in the bowels of the earth. It seemed to shake the entire panorama, and cause even the monstrous mouth of the Tortoise to tremble. It was followed by a lengthened rumbling which, echoing among the hills, could be distinctly heard above the noise of the instruments. The red and brown vapour shot up, a denser volume, enveloping the Crocodile in cloud, amid which apparently forked lightning played. A faint sulphurous odour was borne across the valley. The leviathan seemed to be vomiting fire and smoke. It was a sight to make men grow pale. Those in the hinder part of the throng had no opportunity for observing the phenomenon, save for the trembling of the earth, which passed almost unheeded by them in the excitement of the moment. But those who stood on the lip of the Tortoise exchanged startled glances. Even Hotan lifted his sullen face, and pointed to the Crocodile warningly. The musicians stopped playing. A murmur was heard of "Ximal yani!" (Death is in the day), and there was a movement among the people to hurry proceedings, and depart.

As Anne stood patiently waiting for the end, she felt the touch of warm lips, and of a face wet with tears, upon her bound hands, and saw Semaara kneeling at her feet. The poor girl poured forth incoherent protestations of affection and loyalty, till Ishtal's stern voice bade her cease, and the other Virgins dragged her back to her place among them. Anne felt all the bitterness of death in that farewell, though her mind was growing confused. The clutch of the acolytes was on her shoulders, and, realising that the time was becoming short, she strove to compose her thoughts and lift them to heaven, but her brain was in a whirl. She seemed to see Eric's face in the black cloud that was sweeping up over the valley. Several times she fancied that she heard his voice in the thunderous rumblings. She could remember only that they had parted in pain and anger, and a passionate regret filled her, not that she was about to be flung down on the Death Stone, and cut off in her bloom from the joys of living, but that Eric would never know how dearly she loved him. And then, amid Semaara's sobs, and the mutterings of the wrathful sky, Anne did indeed hear a sound that sent the blood, well-nigh congealed with terror, rushing anew through her body, and caused her heart to leap wildly in her throat. It was in very truth the voice of Hansen speaking in Mayan, but with accents so strange, so stern and menacing, that it seemed like that of some inspired prophet of old calling down vengeance upon a sinning people. The next moment Anne thought that imagination must be deceiving her, for there was no sign of his presence; yet his voice, thundering above the roar of the elements, issued from the dense cloud that now clothed the monolith above her. But with all her senses quickened by this new hope, Anne grasped the meaning of the ringing Mayan words sufficiently to understand that a tremendous denunciation was being hurled at her would-be murderers.

"Hu Aca Tehua! Oh! Virgins of the Flame! Oh! Rebellious Children of Aak! Hear the wrath of the Gods, which I, their Interpreter, proclaim unto you, if ye will slay the Daughter of Dawn, the Chosen of our Lord the Sun."

And thus, Eric Hansen from his post of observation, whence he had suddenly realised what was about to happen, gathering up all the power of which he was capable, strove to strike awe into the superstitious souls of the Acans, and gain if it might be only a brief respite in which to save the woman he loved. Thus he cursed the people—in the names of the Nine Lords of Night, of the Grim Lords of the One Death, and the Seven Deaths; in the names of Tohil and Huracan, Wielder of Thunderbolts, and Ruler of Winds; in the names of Aak the Intercessor, of Viracocha Zazil, and of KU the Unutterable.

He cursed them in their waking, and in their sleeping; in their marrying and in their begetting; in their living and in their dying; in the gardens where they planted, and in the caves wherein they dwelt; in their City of Refuge, and in the Promise of that Land to which no Deliverer should lead them; in the trackless valley of oblivion, and in Ximokasan, realm of shades. So he cursed the Children of Aak.

And the people were swept back like a mighty wave before an opposing wind. They cowered against the rock, veiling their faces, and for the space of a few seconds fear paralysed them. Then the mocking laugh of Keorah, who cared little for her country's gods, echoed, silvery and clear. She had recognised the ring of apprehension in Hansen's voice, and had her own reasons for desiring that there should be no unnecessary delay. At the tinkle of her laugh, Bedo, struggling with his keepers, contrived to turn his fettered body, and bent towards her, frenzied appeal in his staring eyes, and inarticulate jabberings coming from behind the linen cloth over his mouth. Pointing to him, Keorah spoke rapidly to Naquah, who addressed to the unhappy man a few curt phrases. They were wholly unintelligible to Bedo, who believed that Keorah had interceded for him and would once more take him into favour. When at a command from her, the two men drew him round again with his face to the platform, he submitted quietly under the impression that they were about to loose his bonds. But instead of that, they prodded him in the back with the butt end of their javelins, and pushed him to the brink of the death gulf. He gave a gurgling sound that died in his throat as he rolled over, a helpless inert mass. There came a dull thud, and in this manner, without a moment to prepare his soul, Elias Bedo was hurled into eternity.

At the sound of the scuffle, Anne, who had been eagerly gazing upward, glanced down again. She was just in time to see her husband's body disappear over the brink, and shrank back, appalled. It was too late, then! Hope was vain. The moment had come. She shrieked aloud one piercing cry of "Eric! save me!" as she felt her own warders push her forward. Then a great black wall rose suddenly before the ledge of the precipice, blotting out the valley and the mountains. The startled warders relaxed their hold and uttered guttural cries of the vengeance of the gods. Anne, feeling herself free, save for her bound hands, rushed sideways, and cowered in a recess of the cavern. In the confusion that ensued, it was not difficult to hide. Superstitious terror, fairly let loose among the Acans, rendered them almost mad. Faces convulsed with fear showed in the gloom, their starting eyes that saw nothing but the horror that had come upon them, gleaming fiercely in the flare of a few torches. A thrill of dreadful expectancy ran through the crowd; it could be felt like the quiver of a tense wire. Out of the darkness that menacing voice spoke again:—

"Behold! Children of Aak! Our Lord the Sun hideth His face from you. He changeth His glorious vesture for the raiment of mourning and woe. Out of the Place of Death will He of a surety gather His own, but upon you, and upon your children, and your city, shall His vengeance fall. Even now destruction cometh. The four-footed Serpent awaketh. Kan upriseth! See! Ye are delivered over unto the Ancient Enemy."

Hansen's voice trembled with the agony of apprehension that racked him, but his words bore full weight. While he spoke, a terrific flame shot up out of the cloud that enveloped the Crocodile Mountain, and a shower of immense sparks rose and fell, covering the entire heaven. The Tortoise Mountain shook like some great palsied monster. A stench of sulphurous vapour poisoned the air, and through the din of crashing boulders, sounded heart-breaking shrieks, as men and women trampled upon each other in frantic efforts to escape from the death-trap into which they had thronged.

Now above the wailing voices and the roar of elements Anne heard a strange shout—the corroboree whoop of the Moongars, then Kombo's frenzied yell.

"Tulumi Mirrein! Tulumi Mirrein! Debil debil Kelan Yamina! Missa Anne! Missa Anne! Where you sit down? Mine been plenty busy, but mine lookout after you. Mine got-im yarraman. Massa Hansen close-up. Murra—make haste. Ba'al stop! Mine find-im road outside Tortoise. Nalla Yan! Nalla Yan!"

The girl gave a faint cry of relief—she was almost spent—at sound of the familiar tones. She put out her roped hands and touched Kombo's wealed chest. He was close to her—closer than he had known. She felt herself drawn along in his arms, and borne so swiftly that her feet scarcely brushed the ground. Through the darkness they sped, the black boy's unerring instinct leading them right—far along a winding passage, in an opposite direction from the Tortoise's Head, the mountain meanwhile seeming to upheave in a manner something like the living Aak when preparing to rise. Anne laughed hysterically, and shook in the black boy's arms like a terrified child. He tried to cheer her as he ran.

"All right, Missa Anne. Bujeri you! Good boy Kombo! Mine no one fellow dam fool. Mine got him fire-stone—you feel, inside shirt. Mine take-im when big Red Mary tumble down. What for that fellow put on frock belonging to you?"

But Anne's sobbing laugh quavered on. Nevertheless her world was getting a little steadier. She could walk now, and the ground felt firmer, though the mountain trembled still, and the thunder of the Tortoise with the groans of the Acans, and the crash of falling stones came to her muffled by the masses of intervening rock. Livid light flashed through the air-holes of the passage. They were in the tunnel which ran round inside the encircling walls of the great garden of Aak, the passage which led to liberty. Echoing footsteps followed them at a distance, but Anne felt no fear. Her heart told her it was Eric's tread, but Kombo would not let her stop. A joyful grin overspread the black boy's countenance. He brought Anne to a standstill at length, where the passage terminated in a wide-mouthed cave, beyond which a stretch of open, level country could be seen. Fresh winds swept it; the sky in front shone blue and clear;

and here, close at hand, were tethered the stolen horses, with well-stocked saddle-bags beside them.

Anne's happy eyes ran over, but she could not speak till Hansen, hurrying after them, pale and eager, entered the cave. He went straight to Anne, and seeing she was still in bonds, drew out an Acan knife he carried, and cut the rope that bound her hands asunder. Then he took them both in his.

Epilogue

ABOUT a year later a good many extracts such as the following might have been culled from the London daily papers:—

"At the Albert Hall last evening, in the presence of Royalty, and of an immense and appreciative audience, Mr Eric Hansen delivered his very remarkable lecture on the prehistoric antiquities of Northern Australia. This was the Danish explorer's first appearance as a public lecturer in England, though in his own country, and in Germany, he has related before several learned societies the tale of his marvellous exploits, and those of his wife the Baroness Marley, whose recent accession to that old title—so long in abeyance—adds a fresh flavour of romance to the exciting story. Indeed, nothing more thrilling has ever been imagined in fiction than the wanderings, the escapes, and the subsequent marriage of this adventurous pair. It is an open secret that Lady Marley and Mr Eric Hansen have been received with favour in high places, and are in fact the lion and lioness of an exceptionally brilliant season. So that, apart from the enormous scientific value of their discoveries, as demonstrating a connection in past ages between the almost extinct civilisations of the ancient Americas and Australia, it was to be fully expected that the young explorer—himself a fascinating personality—should form a centre of attraction for the representatives of fashion, science, and culture, who crowded the Albert Hall last evening."

There is no need to continue the report verbatim. It may be read by any one who chooses to look through the files of the Daily Recorder, and who may there see the list of celebrities present, including Lady

Marley and her mother and sister to whom several descriptive lines were devoted. The personal appearance, style, and characteristics of the lecturer took up a whole paragraph, and following a summary of the chief points of the address, was an enumeration of the few exhibits which the wanderers had been able to bring away with them in their hurried flight from the cataclysm that had almost overwhelmed them—the Acan costumes they had worn, an obsidian knife, and a huntsman's javelin; specimens of the picture-writing; an ancient MS., together with his own drawings of certain of the hieroglyphics and carvings which Hansen had kept secreted about his person; and—most important relic of all—the great opal worn by the Acan High Priestess. Deeply was it regretted that no fragment had been preserved of the interesting but terrible Death Stone. There were, however, distant allusions to the likelihood of an exploration fund being started, and the foundation of a syndicate to test the wonderful mineral resources of the Land of the Tortoise—unless, indeed, as was darkly hinted, all traces of it had been destroyed by the volcanic eruption which had closed that chapter of adventure.

Then, to use the somewhat elaborate phraseology of the Daily Recorder, we are further informed that "the highly intelligent and humourous aboriginal, Kombo, whose occasional ejaculations in the native tongue were a source of diversion to the audience, was seated during the lecture on the platform behind his master, and afterwards received a special share of attention." We are indeed led to imagine that for some time later Kombo was the delight and despair of interviewers!

So much for the newspapers. But for a full and scientific exposition of the results of Eric Hansen's and Anne Marley's explorations, the reader is referred to the work they are about to publish entitled, "With Cannibals and Acans in Unknown Australia."

THE END

CPSIA information can be obtained
at www.ICGtesting.com
Printed in the USA
BVHW060944090221
599701BV00001B/108

9 781715 585358